# NEBULA
# AWARD
# STORIES

# NEBULA AWARD STORIES

## EDITED BY
## DAMON KNIGHT

STEALTH PRESS

PUBLISHER'S NOTE
This is a work of fiction. Names, characters, places and incidents either are a product of the author's imagination or are used fictitiously, and any resemblance to actual persons, living or dead, events, or locales is entirely coincidental.

ISBN 1-58881-018-6

FIRST STEALTH EDITION FEBRUARY 2001

Stealth Press books are published by Stealth Media Corporation. Its trademark, consisting of the words "Stealth Press" and/or bomber logo is registered in the U.S. Patent & Trademark Office and in other countries. Marca Registrata.

Nebula Awards® is a registered trademark of The Science Fiction and Fantasy Writers of America, Inc.

# Contents

# Nebula Awards 1965

Best Novel: *Dune,* by Frank Herbert (Chilton, Philadelphia).

Best Novella (tie): "The Saliva Tree," by Brian W. Aldiss (*The Magazine of Fantasy and Science Fiction,* September 1965); "He Who Shapes," by Roger Zelazny (*Amazing Stories,* January and February 1965).

Best Novelette: "The Doors of His Face, the Lamps of His Mouth," by Roger Zelazny (*The Magazine of Fantasy and Science Fiction,* March 1965).

Best Short Story: " 'Repent, Harlequin!' Said the Ticktockman," by Harlan Ellison (*Galaxy,* December 1965).

## ROLL OF HONOR

"Balanced Ecology," by James H. Schmitz (*Analog Science Fiction/Science Fact,* March 1965).

"Computers Don't Argue," by Gordon R. Dickson (*Analog Science Fiction/Science Fact,* September 1965).

"Becalmed in Hell," by Larry Niven (*The Magazine of Fantasy and Science Fiction,* July 1965).

"The Drowned Giant," by J. G. Ballard (*Playboy,* May 1965, as "Souvenir").

# Introduction

This book is the result of a happy inspiration. When Science Fiction Writers of America was a few months old, Lloyd Biggle, its Secretary-Treasurer, proposed an annual SFWA anthology as a means of raising money. When Doubleday's Lawrence P. Ashmead agreed to publish the book, we realized that with our share of the royalties (ten per cent), we could do something rather handsome in the way of awards for the best stories of the year. The anthology project, first as small as a man's hand, rapidly grew into an annual ballot of SFWA's members to choose the best stories, an annual series of Nebula Awards, and an annual Awards Banquet. In the process, we lost sight of the original objective—we've spent all our advance royalties and more on the trophies.

We are proud of these trophies. They were designed by Judith Ann Lawrence, James Blish's wife, from a sketch by my wife, Kate Wilhelm. Each consists of a spiral nebula made of metallic glitter, and a specimen of rock crystal, both embedded in a block of clear Lucite. They are strikingly beautiful, hand-made, and costly.

The 1965 Nebulas were presented to the winners on March 11, 1966, at the Overseas Press Club in New York and at McHenry's Tail O' the Cock in Beverly Hills, California. Frank Herbert and Harlan Ellison received their awards at the California banquet; Roger Zelazny and Brian Aldiss (who flew from England to be present) in New York.

Many of us regretted that several previous attempts to found an organization of professional science fiction writers came to nothing. If times had been more propitious, we might have had the first of these annual awards and anthologies more than ten years ago. But it may be, after all, that this is precisely the right time to begin.

Forty years before our banquet in March 1966, Hugo Gernsback launched the first science fiction magazine in the world. Since then we have seen science fiction grow from its primitive beginnings into a flourishing, vigorous, and increasingly respected field of literature.

The stories in this book—the award-winners (except for the novel) plus four distinguished runners-up—show the quality of modern science fiction, its range, and, I think, its growing depth and maturity. Science fiction has come a long way.

DAMON KNIGHT, *Former President*
Science Fiction Writers of America

Nebula Award, Best Novelette 1965

# The Doors of His Face, The Lamps of His Mouth

## Roger Zelazny

*We begin with a fish story.*

*The locale is Venus; the "fish" is* Ichthysaurus elasmognathus, *a three-hundred-foot monster that has never been landed and perhaps never will be, in spite of powered equipment built to the scale of a floating platform as big as an aircraft carrier.*

*This story won overwhelmingly in the novelette category: it got five nominations, and more votes than the next four stories combined.*

*I ' m a* baitman. No one is born a baitman, except in a French novel where everyone is. (In fact, I think that's the title, *We Are All Bait*. Pfft!) How I got that way is barely worth the telling and has nothing to do with neo-exes, but the days of the beast deserve a few words, so here they are.

The Lowlands of Venus lie between the thumb and forefinger of the continent known as Hand. When you break into Cloud Alley it swings its silverblack bowling ball toward you without a warn-ing. You jump then, inside that firetailed tenpin they ride you down in, but the straps keep you from making a fool of yourself. You generally chuckle afterwards, but you always jump first.

Next, you study Hand to lay its illusion and the two middle fingers become dozen-ringed archipelagoes as the outers resolve into greengray peninsulas; the thumb is too short, and curls like the embryo tail of Cape Horn.

You suck pure oxygen, sigh possibly, and begin the long topple to the Lowlands.

There, you are caught like an infield fly at the Lifeline land-ing area—so named because of its nearness to the great delta in the Eastern Bay—located between the first peninsula and "thumb." For a minute it seems as if you're going to miss Lifeline and wind up as canned seafood, but afterwards—shaking off the metaphors—you descend to scorched concrete and present your middle-sized telephone directory of authorizations to the short, fat man in the gray cap. The papers show that you are not sub-ject to mysterious inner rottings and etcetera. He then smiles you a short, fat, gray smile and motions you toward the bus which hauls you to the Reception Area. At the R.A. you spend three days proving that, indeed, you are not subject to myste-rious inner rottings and etcetera.

Boredom, however, is another rot. When your three days are up, you generally hit Lifeline hard, and it returns the compliment as a matter of reflex. The effects of alcohol in variant atmos-pheres is a subject on which the connoisseurs have written numerous volumes, so I will confine my remarks to noting that a good binge is worthy of at least a week's time and often warrants a lifetime study.

I had been a student of exceptional promise (strictly undergraduate) for going on two years when the *Bright Water* fell through our marble ceiling and poured its people like targets into the city.

Pause. The Worlds Almanac re Lifeline: ". . . Port city on the eastern coast of Hand. Employees of the Agency for Nonterrestrial Research comprise approximately 85 % of its 100,000 population (2010 Census). Its other residents are primarily personnel maintained by several industrial corporations engaged in basic research. Independent marine biologists, wealthy fishing enthusiasts, and waterfront entrepreneurs make up the remainder of its inhabitants."

I turned to Mike Perrin, a fellow entrepreneur, and commented on the lousy state of basic research.

"Not if the mumbled truth be known."

He paused behind his glass before continuing the slow swallowing process calculated to obtain my interest and a few oaths, before he continued.

"Carl," he finally observed, poker playing, "they're shaping Tensquare."

I could have hit him. I might have refilled his glass with sulfuric acid and looked on with glee as his lips blackened and cracked. Instead, I grunted a noncommittal: "Who's fool enough to shell out fifty grand a day? ANR?"

He shook his head.

"Jean Luharich," he said, "the girl with the violet contacts and fifty or sixty perfect teeth. I understand her eyes are really brown."

"Isn't she selling enough facecream these days?"

He shrugged.

"Publicity makes the wheels go 'round. Luharich Enterprises

jumped sixteen points when she picked up the Sun Trophy. You ever play golf on Mercury?"

I had, but I overlooked it and continued to press.

"So she's coming here with a blank check and a fishhook?"

"*Bright Water*, today," he nodded. "Should be down by now. Lots of cameras. She wants an Ikky, bad."

"Hmm," I hmmed. "How bad?"

"Sixty day contract, Tensquare. Indefinite extension clause. Million and a half deposit," he recited.

"You seem to know a lot about it."

"I'm Personnel Recruitment. Luharich Enterprises approached me last month. It helps to drink in the right places.

"Or own them," he smirked, after a moment.

I looked away, sipping my bitter brew. After awhile I swallowed several things and asked Mike what he expected to be asked, leaving myself open for his monthly temperance lecture.

"They told me to try getting you," he mentioned. "When's the last time you sailed?"

"Month and a half ago. The *Corning*."

"Small stuff," he snorted. "When have you been under, yourself?"

"It's been awhile."

"It's been over a year, hasn't it? That time you got cut by the screw, under the *Dolphin*?"

I turned to him.

"I was in the river last week, up at Angleford where the currents are strong. I can still get around."

"Sober," he added.

"I'd stay that way," I said, "on a job like this."

A doubting nod.

"Straight union rates. Triple time for extraordinary circumstances," he narrated. "Be at Hangar Sixteen with your gear, Friday morning, five hundred hours. We push off Saturday, daybreak."

"You're sailing?"

"I'm sailing."

"How come?"

"Money."

"Ikky guano."

"The bar isn't doing so well and baby needs new minks."

"I repeat—"

". . . And I want to get away from baby, renew my contact with basics—fresh air, exercise, make cash . . ."

"All right, sorry I asked."

I poured him a drink, concentrating on $H_2SO_4$, but it didn't transmute. Finally I got him soused and went out into the night to walk and think things over.

Around a dozen serious attempts to land *Ichthysaurus elasmognathus*, generally known as "Ikky," had been made over the past five years. When Ikky was first sighted, whaling techniques were employed. These proved either fruitless or disastrous, and a new procedure was inaugurated. Tensquare was constructed by a wealthy sportsman named Michael Jandt, who blew his entire roll on the project.

After a year on the Eastern Ocean, he returned to file bankruptcy. Carlton Davits, a playboy fishing enthusiast, then purchased the huge raft and laid a wake for Ikky's spawning grounds. On the nineteenth day out he had a strike and lost one hundred and fifty bills' worth of untested gear, along with one *Ichthysaurus elasmognathus*. Twelve days later, using tripled lines, he hooked, narcotized, and began to hoist the huge beast. It awakened then, destroyed a control tower, killed six men, and worked general hell over five square blocks of Tensquare. Carlton was left with partial hemiplegia and a bankruptcy suit of his own. He faded into waterfront atmosphere and Tensquare changed hands four more times, with less spectacular but equally expensive results.

Finally, the big raft, built only for one purpose, was purchased at auction by ANR for "marine research." Lloyd's still won't insure it, and the only marine research it has ever seen is an occasional rental at fifty bills a day—to people anxious to tell Leviathan fish stories. I've been baitman on three of the voyages, and I've been close enough to count Ikky's fangs on two occasions. I want one of them to show my grandchildren, for personal reasons.

I faced the direction of the landing area and resolved a resolve.

"You want me for local coloring, gal. It'll look nice on the feature page and all that. But clear this—If anyone gets you an Ikky, it'll be me. I promise."

I stood in the empty Square. The foggy towers of Lifeline shared their mists.

Shoreline a couple eras ago, the western slope above Lifeline stretches as far as forty miles inland in some places. Its angle of rising is not a great one, but it achieves an elevation of several thousand feet before it meets the mountain range which separates us from the Highlands. About four miles inland and five hundred feet higher than Lifeline are set most of the surface airstrips and privately owned hangars. Hangar Sixteen houses Cal's Contract Cab, hop service, shore to ship. I do not like Cal, but he wasn't around when I climbed from the bus and waved to a mechanic.

Two of the hoppers tugged at the concrete, impatient beneath flywing haloes. The one on which Steve was working belched deep within its barrel carburetor and shuddered spasmodically.

"Bellyache?" I inquired.

"Yeah, gas pains and heartburn."

He twisted setscrews until it settled into an even keening, and turned to me.

"You're for out?"

I nodded.

"Tensquare. Cosmetics. Monsters. Stuff like that."

He blinked into the beacons and wiped his freckles. The temperature was about twenty, but the big overhead spots served a double purpose.

"Luharich," he muttered. "Then you *are* the one. There's some people want to see you."

"What about?"

"Cameras. Microphones. Stuff like that."

"I'd better stow my gear. Which one am I riding?"

He poked the screwdriver at the other hopper.

"That one. You're on video tape now, by the way. They wanted to get you arriving."

He turned to the hangar, turned back.

"Say 'cheese.' They'll shoot the close closeups later."

I said something other than "cheese." They must have been using telelens and been able to read my lips, because that part of the tape was never shown.

I threw my junk in the back, climbed into a passenger seat, and lit a cigarette. Five minutes later, Cal himself emerged from the office Quonset, looking cold. He came over and pounded on the side of the hopper. He jerked a thumb back at the hangar.

"They want you in there!" he called through cupped hands. "Interview!"

"The show's over!" I yelled back. "Either that, or they can get themselves another baitman!"

His rustbrown eyes became nailheads under blond brows and his glare a spike before he jerked about and stalked off. I wondered how much they had paid him to be able to squat in his hangar and suck juice from his generator.

Enough, I guess, knowing Cal. I never liked the guy, anyway.

Venus at night is a field of stable waters. On the coasts, you can never tell where the sea ends and the sky begins. Dawn is like dumping milk into an inkwell. First, there are erratic curdles of white, then streamers. Shade the bottle for a gray colloid, then watch it whiten a little more. All of a sudden you've got day. Then start heating the mixture.

I had to shed my jacket as we flashed out over the bay. To our rear, the skyline could have been under water for the way it waved and rippled in the heatfall. A hopper can accommodate four people (five, if you want to bend Regs and underestimate weight), or three passengers with the sort of gear a baitman uses. I was the only fare, though, and the pilot was like his machine. He hummed and made no unnecessary noises. Lifeline turned a somersault and evaporated in the rear mirror at about the same time Tensquare broke the forehorizon. The pilot stopped humming and shook his head.

I leaned forward. Feelings played flopdoodle in my guts. I knew every bloody inch of the big raft, but the feelings you once took for granted change when their source is out of reach. Truthfully, I'd had my doubts I'd ever board the hulk again. But now, now I could almost believe in predestination. There it was!

A tensquare football field of a ship. A-powered. Flat as a pancake, except for the plastic blisters in the middle and the "Rooks" fore and aft, port and starboard.

The Rook towers were named for their corner positions— and any two can work together to hoist, co-powering the graffles between them. The graffles—half gaff, half grapple—can raise enormous weights to near water level; their designer had only one thing in mind, though, which accounts for the gaff half. At water level, the Slider has to implement elevation for six to eight feet before the graffles are in a position to push upward, rather than pulling.

The Slider, essentially, is a mobile room—a big box capable of moving in any of Tensquare's crisscross groovings and "anchoring" on the strike side by means of a powerful electromagnetic bond. Its winches could hoist a battleship the necessary distance, and the whole craft would tilt, rather than the Slider come loose, if you want any idea of the strength of that bond.

The Slider houses a section operated control indicator which is the most sophisticated "reel" ever designed. Drawing broadcast power from the generator beside the center blister, it is connected by shortwave with the sonar room, where the movements of the quarry are recorded and repeated to the angler seated before the section control.

The fisherman might play his "lines" for hours, days even, without seeing any more than metal and an outline on the screen. Only when the beast is graffled and the extensor shelf, located twelve feet below waterline, slides out for support and begins to aid the winches, only then does the fisherman see his catch rising before him like a fallen seraph. Then, as Davits learned, one looks into the Abyss itself and is required to act. He didn't, and a hundred meters of unimaginable tonnage, undernarcotized and hurting, broke the cables of the winch, snapped a graffle, and took a half-minute walk across Tensquare.

We circled till the mechanical flag took notice and waved us on down. We touched beside the personnel hatch and I jettisoned my gear and jumped to the deck.

"Luck," called the pilot as the door was sliding shut. Then he danced into the air and the flag clicked blank.

I shouldered my stuff and went below.

Signing in with Malvern, the de facto captain, I learned that most of the others wouldn't arrive for a good eight hours. They had wanted me alone at Cal's so they could pattern the pub footage along twentieth-century cinema lines.

Open: landing strip, dark. One mechanic prodding a contrary hopper. Stark-o-vision shot of slow bus pulling in. Heavily dressed baitman descends, looks about, limps across field. Closeup: he grins. Move in for words: "Do you think this is the time? The time he *will* be landed?" Embarrassment, taciturnity, a shrug. Dub something.—"I see. And why do you think Miss Luharich has a better chance than any of the others? Is it because she's better equipped? [Grin.] Because more is known now about the creature's habits than when you were out before? Or is it because of her will to win, to be a champion? Is it any one of these things, or is it all of them?" Reply: "Yeah, all of them."—"Is that why you signed on with her? Because your instincts say, 'This one will be it'?" Answer: "She pays union rates. I couldn't rent that damned thing myself. And I want in." Erase. Dub something else. Fadeout as he moves toward hopper, etcetera.

"Cheese," I said, or something like that, and took a walk around Tensquare, by myself.

I mounted each Rook, checking out the controls and the underwater video eyes. Then I raised the main lift.

Malvern had no objections to my testing things this way. In fact, he encouraged it. We had sailed together before and our positions had even been reversed once upon a time. So I wasn't surprised when I stepped off the lift into the Hopkins Locker and found him waiting. For the next ten minutes we inspected the big room in silence, walking through its copper coil chambers soon to be Arctic.

Finally, he slapped a wall.

"Well, will we fill it?"

I shook my head.

"I'd like to, but I doubt it. I don't give two hoots and a damn who gets credit for the catch, so long as I have a part in it. But it won't happen. That gal's an egomaniac. She'll want to operate the Slider, and she can't."

"You ever meet her?"

"Yeah."

"How long ago?"

"Four, five years."

"She was a kid then. How do you know what she can do now?"

"I know. She'll have learned every switch and reading by this time. She'll be up on all the theory. But do you remember one time we were together in the starboard Rook, forward, when Ikky broke water like a porpoise?"

"How could I forget?"

11

"Well?"

He rubbed his emery chin.

"Maybe she can do it, Carl. She's raced torch ships and she's scubaed in bad waters back home." He glanced in the direction of invisible Hand. "And she's hunted in the Highlands. She might be wild enough to pull that horror into her lap without flinching.

". . . For Johns Hopkins to foot the bill and shell out seven figures for the corpus," he added. "That's money, even to a Luharich."

I ducked through a hatchway.

"Maybe you're right, but she was a rich witch when I knew her.

"And she wasn't blonde," I added, meanly.

He yawned.

"Let's find breakfast."

We did that.


When I was young I thought that being born a sea creature was the finest choice Nature could make for anyone. I grew up on the Pacific coast and spent my summers on the Gulf or the Mediterranean. I lived months of my life negotiating coral, photographing trench dwellers, and playing tag with dolphins. I fished everywhere there are fish, resenting the fact that they can go places I can't. When I grew older I wanted bigger fish, and there was nothing living that I knew of, excepting a Sequoia, that came any bigger than Ikky. That's part of it . . .

I jammed a couple extra rolls into a paper bag and filled a thermos with coffee. Excusing myself, I left the galley and made my way to the Slider berth. It was just the way I remembered it. I threw a few switches and the shortwave hummed.

"That you, Carl?"

"That's right, Mike. Let me have some juice down here, you doublecrossing rat."

He thought it over, then I felt the hull vibrate as the generators cut in. I poured my third cup of coffee and found a cigarette.

"So why am I a doublecrossing rat this time?" came his voice again.

"You knew about the cameramen at Hangar Sixteen?"

"Yes."

"Then you're a doublecrossing rat. The last thing I want is publicity. 'He who fouled up so often before is ready to try it, nobly, once more.' I can read it now."

"You're wrong. The spotlight's only big enough for one, and she's prettier than you."

My next comment was cut off as I threw the elevator switch and the elephant ears flapped above me. I rose, settling flush with the deck. Retracting the lateral rail, I cut forward into the groove. Amidships, I stopped at a juncture, dropped the lateral, and retracted the longitudinal rail.

I slid starboard, midway between the Rooks, halted, and threw on the coupler.

I hadn't spilled a drop of coffee.

"Show me pictures."

The screen glowed. I adjusted and got outlines of the bottom.

"Okay."

I threw a Status Blue switch and he matched it. The light went on.

The winch unlocked. I aimed out over the waters, extended the arm, and fired a cast.

"Clean one," he commented.

"Status Red. Call strike." I threw a switch.

"Status Red."

The baitman would be on his way with this, to make the barbs tempting.

It's not exactly a fishhook. The cables bear hollow tubes, the tubes convey enough dope for an army of hopheads, Ikky takes

13

the bait, dandled before him by remote control, and the fisherman rams the barbs home.

My hands moved over the console, making the necessary
adjustments. I checked the narco-tank reading. Empty. Good
they hadn't been filled yet. I thumbed the Inject button.

"In the gullet," Mike murmured.

I released the cables. I played the beast imagined. I let him
run, swinging the winch to simulate his sweep.

I had the air conditioner on and my shirt off and it was still
uncomfortably hot, which is how I knew that morning had gone
over into noon. I was dimly aware of the arrivals and departures
of the hoppers. Some of the crew sat in the "shade" of the doors
I had left open, watching the operation. I didn't see Jean arrive
or I would have ended the session and gotten below.

She broke my concentration by slamming the door hard
enough to shake the bond.

"Mind telling me who authorized you to bring up the Slider?"
she asked.

"No one," I replied. "I'll take it below now."

"Just move aside."

I did, and she took my seat. She was wearing brown slacks
and a baggy shirt and she had her hair pulled back in a practical
manner. Her cheeks were flushed, but not necessarily from the
heat. She attacked the panel with a nearly amusing intensity that
I found disquieting.

"Status Blue," she snapped, breaking a violet fingernail on the
toggle.

I forced a yawn and buttoned my shirt slowly. She threw a
side glance my way, checked the registers, and fired a cast.

I monitored the lead on the screen. She turned to me for a
second.

"Status Red," she said levelly.

I nodded my agreement.

She worked the winch sideways to show she knew how. I

didn't doubt she knew how and she didn't doubt that I didn't doubt, but then—

"In case you're wondering," she said, "you're not going to be anywhere near this thing. You were hired as a baitman, remember? Not a Slider operator! A baitman! Your duties consist of swimming out and setting the table for our friend the monster. It's dangerous, but you're getting well paid for it. Any questions?"

She squashed the Inject button and I rubbed my throat.

"Nope," I smiled, "but I am qualified to run that thingamajigger—and if you need me I'll be available, at union rates."

"Mister Davits," she said, "I don't want a loser operating this panel."

"Miss Luharich, there has never been a winner at this game."

She started reeling in the cable and broke the bond at the same time, so that the whole Slider shook as the big yo-yo returned. We skidded a couple feet backwards as it curled into place, and she retracted the arm. She raised the laterals and we shot back along the groove. Slowing, she transferred rails and we jolted to a clanging halt, then shot off at a right angle. The crew scrambled away from the hatch as we skidded onto the elevator.

"In the future, Mister Davits, do not enter the Slider without being ordered," she told me.

"Don't worry. I won't even step inside if I am ordered," I answered. "I signed on as a baitman. Remember? If you want me in here, you'll have to *ask* me."

"That'll be the day," she smiled.

I agreed, as the doors closed above us. We dropped the subject and headed in our different directions after the Slider came to a halt in its berth. She did say "good day," though, which I thought showed breeding as well as determination, in reply to my chuckle.

\* \* \*

Later that night Mike and I stoked our pipes in Malvern's cabin. The winds were shuffling waves, and a steady spattering of rain and hail overhead turned the deck into a tin roof.

"Nasty," suggested Malvern.

I nodded. After two bourbons the room had become a familiar woodcut, with its mahogany furnishings (which I had transported from Earth long ago on a whim) and the dark walls, the seasoned face of Malvern, and the perpetually puzzled expression of Perrin set between the big pools of shadow that lay behind chairs and splashed in corners, all cast by the tiny table light and seen through a glass, brownly.

"Glad I'm in here."

"What's it like underneath on a night like this?"

I puffed, thinking of my light cutting through the insides of a black diamond, shaken slightly. The meteor-dart of a suddenly illuminated fish, the swaying of grotesque ferns, like nebulae—shadow, then green, then gone—swam in a moment through my mind. I guess it's like a spaceship would feel, if a spaceship could feel, crossing between worlds—and quiet, uncannily, preternaturally quiet; and peaceful as sleep.

"Dark," I said, "and not real choppy below a few fathoms."

"Another eight hours and we shove off," commented Mike.

"Ten, twelve days, we should be there," noted Malvern.

"What do you think Ikky's doing?"

"Sleeping on the bottom with Mrs. Ikky, if he has any brains."

"He hasn't. I've seen ANR's skeletal extrapolation from the bones that have washed up—"

"Hasn't everyone?"

". . . Fully fleshed, he'd be over a hundred meters long. That right, Carl?"

I agreed.

". . . Not much of a brain box, though, for his bulk."

"Smart enough to stay out of our locker."

Chuckles, because nothing exists but this room, really. The

world outside is an empty, sleet-drummed deck. We lean back and make clouds.

"Boss lady does not approve of unauthorized fly fishing."

"Boss lady can walk north till her hat floats."

"What did she say in there?"

"She told me that my place, with fish manure, is on the bottom."

"You don't Slide?"

"I bait."

"We'll see."

"That's all I do. If she wants a Slideman she's going to have to ask nicely."

"You think she'll have to?"

"I think she'll have to."

"And if she does, can you do it?"

"A fair question," I puffed. "I don't know the answer, though."

I'd incorporate my soul and trade forty percent of the stock for the answer. I'd give a couple years off my life for the answer. But there doesn't seem to be a lineup of supernatural takers, because no one knows. Supposing when we get out there, luck being with us, we find ourselves an Ikky? Supposing we succeed in baiting him and get lines on him. What then? If we get him shipside will she hold on or crack up? What if she's made of sterner stuff than Davits, who used to hunt sharks with poison-darted air pistols? Supposing she lands him and Davits has to stand there like a video extra.

Worse yet, supposing she asks for Davits and he still stands there like a video extra or something else—say, some yellow-bellied embodiment named Cringe?

It was when I got him up above the eight-foot horizon of steel and looked out at all that body, sloping on and on till it dropped out of sight like a green mountain range . . . And that head. Small for the body, but still immense. Flat, craggy, with lidless roulettes that had spun black and red since before my forefathers decided to try the New Continent. And swaying.

Fresh narco-tanks had been connected. It needed another shot, fast. But I was paralyzed.

It had made a noise like God playing a Hammond organ . . .

*And looked at me!*

I don't know if seeing is even the same process in eyes like those. I doubt it. Maybe I was just a gray blur behind a black rock, with the plexi-reflected sky hurting its pupils. But it fixed on me. Perhaps the snake doesn't really paralyze the rabbit, perhaps it's just that rabbits are cowards by constitution. But it began to struggle and I still couldn't move, fascinated.

Fascinated by all that power, by those eyes, they found me there fifteen minutes later, a little broken about the head and shoulders, the Inject still unpushed.

And I dream about those eyes. I want to face them once more, even if their finding takes forever. I've got to know if there's something inside me that sets me apart from a rabbit, from notched plates of reflexes and instincts that always fall apart in exactly the same way whenever the proper combination is spun.

Looking down, I noticed that my hand was shaking. Glancing up, I noticed that no one else was noticing.

I finished my drink and emptied my pipe. It was late and no songbirds were singing.

I sat whittling, my legs hanging over the aft edge, the chips spinning down into the furrow of our wake. Three days out. No action.

"You!"

"Me?"

"You."

Hair like the end of the rainbow, eyes like nothing in Nature, fine teeth.

"Hello."

"There's a safety rule against what you're doing, you know."

"I know. I've been worrying about it all morning."

A delicate curl climbed my knife, then drifted out behind us. It settled into the foam and was plowed under. I watched her reflection in my blade, taking a secret pleasure in its distortion.

"Are you baiting me?" she finally asked.

I heard her laugh then, and turned, knowing it had been intentional.

"What, me?"

"I could push you off from here, very easily."

"I'd make it back."

"Would you push me off, then—some dark night, perhaps?"

"They're all dark, Miss Luharich. No, I'd rather make you a gift of my carving."

She seated herself beside me then, and I couldn't help but notice the dimples in her knees. She wore white shorts and a halter and still had an offworld tan to her which was awfully appealing. I almost felt a twinge of guilt at having planned the whole scene, but my right hand still blocked her view of the wooden animal.

"Okay, I'll bite. What have you got for me?"

"Just a second. It's almost finished."

Solemnly, I passed her the wooden jackass I had been carving. I felt a little sorry and slightly jackass-ish myself, but I had to follow through. I always do. The mouth was split into a braying grin. The ears were upright.

She didn't smile and she didn't frown. She just studied it.

"It's very good," she finally said, "like most things you do— and appropriate, perhaps."

"Give it to me." I extended a palm.

She handed it back and I tossed it out over the water. It missed the white water and bobbed for awhile like a pigmy seahorse.

"Why did you do that?"

"It was a poor joke. I'm sorry."

"Maybe you are right, though. Perhaps this time I've bitten off a little too much."

19

I snorted.

"Then why not do something safer, like another race?"

She shook her end of the rainbow.

"No. It has to be an Ikky."

"Why?"

"Why did you want one so badly that you threw away a fortune?"

"Man reasons," I said. "An unfrocked analyst who held black therapy sessions in his basement once told me, 'Mister Davits, you need to reinforce the image of your masculinity by catching one of every kind of fish in existence.' Fish are a very ancient masculinity symbol, you know. So I set out to do it. I have one more to go.—Why do you want to reinforce *your* masculinity?"

"I don't," she said. "I don't want to reinforce anything but Luharich Enterprises. My chief statistician once said, 'Miss Luharich, sell all the cold cream and face powder in the System and you'll be a happy girl. Rich, too.' And he was right. I am the proof. I can look the way I do and do anything, and I sell most of the lipstick and face powder in the System—but I have to be *able* to do anything."

"You do look cool and efficient," I observed.

"I don't feel cool," she said, rising. "Let's go for a swim."

"May I point out that we are making pretty good time?"

"If you want to indicate the obvious, you may. You said you could make it back to the ship, unassisted. Change your mind?"

"No."

"Then get us two scuba outfits and I'll race you under Tensquare.

"I'll win, too," she added.

I stood and looked down at her, because that usually makes me feel superior to women.

"Daughter of Lir, eyes of Picasso," I said, "you've got yourself a race. Meet me at the forward Rook, starboard, in ten minutes."

"Ten minutes," she agreed.

And ten minutes it was. From the center blister to the Rook

took maybe two of them, with the load I was carrying. My sandals grew very hot and I was glad to shuck them for flippers when I reached the comparative cool of the corner.

We slid into harnesses and adjusted our gear. She had changed into a trim one-piece green job that made me shade my eyes and look away, then look back again.

I fastened a rope ladder and kicked it over the side. Then I pounded on the wall of the Rook.

"Yeah?"

"You talk to the port Rook, aft?" I called.

"They're all set up," came the answer. "There's ladders and draglines all over that end."

"You sure you want to do this?" asked the sunburnt little gink who was her publicity man, Anderson yclept.

He sat beside the Rook in a deckchair, sipping lemonade through a straw.

"It might be dangerous," he observed, sunken-mouthed. (His teeth were beside him, in another glass.)

"That's right," she smiled. "It *will* be dangerous. Not overly, though."

"Then why don't you let me get some pictures? We'd have them back to Lifeline in an hour. They'd be in New York by tonight. Good copy."

"No," she said, and turned away from both of us.

She raised her hands to her eyes.

"Here, keep these for me."

She passed him a box full of her unseeing, and when she turned back to me they were the same brown that I remembered.

"Ready?"

"No," I said, tautly. "Listen carefully, Jean. If you're going to play this game there are a few rules. First," I counted, "we're going to be directly beneath the hull, so we have to start low and keep moving. If we bump the bottom, we could rupture an air tank . . ."

21

She began to protest that any moron knew that and I cut her down.

"Second," I went on, "there won't be much light, so we'll stay close together and we will *both* carry torches."

Her wet eyes flashed.

"I dragged you out of Govino without—"

Then she stopped and turned away. She picked up a lamp.

"Okay. Torches. Sorry."

". . . And watch out for the drive-screws," I finished. "There'll be strong currents for at least fifty meters behind them."

She wiped her eyes again and adjusted the mask.

"All right, let's go."

We went.

She led the way, at my insistence. The surface layer was pleasantly warm. At two fathoms the water was bracing; at five it was nice and cold. At eight we let go the swinging stairway and struck out. Tensquare sped forward and we raced in the opposite direction, tattooing the hull yellow at ten-second intervals.

The hull stayed where it belonged, but we raced on like two darkside satellites. Periodically, I tickled her frog feet with my light and traced her antennae of bubbles. About a five meter lead was fine; I'd beat her in the home stretch, but I couldn't let her drop behind yet.

Beneath us, black. Immense. Deep. The Mindanao of Venus, where eternity might eventually pass the dead to a rest in cities of unnamed fishes. I twisted my head away and touched the hull with a feeler of light; it told me we were about a quarter of the way along.

I increased my beat to match her stepped-up stroke, and narrowed the distance which she had suddenly opened by a couple meters. She sped up again and I did, too. I spotted her with my beam.

She turned and it caught on her mask. I never knew whether

she'd been smiling. Probably. She raised two fingers in a V-for-Victory and then cut ahead at full speed.

I should have known. I should have felt it coming. It was just a race to her, something else to win. Damn the torpedoes!

So I leaned into it, hard. I don't shake in the water. Or, if I do it doesn't matter and I don't notice it. I began to close the gap again.

She looked back, sped on, looked back. Each time she looked I was nearer, until I'd narrowed it down to the original five meters.

Then she hit the jatoes.

That's what I had been fearing. We were about halfway under and she shouldn't have done it. The powerful jets of compressed air could easily rocket her upward into the hull, or tear something loose if she allowed her body to twist. Their main use is in tearing free from marine plants or fighting bad currents. I had wanted them along as a safety measure, because of the big suck-and-pull windmills behind.

She shot ahead like a meteorite, and I could feel a sudden tingle of perspiration leaping to meet and mix with the churning waters.

I swept ahead, not wanting to use my own guns, and she tripled, quadrupled the margin.

The jets died and she was still on course. Okay, I was an old fuddyduddy. She *could* have messed up and headed toward the top.

I plowed the sea and began to gather back my yardage, a foot at a time. I wouldn't be able to catch her or beat her now, but I'd be on the ropes before she hit deck.

Then the spinning magnets began their insistence and she wavered. It was an awfully powerful drag, even at this distance. The call of the meat grinder.

I'd been scratched up by one once, under the *Dolphin*, a fishing boat of the middle-class. I *had* been drinking, but it was also a rough day, and the thing had been turned on prematurely. Fortunately, it was turned off in time, also, and a tendon-stapler made everything good as new, except in the log, where it only mentioned that I'd been drinking. Nothing about it being off-hours when I had a right to do as I damn well pleased.

She had slowed to half her speed, but she was still moving crosswise, toward the port aft corner. I began to feel the pull myself and had to slow down. She'd made it past the main one, but she seemed too far back. It's hard to gauge distances under water, but each red beat of time told me I was right. She was out of danger from the main one, but the smaller port screw, located about eighty meters in, was no longer a threat but a certainty.

Each air bubble carried a curse to daylight as I moved to flank her from the left.

She had turned and was pulling away from it now. Twenty meters separated us. She was standing still. Fifteen.

Slowly, she began a backward drifting. I hit my jatoes, aiming two meters behind her and about twenty back of the blades.

Straightline! Thankgod! Catching, softbelly, leadpipe on shoulder SWIMLIKEHELL! maskcracked, not broke though AND UP!

We caught a line and I remember brandy.

Into the cradle endlessly rocking I spit, pacing. Insomnia tonight and left shoulder sore again, so let it rain on me—they can cure rheumatism. Stupid as hell. What I said. In blankets and shivering. She: "Carl, I can't say it." Me: "Then call it square for that night in Govino, Miss Luharich. Huh?" She: nothing. Me: "Any more of that brandy?" She: "Give me another, too." Me: sounds of sipping. It had only lasted three months. No alimony. Many $ on both sides. Not sure whether they were happy or not. Wine-dark Aegean. Good fishing. Maybe he should have spent more time on shore. Or perhaps she shouldn't have. Good swimmer, though. Dragged him all the way to Vido to wring out his

lungs. Young. Both. Strong. Both. Rich and spoiled as hell. Ditto.
Corfu should have brought them closer. Didn't. I think that mental cruelty was a trout. He wanted to go to Canada. She: "Go to
hell if you want!" He: "Will you go along?" She: "No." But she
did, anyhow. Many hells. Expensive. He lost a monster or two.
She inherited a couple. Lot of lightning tonight. Stupid as hell.
Civility's the coffin of a conned soul. By whom?—Sounds like a
bloody neo-ex . . . But I hate you, Anderson, with your glass full
of teeth and her new eyes . . . Can't keep this pipe lit, keep sucking tobacco. Spit again!

Seven days out and the scope showed Ikky.

Bells jangled, feet pounded, and some optimist set the thermostat in the Hopkins. Malvern wanted me to sit it out, but I
slipped into my harness and waited for whatever came. The
bruise looked worse than it felt. I had exercised every day and
the shoulder hadn't stiffened on me.

A thousand meters ahead and thirty fathoms deep, it tun-
neled our path. Nothing showed on the surface.

"Will we chase him?" asked an excited crewman.

"Not unless she feels like using money for fuel," I shrugged.

Soon the scope was clear, and it stayed that way. We remained on alert and held our course.

I hadn't said over a dozen words to my boss since the last
time we went drowning together, so I decided to raise the score.

"Good afternoon," I approached. "What's new?"

"He's going north-northeast. We'll have to let this one go.
A few more days and we can afford some chasing. Not yet."

*Sleek head . . .*

I nodded. "No telling where this one's headed."

"How's your shoulder?"

"All right. How about you?"

*Daughter of Lir . . .*

"Fine. By the way, you're down for a nice bonus."

*Eyes of perdition!*

"Don't mention it," I told her back.

Later that afternoon, and appropriately, a storm shattered. (I prefer "shattered" to "broke." It gives a more accurate idea of the behavior of tropical storms on Venus and saves lots of words.) Remember that inkwell I mentioned earlier? Now take it between thumb and forefinger and hit its side with a hammer. Watch yourself! Don't get splashed or cut—

Dry, then drenched. The sky one million bright fractures as the hammer falls. And sounds of breaking.

"Everyone below!" suggested loudspeakers to the already scurrying crew.

Where was I? Who do you think was doing the loudspeaking?

Everything loose went overboard when the water got to walking, but by then no people were loose. The Slider was the first thing below decks. Then the big lifts lowered their shacks.

I had hit it for the nearest Rook with a yell the moment I recognized the pre-brightening of the holocaust. From there I cut in the speakers and spent half a minute coaching the track team.

Minor injuries had occurred, Mike told me over the radio, but nothing serious. I, however, was marooned for the duration. The Rooks do not lead anywhere; they're set too far out over the hull to provide entry downwards, what with the extensor shelves below.

So I undressed myself of the tanks which I had worn for the past several hours, crossed my flippers on the table, and leaned back to watch the hurricane. The top was black as the bottom and we were in between, and somewhat illuminated because of all that flat, shiny space. The waters above didn't rain down— they just sort of got together and dropped.

The Rooks were secure enough—they'd weathered any number of these onslaughts—it's just that their positions gave them a greater arc of rise and descent when Tensquare makes like the rocker of a very nervous grandma. I had used the belts from my rig to strap myself into the bolted-down chair, and I removed several years in purgatory from the soul of whoever left a pack of cigarettes in the table drawer.

I watched the water make teepees and mountains and hands and trees until I started seeing faces and people. So I called Mike.

"What are you doing down there?"

"Wondering what you're doing up there," he replied. "What's it like?"

"You're from the midwest, aren't you?"

"Yeah."

"Get bad storms out there?"

"Sometimes."

"Try to think of the worst one you were ever in. Got a slide rule handy?"

"Right here."

"Then put a one under it, imagine a zero or two following after, and multiply the thing out."

"I can't imagine the zeroes."

"Then retain the multiplicand—that's all you can do."

"So what are you doing up there?"

"I've strapped myself in the chair. I'm watching things roll around the floor right now."

I looked up and out again. I saw one darker shadow in the forest.

"Are you praying or swearing?"

"Damned if I know. But if this were the Slider—if only this were the Slider!"

*"He's out there?"*

I nodded, forgetting that he couldn't see me.

Big, as I remembered him. He'd only broken surface for a few moments, to look around. *There is no power on Earth that can be compared with him who was made to fear no one.* I dropped my cigarette. It was the same as before. Paralysis and an unborn scream.

"You all right, Carl?"

He had looked at me again. Or seemed to. Perhaps that

27

mindless brute had been waiting half a millennium to ruin the life of a member of the most highly developed species in business . . .

"You okay?"

. . . Or perhaps it had been ruined already, long before their encounter, and theirs was just a meeting of beasts, the stronger bumping the weaker aside, body to psyche . . .

"Carl, dammit! Say something!"

He broke again, this time nearer. Did you ever see the trunk of a tornado? It seems like something alive, moving around in all that dark. Nothing has a right to be so big, so strong, and moving. It's a sickening sensation.

"Please answer me."

He was gone and did not come back that day. I finally made a couple wisecracks at Mike, but I held my next cigarette in my right hand.

The next seventy or eighty thousand waves broke by with a monotonous similarity. The five days that held them were also without distinction. The morning of the thirteenth day out, though, our luck began to rise. The bells broke our coffee-drenched lethargy into small pieces, and we dashed from the galley without hearing what might have been Mike's finest punchline.

"Aft!" cried someone. "Five hundred meters!"

I stripped to my trunks and started buckling. My stuff is always within grabbing distance.

I flipflopped across the deck, girding myself with a deflated squiggler.

"Five hundred meters, twenty fathoms!" boomed the speakers.

The big traps banged upward and the Slider grew to its full height, m'lady at the console. It rattled past me and took root ahead. Its one arm rose and lengthened.

I breasted the Slider as the speakers called, "Four-eighty, twenty!"

"Status Red!"

A belch like an emerging champagne cork and the line arced high over the waters.

"Four-eighty, twenty!" it repeated, all Malvern and static. "Baitman, attend!"

I adjusted my mask and hand-over-handed it down the side. Then warm, then cool, then away.

Green, vast, down. Fast. This is the place where I am equal to a squiggler. If something big decides a baitman looks tastier than what he's carrying, then irony colors his title as well as the water about it.

I caught sight of the drifting cables and followed them down. Green to dark green to black. It had been a long cast, too long. I'd never had to follow one this far down before. I didn't want to switch on my torch.

But I had to.

Bad! I still had a long way to go. I clenched my teeth and stuffed my imagination into a straitjacket.

Finally the line came to an end.

I wrapped one arm about it and unfastened the squiggler. I attached it, working as fast as I could, and plugged in the little insulated connections which are the reason it can't be fired with the line. Ikky could break them, but by then it wouldn't matter.

My mechanical eel hooked up, I pulled its section plugs and watched it grow. I had been dragged deeper during this operation, which took about a minute and a half. I was near—too near—to where I never wanted to be.

Loath as I had been to turn on my light, I was suddenly afraid to turn it off. Panic gripped me and I seized the cable with both hands. The squiggler began to glow, pinkly. It started to twist. It was twice as big as I am and doubtless twice as attractive to pink squiggler-eaters. I told myself this until I believed it, then I switched off my light and started up.

If I bumped into something enormous and steel-hided my

heart had orders to stop beating immediately and release me—
to dart fitfully forever along Acheron, and gibbering.

Ungibbering, I made it to green water and fled back to the
nest.

As soon as they hauled me aboard I made my mask a necklace, shaded my eyes, and monitored for surface turbulence. My
first question, of course, was: "Where is he?"

"Nowhere," said a crewman, "we lost him right after you went
over. Can't pick him up on the scope now. Musta dived."

"Too bad."

The squiggler stayed down, enjoying its bath. My job ended
for the time being, I headed back to warm my coffee with rum.

From behind me, a whisper: "Could you laugh like that afterwards?"

Perceptive Answer: "Depends on what he's laughing at."

Still chuckling, I made my way into the center blister with
two cupfuls.

"Still hell and gone?"

Mike nodded. His big hands were shaking, and mine were
steady as a surgeon's when I set down the cups.

He jumped as I shrugged off the tanks and looked for a
bench.

"Don't drip on that panel! You want to kill yourself and blow
expensive fuses?"

I toweled down, then settled down to watching the unfilled
eye on the wall. I yawned happily; my shoulder seemed good as
new.

The little box that people talk through wanted to say something, so Mike lifted the switch and told it to go ahead.

"Is Carl there, Mister Perrin?"

"Yes, ma'am."

"Then let me talk to him."

Mike motioned and I moved.

"Talk," I said.

"Are you all right?"

"Yes, thanks. Shouldn't I be?"

"That was a long swim. I—I guess I overshot my cast."

"I'm happy," I said. "More triple-time for me. I really clean up on that hazardous duty clause."

"I'll be more careful next time," she apologized. "I guess I was too eager. Sorry—" Something happened to the sentence, so she ended it there, leaving me with half a bagful of replies I'd been saving.

I lifted the cigarette from behind Mike's ear and got a light from the one in the ashtray.

"Carl, she was being nice," he said, after turning to study the panels.

"I know," I told him. "I wasn't."

"I mean, she's an awfully pretty kid, pleasant. Headstrong and all that. But what's she done to you?"

"Lately?" I asked.

He looked at me, then dropped his eyes to his cup.

"I know it's none of my bus—" he began.

"Cream and sugar?"

Ikky didn't return that day, or that night. We picked up some Dixieland out of Lifeline and let the muskrat ramble while Jean had her supper sent to the Slider. Later she had a bunk assembled inside. I piped in "Deep Water Blues" when it came over the air and waited for her to call up and cuss us out. She didn't, though, so I decided she was sleeping.

Then I got Mike interested in a game of chess that went on until daylight. It limited conversation to several "checks," one "checkmate," and a "damn!" Since he's a poor loser it also effectively sabotaged subsequent talk, which was fine with me. I had a steak and fried potatoes for breakfast and went to bed.

Ten hours later someone shook me awake and I propped myself on one elbow, refusing to open my eyes.

"Whassamadder?"

"I'm sorry to get you up," said one of the younger crewmen,

31

"but Miss Luharich wants you to disconnect the squiggler so we can move on."

I knuckled open one eye, still deciding whether I should be amused.

"Have it hauled to the side. Anyone can disconnect it."

"It's at the side now, sir. But she said it's in your contract and we'd better do things right."

"That's very considerate of her. I'm sure my Local appreciates her remembering."

"Uh, she also said to tell you to change your trunks and comb your hair, and shave, too. Mister Anderson's going to film it."

"Okay. Run along, tell her I'm on my way—and ask if she has some toenail polish I can borrow."

I'll save on details. It took three minutes in all, and I played it properly, even pardoning myself when I slipped and bumped into Anderson's white tropicals with the wet squiggler. He smiled, brushed it off; she smiled, even though Luharich Complectacolor couldn't completely mask the dark circles under her eyes; and I smiled, waving to all our fans out there in video-land.—Remember, Mrs. Universe, you, too, can look like a monster-catcher. Just use Luharich facecream.

I went below and made myself a tuna sandwich, with mayonnaise.

Two days like icebergs—bleak, blank, half-melting, all frigid, mainly out of sight, and definitely a threat to peace of mind—drifted by and were good to put behind. I experienced some old guilt feelings and had a few disturbing dreams. Then I called Lifeline and checked my bank balance.

"Going shopping?" asked Mike, who had put the call through for me.

"Going home," I answered.

"Huh?"

"I'm out of the baiting business after this one, Mike. The

Devil with Ikky! The Devil with Venus and Luharich Enterprises! And the Devil with you!"

Up eyebrows.

"What brought that on?"

"I waited over a year for this job. Now that I'm here, I've decided the whole thing stinks."

"You knew what it was when you signed on. No matter what else you're doing, you're selling facecream when you work for facecream sellers."

"Oh, that's not what's biting me. I admit the commercial angle irritates me, but Tensquare has always been a publicity spot, ever since the first time it sailed."

"What, then?"

"Five or six things, all added up. The main one being that I don't care any more. Once it meant more to me than anything else to hook that critter, and now it doesn't. I went broke on what started out as a lark and I wanted blood for what it cost me. Now I realize that maybe I had it coming. I'm beginning to feel sorry for Ikky."

"And you don't want him now?"

"I'll take him if he comes peacefully, but I don't feel like sticking out my neck to make him crawl into the Hopkins."

"I'm inclined to think it's one of the four or five other things you said you added."

"Such as?"

He scrutinized the ceiling.

I growled.

"Okay, but I won't say it, not just to make you happy you guessed right."

He, smirking: "That look she wears isn't just for Ikky."

"No good, no good," I shook my head. "We're both fission chambers by nature. You can't have jets on both ends of the rocket and expect to go anywhere—what's in the middle just gets smashed."

"That's how it *was*. None of my business, of course—"

"Say that again and you'll say it without teeth."

"Any day, big man," he looked up, "any place . . ."

"So go ahead. Get it said!"

"She doesn't care about that bloody reptile, she came here to drag you back where you belong. You're not the baitman this trip."

"Five years is too long."

"There must be something under that cruddy hide of yours that people like," he muttered, "or I wouldn't be talking like this. Maybe you remind us humans of some really ugly dog we felt sorry for when we were kids. Anyhow, someone wants to take you home and raise you—also, something about beggars not getting menus."

"Buddy," I chuckled, "do you know what I'm going to do when I hit Lifeline?"

"I can guess."

"You're wrong. I'm torching it to Mars, and then I'll cruise back home, first class. Venus bankruptcy provisions do not apply to Martian trust funds, and I've still got a wad tucked away where moth and corruption enter not. I'm going to pick up a big old mansion on the Gulf, and if you're ever looking for a job you can stop around and open bottles for me."

"You are a yellowbellied fink," he commented.

"Okay," I admitted, "but it's her I'm thinking of, too."

"I've heard the stories about you both," he said. "So you're a heel and a goofoff and she's a bitch. That's called compatibility these days. I dare you, baitman, try keeping something you catch."

I turned.

"If you ever want that job, look me up."

I closed the door quietly behind me and left him sitting there waiting for it to slam.

*    *    *

The day of the beast dawned like any other. Two days after my gutless flight from empty waters I went down to rebait. Nothing on the scope. I was just making things ready for the routine attempt.

I hollered a "good morning" from outside the Slider and received an answer from inside before I pushed off. I had reappraised Mike's words, sans sound, sans fury, and while I did not approve of their sentiment or significance, I had opted for civility anyhow.

So down, under, and away. I followed a decent cast about two hundred ninety meters out. The snaking cables burned black to my left and I paced their undulations from the yellow-green down into the darkness. Soundless lay the wet night, and I bent my way through it like a cockeyed comet, bright tail before.

I caught the line, slick and smooth, and began baiting. An icy world swept by me then, ankles to head. It was a draft, as if someone had opened a big door beneath me. I wasn't drifting downwards that fast either.

Which meant that something might be moving up, something big enough to displace a lot of water. I still didn't think it was Ikky. A freak current of some sort, but not Ikky. Ha!

I had finished attaching the leads and pulled the first plug when a big, rugged, black island grew beneath me . . .

I flicked the beam downwards. His mouth was opened.

I was rabbit.

Waves of the death-fear passed downwards. My stomach imploded. I grew dizzy.

Only one thing, and one thing only. Left to do. I managed it, finally. I pulled the rest of the plugs.

I could count the scaly articulations ridging his eyes by then.

The squiggler grew, pinked into phosphorence . . . squiggled!

Then my lamp. I had to kill it, leaving just the bait before him.

One glance back as I jammed the jatoes to life.

He was so near that the squiggles reflected on his teeth, in his eyes. Four meters, and I kissed his lambent jowls with two jets of backwash as I soared. Then I didn't know whether he was following or had halted. I began to black out as I waited to be eaten.

The jatoes died and I kicked weakly.

Too fast, I felt a cramp coming on. One flick of the beam, cried rabbit. One second, to know . . .

Or end things up, I answered. No, rabbit, we don't dart before hunters. Stay dark.

Green water, finally, to yellowgreen, then top.

Doubling, I beat off toward Tensquare. The waves from the explosion behind pushed me on ahead. The world closed in, and a screamed, "He's alive!" in the distance.

A giant shadow and a shock wave. The line was alive, too.

—Good-bye Perrin, Violet Eyes, Ikky. I go to the Happy Fishing Grounds. Maybe I did something wrong . . .

Somewhere Hand was clenched. What's bait?

A few million years. I remember starting out as a one-celled organism and painfully becoming an amphibian, then an air-breather. From somewhere high in the treetops I heard a voice.

"He's coming around."

I evolved back into homo sapience, then a step further into a hangover.

"Don't try to get up yet."

"Have we got him?" I slurred.

"Still fighting, but he's hooked. We thought he took you for an appetizer."

"So did I."

"Breathe some of this and shut up."

A funnel over my face. Good. Lift your cups and drink . . .

"He was awfully deep. Below scope range. We didn't catch him till he started up. Too late, then."

I began to yawn.

"We'll get you inside now."

I managed to uncase my ankle knife.

"Try it and you'll be minus a thumb."

"You need rest."

"Then bring me a couple more blankets. I'm staying."

I fell back and closed my eyes.

Someone was shaking me. Gloom and cold. Spotlights bled yellow on the deck. I was in a jury-rigged bunk, bulked against the center blister. Swaddled in wool, I still shivered.

"It's been eleven hours. You're not going to see anything now."

I tasted blood.

"Drink this."

Water. I had a remark but I couldn't mouth it.

"Don't ask how I feel," I croaked. "I know that comes next, but don't ask me. Okay?"

"Okay. Want to go below now?"

"No. Just get me my jacket."

"Right here."

"What's he doing?"

"Nothing. He's deep, he's doped but he's staying down."

"How long since last time he showed?"

"Two hours, about."

"Jean?"

"She won't let anyone in the Slider. Listen, Mike says come on in. He's right behind you in the blister."

I sat up and turned. Mike was watching. He gestured; I gestured back.

I swung my feet over the edge and took a couple deep breaths. Pains in my stomach. I got to my feet and made it into the blister.

"Howza gut?" queried Mike.

I checked the scope. No Ikky. Too deep.

"You buying?"

"Yeah, coffee."

"Not coffee."

"You're ill. Also, coffee is all that's allowed in here."

"Coffee is a brownish liquid that burns your stomach. You have some in the bottom drawer."

"No cups. You'll have to use a glass."

"Tough."

He poured.

"You do that well. Been practicing for that job?"

"What job?"

"The one I offered you—"

A blot on the scope!

"Rising, ma'am! Rising!" he yelled into the box.

"Thanks, Mike. I've got it in here," she crackled.

"Jean!"

"Shut up! She's busy!"

"Was that Carl?"

"Yeah," I called. "Talk later," and I cut it.

Why did I do that?

"Why did you do that?"

I didn't know.

"I don't know."

Damned echoes! I got up and walked outside.

Nothing. Nothing.

Something?

Tensquare actually rocked! He must have turned when he saw the hull and started downward again. White water to my left, and boiling. An endless spaghetti of cable roared hotly into the belly of the deep.

I stood awhile, then turned and went back inside.

Two hours sick. Four, and better.

"The dope's getting to him."

"Yeah."

"What about Miss Luharich?"

"What about her?"

"She must be half dead."

"Probably."

"What are you going to do about it?"

"She signed the contract for this. She knew what might happen. It did."

"I think you could land him."

"So do I."

"So does she."

"Then let her ask me."

Ikky was drifting lethargically, at thirty fathoms.

I took another walk and happened to pass behind the Slider. She wasn't looking my way.

"Carl, come in here!"

Eyes of Picasso, that's what, and a conspiracy to make me Slide . . .

"Is that an order?"

"Yes—No! Please."

I dashed inside and monitored. He was rising.

"Push or pull?"

I slammed the "wind" and he came like a kitten.

"Make up your own mind now."

He balked at ten fathoms.

"Play him?"

"No!"

She wound him upwards—five fathoms, four . . .

She hit the extensors at two, and they caught him. Then the graffles.

Cries without and a heat lightning of flashbulbs.

The crew saw Ikky.

He began to struggle. She kept the cables tight, raised the graffles . . .

Up.

Another two feet and the graffles began pushing.

Screams and fast footballs.

Giant beanstalk in the wind, his neck, waving. The green hills of his shoulders grew.

"He's big, Carl!" she cried.

And he grew, and grew, and grew uneasy . . .

*"Now!"*

He looked down.

He looked down, as the god of our most ancient ancestors might have looked down. Fear, shame, and mocking laughter rang in my head. Her head, too?

"Now!"

She looked up at the nascent earthquake.

"I can't!"

It was going to be so damnably simple this time, now the rabbit had died. I reached out.

I stopped.

"Push it yourself."

"I can't. You do it. Land him, Carl!"

"No. If I do, you'll wonder for the rest of your life whether you could have. You'll throw away your soul finding out. I know you will, because we're alike, and I did it that way. Find out now!"

She stared.

I gripped her shoulders.

"Could be that's me out there," I offered. "I am a green sea serpent, a hateful, monstrous beast, and out to destroy you. I am answerable to no one. Push the Inject."

Her hand moved to the button, jerked back.

"Now!"

She pushed it.

I lowered her still form to the floor and finished things up with Ikky.

It was a good seven hours before I awakened to the steady, sea-chewing grind of Tensquare's blades.

"You're sick," commented Mike.

"How's Jean?"

"The same."

"Where's the beast?"

"Here."

"Good." I rolled over. ". . . Didn't get away this time."

So that's the way it was. No one is born a baitman, I don't think, but the rings of Saturn sing epithalamium the sea-beast's dower.

# Balanced Ecology
## James H. Schmitz

*Next is a farm story, if you like—but this is no ordinary farm.*

*Under the bucolic surface of this tale of another planet, with its consistent and beautifully worked out details, there is a tricky problem, about which I will give you one or two hints:*

*Ecology is something human beings can adapt to suit their own purposes; right? But human beings in an environment are part of its ecology . . .*

*Or: if an experimental animal alters its responses in order to get food from the experimenter—who is conditioning whom?*

*The diamondwood* tree farm was restless this morning. Ilf Cholm had been aware of it for about an hour but had said nothing to Auris, thinking he might be getting a summer fever or a stomach upset and imagining things and that Auris would decide they should go back to the house so Ilf's grandmother could dose him. But the feeling continued to grow, and by now Ilf knew it was the farm.

Outwardly, everyone in the forest appeared to be going about their usual business. There had been a rainfall earlier in the day, and the tumbleweeds had uprooted themselves and were moving about in the bushes, lapping water off the leaves. Ilf had noticed a small one rolling straight towards a waiting slurp and stopped for a moment to watch the slurp catch it. The slurp was of average size, which gave it a tongue-reach of between twelve and fourteen feet, and the tumbleweed was already within range.

The tongue shot out suddenly, a thin, yellow flash. Its tip flicked twice around the tumbleweed, jerked it off the ground and back to the feed opening in the imitation tree stump within which the rest of the slurp was concealed. The tumbleweed said "Oof!" in the surprised way they always did when something caught them, and went in through the opening. After a moment, the slurp's tongue tip appeared in the opening again and waved gently around, ready for somebody else of the right size to come within reach.

Ilf, just turned eleven and rather small for his age, was the right size for this slurp, though barely. But, being a human boy, he was in no danger. The slurps of the diamondwood farms on Wrake didn't attack humans. For a moment, he was tempted to tease the creature into a brief fencing match. If he picked up a stick and banged on the stump with it a few times, the slurp would become annoyed and dart its tongue out and try to knock the stick from his hand.

But it wasn't the day for entertainment of that kind. Ilf couldn't shake off his crawly, uncomfortable feeling, and while he had been standing there, Auris and Sam had moved a couple

45

of hundred feet farther uphill, in the direction of the Queen Grove, and home. He turned and sprinted after them, caught up with them as they came out into one of the stretches of grassland which lay between the individual groves of diamondwood trees.

Auris, who was two years, two months, and two days older than Ilf, stood on top of Sam's semiglobular shell, looking off to the right towards the valley where the diamondwood factory was. Most of the world of Wrake was on the hot side, either rather dry or rather steamy; but this was cool mountain country. Far to the south, below the valley and the foothills behind it, lay the continental plain, shimmering like a flat, green-brown sea. To the north and east were higher plateaus, above the level where the diamondwood liked to grow. Ilf ran past Sam's steadily moving bulk to the point where the forward rim of the shell made a flat upward curve, close enough to the ground so he could reach it.

Sam rolled a somber brown eye back for an instant as Ilf caught the shell and swung up on it, but his huge beaked head didn't turn. He was a mossback, Wrake's version of the turtle pattern, and except for the full-grown trees and perhaps some members of the clean-up squad, the biggest thing on the farm. His corrugated shell was overgrown with a plant which had the appearance of long green fur; and occasionally when Sam fed, he would extend and use a pair of heavy arms with three-fingered hands, normally held folded up against the lower rim of the shell.

Auris had paid no attention to Ilf's arrival. She still seemed to be watching the factory in the valley. She and Ilf were cousins but didn't resemble each other. Ilf was small and wiry, with tight-curled red hair. Auris was slim and blond, and stood a good head taller than he did. He thought she looked as if she owned everything she could see from the top of Sam's shell; and she did, as a matter of fact, own a good deal of it—nine tenths of the diamondwood farm and nine tenths of the factory. Ilf owned the remaining tenth of both.

He scrambled up the shell, grabbing the moss-fur to haul himself along, until he stood beside her. Sam, awkward as he looked when walking, was moving at a good ten miles an hour, clearly headed for the Queen Grove. Ilf didn't know whether it was Sam or Auris who had decided to go back to the house. Whichever it had been, he could feel the purpose of going there.

"They're nervous about something," he told Auris, meaning the whole farm. "Think there's a big storm coming?"

"Doesn't look like a storm," Auris said.

Ilf glanced about the sky, agreed silently. "Earthquake, maybe?"

Auris shook her head. "It doesn't feel like earthquake."

She hadn't turned her gaze from the factory. Ilf asked, "Something going on down there?"

Auris shrugged. "They're cutting a lot today," she said. "They got in a limit order."

Sam swayed on into the next grove while Ilf considered the information. Limit orders were fairly unusual; but it hardly explained the general uneasiness. He sighed, sat down, crossed his legs, and looked about. This was a grove of young trees, fifteen years and less. There was plenty of open space left between them. Ahead, a huge tumbleweed was dying, making happy, chuckling sounds as it pitched its scarlet seed pellets far out from its slowly unfolding leaves. The pellets rolled hurriedly farther away from the old weed as soon as they touched the ground. In a twelve-foot circle about their parent, the earth was being disturbed, churned, shifted steadily about. The clean-up squad had arrived to dispose of the dying tumbleweed; as Ilf looked, it suddenly settled six or seven inches deeper into the softened dirt. The pellets were hurrying to get beyond the reach of the clean-up squad so they wouldn't get hauled down, too. But half-grown tumbleweeds, speckled yellow-green and ready to start their rooted period, were rolling through the grove towards the disturbed area. They would wait around the edge of the circle until the clean-up squad finished, then move in and put down

47

their roots. The ground where the squad had worked recently was always richer than any other spot in the forest.

Ilf wondered, as he had many times before, what the clean-up squad looked like. Nobody ever caught so much as a glimpse of them. Riquol Cholm, his grandfather, had told him of attempts made by scientists to catch a member of the squad with digging machines. Even the smallest ones could dig much faster than the machines could dig after them, so the scientists always gave up finally and went away.

"Ilf, come in for lunch!" called Ilf's grandmother's voice.

Ilf filled his lungs, shouted, "Coming, Grand—"

He broke off, looked up at Auris. She was smirking.

"Caught me again," Ilf admitted. "Dumb humbugs!" He yelled, "Come out, Lying Lou! I know who it was."

Meldy Cholm laughed her low, sweet laugh, a silverbell called, the giant greenweb of the Queen Grove sounded its deep harp note, more or less all together. Then Lying Lou and Gabby darted into sight, leaped up on the mossback's hump. The humbugs were small, brown, bobtailed animals, built with spider leanness and very quick. They had round skulls, monkey faces, and the pointed teeth of animals who lived by catching and killing other animals. Gabby sat down beside Ilf, inflating and deflating his voice pouch, while Lou burst into a series of rattling, clicking, spitting sounds.

"They've been down at the factory?" Ilf asked.

"Yes," Auris said. "Hush now. I'm listening."

Lou was jabbering along at the rate at which the humbugs chattered among themselves, but this sounded like, and was, a recording of human voices played back at high speed. When Auris wanted to know what people somewhere were talking about, she sent the humbugs off to listen. They remembered everything they heard, came back and repeated it to her at their own speed, which saved time. Ilf, if he tried hard, could understand scraps of it. Auris understood it all. She was hearing now what the people at the factory had been saying during the morning.

Gabby inflated his voice pouch part way, remarked in Grandfather Riquol's strong, rich voice, "My, my! We're not being quite on our best behavior today, are we, Ilf?"

"Shut up," said Ilf.

"Hush now," Gabby said in Auris' voice. "I'm listening." He added in Ilf's voice, sounding crestfallen, "Caught me again!" then chuckled nastily.

Ilf made a fist of his left hand and swung fast. Gabby became a momentary brown blur, and was sitting again on Ilf's other side. He looked at Ilf with round, innocent eyes, said in a solemn tone, "We must pay more attention to details, men. Mistakes can be expensive!"

He'd probably picked that up at the factory. Ilf ignored him. Trying to hit a humbug was a waste of effort. So was talking back to them. He shifted his attention to catching what Lou was saying; but Lou had finished up at that moment. She and Gabby took off instantly in a leap from Sam's back and were gone in the bushes. Ilf thought they were a little jittery and erratic in their motions today, as if they, too, were keyed up even more than usual. Auris walked down to the front lip of the shell and sat on it, dangling her legs. Ilf joined her there.

"What were they talking about at the factory?" he asked.

"They did get in a limit order yesterday," Auris said. "And another one this morning. They're not taking any more orders until they've filled those two."

"That's good, isn't it?" Ilf asked.

"I guess so."

After a moment, Ilf asked, "Is that what *they're* worrying about?"

"I don't know," Auris said. But she frowned.

Sam came lumbering up to another stretch of open ground, stopped while he was still well back among the trees. Auris

49

slipped down from the shell, said, "Come on but don't let them see you," and moved ahead through the trees until she could look into the open. Ilf followed her as quietly as he could.

"What's the matter?" he inquired. A hundred and fifty yards away, on the other side of the open area, towered the Queen Grove, its tops dancing gently like armies of slender green spears against the blue sky. The house wasn't visible from here; it was a big one-story bungalow built around the trunks of a number of trees deep within the grove. Ahead of them lay the road which came up from the valley and wound on through the mountains to the west.

Auris said, "An aircar came down here a while ago . . . There it is!"

They looked at the aircar parked at the side of the road on their left, a little distance away. Opposite the car was an opening in the Queen Grove where a path led to the house. Ilf couldn't see anything very interesting about the car. It was neither new nor old, looked like any ordinary aircar. The man sitting inside it was nobody they knew.

"Somebody's here on a visit," Ilf said.

"Yes," Auris said. "Uncle Kugus has come back."

Ilf had to reflect an instant to remember who Uncle Kugus was. Then it came to his mind in a flash. It had been some while ago, a year or so. Uncle Kugus was a big, handsome man with thick, black eyebrows, who always smiled. He wasn't Ilf's uncle but Auris'; but he'd had presents for both of them when he arrived. He had told Ilf a great many jokes. He and Grandfather Riquol had argued on one occasion for almost two hours about something or other; Ilf couldn't remember now what it had been. Uncle Kugus had come and gone in a tiny, beautiful, bright yellow aircar, had taken Ilf for a couple of rides in it, and told him about winning races with it. Ilf hadn't had too bad an impression of him.

"That isn't him," he said "and that isn't his car."

"I know. He's in the house," Auris said. "He's got a couple of people with him. They're talking with Riquol and Meldy."

A sound rose slowly from the Queen Grove as she spoke, deep and resonant, like the stroke of a big, old clock or the hum of a harp. The man in the aircar turned his head towards the grove to listen. The sound was repeated twice. It came from the giant greenweb at the far end of the grove and could be heard all over the farm, even, faintly, down in the valley when the wind was favorable. Ilf said, "Lying Lou and Gabby were up here?"

"Yes. They went down to the factory first, then up to the house."

"What are they talking about in the house?" Ilf inquired.

"Oh, a lot of things." Auris frowned again. "We'll go and find out, but we won't let them see us right away."

Something stirred beside Ilf. He looked down and saw Lying Lou and Gabby had joined them again. The humbugs peered for a moment at the man in the aircar, then flicked out into the open, on across the road, and into the Queen Grove, like small, flying shadows, almost impossible to keep in sight. The man in the aircar looked about in a puzzled way, apparently uncertain whether he'd seen something move or not.

"Come on," Auris said.

Ilf followed her back to Sam. Sam lifted his head and extended his neck. Auris swung herself upon the edge of the undershell beside the neck, crept on hands and knees into the hollow between the upper and lower shells. Ilf climbed in after her. The shell-cave was a familiar place. He'd scuttled in there many times when they'd been caught outdoors in one of the violent electric storms which came down through the mountains from the north or when the ground began to shudder in an earthquake's first rumbling. With the massive curved shell about him and the equally massive flat shell below, the angle formed by the cool, leathery wall which was the side of Sam's neck and the front of his shoulder seemed like the safest place in the world to be on such occasions.

The undershell tilted and swayed beneath Ilf now as the mossback started forward. He squirmed around and looked out through the opening between the shells. They moved out of the grove, headed towards the road at Sam's steady walking pace. Ilf couldn't see the aircar and wondered why Auris didn't want the man in the car to see them. He wriggled uncomfortably. It was a strange, uneasy-making morning in every way.

They crossed the road, went swishing through high grass with Sam's ponderous side-to-side sway like a big ship sailing over dry land, and came to the Queen Grove. Sam moved on into the green-tinted shade under the Queen Trees. The air grew cooler. Presently he turned to the right, and Ilf saw a flash of blue ahead. That was the great thicket of flower bushes, in the center of which was Sam's sleeping pit.

Sam pushed through the thicket, stopped when he reached the open space in the center to let Ilf and Auris climb out of the shell-cave. Sam then lowered his forelegs, one after the other, into the pit, which was lined so solidly with tree roots that almost no earth showed between them, shaped like a mold to fit the lower half of his body; he tilted forward, drawing neck and head back under his shell, slid slowly into the pit, straightened out, and settled down. The edge of his upper shell was now level with the edge of the pit, and what still could be seen of him looked simply like a big, moss-grown boulder. If nobody came to disturb him, he might stay there unmoving the rest of the year. There were mossbacks in other groves of the farm which had never come out of their sleeping pits or given any indication of being awake since Ilf could remember. They lived an enormous length of time and a nap of half a dozen years apparently meant nothing to them.

Ilf looked questioningly at Auris. She said, "We'll go up to the house and listen to what Uncle Kugus is talking about."

They turned into a path which led from Sam's place to the house. It had been made by six generations of human children, all of whom had used Sam for transportation about the diamondwood farm. He was half again as big as any other mossback around and the only one whose sleeping pit was in the Queen Grove. Everything about the Queen Grove was special, from the trees themselves, which were never cut and twice as thick and almost twice as tall as the trees of other groves, to Sam and his blue flower thicket, the huge stump of the Grandfather Slurp not far away, and the giant greenweb at the other end of the grove. It was quieter here; there were fewer of the other animals. The Queen Grove, from what Riquol Cholm had told Ilf, was the point from which the whole diamondwood forest had started a long time ago.

Auris said, "We'll go around and come in from the back. They don't have to know right away that we're here . . ."

"Mr. Terokaw," said Riquol Cholm, "I'm sorry Kugus Ovin persuaded you and Mr. Bliman to accompany him to Wrake on this business. You've simply wasted your time. Kugus should have known better. I've discussed the situation quite thoroughly with him on other occasions."

"I'm afraid I don't follow you, Mr. Cholm," Mr. Terokaw said stiffly. "I'm making you a businesslike proposition in regard to this farm of diamondwood trees—a proposition which will be very much to your advantage as well as to that of the children whose property the Diamondwood is. Certainly you should at least be willing to listen to my terms!"

Riquol shook his head. It was clear that he was angry with Kugus but attempting to control his anger.

"Your terms, whatever they may be, are not a factor in this," he said. "The maintenance of a diamondwood forest is not entirely a business proposition. Let me explain that to you—as Kugus should have done.

"No doubt you're aware that there are less than forty such

53

forests on the world of Wrake and that attempts to grow the trees elsewhere have been uniformly unsuccessful. That and the unique beauty of diamondwood products, which has never been duplicated by artificial means, is, of course, the reason that such products command a price which compares with that of precious stones and similar items."

Mr. Terokaw regarded Riquol with a bleak blue eye, nodded briefly. "Please continue, Mr. Cholm."

"A diamondwood forest," said Riquol, "is a great deal more than an assemblage of trees. The trees are a basic factor, but still only a factor, of a closely integrated, balanced natural ecology. The manner of interdependence of the plants and animals that make up a diamondwood forest is not clear in all details, but the interdependence is a very pronounced one. None of the involved species seem able to survive in any other environment. On the other hand, plants and animals not naturally a part of this ecology will not thrive if brought into it. They move out or vanish quickly. Human beings appear to be the only exception to that rule."

"Very interesting," Mr. Terokaw said dryly.

"It is," said Riquol. "It is a very interesting natural situation and many people, including Mrs. Cholm and myself, feel it should be preserved. The studied, limited cutting practiced on the diamondwood farms at present acts towards its preservation. That degree of harvesting actually is beneficial to the forests, keeps them moving through an optimum cycle of growth and maturity. They are flourishing under the hand of man to an extent which was not usually attained in their natural, untouched state. The people who are at present responsible for them—the farm owners and their associates—have been working for some time to have all diamondwood forests turned into Federation preserves, with the right to harvest them retained by the present owners and their heirs under the same carefully supervised conditions. When Auris and Ilf come of age and can sign an agreement to that effect, the farms will in fact become Federation preserves. All other steps to that end have been taken by now.

"That, Mr. Terokaw, is why we're not interested in your business proposition. You'll discover, if you wish to sound them out on it, that the other diamondwood farmers are not interested in it either. We are all of one mind in that matter. If we weren't, we would long since have accepted propositions essentially similar to yours."

There was silence for a moment. Then Kugus Ovin said pleasantly, "I know you're annoyed with me, Riquol, but I'm thinking of Auris and Ilf in this. Perhaps in your concern for the preservation of a natural phenomenon, you aren't sufficiently considering their interests."

Riquol looked at him, said, "When Auris reaches maturity, she'll be an extremely wealthy young woman, even if this farm never sells another cubic foot of diamondwood from this day on. Ilf would be sufficiently well to-do to make it unnecessary for him ever to work a stroke in his life—though I doubt very much he would make such a choice."

Kugus smiled. "There are degrees even to the state of being extremely wealthy," he remarked. "What my niece can expect to gain in her lifetime from this careful harvesting you talk about can't begin to compare with what she would get at one stroke through Mr. Terokaw's offer. The same, of course, holds true of Ilf."

"Quite right," Mr. Terokaw said heavily. "I'm generous in my business dealings, Mr. Cholm. I have a reputation for it. And I can afford to be generous because I profit well from my investments. Let me bring another point to your attention. Interest in diamondwood products throughout the Federation waxes and wanes, as you must be aware. It rises and falls. There are fashions and fads. At present, we are approaching the crest of a new wave of interest in these products. This interest can be properly stimulated and exploited, but in any event we must expect it will have passed its peak in another few months. The next interest peak might develop six years from now, or twelve years from now. Or it might never develop since there are very few natural products which cannot eventually be duplicated and usually surpassed by artificial methods, and there is no good reason to assume that diamondwood will remain an exception indefinitely.

"We should be prepared, therefore, to make the fullest use of this bonanza while it lasts. I am prepared to do just that, Mr. Cholm. A cargo ship full of cutting equipment is at present stationed a few hours' flight from Wrake. This machinery can be landed and in operation here within a day after the contract I am offering you is signed. Within a week, the forest can be leveled. We shall make no use of your factory here, which would be entirely inadequate for my purpose. The diamondwood will be shipped at express speeds to another world where I have adequate processing facilities set up. And we can hit the Federation's main markets with the finished products the following month."

Riquol Cholm said, icily polite now, "And what would be the reason for all that haste, Mr. Terokaw?"

Mr. Terokaw looked surprised. "To insure that we have no competition, Mr. Cholm. What else? When the other diamondwood farmers here discover what has happened, they may be tempted to follow our example. But we'll be so far ahead of them that the diamondwood boom will be almost entirely to our exclusive advantage. We have taken every precaution to see to that. Mr. Bliman, Mr. Ovin, and I arrived here in the utmost secrecy today. No one so much as suspects that we are on Wrake, much less what our purpose is. I make no mistakes in such matters, Mr. Cholm!"

He broke off and looked around as Meldy Cholm said in a troubled voice, "Come in, children. Sit down over there. We're discussing a matter which concerns you."

"Hello, Auris!" Kugus said heartily. "Hello, Ilf! Remember old Uncle Kugus?"

"Yes," Ilf said. He sat down on the bench by the wall beside Auris, feeling scared.

"Auris," Riquol Cholm said, "did you happen to overhear anything of what was being said before you came into the room?"

Auris nodded. "Yes." She glanced at Mr. Terokaw, looked at Riquol again. "He wants to cut down the forest."

"It's your forest and Ilf's, you know. Do you want him to do it?"

"Mr. Cholm, please!" Mr. Terokaw protested. "We must approach this properly. Kugus, show Mr. Cholm what I'm offering."

Riquol took the document Kugus held out to him, looked over it. After a moment, he gave it back to Kugus. "Auris," he said, "Mr. Terokaw, as he's indicated, is offering you more money than you would ever be able to spend in your life for the right to cut down your share of the forest. Now . . . do you want him to do it?"

"No," Auris said.

Riquol glanced at Ilf, who shook his head. Riquol turned back to Mr. Terokaw.

"Well, Mr. Terokaw," he said, "there's your answer. My wife and I don't want you to do it, and Auris and Ilf don't want you to do it. Now . . ."

"Oh, come now, Riquol!" Kugus said, smiling. "No one can expect either Auris or Ilf to really understand what's involved here. When they come of age—"

"When they come of age," Riquol said, "they'll again have the opportunity to decide what they wish to do." He made a gesture of distaste. "Gentlemen, let's conclude this discussion. Mr. Terokaw, we thank you for your offer, but it's been rejected."

Mr. Terokaw frowned, pursed his lips.

"Well, not so fast, Mr. Cholm," he said. "As I told you, I make no mistakes in business matters. You suggested a few minutes ago that I might contact the other diamondwood farmers on the planet on the subject but predicted that I would have no better luck with them."

"So I did," Riquol agreed. He looked puzzled.

"As a matter of fact," Mr. Terokaw went on, "I already have contacted a number of these people. Not in person, you understand, since I did not want to tip off certain possible competitors that I was interested in diamondwood at present. The offer was rejected, as you indicated it would be. In fact, I learned that the owners of the Wrake diamondwood farms are so involved in legally binding agreements with one another that it would be very difficult for them to accept such an offer even if they wished to do it."

Riquol nodded, smiled briefly. "We realized that the temptation to sell out to commercial interests who would not be willing to act in accordance with our accepted policies could be made very strong," he said. "So we've made it as nearly impossible as we could for any of us to yield to temptation."

"Well," Mr. Terokaw continued, "I am not a man who is easily put off. I ascertained that you and Mrs. Cholm are also bound by such an agreement to the other diamondwood owners of Wrake not to be the first to sell either the farm or its cutting rights to outside interests, or to exceed the established limits of cutting. But you are not the owners of this farm. These two children own it between them."

Riquol frowned. "What difference does that make?" he demanded. "Ilf is our grandson. Auris is related to us and our adopted daughter."

Mr. Terokaw rubbed his chin.

"Mr. Bliman," he said, "please explain to these people what the legal situation is."

Mr. Bliman cleared his throat. He was a tall, thin man with fierce dark eyes, like a bird of prey. "Mr. and Mrs. Cholm," he began, "I work for the Federation Government and am a specialist in adoptive procedures. I will make this short. Some months ago, Mr. Kugus Ovin filed the necessary papers to adopt his niece, Auris Luteel, citizen of Wrake. I conducted the investigation which is standard in such cases and can assure you that no official record exists that you have at any time gone through the steps of adopting Auris."

"*What?*" Riquol came half to his feet. Then he froze in position for a moment, settled slowly back in his chair. "What is this? Just what kind of trick are you trying to play?" he said. His face had gone white.

Ilf had lost sight of Mr. Terokaw for a few seconds, because Uncle Kugus had suddenly moved over in front of the bench on which he and Auris were sitting. But now he saw him again and he had a jolt of fright. There was a large blue and silver gun in Mr. Terokaw's hand, and the muzzle of it was pointed very steadily at Riquol Cholm.

"Mr. Cholm," Mr. Terokaw said, "before Mr. Bliman concludes his explanation, allow me to caution you! I do not wish to kill you. This gun, in fact, is not designed to kill. But if I pull the trigger, you will be in excruciating pain for some minutes. You are an elderly man and it is possible that you would not survive the experience. This would not inconvenience us very seriously. Therefore, stay seated and give up any thoughts of summoning help . . . Kugus, watch the children. Mr. Bliman, let me speak to Mr. Het before you resume."

He put his left hand up to his face, and Ilf saw he was wearing a wrist-talker. "Het," Mr. Terokaw said to the talker without taking his eyes off Riquol Cholm, "you are aware, I believe, that the children are with us in the house?"

The wrist-talker made murmuring sounds for a few seconds, then stopped.

"Yes," Mr. Terokaw said. "There should be no problem about it. But let me know if you see somebody approaching the area . . ." He put his hand back down on the table. "Mr. Bliman, please continue."

Mr. Bliman cleared his throat again.

"Mr. Kugus Ovin," he said, "is now officially recorded as the parent by adoption of his niece, Auris Luteel. Since Auris has not yet reached the age where her formal consent to this action would be required, the matter is settled."

"Meaning," Mr. Terokaw added, "that Kugus can act for Auris in such affairs as selling the cutting rights on this tree farm. Mr. Cholm, if you are thinking of taking legal action against us, forget it. You may have had certain papers purporting to show that the girl was your adopted child filed away in the deposit vault of a bank. If so, those papers have been destroyed. With enough money, many things become possible. Neither you nor Mrs. Cholm nor the two children will do or say anything that might cause trouble to me. Since you have made no rash moves, Mr. Bliman will now use an instrument to put you and Mrs. Cholm painlessly to sleep for the few hours required to get you off this planet. Later, if you should be questioned in connection with this situation, you will say about it only what certain psychological experts will have impressed on you to say, and within a few months, nobody will be taking any further interest whatever in what is happening here today.

"Please do not think that I am a cruel man. I am not. I merely take what steps are required to carry out my purpose. Mr. Bliman, please proceed!"

Ilf felt a quiver of terror. Uncle Kugus was holding his wrist with one hand and Auris' wrist with the other, smiling reassuringly down at them. Ilf darted a glance over to Auris' face. She looked as white as his grandparents but she was making no attempt to squirm away from Kugus, so Ilf stayed quiet, too. Mr. Bliman stood up, looking more like a fierce bird of prey than ever, and stalked over to Riquol Cholm, holding something in his hand that looked unpleasantly like another gun. Ilf shut his eyes. There was a moment of silence, then Mr. Terokaw said, "Catch him before he falls out of the chair. Mrs. Cholm, if you will just settle back comfortably . . ."

There was another moment of silence. Then, from beside him, Ilf heard Auris speak.

It wasn't regular speech but a quick burst of thin, rattling gabble, like human speech speeded up twenty times or so. It ended almost immediately.

"What's that? What's that?" Mr. Terokaw said, surprised.

Ilf's eyes flew open as something came in through the window with a whistling shriek. The two humbugs were in the room, brown blurs flicking here and there, screeching like demons. Mr. Terokaw exclaimed something in a loud voice and jumped up from the chair, his gun swinging this way and that. Something scuttled up Mr. Bliman's back like a big spider, and he yelled and spun away from Meldy Cholm lying slumped back in her chair. Something ran up Uncle Kugus' back. He yelled, letting go of Ilf and Auris, and pulled out a gun of his own. "Wide aperture!" roared Mr. Terokaw, whose gun was making loud, thumping noises. A brown shadow swirled suddenly about his knees. Uncle Kugus cursed, took aim at the shadow, and fired.

"Come," whispered Auris, grabbing Ilf's arm. They sprang up from the bench and darted out the door behind Uncle Kugus' broad back.

"Het!" Mr. Terokaw's voice came bellowing down the hall behind them. "Up in the air and look out for those children! They're trying to get away. If you see them start to cross the road, knock 'em out. Kugus—after them! They may try to hide in the house."

Then he yowled angrily, and his gun began making the thumping noises again. The humbugs were too small to harm people, but their sharp little teeth could hurt and they seemed to be using them now.

"In here," Auris whispered, opening a door. Ilf ducked into the room with her, and she closed the door softly behind them. Ilf looked at her, his heart pounding wildly.

Auris nodded at the barred window. "Through there! Run and hide in the grove. I'll be right behind you . . ."

61

"Auris! Ilf!" Uncle Kugus called in the hall. "Wait—don't be afraid. Where are you?" His voice still seemed to be smiling. Ilf heard his footsteps hurrying along the hall as he squirmed quickly sideways between two of the thick wooden bars over the window, dropped to the ground. He turned, darted off towards the nearest bushes. He heard Auris gabble something to the humbugs again, high and shrill, looked back as he reached the bushes, and saw her already outside, running towards the shrubbery on his right. There was a shout from the window. Uncle Kugus was peering out from behind the bars, pointing a gun at Auris. He fired. Auris swerved to the side, was gone among the shrubs. Ilf didn't think she had been hit.

"They're outside!" Uncle Kugus yelled. He was too big to get through the bars himself.

Mr. Terokaw and Mr. Bliman were also shouting within the house. Uncle Kugus turned around, disappeared from the window.

"Auris!" Ilf called, his voice shaking with fright.

"Run and hide, Ilf!" Auris seemed to be on the far side of the shrubbery, deeper in the Queen Grove.

Ilf hesitated, started running along the path that led to Sam's sleeping pit, glancing up at the open patches of sky among the treetops. He didn't see the aircar with the man Het in it. Het would be circling around the Queen Grove now, waiting for the other men to chase them into sight so he could knock them out with something. But they could hide inside Sam's shell and Sam would get them across the road. "Auris, where are you?" Ilf cried.

Her voice came low and clear from behind him. "Run and hide, Ilf!"

Ilf looked back. Auris wasn't there but the two humbugs were loping up the path a dozen feet away. They darted past Ilf without stopping, disappeared around the turn ahead. He could hear the three men yelling for him and Auris to come back. They were outside, looking around for them now, and they seemed to be coming closer.

Ilf ran on, reached Sam's sleeping place. Sam lay there unmoving, like a great mossy boulder filling the pit. Ilf picked up
a stone and pounded on the front part of the shell.

"Wake up!" he said desperately. "Sam, wake up!"

Sam didn't stir. And the men were getting closer. Ilf looked
this way and that, trying to decide what to do.

"Don't let them see you," Auris called suddenly.

"That was the girl over there," Mr. Terokaw's voice shouted.
"Go after her, Bliman!"

"Auris, watch out!" Ilf screamed, terrified.

"Aha! And here's the boy, Kugus. This way! Het," Mr. Terokaw yelled triumphantly, "come down and help us catch them!
We've got them spotted . . ."

Ilf dropped to hands and knees, crawled away quickly under
the branches of the blue flower thicket, and waited, crouched
low. He heard Mr. Terokaw crashing through the bushes towards
him and Mr. Bliman braying, "Hurry up, Het! Hurry up!" Then
he heard something else. It was the sound the giant greenweb
sometimes made to trick a flock of silverbells into fluttering
straight towards it, a deep drone which suddenly seemed to be
pouring down from the trees and rising up from the ground.

Ilf shook his head dizzily. The drone faded, grew up again.
For a moment, he thought he heard his own voice call, "Auris,
where are you?" from the other side of the blue flower thicket.
Mr. Terokaw veered off in that direction, yelling something to
Mr. Bliman and Kugus. Ilf backed farther away through the
thicket, came out on the other side, climbed to his feet, and
turned.

He stopped. For a stretch of twenty feet ahead of him, the
forest floor was moving, shifting and churning with a slow, cir-
cular motion, turning lumps of deep brown mold over and over.

Mr. Terokaw came panting into Sam's sleeping place, redfaced,
glaring about, the blue and silver gun in his hand. He shook his
head to clear the resonance of the humming air from his brain.

He saw a huge, moss-covered boulder tilted at a slant away from him but no sign of Ilf.

Then something shook the branches of the thicket behind the boulder. "Auris!" Ilf's frightened voice called.

Mr. Terokaw ran around the boulder, leveling the gun. The droning in the air suddenly swelled to a roar. Two big gray, three-fingered hands came out from the boulder on either side of Mr. Terokaw and picked him up.

"Awk!" he gasped, then dropped the gun as the hands folded him, once, twice, and lifted him towards Sam's descending head. Sam opened his large mouth, closed it, swallowed. His neck and head drew back under his shell and he settled slowly into the sleeping pit again.

The greenweb's roar ebbed and rose continuously now, like a thousand harps being struck together in a bewildering, quickening beat. Human voices danced and swirled through the din, crying, wailing, screeching. Ilf stood at the edge of the twenty-foot circle of churning earth outside the blue flower thicket, half stunned by it all. He heard Mr. Terokaw bellow to Mr. Bliman to go after Auris, and Mr. Bliman squalling to Het to hurry. He heard his own voice nearby call Auris frantically and then Mr. Terokaw's triumphant yell: "This way! Here's the boy, Kugus!"

Uncle Kugus bounded out of some bushes thirty feet away, eyes staring, mouth stretched in a wide grin. He saw Ilf, shouted excitedly and ran towards him. Ilf watched, suddenly unable to move. Uncle Kugus took four long steps out over the shifting loam between them, sank ankle-deep, knee-deep. Then the brown earth leaped in cascades about him, and he went sliding straight down into it as if it were water, still grinning, and disappeared. In the distance, Mr. Terokaw roared, "This way!" and Mr. Bliman yelled to Het to hurry up. A loud, slapping sound came from the direction of the stump of the Grandfather Slurp. It was followed by a great commotion in the bushes around there; but that only lasted a moment. Then, a few seconds later, the greenweb's drone rose and thinned to the wild shriek it made when it had caught something big and faded slowly away . . .

Ilf came walking shakily through the opening in the thickets to Sam's sleeping place. His head still seemed to hum inside with the greenweb's drone but the Queen Grove was quiet again; no voices called anywhere. Sam was settled into his pit. Ilf saw something gleam on the ground near the front end of the pit. He went over and looked at it, then at the big, moss-grown dome of Sam's shell.

"Oh, Sam," he whispered, "I'm not sure we should have done it . . ."

Sam didn't stir. Ilf picked up Mr. Terokaw's blue and silver gun gingerly by the barrel and went off with it to look for Auris. He found her at the edge of the grove, watching Het's aircar on the other side of the road. The aircar was turned on its side and about a third of it was sunk in the ground. At work around and below it was the biggest member of the clean-up squad Ilf had ever seen in action.

They went up to the side of the road together and looked on while the aircar continued to shudder and turn and sink deeper into the earth. Ilf suddenly remembered the gun he was holding and threw it over on the ground next to the aircar. It was swallowed up instantly there. Tumbleweeds came rolling up to join them and clustered around the edge of the circle, waiting. With a final jerk, the aircar disappeared. The disturbed section of earth began to smooth over. The tumbleweeds moved out into it.

There was a soft whistling in the air, and from a Queen Tree at the edge of the grove a hundred and fifty feet away, a diamondwood seedling came lancing down, struck at a slant into the center of the circle where the aircar had vanished, stood trembling a moment, then straightened up. The tumbleweeds nearest it moved respectfully aside to give it room. The seedling shuddered and unfolded its first five-fingered cluster of silver-green leaves. Then it stood still.

Ilf looked over at Auris. "Auris," he said, "should we have done it?"

Auris was silent a moment.

"Nobody did anything," she said then. "They've just gone away again." She took Ilf's hand. "Let's go back to the house and wait for Riquol and Meldy to wake up."

The organism that was the diamondwood forest grew quiet again. The quiet spread back to its central mind unit in the Queen Grove, and the unit began to relax towards somnolence. A crisis had been passed—perhaps the last of the many it had foreseen when human beings first arrived on the world of Wrake.

The only defense against Man was Man. Understanding that, it had laid its plans. On a world now owned by Man, it adopted Man, brought him into its ecology, and its ecology into a new and again successful balance.

This had been a final flurry. A dangerous attack by dangerous humans. But the period of danger was nearly over, would soon be for good a thing of the past.

It had planned well, the central mind unit told itself drowsily. But now, since there was no further need to think today, it would stop thinking . . .

Sam the mossback fell gratefully asleep.

Nebula Award, Best Short Story 1965

# "Repent, Harlequin!" Said the Ticktockman

## Harlan Ellison

*Multiple award-winning author, TV and movie scripter Harlan Ellison is a small, intense, muscular young man, something like a miniature Rod Serling, who never gets anywhere on time.*

*Here is a story written to the rhythm of a clock without a balance wheel, out of whack, out of synch, tock-tick, tick-tock.*

*T h e r e   a r e*   always those who ask, what is it all about? For those who need to ask, for those who need points sharply made, who need to know "where it's at," this:

> *The mass of men serve the state thus, not as men mainly, but as machines, with their bodies. They are the standing army, and the militia, jailors, constables,* posse comitatus, *etc. In most cases there is no free exercise whatever of the judgment or of the moral sense; but they put themselves on a level with wood and earth and stones; and wooden men can perhaps be manufactured that will serve the purpose as well. Such command no more respect than men of straw or a lump of dirt. They have the same sort of worth only as horses and dogs. Yet such as these even are commonly esteemed good citizens. Others—as most legislators, politicians, lawyers, ministers, and officeholders—serve the state chiefly with their heads; and, as they rarely make any moral distinctions, they are as likely to serve the Devil, without intending it, as God. A very few, as heroes, patriots, martyrs, reformers in the great sense, and* men, *serve the state with their consciences also, and so necessarily resist it for the most part; and they are commonly treated as enemies by it.*

Henry David Thoreau,
CIVIL DISOBEDIENCE

That is the heart of it. Now begin in the middle, and later learn the beginning; the end will take care of itself.

But because it was the very world it was, the very world they had allowed it to *become,* for months his activities did not come to the alarmed attention of The Ones Who Kept The Machine Functioning Smoothly, the ones who poured the very best butter over the cams and mainsprings of the culture. Not until it had become obvious that somehow, someway, he had become a notoriety, a celebrity, perhaps even a hero for (what Officialdom inescapably tagged) "an emotionally disturbed segment of the

populace," did they turn it over to the Ticktockman and his legal
machinery. But by then, because it was the very world it was,
and they had no way to predict he would happen—possibly a
strain of disease long-defunct, now, suddenly, reborn in a system
where immunity had been forgotten, had lapsed—he had been
allowed to become too real. Now he had form and substance.

He had become a *personality*, something they had filtered out
of the system many decades before. But there it was, and there
*he* was, a very definitely imposing personality. In certain circles—
middle-class circles—it was thought disgusting. Vulgar ostenta-
tion. Anarchistic. Shameful. In others, there was only sniggering:
those strata where thought is subjugated to form and ritual,
niceties, proprieties. But down below, ah, down below, where
the people always needed their saints and sinners, their bread
and circuses, their heroes and villains, he was considered a Bo-
livar; a Napoleon; a Robin Hood; a Dick Bong (Ace of Aces); a
Jesus; a Jomo Kenyatta.

And at the top—where, like socially-attuned Shipwreck Kel-
lys, every tremor and vibration threatening to dislodge the
wealthy, powerful, and titled from their flagpoles—he was considered a menace; a heretic; a rebel; a disgrace; a peril. He was
known down the line, to the very heartmeat core, but the important reactions were high above and far below. At the very
top, at the very bottom.

So his file was turned over, along with his time-card and his
cardioplate, to the office of the Ticktockman.

The Ticktockman: very much over six feet tall, often silent,
a soft purring man when things went timewise. The Ticktockman.

Even in the cubicles of the hierarchy, where fear was generated, seldom suffered, he was called the Ticktockman. But no
one called him that to his mask.

You don't call a man a hated name, not when that man,
behind his mask, is capable of revoking the minutes, the hours,

the days and nights, the years of your life. He was called the Master Timekeeper to his mask. It was safer that way.

"This is *what* he is," said the Ticktockman with genuine softness, "but not *who* he is? This time-card I'm holding in my left hand has a name on it, but it is the name of *what* he is, not *who* he is. The cardioplate here in my right hand is also named, but not *whom* named, merely *what* named. Before I can exercise proper revocation, I have to know *who* this *what* is."

To his staff, all the ferrets, all the loggers, all the finks, all the commex, even the mineez, he said, "Who is this Harlequin?"

He was not purring smoothly. Timewise, it was jangle.

However, it *was* the longest speech they had ever heard him utter at one time, the staff, the ferrets, the loggers, the finks, the commex, but not the mineez, who usually weren't around to know, in any case. But even they scurried to find out.

Who is the Harlequin?

High above the third level of the city, he crouched on the humming aluminum-frame platform of the air-boat (foof! air-boat, indeed! swizzleskid is what it was, with a tow-rack jerry-rigged) and he stared down at the neat Mondrian arrangement of the buildings.

Somewhere nearby, he could hear the metronomic left-right-left of the 2:47 P.M. shift, entering the Timkin roller-bearing plant in their sneakers. A minute later, precisely, he heard the softer right-left-right of the 5:00 A.M. formation, going home.

An elfin grin spread across his tanned features, and his dimples appeared for a moment. Then, scratching at his thatch of auburn hair, he shrugged within his motley, as though girding himself for what came next, and threw the joystick forward, and bent into the wind as the air-boat dropped. He skimmed over a slidewalk, purposely dropping a few feet to crease the tassels of the ladies of fashion, and—inserting thumbs in large ears—he stuck out his tongue, rolled his eyes, and went wugga-wugga-

71

wugga. It was a minor diversion. One pedestrian skittered and tumbled, sending parcels everywhichway, another wet herself, a third keeled slantwise and the walk was stopped automatically by the servitors till she could be resuscitated. It was a minor diversion.

Then he swirled away on a vagrant breeze, and was gone. Hi-ho.

As he rounded the cornice of the Time-Motion Study Building, he saw the shift, just boarding the slidewalk. With practiced motion and an absolute conservation of movement, they sidestepped up onto the slow-strip and (in a chorus line reminiscent of a Busby Berkeley film of the antediluvian 1930s) advanced across the strips ostrich-walking till they were lined up on the expresstrip.

Once more, in anticipation, the elfin grin spread, and there was a tooth missing back there on the left side. He dipped, skimmed, and swooped over them; and then, scrunching about on the air-boat, he released the holding pins that fastened shut the ends of the home-made pouring troughs that kept his cargo from dumping prematurely. And as he pulled the trough-pins, the air-boat slid over the factory workers and one hundred and fifty thousand dollars' worth of jelly beans cascaded down on the expresstrip.

Jelly beans! Millions and billions of purples and yellows and greens and licorice and grape and raspberry and mint and round and smooth and crunchy outside and soft-mealy inside and sugary and bouncing jouncing tumbling clittering clattering skittering fell on the heads and shoulders and hardhats and carapaces of the Timkin workers, tinkling on the slidewalk and bouncing away and rolling about underfoot and filling the sky on their way down with all the colors of joy and childhood and holidays, coming down in a steady rain, a solid wash, a torrent of color and sweetness out of the sky from above, and entering a universe of sanity and metronomic order with quite-mad coocoo newness.

Jelly beans!

The shift workers howled and laughed and were pelted, and broke ranks, and the jelly beans managed to work their way into the mechanism of the slidewalks after which there was a hideous scraping as the sound of a million fingernails rasped down a quarter of a million blackboards, followed by a coughing and a sputtering, and then the slidewalks all stopped and everyone was dumped thisawayandthataway in a jackstraw tumble, still laughing and popping little jelly bean eggs of childish color into their mouths. It was a holiday, and a jollity, an absolute insanity, a giggle. But . . .

The shift was delayed seven minutes.

They did not get home for seven minutes.

The master schedule was thrown off by seven minutes.

Quotas were delayed by inoperative slidewalks for seven minutes.

He had tapped the first domino in the line, and one after another, like chik chik chik, the others had fallen.

The System had been seven minutes' worth of disrupted. It was a tiny matter, one hardly worthy of note, but in a society where the single driving force was order and unity and equality and promptness and clocklike precision and attention to the clock, reverence of the gods of the passage of time, it was a disaster of major importance.

So he was ordered to appear before the Ticktockman. It was broadcast across every channel of the communications web. He was ordered to be *there* at 7:00 dammit on time. And they waited, and they waited, but he didn't show up till almost ten-thirty, at which time he merely sang a little song about moonlight in a place no one had ever heard of, called Vermont, and vanished again. But they had all been waiting since seven, and it wrecked *hell* with their schedules. So the question remained: Who is the Harlequin?

But the *unasked* question (more important of the two) was: how did we get *into* this position, where a laughing, irresponsible japer of jabberwocky and jive could disrupt our entire economic and cultural life with a hundred and fifty thousand dollars' worth of jelly beans . . .

*Jelly* for God's sake *beans!* This is madness! Where did he get the money to buy a hundred and fifty thousand dollars' worth of jelly beans? (They knew it would have cost that much, because they had a team of Situation Analysts pulled off another assignment, and rushed to the slidewalk scene to sweep up and count the candies, and produce findings, which disrupted *their* schedules and threw their entire branch at least a day behind.) Jelly beans! Jelly . . . *beans?* Now wait a second—a second accounted for— no one has manufactured jelly beans for over a hundred years. Where did he get jelly beans?

That's another good question. More than likely it will never be answered to your complete satisfaction. But then, how many questions ever are?

The middle you know. Here is the beginning. How it starts:

A DESK PAD. DAY FOR DAY, AND TURN EACH DAY. 9:00— OPEN THE MAIL. 9:45—APPOINTMENT WITH PLANNING COMMISSION BOARD. 10:30—DISCUSS INSTALLATION PROGRESS CHARTS WITH J. L. 11:45—PRAY FOR RAIN. 12:00—LUNCH. *AND SO IT GOES.*

"I'm sorry, Miss Grant, but the time for interviews was set at 2:30, and it's almost five now. I'm sorry you're late, but those are the rules. You'll have to wait till next year to submit application for this college again." *And so it goes.*

The 10:10 local stops at Cresthaven, Galesville, Tonawanda Junction, Selby, and Farnhurst, but not at Indiana City, Lucasville, and Colton, except on Sunday. The 10:35 express stops at Galesville, Selby, and Indiana City, except on Sundays & Holidays, at which time it stops at . . . *and so it goes.*

"I couldn't wait, Fred. I had to be at Pierre Cartain's by 3:00, and you said you'd meet me under the clock in the terminal at 2:45, and you weren't there, so I had to go on. You're always late, Fred. If you'd been there, we could have sewed it up together, but as it was, well, I took the order alone . . ." *And so it goes.*

Dear Mr. and Mrs. Atterley: In reference to your son Gerold's constant tardiness, I am afraid we will have to suspend him from school unless some more reliable method can be instituted guaranteeing he will arrive at his classes on time. Granted he is an exemplary student, and his marks are high, his constant flouting of the schedules of this school makes it impractical to maintain him in a system where the other children seem capable of getting where they are supposed to be on time *and so it goes.*

YOU CANNOT VOTE UNLESS YOU APPEAR AT 8:45 A.M.

"I don't care if the script is *good,* I need it Thursday!"

**CHECK-OUT TIME IS 2:00 P.M.**

"You got here late. The job's taken. Sorry."

YOUR SALARY HAS BEEN DOCKED FOR TWENTY MINUTES TIME LOST.

"God, what time is it, I've gotta run!"

And so it goes. And so it goes. And so it goes. And so it goes goes goes goes goes tick tock tick tock tick tock and one day we no longer let time serve us, we serve time and we are

75

slaves of the schedule, worshippers of the sun's passing, bound into a life predicated on restrictions because the system will not function if we don't keep the schedule tight.

Until it becomes more than a minor inconvenience to be late. It becomes a sin. Then a crime. Then a crime punishable by this:

EFFECTIVE 15 JULY 2389 12:00:00 midnight, the office of the Master Timekeeper will require all citizens to submit their time-cards and cardioplates for processing. In accordance with Statute 555-7-SGH-999 governing the revocation of time per capita, all cardioplates will be keyed to the individual holder and—

What they had done was devise a method of curtailing the amount of life a person could have. If he was ten minutes late, he lost ten minutes of his life. An hour was proportionately worth more revocation. If someone was consistently tardy, he might find himself, on a Sunday night, receiving a communiqué from the Master Timekeeper that his time had run out, and he would be "turned off" at high noon on Monday, please straighten your affairs, sir, madam or bisex,

And so, by this simple scientific expedient (utilizing a scientific process held dearly secret by the Ticktockman's office) the System was maintained. It was the only expedient thing to do. It was, after all, patriotic. The schedules had to be met. After all, there *was* a war on!

But, wasn't there always?

"Now that is really disgusting," the Harlequin said, when Pretty Alice showed him the wanted poster. "Disgusting and *highly* improbable. After all, this isn't the Day of the Desperado. A *wanted* poster!"

"You know," Pretty Alice noted, "you speak with a great deal of inflection."

"I'm sorry," said the Harlequin, humbly.

"No need to be sorry. You're always saying 'I'm sorry.' You have such massive guilt, Everett, it's really very sad."

"I'm sorry," he said again, then pursed his lips so the dimples appeared momentarily. He hadn't wanted to say that at all. "I have to go out again. I have to *do* something."

Pretty Alice slammed her coffee-bulb down on the counter. "Oh for God's *sake*, Everett, can't you stay home just *one* night! Must you always be out in that ghastly clown suit, running around annoying people?"

"I'm—" He stopped, and clapped the jester's hat onto his auburn thatch with a tiny tinkling of bells. He rose, rinsed out his coffee-bulb at the spray, and put it into the dryer for a moment. "I have to go."

She didn't answer. The faxbox was purring, and she pulled a sheet out, read it, threw it toward him on the counter. "It's about you. Of course. You're ridiculous."

He read it quickly. It said the Ticktockman was trying to locate him. He didn't care, he was going out to be late again. At the door, dredging for an exit line, he hurled back petulantly, "Well, *you* speak with inflection, *too!*"

Pretty Alice rolled her pretty eyes heavenward. "You're ridiculous."

The Harlequin stalked out, slamming the door, which sighed shut softly, and locked itself.

There was a gentle knock, and Pretty Alice got up with an exhalation of exasperated breath, and opened the door. He stood there. "I'll be back about ten-thirty, okay?"

She pulled a rueful face. "Why do you tell me that? Why? You *know* you'll be late! You *know it!* You're *always* late, so why do you tell me these dumb things?" She closed the door.

On the other side, the Harlequin nodded to himself. *She's right. She's always right. I'll be late. I'm always late. Why do I tell her these dumb things?*

He shrugged again, and went off to be late once more.

He had fired off the firecracker rockets that said: I will attend the 115th annual International Medical Association Invocation at 8:00 P.M. precisely. I do hope you will all be able to join me.

The words had burned in the sky, and of course the authorities were there, lying in wait for him. They assumed, naturally, that he would be late. He arrived twenty minutes early, while they were setting up the spiderwebs to trap and hold him. Blowing a large bullhorn, he frightened and unnerved them so, their own moisturized encirclement webs sucked closed, and they were hauled up, kicking and shrieking, high above the amphitheater's floor. The Harlequin laughed and laughed, and apologized profusely. The physicians, gathered in solemn conclave, roared with laughter, and accepted the Harlequin's apologies with exaggerated bowing and posturing, and a merry time was had by all, who thought the Harlequin was a regular foofaraw in fancy pants; all, that is, but the authorities, who had been sent out by the office of the Ticktockman; they hung there like so much dockside cargo, hauled up above the floor of the amphitheater in a most unseemly fashion.

(In another part of the same city where the Harlequin carried on his "activities," totally unrelated in every way to what concerns us here, save that it illustrates the Ticktockman's power and import, a man named Marshall Delahanty received his turn-off notice from the Ticktockman's office. His wife received the notification from the gray-suited minee who delivered it, with the traditional "look of sorrow" plastered hideously across his face. She knew what it was, even without unsealing it. It was a billet-doux of immediate recognition to everyone these days. She gasped, and held it as though it were a glass slide tinged with botulism, and prayed it was not for her. Let it be for Marsh, she thought, brutally, realistically, or one of the kids, but not for me, please dear God, not for me. And then she opened it, and it *was* for Marsh, and she was at one and the same time horrified and relieved. The next trooper in the line had caught the bullet. "Marshall," she screamed, "Marshall! Termination, Marshall! OhmiGod, Marshall, whattl we do, whattl we do, Marshall omigodmarshall . . ." and in their home that night was the sound of tearing paper and fear, and the stink of madness went up the flue and there was nothing, absolutely nothing they could do about it.

(But Marshall Delahanty tried to run. And early the next day, when turn-off time came, he was deep in the Canadian forest two hundred miles away, and the office of the Ticktockman blanked his cardioplate, and Marshall Delahanty keeled over, running, and his heart stopped, and the blood dried up on its way to his brain, and he was dead that's all. One light went out on the sector map in the office of the Master Timekeeper, while notification was entered for fax reproduction, and Georgette Delahanty's name was entered on the dole roles till she could remarry. Which is the end of the footnote, and all the point that need be made, except don't laugh, because that is what would happen to the Harlequin if ever the Ticktockman found out his real name. It isn't funny.)

The shopping level of the city was thronged with the Thursday-colors of the buyers. Women in canary yellow chitons and men in pseudo-Tyrolean outfits that were jade and leather and fit very tightly, save for the balloon pants.

When the Harlequin appeared on the still-being-constructed shell of the new Efficiency Shopping Center, his bullhorn to his elfishly-laughing lips, everyone pointed and stared, and he berated them:

"Why let them order you about? Why let them tell you to hurry and scurry like ants or maggots? Take your time! Saunter a while! Enjoy the sunshine, enjoy the breeze, let life carry you at your own pace! Don't be slaves of time, it's a helluva way to die, slowly, by degrees . . . down with the Ticktockman!"

Who's the nut? most of the shoppers wanted to know. Who's the nut oh wow I'm gonna be late I gotta run . . .

And the construction gang on the Shopping Center received an urgent order from the office of the Master Timekeeper that the dangerous criminal known as the Harlequin was atop their spire, and their aid was urgently needed in apprehending him. The work crew said no, they would lose time on their construction schedule, but the Ticktockman managed to pull the proper threads of governmental webbing, and they were told to cease work and catch that nitwit up there on the spire; up there with the bullhorn. So a dozen and more burly workers began climbing into their construction platforms, releasing the a-grav plates, and rising toward the Harlequin.

After the debacle (in which, through the Harlequin's attention to personal safety, no one was seriously injured), the workers tried to reassemble, and assault him again, but it was too late. He had vanished. It had attracted quite a crowd, however, and the shopping cycle was thrown off by hours, simply hours. The purchasing needs of the system were therefore falling behind, and so measures were taken to accelerate the cycle for the rest of the day, but it got bogged down and speeded up and they sold too many float-valves and not nearly enough wegglers, which meant that the popli ratio was off, which made it necessary to rush cases and cases of spoiling Smash-O to stores that usually needed a case only every three or four hours. The shipments were bollixed, the transshipments were misrouted, and in the end, even the swizzleskid industries felt it.

"Don't come back till you have him!" the Ticktockman said, very quietly, very sincerely, extremely dangerously.

They used dogs. They used probes. They used cardioplate crossoffs. They used teepers. They used bribery. They used stiktytes. They used intimidation. They used torment. They used torture. They used finks. They used cops. They used search&seizure. They used fallaron. They used betterment incentive. They used fingerprints. They used the Bertillon system. They used cunning. They used guile. They used treachery. They used Raoul Mitgong, but he didn't help much. They used applied physics. They used techniques of criminology.

And what the hell: they caught him.

After all, his name was Everett C. Marm, and he wasn't much to begin with, except a man who had no sense of time.

"Repent, Harlequin!" said the Ticktockman.

"Get stuffed!" the Harlequin replied, sneering.

"You've been late a total of sixty-three years, five months, three weeks, two days, twelve hours, forty-one minutes, fifty-nine seconds, point oh three six one one one microseconds. You've used up everything you can, and more. I'm going to turn you off."

"Scare someone else. I'd rather be dead than live in a dumb world with a bogeyman like you."

"It's my job."

"You're full of it. You're a tyrant. You have no right to order people around and kill them if they show up late."

"You can't adjust. You can't fit in."

"Unstrap me, and I'll fit my fist into your mouth."

"You're a non-conformist."

"That didn't used to be a felony."

"It is now. Live in the world around you."

"I hate it. It's a terrible world."

"Not everyone thinks so. Most people enjoy order."

"I don't, and most of the people I know don't."

"That's not true. How do you think we caught you?"

"I'm not interested."

"A girl named Pretty Alice told us who you were."

"That's a lie."

"It's true. You unnerve her. She wants to belong; she wants to conform; I'm going to turn you off."

"Then do it already, and stop arguing with me."

"I'm not going to turn you off."

"You're an idiot!"

"Repent, Harlequin!" said the Ticktockman.

"Get stuffed."

                        *   *   *

So they sent him to Coventry. And in Coventry they worked
him over. It was just like what they did to Winston Smith in
NINETEEN EIGHTY-FOUR which was a book none of them knew
about, but the techniques are really quite ancient, and so they
did it to Everett C. Marm; and one day, quite a long time later,
the Harlequin appeared on the communications web, appearing
elfin and dimpled and bright-eyed, and not at all brainwashed,
and he said he had been wrong, that it was a good, a very good
thing indeed, to belong, to be right on time hip-ho and away
we go, and everyone stared up at him on the public screens that
covered an entire city block, and they said to themselves, well,
you see, he was just a nut after all, and if that's the way the
system is run, then let's do it that way, because it doesn't pay to
fight city hall, or in this case, the Ticktockman. So Everett C.
Marm was destroyed, which was a loss, because of what Thoreau
said earlier, but you can't make an omelet without breaking a
few eggs, and in every revolution a few die who shouldn't, but
they have to, because that's the way it happens, and if you make
only a little change, then it seems to be worthwhile. Or, to make
the point lucidly:

"Uh, excuse me, sir, I, uh, don't know how to uh, to uh, tell you
this, but you were three minutes late. The schedule is a little,
uh, bit off."

He grinned sheepishly.

"That's ridiculous!" murmured the Ticktockman behind his
mask. "Check your watch." And then he went into his office,
going *mrmee, mrmee, mrmee, mrmee.*

Nebula Award, Best Novella 1965
(tied with "The Saliva Tree," by Brian W. Aldiss)

# He Who Shapes

## Roger Zelazny

*All science fiction writers know that reality is more fantastic than any publishable fiction. Here is one proof. The story you are about to read was tied on the first ballot with Brian W. Aldiss's "The Saliva Tree." We accordingly held a second ballot. The result? Another tie.*

*Feeling that it would be fruitless to pursue this any further (as well as illegal—the rules made no provision for a third ballot), we gladly awarded Nebulas to both authors.*

*Here is another story only Zelazny could have written: an intricate and subtle marriage of reality and hallucination, delicate eroticism, horror, all turning around a brilliantly imagined new kind of psychiatrist—*

*L o v e l y    a s*  it was, with the blood and all, Render could sense that it was about to end.

Therefore, each microsecond would be better off as a minute, he decided—and perhaps the temperature should be increased . . . Somewhere, just at the periphery of everything, the darkness halted its constriction.

Something, like a crescendo of subliminal thunders, was arrested at one raging note. That note was a distillate of shame and pain, and fear.

The Forum was stifling.

Caesar cowered outside the frantic circle. His forearm covered his eyes but it could not stop the seeing, not this time.

The senators had no faces and their garments were spattered with blood. All their voices were like the cries of birds. With an inhuman frenzy they plunged their daggers into the fallen figure.

All, that is, but Render.

The pool of blood in which he stood continued to widen. His arm seemed to be rising and falling with a mechanical regularity and his throat might have been shaping bird-cries, but he was simultaneously apart from and a part of the scene.

For he was Render, the Shaper.

Crouched, anguished and envious, Caesar wailed his protests.

"You have slain him! You have murdered Marcus Antonius— a blameless, useless fellow!"

Render turned to him, and the dagger in his hand was quite enormous and quite gory.

"Aye," said he.

The blade moved from side to side. Caesar, fascinated by the sharpened steel, swayed to the same rhythm.

"Why?" he cried. "Why?"

"Because," answered Render, "he was a far nobler Roman than yourself."

"You lie! It is not so!"

Render shrugged and returned to the stabbing.

"It is not true!" screamed Caesar. "Not true!"

Render turned to him again and waved the dagger. Puppet-like, Caesar mimicked the pendulum of the blade.

"Not true?" smiled Render. "And who are you to question an assassination such as this? You are no one! You detract from the dignity of this occasion! Begone!"

Jerkily, the pink-faced man rose to his feet, his hair half-wispy, half-wetplastered, a disarray of cotton. He turned, moved away; and as he walked, he looked back over his shoulder.

He had moved far from the circle of assassins, but the scene did not diminish in size. It retained an electric clarity. It made him feel even further removed, ever more alone and apart.

Render rounded a previously unnoticed corner and stood before him, a blind beggar.

Caesar grasped the front of his garment.

"Have you an ill omen for me this day?"

"Beware!" jeered Render.

"Yes! Yes!" cried Caesar. " 'Beware!' That is good! Beware what?"

"The ides—"

"Yes? The ides—"

"—of Octember."

He released the garment.

"What is that you say? What is Octember?"

"A month."

"You lie! There is no month of Octember!"

"And that is the date noble Caesar need fear—the non-existent time, the never-to-be-calendared occasion."

Render vanished around another sudden corner.

"Wait! Come back!"

Render laughed, and the Forum laughed with him. The bird-cries became a chorus of inhuman jeers.

"You mock me!" wept Caesar.

The Forum was an oven, and the perspiration formed like a glassy mask over Caesar's narrow forehead, sharp nose, chinless jaw.

"I want to be assassinated too!" he sobbed. "It isn't fair!"

And Render tore the Forum and the senators and the grinning corpse of Antony to pieces and stuffed them into a black sack—with the unseen movement of a single finger—and last of all went Caesar.

Charles Render sat before the ninety white buttons and the two red ones, not really looking at any of them. His right arm moved in its soundless sling, across the lap-level surface of the console—pushing some of the buttons, skipping over others, moving on, retracing its path to press the next in the order of the Recall Series.

Sensations throttled, emotions reduced to nothing. Representative Erikson knew the oblivion of the womb.

There was a soft click.

Render's hand had glided to the end of the bottom row of buttons. An act of conscious intent—will, if you like—was required to push the red button.

Render freed his arm and lifted off his crown of Medusa-hair leads and microminiature circuitry. He slid from behind his desk-couch and raised the hood. He walked to the window and transpared it, fingering forth a cigarette.

*One minute in the ro-womb*, he decided. *No more. This is a crucial one . . . Hope it doesn't snow till later—those clouds look mean . . .*

It was smooth yellow trellises and high towers, glassy and gray, all smouldering into evening under a shale-colored sky; the city was squared volcanic islands, glowing in the end-of-day light, rumbling deep down under the earth; it was fat, incessant rivers of traffic, rushing.

Render turned away from the window and approached the great egg that lay beside his desk, smooth and glittering. It threw back a reflection that smashed all aquilinity from his nose, turned his eyes to gray saucers, transformed his hair into a light-streaked skyline; his reddish necktie became the wide tongue of a ghoul.

He smiled, reached across the desk. He pressed the second red button.

With a sigh, the egg lost its dazzling opacity and a horizontal crack appeared about its middle. Through the now-transparent shell, Render could see Erikson grimacing, squeezing his eyes tight, fighting against a return to consciousness and the thing it would contain. The upper half of the egg rose vertical to the base, exposing him knobby and pink on half-shell. When his eyes opened he did not look at Render. He rose to his feet and began dressing. Render used this time to check the ro-womb.

He leaned back across his desk and pressed the buttons: temperature control, full range, *check*; exotic sounds—he raised the earphone—*check*, on bells, on buzzes, on violin notes and whistles, on squeals and moans, on traffic noises and the sound of surf; *check*, on the feedback circuit—holding the patient's own voice, trapped earlier in analysis; *check*, on the sound blanket, the moisture spray, the odor banks; *check*, on the couch agitator and the colored lights, the taste stimulants . . .

Render closed the egg and shut off its power. He pushed the unit into the closet, palmed shut the door. The tapes had registered a valid sequence.

"Sit down," he directed Erikson.

The man did so, fidgeting with his collar.

"You have full recall," said Render, "so there is no need for me to summarize what occurred. Nothing can be hidden from me. I was there."

Erikson nodded.

"The significance of the episode should be apparent to you."

Erikson nodded again, finally finding his voice. "But was it valid?" he asked. "I mean, you constructed the dream and you controlled it, all the way. I didn't really *dream* it—in the way I would normally dream. Your ability to make things happen stacks the deck for whatever you're going to say—doesn't it?"

Render shook his head slowly, flicked an ash into the southern hemisphere of his globe-made-ashtray, and met Erikson's eyes.

"It is true that I supplied the format and modified the forms. You, however, filled them with an emotional significance, promoted them to the status of symbols corresponding to your problem. If the dream was not a valid analogue it would not have provoked the reactions it did. It would have been devoid of the anxiety-patterns which were registered on the tapes.

"You have been in analysis for many months now," he continued, "and everything I have learned thus far serves to convince me that your fears of assassination are without any basis in fact."

Erikson glared.

"Then why the hell do I have them?"

"Because," said Render, "you would like very much to be the subject of an assassination."

Erikson smiled then, his composure beginning to return.

"I assure you, doctor, I have never contemplated suicide, nor have I any desire to stop living."

He produced a cigar and applied a flame to it. His hand shook.

"When you came to me this summer," said Render, "You stated that you were in fear of an attempt on your life. You were quite vague as to why anyone should want to kill you—"

"My position! You can't be a Representative as long as I have and make no enemies!"

"Yet," replied Render, "it appears that you have managed it. When you permitted me to discuss this with your detectives I was informed that they could unearth nothing to indicate that your fears might have any real foundation. Nothing."

"They haven't looked far enough—or in the right places. They'll turn up something."

"I'm afraid not."

"Why?"

"Because, I repeat, your feelings are without any objective basis.—Be honest with me. Have you any information whatsoever indicating that someone hates you enough to want to kill you?"

"I receive many threatening letters . . ."

"As do all Representatives—and all of those directed to you during the past year have been investigated and found to be the work of cranks. Can you offer me *one* piece of evidence to substantiate your claims?"

Erikson studied the tip of his cigar.

"I came to you on the advice of a colleague," he said, "came to you to have you poke around inside my mind to find me something of that sort, to give my detectives something to work with.—Someone I've injured severely perhaps—or some damaging piece of legislation I've dealt with . . ."

"—And I found nothing," said Render, "nothing, that is, but the cause of your discontent. Now, of course, you are afraid to hear it, and you are attempting to divert me from explaining my diagnosis—"

"I am not!"

"Then listen. You can comment afterwards if you want, but you've poked and dawdled around here for months, unwilling to accept what I presented to you in a dozen different forms. Now I am going to tell you outright what it is, and you can do what you want about it."

"Fine."

"First," he said, "you would like very much to have an enemy or enemies—"

"Ridiculous!"

"—Because it is the only alternative to having friends—"

"I have lots of friends!"

"—Because nobody wants to be completely ignored, to be an object for whom no one has really strong feelings. Hatred and love are the ultimate forms of human regard. Lacking one, and unable to achieve it, you sought the other. You wanted it so badly that you succeeded in convincing yourself it existed. But there is always a psychic pricetag on these things. Answering a genuine emotional need with a body of desire-surrogates does not produce real satisfaction, but anxiety, discomfort—because in these matters the psyche should be an open system. You did not seek outside yourself for human regard. You were closed off. You created that which you needed from the stuff of your own being. You are a man very much in need of strong relationships with other people."

"Manure!"

"Take it or leave it," said Render. "I suggest you take it."

"I've been paying you for half a year to help find out who wants to kill me. Now you sit there and tell me I made the whole thing up to satisfy a desire to have someone hate me."

"Hate you, or love you. That's right."

"It's absurd! I meet so many people that I carry a pocket recorder and a lapel-camera, just so I can recall them all . . ."

"Meeting quantities of people is hardly what I was speaking of.—Tell me, *did* that dream sequence have a strong meaning for you?"

Erikson was silent for several tickings of the huge wallclock.

"Yes," he finally conceded, "it did. But your interpretation of the matter is still absurd. Granting though, just for the sake of argument, that what you say is correct—what would I do to get out of this bind?"

Render leaned back in his chair.

"Rechannel the energies that went into producing the thing. Meet some people as yourself, Joe Erikson, rather than Representative Erikson. Take up something you can do with other people—something non-political, and perhaps somewhat competitive—and make some real friends or enemies, preferably the former. I've encouraged you to do this all along."

"Then tell me something else."

"Gladly."

"Assuming you *are* right, why is it that I am neither liked nor hated, and never have been? I have a responsible position in the Legislature. I meet people all the time. Why am I so neutral a—thing?"

Highly familiar now with Erikson's career, Render had to push aside his true thoughts on the matter, as they were of no operational value. He wanted to cite him Dante's observations concerning the trimmers—those souls who, denied heaven for their lack of virtue, were also denied entrance to hell for a lack of significant vices—in short, the ones who trimmed their sails to move them with every wind of the times, who lacked direction, who were not really concerned toward which ports they were pushed. Such was Erikson's long and colorless career of migrant loyalties, of political reversals.

Render said:

"More and more people find themselves in such circumstances these days. It is due largely to the increasing complexity of society and the depersonalization of the individual into a sociometric unit. Even the act of cathecting toward other persons has grown more forced as a result. There are so many of us these days."

Erikson nodded, and Render smiled inwardly.

*Sometimes the gruff line, and then the lecture . . .*

"I've got the feeling you could be right," said Erikson. "Sometimes I *do* feel like what you described—a unit, something depersonalized . . ."

Render glanced at the clock.

"What you choose to do about it from here is, of course, your own decision to make. I think you'd be wasting your time to remain in analysis any longer. We are now both aware of the cause of your complaint. I can't take you by the hand and show you how to lead your life. I can indicate, I can commiserate—but no more deep probing. Make an appointment as soon as you feel a need to discuss your activities and relate them to my diagnosis."

"I will," nodded Erikson, "and—damn that dream! It got to me. You can make them seem as vivid as waking life—more vivid . . . It may be a long while before I can forget it."

"I hope so."

"Okay, doctor." He rose to his feet, extended a hand. "I'll probably be back in a couple weeks. I'll give this socializing a fair try." He grinned at the word he normally frowned upon. "In fact, I'll start now. May I buy you a drink around the corner, downstairs?"

Render met the moist palm which seemed as weary of the performance as a lead actor in too successful a play. He felt almost sorry as he said, "Thank you, but I have an engagement."

Render helped him on with his coat then, handed him his hat, saw him to the door.

"Well, good night."

"Good night."

As the door closed soundlessly behind him, Render recrossed the dark Astrakhan to his mahogany fortress and flipped his cigarette into the southern hemisphere. He leaned back in his chair, hands behind his head, eyes closed.

"Of course it was more real than life," he informed no one in particular. "I shaped it."

Smiling, he reviewed the dream sequence step by step, wishing some of his former instructors could have witnessed it. It had been well-constructed and powerfully executed, as well as being precisely appropriate for the case at hand. But then, he was Render, the Shaper—one of the two hundred or so special analysts whose own psychic makeup permitted them to enter into neurotic patterns without carrying away more than an esthetic gratification from the mimesis of aberrance—a Sane Hatter.

Render stirred his recollections. He had been analyzed himself, analyzed and passed upon as a granite-willed, ultrastable outsider—tough enough to weather the basilisk gaze of a fixation, walk unscathed amidst the chimaerae of perversions, force dark Mother Medusa to close her eyes before the caduceus of his art. His own analysis had not been difficult. Nine years before (it seemed much longer) he had suffered a willing injection of novocain into the most painful area of his spirit. It was after the auto wreck, after the death of Ruth, and of Miranda their daughter, that he had begun to feel detached. Perhaps he did not want to recover certain empathies; perhaps his own world was now based upon a certain rigidity of feeling. If this was true, he was wise enough in the ways of the mind to realize it, and perhaps he had decided that such a world had its own compensations.

His son Peter was now ten years old. He was attending a school of quality, and he penned his father a letter every week. The letters were becoming progressively literate, showing signs of a precociousness of which Render could not but approve. He would take the boy with him to Europe in the summer.

As for Jill—Jill DeVille (what a luscious, ridiculous name!— he loved her for it)—she was growing, if anything, more interesting to him. (He wondered if this was an indication of early middle age.) He was vastly taken by her unmusical nasal voice, her sudden interest in architecture, her concern with the unremovable mole on the right side of her otherwise well-designed nose. He should really call her immediately and go in search of a new restaurant. For some reason though, he did not feel like it.

It had been several weeks since he had visited his club, The Partridge and Scalpel, and he felt a strong desire to eat from an oaken table, alone, in the split-level dining room with the three fireplaces, beneath the artificial torches and the boars' heads like gin ads. So he pushed his perforated membership card into the phone-slot on his desk and there were two buzzes behind the voice-screen.

"Hello, Partridge and Scalpel," said the voice. "May I help you?"

"Charles Render," he said. "I'd like a table in about half an hour."

"How many will there be?"

"Just me."

"Very good, sir. Half an hour, then.—That's 'Render'?—R-e-n-d-e-r?"

"Right."

"Thank you."

He broke the connection, rose from his desk. Outside, the day had vanished.

The monoliths and the towers gave forth their own light now. A soft snow, like sugar, was sifting down through the shadows and transforming itself into beads on the windowpane.

Render shrugged into his overcoat, turned off the lights, locked the inner office. There was a note on Mrs. Hedges' blotter.

*Miss DeVille called*, it said.

He crumpled the note and tossed it into the waste-chute. He would call her tomorrow and say he had been working until late on his lecture.

He switched off the final light, clapped his hat onto his head, and passed through the outer door, locking it as he went. The drop took him to the sub-subcellar where his auto was parked.

It was chilly in the sub-sub, and his footsteps seemed loud on the concrete as he passed among the parked vehicles. Beneath the glare of the naked lights, his S-7 Spinner was a sleek gray cocoon from which it seemed turbulent wings might at any moment emerge. The double row of antennae which fanned forward from the slope of its hood added to this feeling. Render thumbed open the door.

He touched the ignition and there was the sound of a lone bee awakening in a great hive. The door swung soundlessly shut as he raised the steering wheel and locked it into place. He spun up the spiral ramp and came to a rolling stop before the big overhead.

As the door rattled upward he lighted his destination screen and turned the knob that shifted the broadcast map.—Left to right, top to bottom, section by section he shifted it, until he located the portion of Carnegie Avenue he desired. He punched out its coordinates and lowered the wheel. The car switched over to monitor and moved out onto the highway marginal. Render lit a cigarette.

Pushing his seat back into the centerspace, he left all the windows transparent. It was pleasant to half-recline and watch the oncoming cars drift past him like swarms of fireflies. He pushed his hat back on his head and stared upward.

He could remember a time when he had loved snow, when it had reminded him of novels by Thomas Mann and music by Scandinavian composers. In his mind now, though, there was another element from which it could never be wholly dissociated. He could visualize so clearly the eddies of milk-white coldness that swirled about his old manual-steer auto, flowing into its fire-charred interior to rewhiten that which had been blackened; so clearly—as though he had walked toward it across a chalky lakebottom—it, the sunken wreck, and he, the diver—unable to open his mouth to speak, for fear of drowning; and he knew, whenever he looked upon falling snow, that somewhere skulls were whitening. But nine years had washed away much of the pain, and he also knew that the night was lovely.

He was sped along the wide, wide roads, shot across high bridges, their surfaces slick and gleaming beneath his lights, was woven through frantic cloverleafs and plunged into a tunnel whose dimly glowing walls blurred by him like a mirage. Finally, he switched the windows to opaque and closed his eyes.

He could not remember whether he had dozed for a moment or not, which meant he probably had. He felt the car slowing, and he moved the seat forward and turned on the windows again. Almost simultaneously, the cutoff buzzer sounded. He raised the

steering wheel and pulled into the parking dome, stepped out
onto the ramp, and left the car to the parking unit, receiving his
ticket from that box-headed robot which took its solemn revenge
on mankind by sticking forth a cardboard tongue at everyone it
served.

As always, the noises were as subdued as the lighting. The place
seemed to absorb sound and convert it into warmth, to lull the
tongue with aromas strong enough to be tasted, to hypnotize
the ear with the vivid crackle of the triple hearths.

Render was pleased to see that his favorite table, in the corner off to the right of the smaller fireplace, had been held for
him. He knew the menu from memory, but he studied it with
zeal as he sipped a Manhattan and worked up an order to match
his appetite. Shaping sessions always left him ravenously hungry.

"Doctor Render . . . ?"

"Yes?" He looked up.

"Doctor Shallot would like to speak with you," said the
waiter.

"I don't know anyone named Shallot," he said. "Are you sure
he doesn't want Bender? He's a surgeon from Metro who sometimes eats here . . ."

The waiter shook his head.

"No sir—'Render'. See here?" He extended a three-by-five
card on which Render's full name was typed in capital letters.
"Doctor Shallot has dined here nearly every night for the past
two weeks," he explained, "and on each occasion has asked to
be notified if you came in."

"Hm?" mused Render. "That's odd. Why didn't he just call
me at my office?"

The waiter smiled and made a vague gesture.

"Well, tell him to come on over," he said, gulping his Manhattan, "and bring me another of these."

"Unfortunately, Doctor Shallot is blind," explained the
waiter. "It would be easier if you—"

"All right, sure." Render stood up, relinquishing his favorite table with a strong premonition that he would not be returning to it that evening.

"Lead on."

They threaded their way among the diners, heading up to the next level. A familiar face said "hello" from a table set back against the wall, and Render nodded a greeting to a former seminar pupil whose name was Jurgens or Jirkans or something like that.

He moved on, into the smaller dining room wherein only two tables were occupied. No, three. There was one set in the corner at the far end of the darkened bar, partly masked by an ancient suit of armor. The waiter was heading him in that direction.

They stopped before the table and Render stared down into the darkened glasses that had tilted upward as they approached. Doctor Shallot was a woman, somewhere in the vicinity of her early thirties. Her low bronze bangs did not fully conceal the spot of silver which she wore on her forehead like a castemark. Render inhaled, and her head jerked slightly as the tip of his cigarette flared. She appeared to be staring straight up into his eyes. It was an uncomfortable feeling, even knowing that all she could distinguish of him was that which her minute photo-electric cell transmitted to her visual cortex over the hair-fine wire implants attached to that oscillator-convertor: in short, the glow of his cigarette.

"Doctor Shallot, this is Doctor Render," the waiter was saying.

"Good evening," said Render.

"Good evening," she said. "My name is Eileen and I've wanted very badly to meet you." He thought he detected a slight quaver in her voice. "Will you join me for dinner?"

"My pleasure," he acknowledged, and the waiter drew out the chair.

98

Render sat down, noting that the woman across from him

already had a drink. He reminded the waiter of his second Manhattan.

"Have you ordered yet?" he inquired.

"No."

". . . And two menus—" he started to say, then bit his tongue.

"Only one," she smiled.

"Make it none," he amended, and recited the menu.

They ordered. Then:

"Do you always do that?"

"What?"

"Carry menus in your head."

"Only a few," he said, "for awkward occasions. What was it you wanted to see—talk to me about?"

"You're a neuroparticipant therapist," she stated, "a Shaper."

"And you are—?"

"—a resident in psychiatry at State Psych. I have a year remaining."

"You knew Sam Riscomb then."

"Yes, he helped me get my appointment. He was my adviser."

"He was a very good friend of mine. We studied together at Menninger."

She nodded.

"I'd often heard him speak of you—that's one of the reasons I wanted to meet you. He's responsible for encouraging me to go ahead with my plans, despite my handicap."

Render stared at her. She was wearing a dark green dress which appeared to be made of velvet. About three inches to the left of the bodice was a pin which might have been gold. It displayed a red stone which could have been a ruby, around which the outline of a goblet was cast. Or was it really two profiles that were outlined, staring through the stone at one another? It seemed vaguely familiar to him, but he could not place it at the moment. It glittered expensively in the dim light.

Render accepted his drink from the waiter.

"I want to become a neuroparticipant therapist," she told him.

And if she had possessed vision Render would have thought she was staring at him, hoping for some response in his expression. He could not quite calculate what she wanted him to say.

"I commend your choice," he said, "and I respect your ambition." He tried to put his smile into his voice. "It is not an easy thing, of course, not all of the requirements being academic ones."

"I know," she said. "But then, I have been blind since birth and it was not an easy thing to come this far."

"Since birth?" he repeated. "I thought you might have lost your sight recently. You did your undergrad work then, and went on through med school without eyes . . . That's—rather impressive."

"Thank you," she said, "but it isn't. Not really. I heard about the first neuroparticipants—Bartelmetz and the rest—when I was a child, and I decided then that I wanted to be one. My life ever since has been governed by that desire."

"What did you do in the labs?" he inquired. "—Not being able to see a specimen, look through a microscope . . . ? Or all that reading?"

"I hired people to read my assignments to me. I taped everything. The school understood that I wanted to go into psychiatry, and they permitted a special arrangement for labs. I've been guided through the dissection of cadavers by lab assistants, and I've had everything described to me. I can tell things by touch . . . and I have a memory like yours with the menu," she smiled. " 'The quality of psychoparticipation phenomena can only be gauged by the therapist himself, at that moment outside of time and space as we normally know it, when he stands in the midst of a world erected from the stuff of another man's dreams, recognizes there the non-Euclidian architecture of aberrance, and then takes his patient by the hand and tours the landscape . . . If he can lead him back to the common earth, then his judgments were sound, his actions valid.' "

"From *Why No Psychometrics in This Place*," reflected Render.

"—by Charles Render, M.D."

"Our dinner is already moving in this direction," he noted, picking up his drink as the speed-cooked meal was pushed toward them in the kitchen-buoy.

"That's one of the reasons I wanted to meet you," she continued, raising her glass as the dishes rattled before her. "I want you to help me become a Shaper."

Her shaded eyes, as vacant as a statue's, sought him again.

"Yours is a completely unique situation," he commented. "There has never been a congenitally blind neuroparticipant— for obvious reasons. I'd have to consider all the aspects of the situation before I could advise you. Let's eat now, though. I'm starved."

"All right. But my blindness does not mean that I have never seen."

He did not ask her what she meant by that, because prime ribs were standing in front of him now and there was a bottle of Chambertin at his elbow. He did pause long enough to notice though, as she raised her left hand from beneath the table, that she wore no rings.

"I wonder if it's still snowing," he commented as they drank their coffee. "It was coming down pretty hard when I pulled into the dome."

"I hope so," she said, "even though it diffuses the light and I can't 'see' anything at all through it. I like to feel it falling about me and blowing against my face."

"How do you get about?"

"My dog, Sigmund—I gave him the night off," she smiled, "—he can guide me anywhere. He's a mutie Shepherd."

"Oh?" Render grew curious. "Can he talk much?"

She nodded.

"That operation wasn't as successful on him as on some of them, though. He has a vocabulary of about four hundred words,

101

but I think it causes him pain to speak. He's quite intelligent. You'll have to meet him sometime."

Render began speculating immediately. He had spoken with such animals at recent medical conferences, and had been startled by their combination of reasoning ability and their devotion to their handlers. Much chromosome tinkering, followed by delicate embryo-surgery, was required to give a dog a brain capacity greater than a chimpanzee's. Several followup operations were necessary to produce vocal abilities. Most such experiments ended in failure, and the dozen or so puppies a year on which they succeeded were valued in the neighborhood of a hundred thousand dollars each. He realized then, as he lit a cigarette and held the light for a moment, that the stone in Miss Shallot's medallion was a genuine ruby. He began to suspect that her admission to a medical school might, in addition to her academic record, have been based upon a sizeable endowment to the college of her choice. Perhaps he was being unfair though, he chided himself.

"Yes," he said, "we might do a paper on canine neuroses. Does he ever refer to his father as 'that son of a female Shepherd?'"

"He never met his father," she said, quite soberly. "He was raised apart from other dogs. His attitude could hardly be typical. I don't think you'll ever learn the functional psychology of the dog from a mutie."

"I imagine you're right," he dismissed it. "More coffee?"

"No, thanks."

Deciding it was time to continue the discussion, he said, "So you want to be a Shaper . . ."

"Yes."

"I hate to be the one to destroy anybody's high ambitions," he told her. "Like poison, I hate it. Unless they have no foundation at all in reality. Then I can be ruthless. So—honestly, frankly, and in all sincerity, I do not see how it could ever be managed. Perhaps you're a fine psychiatrist—but in my opinion, it is a physical and mental impossibility for you ever to become a neuroparticipant. As for my reasons—"

"Wait," she said. "Not here, please. Humor me. I'm tired of this stuffy place—take me somewhere else to talk. I think I might be able to convince you there *is* a way."

"Why not?" he shrugged. "I have plenty of time. Sure—you call it. Where?"

"Blindspin?"

He suppressed an unwilling chuckle at the expression, but she laughed aloud.

"Fine," he said, "but I'm still thirsty."

A bottle of champagne was tallied and he signed the check despite her protests. It arrived in a colorful "Drink While You Drive" basket, and they stood then, and she was tall, but he was taller.

Blindspin.

A single name of a multitude of practices centered about the auto-driven auto. Flashing across the country in the sure hands of an invisible chauffeur, windows all opaque, night dark, sky high, tires assailing the road below like four phantom buzzsaws— and starting from scratch and ending in the same place, and never knowing where you are going or where you have been—it is possible, for a moment, to kindle some feeling of individuality in the coldest brainpan, to produce a momentary awareness of self by virtue of an apartness from all but a sense of motion. This is because movement through darkness is the ultimate abstraction of life itself—at least that's what one of the Vital Comedians said, and everybody in the place laughed.

Actually now, the phenomenon known as blindspin first became prevalent (as might be suspected) among certain younger members of the community, when monitored highways deprived them of the means to exercise their automobiles in some of the more individualistic ways which had come to be frowned upon by the National Traffic Control Authority. Something had to be done.

It was.

The first, disastrous reaction involved the simple engineering feat of disconnecting the broadcast control unit after one had entered onto a monitored highway. This resulted in the car's vanishing from the ken of the monitor and passing back into the control of its occupants. Jealous as a deity, a monitor will not tolerate that which denies its programmed omniscience; it will thunder and lightning in the Highway Control Station nearest the point of last contact, sending winged seraphs in search of that which has slipped from sight.

Often, however, this was too late in happening, for the roads are many and well-paved. Escape from detection was, at first, relatively easy to achieve.

Other vehicles, though, necessarily behave as if a rebel has no actual existence. Its presence cannot be allowed for.

Boxed-in, on a heavily-traveled section of roadway, the offender is subject to immediate annihilation in the event of any overall speedup or shift in traffic pattern which involves movement through his theoretically vacant position. This, in the early days of monitor-controls, caused a rapid series of collisions. Monitoring devices later became far more sophisticated, and mechanized cutoffs reduced the collision incidence subsequent to such an action. The quality of the pulpefactions and contusions which did occur, however, remained unaltered.

The next reaction was based on a thing which had been overlooked because it was obvious. The monitors took people where they wanted to go only because people told them they wanted to go there. A person pressing a random series of coordinates, without reference to any map, would either be left with a stalled automobile and a "RECHECK YOUR COORDINATES" light, or would suddenly be whisked away in any direction. The latter possesses a certain romantic appeal in that it offers speed, unexpected sights, and free hands. Also, it is perfectly legal; and it is possible to navigate all over two continents in this manner, if one is possessed of sufficient wherewithal and gluteal stamina.

As is the case in all such matters, the practice diffused upwards through the age brackets. Schoolteachers who only drove on Sundays fell into disrepute as selling points for used autos. Such is the way a world ends, said the entertainer.

End or no, the car designed to move on monitored highways is a mobile efficiency unit, complete with latrine, cupboard, refrigerator compartment, and gaming table. It also sleeps two with ease and four with some crowding. On occasion, three can be a real crowd.

Render drove out of the dome and into the marginal aisle. He halted the car.

"Want to jab some coordinates?" he asked.

"You do it. My fingers know too many."

Render punched random buttons. The Spinner moved onto the highway. Render asked speed of the vehicle then, and it moved into the high-acceleration lane.

The Spinner's lights burnt holes in the darkness. The city backed away fast; it was a smouldering bonfire on both sides of the road, stirred by sudden gusts of wind, hidden by white swirlings, obscured by the steady fall of gray ash. Render knew his speed was only about sixty percent of what it would have been on a clear, dry night.

He did not blank the windows, but leaned back and stared out through them. Eileen "looked" ahead into what light there was. Neither of them said anything for ten or fifteen minutes.

The city shrank to sub-city as they sped on. After a time, short sections of open road began to appear.

"Tell me what it looks like outside," she said.

"Why didn't you ask me to describe your dinner, or the suit of armor beside our table?"

"Because I tasted one and felt the other. This is different."

"There is snow falling outside. Take it away and what you have left is black."

"What else?"

"There is slush on the road. When it starts to freeze, traffic will drop to a crawl unless we outrun this storm. The slush looks like an old, dark syrup, just starting to get sugary on top."

"Anything else?"

"That's it, lady."

"Is it snowing harder or less hard than when we left the club?"

"Harder, I should say."

"Would you pour me a drink?" she asked him.

"Certainly."

They turned their seats inward and Render raised the table. He fetched two glasses from the cupboard.

"Your health," said Render, after he had poured.

"Here's looking at you."

Render downed his drink. She sipped hers. He waited for her next comment. He knew that two cannot play at the Socratic game, and he expected more questions before she said what she wanted to say.

She said: "What is the most beautiful thing you have ever seen?"

Yes, he decided, he had guessed correctly.

He replied without hesitation: "The sinking of Atlantis."

"I was serious."

"So was I."

"Would you care to elaborate?"

"I sank Atlantis," he said, "personally.

"It was about three years ago. And God! it was lovely! It was all ivory towers and golden minarets and silver balconies. There were bridges of opal, and crimson pennants and a milk-white river flowing between lemon-colored banks. There were jade steeples, and trees as old as the world tickling the bellies of clouds, and ships in the great sea-harbor of Xanadu, as delicately constructed as musical instruments, all swaying with the tides. The twelve princes of the realm held court in the dozen-pillared Coliseum of the Zodiac, to listen to a Greek tenor sax play at sunset.

"The Greek, of course, was a patient of mine—paranoiac. The etiology of the thing is rather complicated, but that's what I wandered into inside his mind. I gave him free rein for awhile, and in the end I had to split Atlantis in half and sink it full fathom five. He's playing again and you've doubtless heard his sounds, if you like such sounds at all. He's good. I still see him periodically, but he is no longer the last descendant of the greatest minstrel of Atlantis. He's just a fine, late twentieth-century saxman.

"Sometimes though, as I look back on the apocalypse I worked within his vision of grandeur, I experience a fleeting sense of lost beauty—because, for a single moment, his abnormally intense feelings were my feelings, and he felt that his dream was the most beautiful thing in the world."

He refilled their glasses.

"That wasn't exactly what I meant," she said.

"I know."

"I meant something real."

"It was more real than real, I assure you."

"I don't doubt it, but . . ."

"—But I destroyed the foundation you were laying for your argument. Okay, I apologize. I'll hand it back to you. Here's something that could be real:

"We are moving along the edge of a great bowl of sand," he said. "Into it, the snow is gently drifting. In the spring the snow will melt, the waters will run down into the earth, or be evaporated away by the heat of the sun. Then only the sand will remain. Nothing grows in the sand, except for an occasional cactus. Nothing lives here but snakes, a few birds, insects, burrowing things, and a wandering coyote or two. In the afternoon these things will look for shade. Any place where there's an old fence post or a rock or a skull or a cactus to block out the sun, there you will witness life cowering before the elements. But the colors are beyond belief, and the elements are more lovely, almost, than the things they destroy."

"There is no such place near here," she said.

"If I say it, then there is. Isn't there? I've seen it."

"Yes . . . You're right."

"And it doesn't matter if it's a painting by a woman named O'Keefe, or something right outside our window, does it? If I've seen it?"

"I acknowledge the truth of the diagnosis," she said. "Do you want to speak it for me?"

"No, go ahead."

He refilled the small glasses once more.

"The damage is in my eyes," she told him, "not my brain."

He lit her cigarette.

"I can see with other eyes if I can enter other brains."

He lit his own cigarette.

"Neuroparticipation is based upon the fact that two nervous systems can share the same impulses, the same fantasies . . ."

"*Controlled* fantasies."

"I could perform therapy and at the same time experience genuine visual impressions."

"No," said Render.

"You don't know what it's like to be cut off from a whole area of stimuli! To know that a Mongoloid idiot can experience something you can never know—and that he cannot appreciate it because, like you, he was condemned before birth in a court of biological happenstance, in a place where there is no justice— only fortuity, pure and simple."

"The universe did not invent justice. Man did. Unfortunately, man must reside in the universe."

"I'm not asking the universe to help me—I'm asking you."

"I'm sorry," said Render.

108    "Why won't you help me?"

"At this moment you are demonstrating my main reason."

"Which is . . . ?"

"Emotion. This thing means far too much to you. When the therapist is in-phase with a patient he is narco-electrically removed from most of his own bodily sensations. This is necessary—because his mind must be completely absorbed by the task at hand. It is also necessary that his emotions undergo a similar suspension. This, of course, is impossible in the one sense that a person always emotes to some degree. But the therapist's emotions are sublimated into a generalized feeling of exhilaration— or, as in my own case, into an artistic reverie. With you, however, the 'seeing' would be too much. You would be in constant danger of losing control of the dream."

"I disagree with you."

"Of course you do. But the fact remains that you would be dealing, and dealing constantly, with the abnormal. The power of a neurosis is unimaginable to ninety-nine point etcetera percent of the population, because we can never adequately judge the intensity of our own—let alone those of others, when we only see them from the outside. That is why no neuroparticipant will ever undertake to treat a full-blown psychotic. The few pioneers in that area are all themselves in therapy today. It would be like diving into a maelstrom. If the therapist loses the upper hand in an intense session he becomes the Shaped rather than the Shaper. The synapses respond like a fission reaction when nervous impulses are artificially augmented. The transference effect is almost instantaneous.

"I did an awful lot of skiing five years ago. This is because I was a claustrophobe. I had to run and it took me six months to beat the thing—all because of one tiny lapse that occurred in a measureless fraction of an instant. I had to refer the patient to another therapist. And this was only a minor repercussion.—If you were to go ga-ga over the scenery, girl, you could wind up in a rest home for life."

She finished her drink and Render refilled the glass. The 109 night raced by. They had left the city far behind them, and the road was open and clear. The darkness eased more and more of itself between the falling flakes. The Spinner picked up speed.

"All right," she admitted, "maybe you're right. Still, though, I think you can help me."

"How?" he asked.

"Accustom me to seeing, so that the images will lose their novelty, the emotions wear off. Accept me as a patient and rid me of my sight-anxiety. Then what you have said so far will cease to apply. I will be able to undertake the training then, and give my full attention to therapy. I'll be able to sublimate the sight-pleasure into something else."

Render wondered.

Perhaps it could be done. It would be a difficult undertaking, though.

It might also make therapeutic history.

No one was really qualified to try it, because no one had ever tried it before.

But Eileen Shallot was a rarity—no, a unique item—for it was likely she was the only person in the world who combined the necessary technical background with the unique problem.

He drained his glass, refilled it, refilled hers.

He was still considering the problem as the "RE-COOR-DINATE" light came on and the car pulled into a cutoff and stood there. He switched off the buzzer and sat there for a long while, thinking.

It was not often that other persons heard him acknowledge his feelings regarding his skill. His colleagues considered him modest. Offhand, though, it might be noted that he was aware that the day a better neuroparticipant began practicing would be the day that a troubled homo sapiens was to be treated by something but immeasurably less than angels.

Two drinks remained. Then he tossed the emptied bottle into the backbin.

"You know something?" he finally said.

"What?"

"It might be worth a try."

He swiveled about then and leaned forward to re-coordinate, but she was there first. As he pressed the buttons and the S-7 swung around, she kissed him. Below her dark glasses her cheeks were moist.

## II

The suicide bothered him more than it should have, and Mrs. Lambert had called the day before to cancel her appointment. So Render decided to spend the morning being pensive. Accordingly, he entered the office wearing a cigar and a frown.

"Did you see . . . ?" asked Mrs. Hedges.

"Yes." He pitched his coat onto the table that stood in the far corner of the room. He crossed to the window, stared down. "Yes," he repeated, "I was driving by with my windows clear. They were still cleaning up when I passed."

"Did you know him?"

"I don't even know the name yet. How could I?"

"Priss Tully just called me—she's a receptionist for that engineering outfit up on the eighty-sixth. She says it was James Irizarry, an ad designer who had offices down the hall from them.—That's a long way to fall. He must have been unconscious when he hit, huh? He bounced off the building. If you open the window and lean out you can see—off to the left there where . . ."

"Never mind, Bennie—Your friend have any idea why he did it?"

"Not really. His secretary came running up the hall, screaming. Seems she went in his office to see him about some drawings, just as he was getting up over the sill. There was a note on his board. 'I've had everything I wanted,' it said. 'Why wait around?' Sort of funny, huh? I don't mean *funny* . . ."

"Yeah.—Know anything about his personal affairs?"

"Married. Coupla kids. Good professional rep. Lots of business. Sober as anybody.—He could afford an office in this building."

"Good Lord!" Render turned. "Have you got a case file there or something?"

"You know," she shrugged her thick shoulders, "I've got friends all over this hive. We always talk when things go slow. Prissy's my sister-in-law anyhow—"

"You mean that if I dived through this window right now, my current biography would make the rounds in the next five minutes?"

"Probably," she twisted her bright lips into a smile, "give or take a couple. But don't do it today, huh?—You know, it would be kind of anticlimactic, and it wouldn't get the same coverage as a solus.

"Anyhow," she continued, "you're a mind-mixer. You wouldn't do it."

"You're betting against statistics," he observed. "The medical profession, along with attorneys, manages about three times as many as most other work areas."

"Hey!" She looked worried. "Go 'way from my window!

"I'd have to go to work for Doctor Hanson then," she added, "and he's a slob."

He moved to her desk.

"I never know when to take you seriously," she decided.

"I appreciate your concern," he nodded, "indeed I do. As a matter of fact, I have never been statistic-prone—I should have repercussed out of the neuropy game four years ago."

"You'd be a headline, though," she mused. "All those reporters asking me about you . . . Hey, why do they do it, huh?"

"Who?"

"Anybody."

"How should I know, Bennie? I'm only a humble psychestirrer. If I could pinpoint a general underlying cause—and then maybe figure a way to anticipate the thing—why, it might even be better than my jumping, for newscopy. But I can't do it, because there is no single, simple reason—I don't think."

"Oh."

"About thirty-five years ago it was the ninth leading cause of death in the United States. Now it's number six for North and South America. I think it's seventh in Europe."

"And nobody will ever really know why Irizarry jumped?"

Render swung a chair backwards and seated himself. He knocked an ash into her petite and gleaming tray. She emptied it into the waste-chute, hastily, and coughed a significant cough.

"Oh, one can always speculate," he said, "and one in my profession will. The first thing to consider would be the personality traits which might predispose a man to periods of depression. People who keep their emotions under rigid control, people who are conscientious and rather compulsively concerned with small matters . . ." He knocked another fleck of ash into her tray and watched as she reached out to dump it, then quickly drew her hand back again. He grinned an evil grin. "In short," he finished, "some of the characteristics of people in professions which require individual, rather than group performance—medicine, law, the arts."

She regarded him speculatively.

"Don't worry though," he chuckled, "I'm pleased as hell with life."

"You're kind of down in the mouth this morning."

"Pete called me. He broke his ankle yesterday in gym class. They ought to supervise those things more closely. I'm thinking of changing his school."

"Again?"

"Maybe. I'll see. The headmaster is going to call me this afternoon. I don't like to keep shuffling him, but I do want him to finish school in one piece."

"A kid can't grow up without an accident or two. It's—statistics."

"Statistics aren't the same thing as destiny, Bennie. Everybody makes his own."

"Statistics or destiny?"

"Both, I guess."

"I think that if something's going to happen, it's going to happen."

"I don't. I happen to think that the human will, backed by a sane mind can exercise some measure of control over events. If I didn't think so, I wouldn't be in the racket I'm in."

"The world's a machine—you know—cause, effect. Statistics do imply the prob—"

"The human mind is not a machine, and I do not know cause and effect. Nobody does."

"You have a degree in chemistry, as I recall. You're a scientist, Doc."

"So I'm a Trotskyite deviationist," he smiled, stretching, "and you were once a ballet teacher." He got to his feet and picked up his coat.

"By the way, Miss DeVille called, left a message, She said: 'How about St. Moritz?' "

"Too ritzy," he decided aloud. "It's going to be Davos."

Because the suicide bothered him more than it should have, Render closed the door to his office and turned off the windows and turned on the phonograph. He put on the desk light only.

*How has the quality of human life been changed, he wrote, since the beginnings of the industrial revolution?*

He picked up the paper and re-read the sentence. It was the topic he had been asked to discuss that coming Saturday. As was typical in such cases he did not know what to say because he had too much to say, and only an hour to say it in.

He got up and began to pace the office, now filled with Beethoven's Eighth Symphony.

"The power to hurt," he said, snapping on a lapel microphone and activating his recorder, "has evolved in a direct relationship to technological advancement." His imaginary audience grew quiet. He smiled. "Man's potential for working simple mayhem has been multiplied by mass-production; his capacity for injuring the psyche through personal contacts has expanded in an exact ratio to improved communication facilities. But these are all matters of common knowledge, and are not the things I wish to consider tonight. Rather, I should like to discuss what I choose to call autopsychomimesis—the self-generated anxiety complexes which on first scrutiny appear quite similar to classic patterns, but which actually represent radical dispersions of psychic energy. They are peculiar to our times . . ."

He paused to dispose of his cigar and formulate his next words.

"Autopsychomimesis," he thought aloud, "a self-perpetuated imitation complex—almost an attention-getting affair.—A jazzman, for example, who acted hopped-up half the time, even though he had never used an addictive narcotic and only dimly remembered anyone who had—because all the stimulants and tranquilizers of today are quite benign. Like Quixote, he aspired after a legend when his music alone should have been sufficient outlet for his tensions.

"Or my Korean War Orphan, alive today by virtue of the Red Cross and UNICEF and foster parents whom he never met. He wanted a family so badly that he made one up. And what then?—He hated his imaginary father and he loved his imaginary mother quite dearly—for he was a highly intelligent boy, and he too longed after the half-true complexes of tradition. Why?

"Today, everyone is sophisticated enough to understand the time-honored patterns of psychic disturbance. Today, many of the reasons for those disturbances have been removed—not as radically as my now-adult war orphan's, but with as remarkable an effect. We are living in a neurotic past.—Again, why? Because our present times are geared to physical health, security, and well-being. We have abolished hunger, though the backwoods orphan would still rather receive a package of food concentrates from a human being who cares for him than to obtain a warm meal from an automat unit in the middle of the jungle.

"Physical welfare is now every man's right, in excess. The reaction to this has occurred in the area of mental health. Thanks to technology, the reasons for many of the old social problems have passed, and along with them went many of the reasons for psychic distress. But between the black of yesterday and the white of tomorrow is the great gray of today, filled with nostalgia, and fear of the future, which cannot be expressed on a purely material plane, is now being represented by a willful seeking after historical anxiety-modes . . ."

The phone-box buzzed briefly. Render did not hear it over the Eighth.

"We are afraid of what we do not know," he continued, "and tomorrow is a very great unknown. My own specialized area of psychiatry did not even exist thirty years ago. Science is capable of advancing itself so rapidly now that there is a genuine public uneasiness—I might even say 'distress'—as to the logical outcome: the total mechanization of everything in the world . . ."

He passed near the desk as the phone buzzed again. He switched off his microphone and softened the Eighth.

"Hello?"

"Saint Moritz," she said.

"Davos," he replied firmly.

"Charlie, you are most exasperating!"

"Jill, dear—so are you."

"Shall we discuss it tonight?"

"There is nothing to discuss!"

"You'll pick me up at five, though?"

He hesitated, then:

"Yes, at five. How come the screen is blank?"

"I've had my hair fixed. I'm going to surprise you again."

He suppressed an idiot chuckle, said, "Pleasantly, I hope.

Okay, see you then," waited for her "goodbye," and broke the connection.

He transpared the windows, turned off the light on his desk, and looked outside.

Gray again overhead, and many slow flakes of snow—wandering, not being blown about much—moving downwards and then losing themselves in the tumult . . .

He also saw, when he opened the window and leaned out, the place off to the left where Irizarry had left his next-to-last mark on the world.

He closed the window and listened to the rest of the symphony. It had been a week since he had gone blindspinning with Eileen. Her appointment was for one o'clock.

He remembered her fingertips brushing over his face, like leaves, or the bodies of insects, learning his appearance in the ancient manner of the blind. The memory was not altogether pleasant. He wondered why.

Far below, a patch of hosed pavement was blank once again; under a thin, fresh shroud of white, it was slippery as glass. A building custodian hurried outside and spread salt on it, before someone slipped and hurt himself.

Sigmund was the myth of Fenris come alive. After Render had instructed Mrs. Hedges, "Show them in," the door had begun to open, was suddenly pushed wider, and a pair of smoky-yellow eyes stared in at him. The eyes were set in a strangely misshapen dog-skull.

Sigmund's was not a low canine brow, slanting up slightly from the muzzle; it was a high, shaggy cranium, making the eyes appear even more deep-set than they actually were. Render shivered slightly at the size and aspect of that head. The muties he had seen had all been puppies. Sigmund was full grown, and his gray-black fur had a tendency to bristle, which made him appear somewhat larger than a normal specimen of the breed.

117

He stared in at Render in a very un-doglike way and made a growling noise which sounded too much like, "Hello, doctor," to have been an accident.

Render nodded and stood.

"Hello, Sigmund," he said. "Come in."

The dog turned his head, sniffing the air of the room—as though deciding whether or not to trust his ward within its confines. Then he returned his stare to Render, dipped his head in an affirmative, and shouldered the door open. Perhaps the entire encounter had taken only one disconcerting second.

Eileen followed him, holding lightly to the double-leashed harness. The dog padded soundlessly across the thick rug—head low, as though he was stalking something. His eyes never left Render's.

"So this is Sigmund . . . ? How are you, Eileen?"

"Fine.—Yes, he wanted very badly to come along, and *I* wanted you to meet him."

Render led her to a chair and seated her. She unsnapped the double guide from the dog's harness and placed it on the floor. Sigmund sat down beside it and continued to stare at Render.

"How is everything at State Psych?"

"Same as always.—May I bum a cigarette, doctor? I forgot mine."

He placed it between her fingers, furnished a light. She was wearing a dark blue suit and her glasses were flame blue. The silver spot on her forehead reflected the glow of his lighter; she continued to stare at that point in space after he had withdrawn his hand. Her shoulder-length hair appeared a trifle lighter than it had seemed on the night they met; today it was like a fresh-minted copper coin.

Render seated himself on the corner of his desk, drawing up his world-ashtray with his toe.

"You told me before that being blind did not mean that you had never seen. I didn't ask you to explain it then. But I'd like to ask you now."

"I had a neuroparticipation session with Doctor Riscomb," she told him, "before he had his accident. He wanted to accommodate my mind to visual impressions. Unfortunately, there was never a second session."

"I see. What did you do in that session?"

She crossed her ankles and Render noted they were well-turned.

"Colors, mostly. The experience was quite overwhelming."

"How well do you remember them? How long ago was it?"

"About six months ago—and I shall never forget them. I have even dreamt in color patterns since then."

"How often?"

"Several times a week."

"What sort of associations do they carry?"

"Nothing special. They just come into my mind along with other stimuli now—in a pretty haphazard way."

"How?"

"Well, for instance, when you ask me a question it's a sort of yellowish-orangish pattern that I 'see.' Your greeting was a kind of silvery thing. Now that you're just sitting there listening to me, saying nothing, I associate you with a deep, almost violet, blue."

Sigmund shifted his gaze to the desk and stared at the side panel.

*Can he hear the recorder spinning inside?* wondered Render. *And if he can, can he guess what it is and what it's doing?*

If so, the dog would doubtless tell Eileen—not that she was unaware of what was now an accepted practice—and she might not like being reminded that he considered her case as therapy, rather than a mere mechanical adaptation process. If he thought it would do any good (he smiled inwardly at the notion), he would talk to the dog in private about it.

Inwardly, he shrugged.

"I'll construct a rather elementary fantasy world then," he said finally, "and introduce you to some basic forms today."

She smiled; and Render looked down at the myth who crouched by her side, its tongue a piece of beefsteak hanging over a picket fence.

*Is he smiling too?*

"Thank you," she said.

Sigmund wagged his tail.

"Well then," Render disposed of his cigarette near Madagascar, "I'll fetch out the 'egg' now and test it. In the meantime," he pressed an unobtrusive button, "perhaps some music would prove relaxing."

She started to reply, but a Wagnerian overture snuffed out the words. Render jammed the button again, and there was a moment of silence during which he said, "Heh heh. Thought Respighi was next."

It took two more pushes for him to locate some Roman pines.

"You could have left him on," she observed. "I'm quite fond of Wagner."

"No thanks," he said, opening the closet, "I'd keep stepping in all those piles of leitmotifs."

The great egg drifted out into the office, soundless as a cloud. Render heard a soft growl behind as he drew it toward the desk. He turned quickly.

Like the shadow of a bird, Sigmund had gotten to his feet, crossed the room, and was already circling the machine and sniffing at it—tail taut, ears flat, teeth bared.

"Easy, Sig," said Render. "It's an Omnichannel Neural T & R Unit. It won't bite or anything like that. It's just a machine, like a car, or a teevee, or a dishwasher. That's what we're going to use today to show Eileen what some things look like."

"Don't like it," rumbled the dog.

"Why?"

Sigmund had no reply, so he stalked back to Eileen and laid his head in her lap.

"Don't like it," he repeated, looking up at her.

"Why?"

"No words," he decided. "We go home now?"

"No," she answered him. "You're going to curl up in the corner and take a nap, and I'm going to curl up in that machine and do the same thing—sort of."

"No good," he said, tail drooping.

"Go on now," she pushed him, "lie down and behave yourself."

He acquiesced, but he whined when Render blanked the windows and touched the button which transformed his desk into the operator's seat.

He whined once more—when the egg, connected now to an outlet, broke in the middle and the top slid back and up, revealing the interior.

Render seated himself. His chair became a contour couch and moved in halfway beneath the console. He sat upright and it moved back again, becoming a chair. He touched a part of the desk and half the ceiling disengaged itself, reshaped itself, and lowered to hover overhead like a huge bell. He stood and moved around to the side of the ro-womb. Respighi spoke of pines and such, and Render disengaged an earphone from beneath the egg and leaned back across his desk. Blocking one ear with his shoulder and pressing the microphone to the other, he played upon the buttons with his free hand. Leagues of surf drowned the tone poem; miles of traffic overrode it; a great clanging bell sent fracture lines running through it; and the feedback said: ". . . Now that you are just sitting there listening to me, saying nothing, I associate you with a deep, almost violet, blue . . ."

He switched to the face mask and monitored, *one*—cinnamon, *two*—leaf mold, *three*—deep reptilian musk . . . and down through thirst, and the tastes of honey and vinegar and salt, and back on up through lilacs and wet concrete, a before-the-storm whiff of ozone, and all the basic olfactory and gustatory cues for morning, afternoon, and evening in the town.

The couch floated normally in its pool of mercury, magnetically stabilized by the walls of the egg. He set the tapes.

The ro-womb was in perfect condition.

"Okay," said Render, turning, "everything checks."

She was just placing her glasses atop her folded garments. She had undressed while Render was testing the machine. He was perturbed by her narrow waist, her large, dark-pointed breasts, her long legs. She was too well-formed for a woman her height, he decided.

He realized though, as he stared at her, that his main annoyance was, of course, the fact that she was his patient.

"Ready here," she said, and he moved to her side.

He took her elbow and guided her to the machine. Her fingers explored its interior. As he helped her enter the unit, he saw that her eyes were a vivid seagreen. Of this, too, he disapproved.

"Comfortable?"

"Yes."

"Okay then, we're set. I'm going to close it now. Sweet dreams."

The upper shell dropped slowly. Closed, it grew opaque, then dazzling. Render was staring down at his own distorted reflection.

He moved back in the direction of his desk.

Sigmund was on his feet, blocking the way.

Render reached down to pat his head, but the dog jerked it aside.

"Take me, with," he growled.

"I'm afraid that can't be done, old fellow," said Render. "Besides, we're not really going anywhere. We'll just be dozing right here, in this room."

The dog did not seem mollified.

"Why?"

Render sighed. An argument with a dog was about the most
122   ludicrous thing he could imagine when sober.

"Sig," he said, "I'm trying to help her learn what things look like. You doubtless do a fine job guiding her around in this world which she cannot see—but she needs to know what it looks like now, and I'm going to show her."

"Then she, will not, need me."

"Of course she will." Render almost laughed. The pathetic thing was here bound so closely to the absurd thing that he could not help it. "I can't restore her sight," he explained. "I'm just going to transfer her some sight-abstractions—sort of lend her my eyes for a short time. Savvy?"

"No," said the dog. "Take mine."

Render turned off the music.

*The whole mutie-master relationship might be worth six volumes,* he decided, *in German.*

He pointed to the far corner.

"Lie down, over there, like Eileen told you. This isn't going to take long, and when it's all over you're going to leave the same way you came—you leading. Okay?"

Sigmund did not answer, but he turned and moved off to the corner, tail drooping again.

Render seated himself and lowered the hood, the operator's modified version of the ro-womb. He was alone before the ninety white buttons and the two red ones. The world ended in the blackness beyond the console. He loosened his necktie and unbuttoned his collar.

He removed the helmet from its receptacle and checked its leads. Donning it then, he swung the halfmask up over his lower face and dropped the darksheet down to meet with it. He rested his right arm in the sling, and with a single tapping gesture, he eliminated his patient's consciousness.

A Shaper does not press white buttons consciously. He wills conditions. Then deeply-implanted muscular reflexes exert an almost imperceptible pressure against the sensitive arm-sling, which glides into the proper position and encourages an

123

extended finger to move forward. A button is pressed. The sling moves on.

Render felt a tingling at the base of his skull; he smelled fresh-cut grass.

Suddenly he was moving up the great gray alley between the worlds.

After what seemed a long time, Render felt that he was footed on a strange Earth. He could see nothing; it was only a sense of presence that informed him he had arrived. It was the darkest of all the dark nights he had ever known.

He willed that the darkness disperse. Nothing happened.

A part of his mind came awake again, a part he had not realized was sleeping; he recalled whose world he had entered.

He listened for her presence. He heard fear and anticipation.

He willed color. First, red . . .

He felt a correspondence. Then there was an echo.

Everything became red; he inhabited the center of an infinite ruby.

Orange. Yellow . . .

He was caught in a piece of amber.

Green now, and he added the exhalations of a sultry sea. Blue, and the coolness of evening.

He stretched his mind then, producing all the colors at once. They came in great swirling plumes.

Then he tore them apart and forced a form upon them.

An incandescent rainbow arched across the black sky.

He fought for browns and grays below him. Self-luminescent, they appeared—in shimmering, shifting patches.

Somewhere, a sense of awe. There was no trace of hysteria though, so he continued with the Shaping.

He managed a horizon, and the blackness drained away beyond it. The sky grew faintly blue, and he ventured a herd of dark clouds. There was resistance to his efforts at creating distance and depth, so he reinforced the tableau with a very faint sound of surf. A transference from an auditory concept of distance came on slowly then, as he pushed the clouds about. Quickly, he threw up a high forest to offset a rising wave of acrophobia.

The panic vanished.

Render focused his attention on tall trees—oaks and pines, poplars and sycamores. He hurled them about like spears, in ragged arrays of greens and browns and yellows, unrolled a thick mat of morning-moist grass, dropped a series of gray boulders and greenish logs at irregular intervals, and tangled and twined the branches overhead, casting a uniform shade throughout the glen.

The effect was staggering. It seemed as if the entire world was shaken with a sob, then silent.

Through the stillness he felt her presence. He had decided it would be best to lay the groundwork quickly, to set up a tangible headquarters, to prepare a field for operations. He could backtrack later, he could repair and amend the results of the trauma in the sessions yet to come; but this much, at least, was necessary for a beginning.

With a start, he realized that the silence was not a withdrawal. Eileen had made herself immanent in the trees and the grass, the stones and the bushes; she was personalizing their forms, relating them to tactile sensations, sounds, temperatures, aromas.

With a soft breeze, he stirred the branches of the trees. Just beyond the bounds of seeing he worked out the splashing sounds of a brook.

There was a feeling of joy. He shared it.

She was bearing it extremely well, so he decided to extend the scope of the exercise. He let his mind wander among the trees, experiencing a momentary doubling of vision, during which time he saw an enormous hand riding in an aluminum carriage toward a circle of white.

He was beside the brook now and he was seeking her, carefully.

He drifted with the water. He had not yet taken on a form. The splashes became a gurgling as he pushed the brook through shallow places and over rocks. At his insistence, the waters became more articulate.

"Where are you?" asked the brook.

*Here! Here!*

*Here!*

*. . . and here!* replied the trees, the bushes, the stones, the grass.

"Choose one," said the brook, as it widened, rounded a mass of rock, then bent its way toward a slope, heading toward a blue pool.

*I cannot,* was the answer from the wind.

"You must." The brook widened and poured itself into the pool, swirled about the surface, then stilled itself and reflected branches and dark clouds. "Now!"

*Very well,* echoed the wood, *in a moment.*

The mist rose above the lake and drifted to the bank of the pool.

"Now," tinkled the mist.

*Here, then . . .*

She had chosen a small willow. It swayed in the wind; it trailed its branches in the water.

"Eileen Shallot," he said, "regard the lake."

The breezes shifted; the willow bent.

It was not difficult for him to recall her face, her body. The tree spun as though rootless. Eileen stood in the midst of a quiet explosion of leaves; she stared, frightened, into the deep blue mirror of Render's mind, the lake.

She covered her face with her hands, but it could not stop the seeing.

"Behold yourself," said Render.

She lowered her hands and peered downwards. Then she turned in every direction, slowly; she studied herself. Finally:

"I feel I am quite lovely," she said. "Do I feel so because you want me to, or is it true?"

She looked all about as she spoke, seeking the Shaper.

"It is true," said Render, from everywhere.

"Thank you."

There was a swirl of white and she was wearing a belted garment of damask. The light in the distance brightened almost imperceptibly. A faint touch of pink began at the base of the lowest cloudbank.

"What is happening there?" she asked, facing that direction.

"I am going to show you a sunrise," said Render, "and I shall probably botch it a bit—but then, it's my first professional sunrise under these circumstances."

"Where are *you*?" she asked.

"Everywhere," he replied.

"Please take on a form so that I can see you."

"All right."

"Your natural form."

He willed that he be beside her on the bank, and he was.

Startled by a metallic flash, he looked downward. The world receded for an instant, then grew stable once again. He laughed, and the laugh froze as he thought of something.

He was wearing the suit of armor which had stood beside their table in The Partridge and Scalpel on the night they met.

She reached out and touched it.

"The suit of armor by our table," she acknowledged, running her fingertips over the plates and the junctures. "I associated it with you that night."

". . . And you stuffed me into it just now," he commented. "You're a strong-willed woman."

The armor vanished and he was wearing his graybrown suit and looseknit bloodclot necktie and a professional expression.

"Behold the real me," he smiled faintly. "Now, to the sunset. I'm going to use all the colors. Watch!"

They seated themselves on the green park bench which had

127

appeared behind them, and Render pointed in the direction he had decided upon as east.

Slowly, the sun worked through its morning attitudes. For the first time in this particular world it shone down like a god, and reflected off the lake, and broke the clouds, and set the landscape to smouldering beneath the mist that arose from the moist wood.

Watching, watching intently, staring directly into the ascending bonfire, Eileen did not move for a long while, nor speak. Render could sense her fascination.

She was staring at the source of all light; it reflected back from the gleaming coin on her brow, like a single drop of blood.

Render said, "That is the sun, and those are clouds," and he clapped his hands and the clouds covered the sun and there was a soft rumble overhead, "and that is thunder," he finished.

The rain fell then, shattering the lake and tickling their faces, making sharp striking sounds on the leaves, then soft tapping sounds, dripping down from the branches overhead, soaking their garments and plastering their hair, running down their necks and falling into their eyes; turning patches of brown earth to mud.

A splash of lightning covered the sky, and a second later there was another peal of thunder.

". . . And this is a summer storm," he lectured. "You see how the rain affects the foliage, and ourselves. What you just saw in the sky before the thunderclap was lightning."

". . . Too much," she said. "Let up on it for a moment, please."

The rain stopped instantly and the sun broke through the clouds.

"I have the damnedest desire for a cigarette," she said, "but I left mine in another world."

As she said it one appeared, already lighted, between her fingers.

"It's going to taste rather flat," said Render strangely.

He watched her for a moment, then:

"I didn't give you that cigarette," he noted. "You picked it from my mind."

The smoke laddered and spiraled upward, was swept away.

". . . Which means that, for the second time today, I have underestimated the pull of that vacuum in your mind—in the place where sight ought to be. You are assimilating these new impressions very rapidly. You're even going to the extent of groping after new ones. Be careful. Try to contain that impulse."

"It's like a hunger," she said.

"Perhaps we had best conclude this session now."

Their clothing was dry again. A bird began to sing.

"No, wait! Please! I'll be careful. I want to see more things."

"There is always the next visit," said Render. "But I suppose we can manage one more. Is there something you want very badly to see?"

"Yes. Winter. Snow."

"Okay," smiled the Shaper, "then wrap yourself in that fur-piece . . ."

The afternoon slipped by rapidly after the departure of his patient. Render was in a good mood. He felt emptied and filled again. He had come through the first trial without suffering any repercussions. He decided that he was going to succeed. His satisfaction was greater than his fear. It was with a sense of exhilaration that he returned to working on his speech.

". . . And what is the power to hurt?" he inquired of the microphone.

"We live by pleasure and we live by pain," he answered himself. "Either can frustrate and either can encourage. But while pleasure and pain are rooted in biology, they are conditioned by society: thus are values to be derived. Because of the enormous masses of humanity, hectically changing positions in space every day throughout the cities of the world, there has come into necessary being a series of totally inhuman controls upon these movements. Every day they nibble their way into new areas—

driving our cars, flying our planes, interviewing us, diagnosing our diseases—and I cannot even venture a moral judgment upon these intrusions. They have become necessary. Ultimately, they may prove salutary.

"The point I wish to make, however, is that we are often unaware of our own values. We cannot honestly tell what a thing means to us until it is removed from our life-situation. If an object of value ceases to exist, then the psychic energies which were bound up in it are released. We seek after new objects of value in which to invest this—mana, if you like, or libido, if you don't. And no one thing which has vanished during the past three or four or five decades was, in itself, massively significant; and no new thing which came into being during that time is massively malicious toward the people it has replaced or the people it in some manner controls. A society, though, is made up of many things, and when these things are changed too rapidly the results are unpredictable. An intense study of mental illness is often quite revealing as to the nature of the stresses in the society where the illness was made. If anxiety-patterns fall into special groups and classes, then something of the discontent of society can be learned from them. Carl Jung pointed out that when consciousness is repeatedly frustrated in a quest for values it will turn its search to the unconscious; failing there, it will proceed to quarry its way into the hypothetical collective unconscious. He noted, in the postwar analyses of ex-Nazis, that the longer they searched for something to erect from the ruins of their lives—having lived through a period of classical iconoclasm, and then seen their new ideals topple as well—the longer they searched, the further back they seemed to reach into the collective unconscious of their people. Their dreams themselves came to take on patterns out of the Teutonic mythos.

"This, in a much less dramatic sense, is happening today. There are historical periods when the group tendency for the mind to turn in upon itself, to turn back, is greater than at other times. We are living in such a period of Quixotism, in the original sense of the term. This is because the power to hurt, in our time, is the power to ignore, to baffle—and it is no longer the exclusive property of human beings—"

A buzz interrupted him then. He switched off the recorder, touched the phone-box.

"Charles Render speaking," he told it.

"This is Paul Charter," lisped the box. "I am headmaster at Dilling."

"Yes?"

The picture cleared. Render saw a man whose eyes were set close together beneath a high forehead. The forehead was heavily creased; the mouth twitched as it spoke.

"Well, I want to apologize again for what happened. It was a faulty piece of equipment that caused—"

"Can't you afford proper facilities? Your fees are high enough."

"It was a *new* piece of equipment. It was a factory defect—"

"Wasn't there anybody in charge of the class?"

"Yes, but—"

"Why didn't he inspect the equipment? Why wasn't he on hand to prevent the fall?"

"He *was* on hand, but it happened too fast for him to do anything. As for inspecting the equipment for factory defects, that isn't his job. Look, I'm very sorry. I'm quite fond of your boy. I can assure you nothing like this will ever happen again."

"You're right, there. But that's because I'm picking him up tomorrow morning and enrolling him in a school that exercises proper safety precautions."

Render ended the conversation with a flick of his finger.

After several minutes had passed he stood and crossed the room to his small wall safe, which was partly masked, though not concealed, by a shelf of books. It took only a moment for him to open it and withdraw a jewel box containing a cheap necklace and a framed photograph of a man resembling himself, though somewhat younger, and a woman whose upswept hair was dark and whose chin was small, and two youngsters between them—the girl holding the baby in her arms and forcing her bright bored smile on ahead. Render always stared for only a few seconds on such occasions, fondling the necklace, and then he shut the box and locked it away again for many months.

*Whump! Whump!* went the bass. *Tchg-tchg-tchga-tchg,* the gourds.

The gelatins splayed reds, greens, blues, and godawful yellows about the amazing metal dancers.

HUMAN? asked the marquee.

ROBOTS? (immediately below).

COME SEE FOR YOURSELF! (across the bottom, cryptically).

So they did.

Render and Jill were sitting at a microscopic table, thankfully set back against a wall, beneath charcoal caricatures of personalities largely unknown (there being so many personalities among the subcultures of a city of 14 million people). Nose crinkled with pleasure, Jill stared at the present focal point of this particular subculture, occasionally raising her shoulders to ear level to add emphasis to a silent laugh or a small squeal, because the performers were just *too* human—the way the ebon robot ran his fingers along the silver robot's forearm as they parted and passed . . .

Render alternated his attention between Jill and the dancers and a wicked-looking decoction that resembled nothing so much as a small bucket of whisky sours strewn with seaweed (through which the Kraken might at any moment arise to drag some hapless ship down to its doom).

"Charlie, I think they're really people!"

Render disentangled his gaze from her hair and bouncing earrings.

He studied the dancers down on the floor, somewhat below the table area, surrounded by music.

There *could* be humans within those metal shells. If so, their dance was a thing of extreme skill. Though the manufacture of

sufficiently light alloys was no problem, it would be some trick
for a dancer to cavort so freely—and for so long a period of
time, and with such effortless-seeming ease—within a head-to-
toe suit of armor, without so much as a grate or a click or a
clank.

Soundless . . .

They glided like two gulls; the larger, the color of polished
anthracite, and the other, like a moonbeam falling through a
window upon a silk-wrapped manikin.

Even when they touched there was no sound—or if there
was, it was wholly masked by the rhythms of the band.

*Whump-whump! Tchga-tchg!*

Render took another drink.

Slowly, it turned into an apache-dance. Render checked his
watch. Too long for normal entertainers, he decided. They must
be robots. As he looked up again the black robot hurled the
silver robot perhaps ten feet and turned his back on her.

There was no sound of striking metal.

*Wonder what a setup like that costs?* he mused.

"Charlie! There was no sound! How do they do that?"

"Really?" asked Render.

The gelatins were yellow again, then red, then blue, then
green.

"You'd think it would damage their mechanisms, wouldn't
you?"

The white robot crawled back and the other swiveled his
wrist around and around, a lighted cigarette between the fingers.
There was laughter as he pressed it mechanically to his lipless
faceless face. The silver robot confronted him. He turned away
again, dropped the cigarette, ground it out slowly, soundlessly,
then suddenly turned back to his partner. Would he throw her
again? No . . .

Slowly then, like the great-legged birds of the East, they
recommenced their movement, slowly, and with many turnings
away.

Something deep within Render was amused, but he was too far gone to ask it what was funny. So he went looking for the Kraken in the bottom of the glass instead.

Jill was clutching his bicep then, drawing his attention back to the floor.

As the spotlight tortured the spectrum, the black robot raised the silver one high above his head, slowly, slowly, and then commenced spinning with her in that position—arms outstretched, back arched, legs scissored—very slowly, at first. Then faster.

Suddenly they were whirling with an unbelievable speed, and the gelatins rotated faster and faster.

Render shook his head to clear it.

They were moving so rapidly that they *had* to fall—human or robot. But they didn't. They were a mandala. They were a gray-form uniformity. Render looked down.

Then slowing, and slower, slower. Stopped.

The music stopped.

Blackness followed. Applause filled it.

When the lights came on again the two robots were standing statue-like, facing the audience. Very, very slowly, they bowed.

The applause increased.

Then they turned and were gone.

Then the music came on and the light was clear again. A babble of voices arose. Render slew the Kraken.

"What d'you think of that?" she asked him.

Render made his face serious and said: "Am I a man dreaming I am a robot, or a robot dreaming I am a man?" He grinned, then added: "I don't know."

She punched his shoulder gaily at that and he observed that she was drunk.

"I am not," she protested. "Not much, anyhow. Not as much as you."

"Still, I think you ought to see a doctor about it. Like me. Like now. Let's get out of here and go for a drive."

"Not yet, Charlie. I want to see them once more, huh? Please?"

"If I have another drink I won't be able to see that far."

"Then order a cup of coffee."

"Yaagh!"

"Then order a beer."

"I'll suffer without."

There were people on the dance floor now, but Render's feet felt like lead.

He lit a cigarette.

"So you had a dog talk to you today?"

"Yes. Something very disconcerting about that . . ."

"Was she pretty?"

"It was a boy dog. And boy, was he ugly!"

"Silly. I mean his mistress."

"You know I never discuss cases, Jill."

"You told me about her being blind and about the dog. All I want to know is if she's pretty."

"Well . . . Yes and no." He bumped her under the table and gestured vaguely. "Well, you know . . ."

"Same thing all the way around," she told the waiter who had appeared suddenly out of an adjacent pool of darkness, nodded, and vanished as abruptly.

"There go my good intentions," sighed Render. "See how you like being examined by a drunken sot, that's all I can say."

"You'll sober up fast, you always do. Hippocratics and all that."

He sniffed, glanced at his watch.

"I have to be in Connecticut tomorrow. Pulling Pete out of that damned school . . ."

She sighed, already tired of the subject.

"I think you worry too much about him. Any kid can bust an ankle. It's a part of growing up. I broke my wrist when I was seven. It was an accident. It's not the school's fault those things sometimes happen."

135

"Like hell," said Render, accepting his dark drink from the dark tray the dark man carried. "If they can't do a good job I'll find someone who can."

She shrugged.

"You're the boss. All I know is what I read in the papers.

"—And you're still set on Davos, even though you know you meet a better class of people at Saint Moritz?" she added.

"We're going there to ski, remember? I like the runs better at Davos."

"I can't score any tonight, can I?"

He squeezed her hand.

"You always score with me, honey."

And they drank their drinks and smoked their cigarettes and held their hands until the people left the dance floor and filed back to their microscopic tables, and the gelatins spun round and round, tinting clouds of smoke from hell to sunrise and back again, and the bass went *whump!*

*Tchga-tchgat!*

"Oh, Charlie! Here they come again!"

The sky was clear as crystal. The roads were clean. The snow had stopped.

Jill's breathing was the breathing of a sleeper. The S-7 arced across the bridges of the city. If Render sat very still he could convince himself that only his body was drunk; but whenever he moved his head the universe began to dance about him. As it did so, he imagined himself within a dream, and Shaper of it all.

For one instant this was true. He turned the big clock in the sky backward, smiling as he dozed. Another instant and he was awake again, and unsmiling.

The universe had taken revenge for his presumption. For one reknown moment with the helplessness which he had loved beyond helping, it had charged him the price of the lake-bottom vision once again; and as he had moved once more toward the wreck at the bottom of the world—like a swimmer, as unable to

speak—he heard, from somewhere high over the Earth, and filtered down to him through the waters above the Earth, the howl
of the Fenris Wolf as it prepared to devour the moon; and as
this occurred, he knew that the sound was as like to the trump
of a judgment as the lady by his side was unlike the moon. Every
bit. In all ways. And he was afraid.

## III

". . . The plain, the direct, and the blunt. This is Winchester
Cathedral," said the guidebook. "With its floor-to-ceiling shafts,
like so many huge treetrunks, it achieves a ruthless control over
its spaces: the ceilings are flat; each bay, separated by those
shafts, is itself a thing of certainty and stability. It seems, indeed,
to reflect something of the spirit of William the Conqueror. Its
disdain of mere elaboration and its passionate dedication to the
love of another world would make it seem, too, an appropriate
setting for some tale out of Mallory . . ."

"Observe the scalloped capitals," said the guide. "In their
primitive fluting they anticipated what was later to become a
common motif . . ."

"Faugh!" said Render—softly though, because he was in a
group inside a church.

"Shh!" said Jill (Fotlock—that was her real last name) De-
Ville.

But Render was impressed as well as distressed.

Hating Jill's hobby though, had become so much of a reflex
with him that he would sooner have taken his rest seated beneath
an oriental device which dripped water on his head than to admit
he occasionally enjoyed walking through the arcades and the
galleries, the passages and the tunnels, and getting all out of
breath climbing up the high twisty stairways of towers.

So he ran his eyes over everything, burnt everything down
by shutting them, then built the place up again out of the still
smouldering ashes of memory, all so that at a later date he would     137

be able to repeat the performance, offering the vision to his one patient who could see only in this manner. This building he disliked less than most. Yes, he would take it back to her.

The camera in his mind photographing the surroundings, Render walked with the others, overcoat over his arm, his fingers anxious to reach after a cigarette. He kept busy ignoring his guide, realizing this to be the nadir of all forms of human protest. As he walked through Winchester he thought of his last two sessions with Eileen Shallot. He recalled his almost unwilling Adam-attitude as he had named all the animals passing before them, led of course by the *one* she had wanted to see, colored fearsome by his own unease. He had felt pleasantly bucolic after boning up on an old botany text and then proceeding to Shape and name the flowers of the fields.

So far they had stayed out of the cities, far away from the machines. Her emotions were still too powerful at the sight of the simple, carefully introduced objects to risk plunging her into so complicated and chaotic a wilderness yet; he would build her city slowly.

Something passed rapidly, high above the cathedral, uttering a sonic boom. Render took Jill's hand in his for a moment and smiled as she looked up at him. Knowing she verged upon beauty, Jill normally took great pains to achieve it. But today her hair was simply drawn back and knotted behind her head, and her lips and her eyes were pale; and her exposed ears were tiny and white and somewhat pointed.

"Observe the scalloped capitals," he whispered. "In their primitive fluting they anticipated what was later to become a common motif."

"Faugh!" said she.

"Shh!" said a sunburnt little woman nearby, whose face seemed to crack and fall back together again as she pursed and unpursed her lips.

Later, as they strolled back toward their hotel, Render said, "Okay on Winchester?"

"Okay on Winchester."

"Happy?"

"Happy."

"Good, then we can leave this afternoon."

"All right."

"For Switzerland . . ."

She stopped and toyed with a button on his coat.

"Couldn't we just spend a day or two looking at some old chateaux first? After all, they're just across the Channel, and you could be sampling all the local wines while I looked . . ."

"Okay," he said.

She looked up—a trifle surprised.

"What? No argument?" she smiled. "Where is your fighting spirit?—to let me push you around like this?"

She took his arm then and they walked on as he said, "Yesterday, while we were galloping about in the innards of that old castle, I heard a weak moan, and then a voice cried out, 'For the love of God, Montresor!' I think it was my fighting spirit, because I'm certain it was my voice. I've given up der geist der stets verneint. Pax vobiscum! Let us be gone to France. Alors!"

"Dear Rendy, it'll only be another day or two . . ."

"Amen," he said, "though my skis that were waxed are already waning."

So they did that, and on the morn of the third day, when she spoke to him of castles in Spain, he reflected aloud that while psychologists drink and only grow angry, psychiatrists have been known to drink, grow angry, and break things. Construing this as a veiled threat aimed at the Wedgwoods she had collected, she acquiesced to his desire to go skiing.

Free! Render almost screamed it.

His heart was pounding inside his head. He leaned hard. He cut to the left. The wind strapped at his face; a shower of ice crystals, like bullets of emery, fired by him, scraped against his cheek.

He was moving. Aye—the world had ended at Weissflujoch, and Dorftali led down and away from this portal.

His feet were two gleaming rivers which raced across the stark, curving plains; they could not be frozen in their course. Downward. He flowed. Away from all the rooms of the world. Away from the stifling lack of intensity, from the day's hundred spoon-fed welfares, from the killing pace of the forced amusements that hacked at the Hydra, leisure; away.

And as he fled down the run he felt a strong desire to look back over his shoulder, as though to see whether the world he had left behind and above had set one fearsome embodiment of itself, like a shadow, to trail along after him, hunt him down, and to drag him back to a warm and well-lit coffin in the sky, there to be laid to rest with a spike of aluminum driven through his will and a garland of alternating currents smothering his spirit.

"I hate you," he breathed between clenched teeth, and the wind carried the words back; and he laughed then, for he always analyzed his emotions, as a matter of reflex; and he added, "Exit Orestes, mad, pursued by the Furies . . ."

After a time the slope leveled out and he reached the bottom of the run and had to stop.

He smoked one cigarette then and rode back up to the top so that he could come down it again for non-therapeutic reasons.

That night he sat before a fire in the big lodge, feeling its warmth soaking into his tired muscles. Jill massaged his shoulders as he played Rorschach with the flames, and he came upon a blazing goblet which was snatched away from him in the same instant by the sound of his name being spoken somewhere across the Hall of the Nine Hearths.

"Charles Render!" said the voice (only it sounded more like "Sharlz Runder"), and his head instantly jerked in that direction, but his eyes danced with too many afterimages for him to isolate the source of the calling.

"Maurice?" he queried after a moment, "Bartelmetz?"

"Aye," came the reply, and then Render saw the familiar grizzled visage, set neckless and balding above the red and blue shag sweater that was stretched mercilessly about the wine-keg rotundity of the man who now picked his way in their direction, deftly avoiding the strewn crutches and the stacked skis and the people who, like Jill and Render, disdained sitting in chairs.

Render stood, stretching, and shook hands as he came upon them.

"You've put on more weight," Render observed. "That's unhealthy."

"Nonsense, it's all muscle. How have you been, and what are you up to these days?" He looked down at Jill and she smiled back at him.

"This is Miss DeVille," said Render.

"Jill," she acknowledged.

He bowed slightly, finally releasing Render's aching hand.

". . . And this is Professor Maurice Bartelmetz of Vienna," finished Render, "a benighted disciple of all forms of dialectical pessimism, and a very distinguished pioneer in neuroparticipation—although you'd never guess it to look at him. I had the good fortune to be his pupil for over a year."

Bartelmetz nodded and agreed with him, taking in the Schnappsflasche Render brought forth from a small plastic bag, and accepting the collapsible cup which he filled to the brim.

"Ah, you are a good doctor still," he sighed. "You have diagnosed the case in an instant and you make the proper prescription. Nozdrovia!"

"Seven years in a gulp," Render acknowledged, refilling their glasses.

"Then we shall make time more malleable by sipping it."

They seated themselves on the floor, and the fire roared up through the great brick chimney as the logs burnt themselves back to branches, to twigs, to thin sticks, ring by yearly ring.

Render replenished the fire.

"I read your last book," said Bartelmetz finally, casually, "about four years ago."

Render reckoned that to be correct.

"Are you doing any research work these days?"

Render poked lazily at the fire.

"Yes," he answered, "sort of."

He glanced at Jill, who was dozing with her cheek against the arm of the huge leather chair that held his emergency bag, the planes of her face all crimson and flickering shadow.

"I've hit upon a rather unusual subject and started with a piece of jobbery I eventually intend to write about."

"Unusual? In what way?"

"Blind from birth, for one thing."

"You're using the ONT&R?"

"Yes. She's going to be a Shaper."

"Verfluchter!—Are you aware of the possible repercussions?"

"Of course."

"You've heard of unlucky Pierre?"

"No."

"Good, then it was successfully hushed. Pierre was a philosophy student at the University of Paris, and he was doing a dissertation on the evolution of consciousness. This past summer he decided it would be necessary for him to explore the mind of an ape, for purposes of comparing a moins-nausée mind with his own, I suppose. At any rate, he obtained illegal access to an ONT&R and to the mind of our hairy cousin. It was never ascertained how far along he got in exposing the animal to the stimuli-bank, but it is to be assumed that such items as would not be immediately trans-subjective between man and ape—traffic sounds and so weiter—were what frightened the creature. Pierre is still residing in a padded cell, and all his responses are those of a frightened ape.

"So, while he did not complete his own dissertation," he finished, "he may provide significant material for someone else's."

Render shook his head.

"Quite a story," he said softly, "but I have nothing that dramatic to contend with. I've found an exceedingly stable individual—a psychiatrist, in fact—one who's already spent time in ordinary analysis. She wants to go into neuroparticipation—but the fear of a sight-trauma was what was keeping her out. I've been gradually exposing her to a full range of visual phenomena. When I've finished she should be completely accommodated to sight, so that she can give her full attention to therapy and not be blinded by vision, so to speak. We've already had four sessions."

"And?"

". . . And it's working fine."

"You are certain about it?"

"Yes, as certain as anyone can be in these matters."

"Mm-hm," said Bartelmetz. "Tell me, do you find her excessively strong-willed? By that I mean, say, perhaps an obsessive-compulsive pattern concerning anything to which she's been introduced so far?"

"No."

"Has she ever succeeded in taking over control of the fantasy?"

"No!"

"You lie," he said simply.

Render found a cigarette. After lighting it, he smiled.

"Old father, old artificer," he conceded, "age has not withered your perceptiveness. I may trick me, but never you.—Yes, as a matter of fact, she *is* very difficult to keep under control. She is not satisfied just to see. She wants to Shape things for herself already. It's quite understandable—both to her and to me—but conscious apprehension and emotional acceptance never do seem to get together on things. She has become dominant on several occasions, but I've succeeded in resuming control almost immediately. After all, I *am* master of the bank."

143

"Hm," mused Bartelmetz. "Are you familiar with a Buddhist text—*Shankara's Catechism?*"

"I'm afraid not."

"Then I lecture you on it now. It posits—obviously not for therapeutic purposes—a true ego and a false ego. The true ego is that part of man which is immortal and shall proceed on to nirvana: the soul, if you like. Very good. Well, the false ego, on the other hand, is the normal mind, bound round with the illusions—the consciousness of you and I and everyone we have ever known professionally. Good?—Good. Now, the stuff this false ego is made up of they call skandhas. These include the feelings, the perceptions, the aptitudes, consciousness itself, and even the physical form. Very unscientific. Yes. Now they are not the same thing as neuroses, or one of Mister Ibsen's life-lies, or an hallucination—no, even though they are all wrong, being parts of a false thing to begin with. Each of the five skandhas is a part of the eccentricity that we call identity—then on top come the neuroses and all the other messes which follow after and keep us in business. Okay?—Okay. I give you this lecture because I need a dramatic term for what I will say, because I wish to say something dramatic. View the skandhas as lying at the bottom of the pond; the neuroses, they are ripples on the top of the water; the 'true ego', if there is one, is buried deep beneath the sand at the bottom. So. The ripples fill up the—the—zwischenwelt—between the object and the subject. The skandhas are a part of the subject, basic, unique, the stuff of his being.—So far, you are with me?"

"With many reservations."

"Good. Now I have defined my term somewhat, I will use it. You are fooling around with skandhas, not simple neuroses. You are attempting to adjust this woman's overall conception of herself and of the world. You are using the ONT&R to do it. It is the same thing as fooling with a psychotic, or an ape. All may seem to go well, but—at any moment, it is possible you may do something, show her some sight, or some way of seeing which will break in upon her selfhood, break a skandha—and pouf!—it will be like breaking through the bottom of the pond. A whirlpool will result, pulling you—where? I do not want you for a patient, young man, young artificer, so I counsel you not to proceed with this experiment. The ONT&R should not be used in such a manner."

Render flipped his cigarette into the fire and counted on his fingers:

"One," he said, "you are making a mystical mountain out of a pebble. All I am doing is adjusting her consciousness to accept an additional area of perception. Much of it is simple transference work from the other senses.—Two, her emotions were quite intense initially because it *did* involve a trauma—but we've passed that stage already. Now it is only a novelty to her. Soon it will be a commonplace.—Three, Eileen is a psychiatrist herself; she is educated in these matters and deeply aware of the delicate nature of what we are doing.—Four, her sense of identity and her desires, or her skandhas, or whatever you want to call them, are as firm as the Rock of Gibraltar. Do you realize the intense application required for a blind person to obtain the education she has obtained? It took a will of ten-point steel and the emotional control of an ascetic as well—"

"—And if something that strong should break, in a timeless moment of anxiety," smiled Bartelmetz sadly, "may the shades of Sigmund Freud and Carl Jung walk by your side in the valley of darkness.

"Five," he ticked it off on one finger. "Is she pretty?"

Render looked back into the fire.

"Very clever," sighed Bartelmetz, "I cannot tell whether you are blushing or not, with the rosy glow of the flames upon your face. I fear that you are, though, which would mean that you are aware that you yourself could be the source of the inciting stimulus. I shall burn a candle tonight before a portrait of Adler and pray that he give you the strength to compete successfully in your duel with your patient."

Render looked at Jill, who was still sleeping. He reached out and brushed a lock of her hair back into place.

"Still," said Bartelmetz, "if you do proceed and all goes well, I shall look forward with great interest to the reading of your work. Did I ever tell you that I have treated several Buddhists and never found a 'true ego'?"

Both men laughed.

Like me but not like me, that one on a leash, smelling of fear, small, gray, and unseeing. *Rrowl* and he'll choke on his collar. His head is empty as the oven till She pushes the button and it makes dinner. Make talk and they never understand, but they are like me. One day I will kill one—why? . . . Turn here.

"Three steps. Up. Glass doors. Handle to right."

Why? Ahead, drop-shaft. Gardens under, down. Smells nice, there. Grass, wetdirt, trees, and cleanair. I see. Birds are recorded though. I see all. I.

"Drop-shaft. Four steps."

Down. Yes. Want to make loud noises in throat, feel silly. Clean, smooth, many of trees. God . . . She likes sitting on bench chewing leaves smelling smooth air. Can't see them like me. Maybe now, some . . . ? No.

Can't Bad Sigmund me on grass, trees, here. Must hold it. Pity. Best place . . .

"Watch for steps."

Ahead. To right, to left, to right, to left, trees and grass now. Sigmund sees. Walking . . . Doctor with machine gives her his eyes. *Rrowl* and he will not choke. No fearsmell.

Dig deep hole in ground, bury eyes. God is blind. Sigmund to see. Her eyes now filled, and he is afraid of teeth. Will make her to see and take her high up in the sky to see, away. Leave me here, leave Sigmund with none to see, alone. I will dig a deep hole in the ground . . .

It was after ten in the morning when Jill awoke. She did not have to turn her head to know that Render was already gone. He never slept late. She rubbed her eyes, stretched, turned onto her side and raised herself on her elbow. She squinted at the clock on the bedside table, simultaneously reaching for a cigarette and her lighter.

As she inhaled, she realized there was no ashtray. Doubtless Render had moved it to the dresser because he did not approve of smoking in bed. With a sigh that ended in a snort she slid out of the bed and drew on her wrap before the ash grew too long.

She hated getting up, but once she did she would permit the day to begin and continue on without lapse through its orderly progression of events.

"Damn him," she smiled. She had wanted her breakfast in bed, but it was too late now.

Between thoughts as to what she would wear, she observed an alien pair of skis standing in the corner. A sheet of paper was impaled on one. She approached it.

"Join me?" asked the scrawl.

She shook her head in an emphatic negative and felt somewhat sad. She had been on skis twice in her life and she was afraid of them. She felt that she should really try again, after his being a reasonably good sport about the chateaux, but she could not even bear the memory of the unseemly downward rushing— which, on two occasions, had promptly deposited her in a snowbank—without wincing and feeling once again the vertigo that had seized her during the attempts.

So she showered and dressed and went downstairs for breakfast.

All nine fires were already roaring as she passed the big hall     147 and looked inside. Some red-faced skiers were holding their hands up before the blaze of the central hearth. It was not crowded though. The racks held only a few pairs of dripping boots, bright caps hung on pegs, moist skis stood upright in their place beside the door. A few people were seated in the chairs set further back toward the center of the hall, reading papers, smoking, or talking quietly. She saw no one she knew, so she moved on toward the dining room.

As she passed the registration desk the old man who worked there called out her name. She approached him and smiled.

"Letter," he explained, turning to a rack. "Here it is," he announced, handing it to her. "Looks important."

It had been forwarded three times, she noted. It was a bulky brown envelope, and the return address was that of her attorney.

"Thank you."

She moved off to a seat beside the big window that looked out upon a snow garden, a skating rink, and a distant winding trail dotted with figures carrying skis over their shoulders. She squinted against the brightness as she tore open the envelope.

Yes, it was final. Her attorney's note was accompanied by a copy of the divorce decree. She had only recently decided to end her legal relationship to Mister Fotlock, whose name she had stopped using five years earlier, when they had separated. Now that she had the thing she wasn't sure exactly what she was going to do with it. It would be a hell of a surprise for dear Rendy, though, she decided. She would have to find a reasonably innocent way of getting the information to him. She withdrew her compact and practiced a "Well?" expression. Well, there would be time for that later, she mused. Not too much later, though . . . Her thirtieth birthday, like a huge black cloud, filled an April but four months distant. Well . . . She touched her quizzical lips with color, dusted more powder over her mole, and locked the expression within her compact for future use.

\*    \*    \*

In the dining room she saw Doctor Bartelmetz, seated before an enormous mound of scrambled eggs, great chains of dark sausages, several heaps of yellow toast, and a half-emptied flask of orange juice. A pot of coffee steamed on the warmer at his elbow. He leaned slightly forward as he ate, wielding his fork like a windmill blade.

"Good morning," she said.

He looked up.

"Miss DeVille—Jill . . . Good morning." He nodded at the chair across from him. "Join me, please."

She did so, and when the waiter approached she nodded and said, "I'll have the same thing, only about ninety percent less."

She turned back to Bartelmetz.

"Have you seen Charles today?"

"Alas, I have not," he gestered, open-handed, "and I wanted to continue our discussion while his mind was still in the early stages of wakefulness and somewhat malleable. Unfortunately," he took a sip of coffee, "he who sleeps well enters the day somewhere in the middle of its second act."

"Myself, I usually come in around intermission and ask someone for a synopsis," she explained. "So why not continue the discussion with me?—I'm always malleable, and my skandhas are in good shape."

Their eyes met, and he took a bite of toast.

"Aye," he said, at length, "I had guessed as much. Well— good. What do you know of Render's work?"

She adjusted herself in the chair.

"Mm. He being a special specialist in a highly specialized area, I find it difficult to appreciate the few things he does say about it. I'd like to be able to look inside other people's minds sometimes—to see what they're thinking about *me*, of course— but I don't think I could stand staying there very long. Especially," she gave a mock-shudder, "the mind of somebody with— problems. I'm afraid I'd be too sympathetic or too frightened or

149

something. Then, according to what I've read—pow!—like sympathetic magic, it would be my problem.

"Charles never has problems though," she continued, "at least, none that he speaks to me about. Lately I've been wondering, though. That blind girl and her talking dog seem to be too much with him."

"Talking dog?"

"Yes, her seeing-eye dog is one of those surgical mutants."

"How interesting . . . Have you ever met her?"

"Never."

"So," he mused.

"Sometimes a therapist encounters a patient whose problems are so akin to his own that the sessions become extremely mordant," he noted. "It has always been the case with me when I treat a fellow-psychiatrist. Perhaps Charles sees in this situation a parallel to something which has been troubling him personally. I did not administer his personal analysis. I do not know all the ways of his mind, even though he was a pupil of mine for a long while. He was always self-contained, somewhat reticent; he could be quite authoritative on occasion, however.—What are some of the other things which occupy his attention these days?"

"His son Peter is a constant concern. He's changed the boy's school five times in five years."

Her breakfast arrived. She adjusted her napkin and drew her chair closer to the table.

"—and he has been reading case histories of suicides recently, and talking about them, and talking about them, and talking about them."

"To what end?"

She shrugged and began eating.

"He never mentioned why," she said, looking up again. "Maybe he's writing something . . ."

Bartelmetz finished his eggs and poured more coffee.

"Are you afraid of this patient of his?" he inquired.

150     "No . . . Yes," she responded, "I am."

"Why?"

"I am afraid of sympathetic magic," she said, flushing slightly.

"Many things could fall under that heading."

"Many indeed," she acknowledged. And, after a moment, "We are united in our concern for his welfare and in agreement as to what represents the threat. So, may I ask a favor?"

"You may."

"Talk to him again," she said. "Persuade him to drop the case."

He folded his napkin.

"I intended to do that after dinner," he stated, "because I believe in the ritualistic value of rescue-motions. They shall be made."

Dear Father-Image,

Yes, the school is fine, my ankle is getting that way, and my classmates are a congenial lot. No, I am not short on cash, undernourished, or having difficulty fitting into the new curriculum. Okay?

The building I will not describe, as you have already seen the macabre thing. The grounds I cannot describe, as they are presently residing beneath cold white sheets. Brrr! I trust yourself to be enjoying the arts wint'rish. I do not share your enthusiasm for summer's opposite, except within picture frames or as an emblem on ice cream bars.

The ankle inhibits my mobility and my roommate has gone home for the weekend—both of which are really blessings (saith Pangloss), for I now have the opportunity to catch up on some reading. I will do so forthwith.

> Prodigally,
> Peter

Render reached down to pat the huge head. It accepted the gesture stoically, then turned its gaze up to the Austrian whom Render had asked for a light, as if to say, "Must I endure this indignity?" The man laughed at the expression, snapping shut the engraved lighter on which Render noted the middle initial to be a small *v*.

"Thank you," he said, and to the dog: "What is your name?"

"Bismark," it growled.

Render smiled.

"You remind me of another of your kind," he told the dog. "One Sigmund, by name, a companion and guide to a blind friend of mine, in America."

"My Bismark is a hunter," said the young man. "There is no quarry that can outthink him, neither the deer nor the big cats."

The dog's ears pricked forward and he stared up at Render with proud, blazing eyes.

"We have hunted in Africa and the northern and south-western parts of America. Central America, too. He never loses the trail. He never gives up. He is a beautiful brute, and his teeth could have been made in Solingen."

"You are indeed fortunate to have such a hunting companion."

"I hunt," growled the dog. "I follow . . . Sometimes, I have, the kill . . ."

"You would not know of the one called Sigmund then, or the woman he guides—Miss Eileen Shallot?" asked Render.

The man shook his head.

"No, Bismark came to me from Massachusetts, but I was never to the Center personally. I am not acquainted with other mutie handlers."

"I see. Well, thank you for the light. Good afternoon."

"Good afternoon."

"Good, after, noon . . ."

Render strolled on up the narrow street, hands in his pockets. He had excused himself and not said where he was going. This was because he had had no destination in mind. Bartelmetz' second essay at counseling had almost led him to say things he would later regret. It was easier to take a walk than to continue the conversation.

On a sudden impulse he entered a small shop and bought a cuckoo clock which had caught his eye. He felt certain that Bartelmetz would accept the gift in the proper spirit. He smiled and walked on. And what was that letter to Jill which the desk clerk had made a special trip to their table to deliver at dinner-time? he wondered. It had been forwarded three times, and its return address was that of a law firm. Jill had not even opened it, but had smiled, overtipped the old man, and tucked it into her purse. He would have to hint subtly as to its contents. His curiosity was so aroused that she would be sure to tell him out of pity.

The icy pillars of the sky suddenly seemed to sway before him as a cold wind leapt down out of the north. Render hunched his shoulders and drew his head further below his collar. Clutching the cuckoo clock, he hurried back up the street.

That night the serpent which holds its tail in its mouth belched, the Fenris Wolf made a pass at the moon, the little clock said "cuckoo," and tomorrow came on like Manolete's last bull, shaking the gate of horn with the bellowed promise to tread a river of lions to sand.

Render promised himself he would lay off the gooey fondue.

Later, much later, when they skipped through the skies in a kite-shaped cruiser, Render looked down upon the darkened Earth dreaming its cities full of stars, looked up at the sky where they were all reflected, looked about him at the tapescreens watching all the people who blinked into them, and at the coffee, tea, and mixed drink dispensers who sent their fluids forth to explore the insides of the people they required to push their buttons, then looked across at Jill, whom the old buildings had compelled to walk among their walls—because he knew she felt he should be

153

looking at her then—felt his seat's demand that he convert it into a couch, did so, and slept.

## IV

Her office was full of flowers, and she liked exotic perfumes. Sometimes she burned incense.

She liked soaking in overheated pools, walking through falling snow, listening to too much music, played perhaps too loudly, drinking five or six varieties of liqueurs (usually reeking of anise, sometimes touched with wormwood) every evening. Her hands were soft and lightly freckled. Her fingers were long and tapered. She wore no rings.

Her fingers traced and retraced the floral swellings on the side of her chair as she spoke into the recording unit:

". . . Patient's chief complaints on admission were nervousness, insomnia, stomach pains, and a period of depression. Patient has had a record of previous admissions for short periods of time. He had been in this hospital in 1995 for a manic depressive psychosis, depressed type, and he returned here again, 2-3-96. He was in another hospital, 9-20-97. Physical examination revealed a BP of 170/100. He was normally developed and well-nourished on the date of examination, 12-11-98. On this date patient complained of chronic backache, and there was noted some moderate symptoms of alcohol withdrawal. Physical examination further revealed no pathology except that the patient's tendon reflexes were exaggerated but equal. These symptoms were the result of alcohol withdrawal. Upon admission he was shown to be not psychotic, neither delusional nor hallucinated. He was well-oriented as to place, time, and person. His psychological condition was evaluated and he was found to be somewhat grandiose and expansive and more than a little hostile. He was considered a potential troublemaker. Because of his experience as a cook, he was assigned to work in the kitchen. His

general condition then showed definite improvement. He is less tense and is cooperative. Diagnosis: Manic depressive reaction (external precipitating stress unknown). The degree of psychiatric impairment is mild. He is considered competent. To be continued on therapy and hospitalization."

She turned off the recorder then and laughed. The sound frightened her. Laughter is a social phenomenon and she was alone. She played back the recording then, chewing on the corner of her handkerchief while the soft, clipped words were returned to her. She ceased to hear them after the first dozen or so.

When the recorder stopped talking she turned it off. She was alone. She was very alone. She was so damned alone that the little pool of brightness which occurred when she stroked her forehead and faced the window—that little pool of brightness suddenly became the most important thing in the world. She wanted it to be immense. She wanted it to be an ocean of light. Or else she wanted to grow so small herself that the effect would be the same: she wanted to drown in it.

It had been three weeks, yesterday . . .

*Too long,* she decided, *I should have waited. No! Impossible! But what if he goes as Riscomb went? No! He won't. He would not. Nothing can hurt him. Never. He is all strength and armor. But—but we should have waited till next month to start. Three weeks . . . Sight withdrawal—that's what it is. Are the memories fading? Are they weaker? What does a tree look like? Or a cloud?—I can't remember! What is red? What is green? God! It's hysteria! I'm watching and I can't stop it!—Take a pill! A pill!*

Her shoulders began to shake. She did not take a pill though, but bit down harder on the handkerchief until her sharp teeth tore through its fabric.

"Beware," she recited a personal beatitude, "those who hunger and thirst after justice, for we *will* be satisfied.

"And beware the meek," she continued, "for we shall attempt to inherit the Earth.

"And beware . . ."

There was a brief buzz from the phone-box. She put away her handkerchief, composed her face, turned the unit on.

"Hello . . . ?"

"Eileen, I'm back. How've you been?"

"Good, quite well in fact. How was your vacation?"

"Oh, I can't complain. I had it coming for a long time. I guess I deserve it. Listen, I brought some things back to show you—like Winchester Cathedral. You want to come in this week? I can make it any evening."

*Tonight. No. I want it too badly. It will set me back if he sees . . .*

"How about tomorrow night?" she asked. "Or the one after?"

"Tomorrow will be fine," he said. "Meet you at the P & S, around seven?"

"Yes, that would be pleasant. Same table?"

"Why not?—I'll reserve it."

"All right. I'll see you then."

"Goodbye."

The connection was broken.

Suddenly, then, at that moment, colors swirled again through her head; and she saw trees—oaks and pines, poplars and syca-mores—great, and green and brown, and iron-colored; and she saw wads of fleecy clouds, dipped in paintpots, swabbing a pastel sky; and a burning sun, and a small willow tree, and a lake of a deep, almost violet, blue. She folded her torn handkerchief and put it away.

She pushed a button beside her desk and music filled the office: Scriabin. Then she pushed another button and replayed the tape she had dictated, half-listening to each.

Pierre sniffed suspiciously at the food. The attendant moved away from the tray and stepped out into the hall, locking the door behind him. The enormous salad waited on the floor. Pierre approached cautiously, snatched a handful of lettuce, gulped it.

He was afraid.

*If only the steel would stop crashing, and crashing against steel, some-where in that dark night . . . If only . . .*

Sigmund rose to his feet, yawned, stretched. His hind legs trailed out behind him for a moment, then he snapped to attention and shook himself. She would be coming home soon. Wagging his tail slowly, he glanced up at the human-level clock with the raised numerals, verified his feelings, then crossed the apartment to the teevee. He rose onto his hind legs, rested one paw against the table, and used the other to turn on the set.

It was nearly time for the weather report and the roads would be icy.

"I have driven through county-wide graveyards," wrote Render, "vast forests of stone that spread further every day.

"Why does man so zealously guard his dead? Is it because this is the monumentally democratic way of immortalization, the ultimate affirmation of the power to hurt—that is to say, life—and the desire that it continue on forever? Unamuno has sug-gested that this is the case. If it is, then a greater percentage of the population actively sought immortality last year than ever before in history . . ."

*Tch-tchg, tchga-tchg!*
"Do you think they're really people?"
"Naw, they're too good."

The evening was starglint and soda over ice. Render wound the S-7 into the cold sub-subcellar, found his parking place, nosed into it.

There was a damp chill that emerged from the concrete to gnaw like rats' teeth at their flesh. Render guided her toward the lift, their breath preceding them in dissolving clouds.

"A bit of a chill in the air," he noted.

She nodded, biting her lip.

Inside the lift, he sighed, unwound his scarf, lit a cigarette.

"Give me one, please," she requested, smelling the tobacco. He did.

They rose slowly, and Render leaned against the wall, puffing a mixture of smoke and crystallized moisture.

"I met another mutie shep," he recalled, "in Switzerland. Big as Sigmund. A hunter though, and as Prussian as they come," he grinned.

"Sigmund likes to hunt, too," she observed. "Twice every year we go up to the North Woods and I turn him loose. He's gone for days at a time, and he's always quite happy when he returns. Never says what he's done, but he's never hungry. Back when I got him I guessed that he would need vacations from humanity to stay stable. I think I was right."

The lift stopped, the door opened, and they walked out into the hall, Render guiding her again.

Inside his office, he poked at the thermostat and warm air sighed through the room. He hung their coats in the inner office and brought the great egg out from its nest behind the wall. He connected it to an outlet and moved to convert his desk into a control panel.

"How long do you think it will take?" she asked, running her fingertips over the smooth, cold curves of the egg. "The whole thing, I mean. The entire adaptation to seeing."

He wondered.

"I have no idea," he said, "no idea whatsoever, yet. We got off to a good start, but there's still a lot of work to be done. I think I'll be able to make a good guess in another three months."

She nodded wistfully, moved to his desk, explored the controls with fingerstrokes like ten feathers.

"Careful you don't push any of those."

"I won't. How long do you think it will take me to learn to operate one?"

"Three months to learn it. Six, to actually become proficient enough to use it on anyone; and an additional six under close supervision before you can be trusted on your own.—About a year altogether."

"Uh-huh." She chose a chair.

Render touched the seasons to life, and the phases of day and night, the breath of the country, the city, the elements that raced naked through the skies, and all the dozens of dancing cues he used to build worlds. He smashed the clock of time and tasted the seven or so ages of man.

"Okay," he turned, "everything is ready."

It came quickly, and with a minimum of suggestion on Render's part. One moment there was grayness. Then a dead-white fog. Then it broke itself apart, as though a quick wind had arisen, although he neither heard nor felt a wind.

He stood beside the willow tree beside the lake, and she stood half-hidden among the branches and the lattices of shadow. The sun was slanting its way into evening.

"We have come back," she said, stepping out, leaves in her hair. "For a time I was afraid it had never happened, but I see it all again, and I remember now."

"Good," he said. "Behold yourself." And she looked into the lake.

"I have not changed," she said. "I haven't changed . . ."

"No."

"But you have," she continued, looking up at him. "You are taller, and there is something different . . ."

"No," he answered.

"I am mistaken," she said quickly, "I don't understand everything I see yet. I will though."

"Of course."

"What are we going to do?"

"Watch," he instructed her.

Along a flat, no-colored river of road she just then noticed beyond the trees, came the car. It came from the farthest quarter of the sky, skipping over the mountains, buzzing down the hills,

159

circling through the glades, and splashing them with the colors of its voice—the gray and the silver of synchronized potency—and the lake shivered from its sounds, and the car stopped a hundred feet away, masked by the shrubberies; and it waited. It was the S-7.

"Come with me," he said, taking her hand. "We're going for a ride."

They walked among the trees and rounded the final cluster of bushes. She touched the sleek cocoon, its antennae, its tires, its windows—and the windows transpared as she did so. She stared through them at the inside of the car, and she nodded.

"It is your Spinner."

"Yes." He held the door for her. "Get in. We'll return to the club. The time is now. The memories are fresh, and they should be reasonably pleasant, or neutral."

"Pleasant," she said, getting in.

He closed the door, then circled the car and entered. She watched as he punched imaginary coordinates. The car leapt ahead and he kept a steady stream of trees flowing by them. He could feel the rising tension, so he did not vary the scenery. She swiveled her seat and studied the interior of the car.

"Yes," she finally said, "I can perceive what everything is."

She stared out the window again. She looked at the rushing trees. Render stared out and looked upon rushing anxiety patterns. He opaqued the windows.

"Good," she said, "Thank you. Suddenly it was too much to see—all of it, moving past like a . . ."

"Of course," said Render, maintaining the sensations of forward motion. "I'd anticipated that. You're getting tougher, though."

After a moment, "Relax," he said, "relax now," and somewhere a button was pushed, and she relaxed, and they drove on, and on and on, and finally the car began to slow, and Render said, "Just for one nice, slow glimpse now, look out your window."

She did.

He drew upon every stimulus in the bank which could promote sensations of pleasure and relaxation, and he dropped the city around the car, and the windows became transparent, and she looked out upon the profiles of towers and a block of monolithic apartments, and then she saw three rapid cafeterias, an entertainment palace, a drugstore, a medical center of yellow brick with an aluminum caduceus set above its archway, and a glassed-in high school, now emptied of its pupils, a fifty-pump gas station, another drugstore, and many more cars, parked or roaring by them, and people, people moving in and out of the doorways and walking before the buildings and getting into the cars and getting out of the cars; and it was summer, and the light of late afternoon filtered down upon the colors of the city and the colors of the garments the people wore as they moved along the boulevard, as they loafed upon the terraces, as they crossed the balconies, leaned on balustrades and windowsills, emerged from a corner kiosk, entered one, stood talking to one another; a woman walking a poodle rounded a corner; rockets went to and fro in the high sky.

The world fell apart then and Render caught the pieces.

He maintained an absolute blackness, blanketing every sensation but that of their movement forward.

After a time a dim light occurred, and they were still seated in the Spinner, windows blanked again, and the air as they breathed it became a soothing unguent.

"Lord," she said, "the world is so filled. Did I really see all of that?"

"I wasn't going to do that tonight, but you wanted me to. You seemed ready."

"Yes," she said, and the windows became transparent again. She turned away quickly.

"It's gone," he said. "I only wanted to give you a glimpse."

She looked, and it was dark outside now, and they were crossing over a high bridge. They were moving slowly. There was no other traffic. Below them were the Flats, where an occasional smelter flared like a tiny, drowsing volcano, spitting showers of orange sparks skyward; and there were many stars; they glistened on the breathing water that went beneath the bridge; they silhouetted by pinprick the skyline that hovered dimly below its surface. The slanting struts of the bridge marched steadily by.

"You have done it," she said, "and I thank you." Then: "Who are you, really?" (He must have wanted her to ask that.)

"I am Render," he laughed. And they wound their way through a dark, now-vacant city, coming at last to their club and entering the great parking dome.

Inside, he scrutinized all her feelings, ready to banish the world at a moment's notice. He did not feel he would have to, though.

They left the car, moved ahead. They passed into the club, which he had decided would not be crowded tonight. They were shown to their table at the foot of the bar in the small room with the suit of armor, and they sat down and ordered the same meal over again.

"No," he said, looking down, "it belongs over there."

The suit of armor appeared once again beside the table, and he was once again inside his gray suit and black tie and silver tie clasp shaped like a treelimb.

They laughed.

"I'm just not the type to wear a tin suit, so I wish you'd stop seeing me that way."

"I'm sorry," she smiled. "I don't know how I did that, or why."

"I do, and I decline the nomination. Also, I caution you once again. You are conscious of the fact that this is all an illusion. I had to do it that way for you to get the full benefit of the thing. For most of my patients though, it is the real item while they are experiencing it. It makes a counter-trauma or a symbolic sequence even more powerful. You are aware of the parameters of the game, however, and whether you want it or not this gives you a different sort of control over it than I normally have to deal with. Please be careful."

"I'm sorry. I didn't mean to."

"I know. Here comes the meal we just had."

"Ugh! It looks dreadful! Did we eat all that stuff?"

"Yes," he chuckled. "That's a knife, that's a fork, that's a spoon. That's roast beef, and those are mashed potatoes, those are peas, that's butter . . ."

"Goodness! I don't feel so well."

". . . And those are the salads, and those are the salad dressings. This is a brook trout—mm! These are French fried potatoes. This is a bottle of wine. Hmm—let's see—Romanée-Conti, since I'm not paying for it—and a bottle of Yquem for the trou— Hey!"

The room was wavering.

He bared the table, he banished the restaurant. They were back in the glade. Through the transparent fabric of the world he watched a hand moving along a panel. Buttons were being pushed. The world grew substantial again. Their emptied table was set beside the lake now, and it was still nighttime and summer, and the tablecloth was very white under the glow of the giant moon that hung overhead.

"That was stupid of me," he said. "Awfully stupid. I should have introduced them one at a time. The actual sight of basic, oral stimuli can be very distressing to a person seeing them for the first time. I got so wrapped up in the Shaping that I forgot the patient, which is just dandy! I apologize."

"I'm okay now. Really I am."

He summoned a cool breeze from the lake.

". . . And that is the moon," he added lamely.

She nodded, and she was wearing a tiny moon in the center of her forehead; it glowed like the one above them, and her hair and dress were all of silver.

163

The bottle of Romanee-Conti stood on the table, and two glasses.

"Where did that come from?"

She shrugged. He poured out a glassful.

"It may taste kind of flat," he said.

"It doesn't. Here—" She passed it to him.

As he sipped it he realized it had a taste—a *fruite* such as might be quashed from the grapes grown in the Isles of the Blest, a smooth, muscular *charnu*, and a *capiteux* centrifuged from the fumes of a field of burning poppies. With a start, he knew that his hand must be traversing the route of the perceptions, symphonizing the sensual cues of a transference and a countertransference which had come upon him all unawares, there beside the lake.

"So it does," he noted, "and now it is time we returned."

"So soon? I haven't seen the cathedral yet . . ."

"So soon."

He willed the world to end, and it did.

"It is cold out there," she said as she dressed, "and dark."

"I know. I'll mix us something to drink while I clear the unit."

"Fine."

He glanced at the tapes and shook his head. He crossed to his bar cabinet.

"It's not exactly Romanee-Conti," he observed, reaching for a bottle.

"So what? I don't mind."

Neither did he, at that moment. So he cleared the unit, they drank their drinks, and he helped her into her coat and they left.

As they rode the lift down to the sub-sub he willed the world to end again, but it didn't.

Dad,

    I hobbled from school to taxi and taxi to spaceport, for the local Air Force Exhibit—Outward, it was called. (Okay, I exaggerated the hobble. It got me extra attention though.)

The whole bit was aimed at seducing young manhood into a five-year hitch, as I saw it. But it worked. I wanna join up. I wanna go Out There. Think they'll take me when I'm old enuff? I mean take me Out—not some crummy desk job. Think so?

I do.

There was this dam lite colonel ('scuse the French) who saw this kid lurching around and pressing his nose 'gainst the big windowpanes, and he decided to give him the sub-liminal sell. Great! He pushed me through the gallery and showed me all the pitchers of AF triumphs, from Moonbase to Marsport. He lectured me on the Great Traditions of the Service, and marched me into a flic room where the Corps had good clean fun on tape, wrestling one another in null-G "where it's all skill and no brawn," and making tinted water sculpture-work way in the middle of the air and doing dismounted drill on the skin of a cruiser. Oh joy!

Seriously though, I'd like to be there when they hit the Outer Five—and On Out. Not because of the bogus bal-onus in the throwaways, and suchlike crud, but because I think someone of sensibility should be along to chronicle the thing in the proper way. You know, raw frontier ob-server. Francis Parkman. Mary Austin, like that. So I de-cided I'm going.

The AF boy with the chicken stuff on his shoulders wasn't in the least way patronizing, gods be praised. We stood on the balcony and watched ships lift off and he told me to go forth and study real hard and I might be riding them some day. I did not bother to tell him that I'm hardly intellectually deficient and that I'll have my B.A. before I'm old enough to do anything with it, even join his Corps. I just watched the ships lift off and said, "Ten years from now I'll be looking down, not up." Then he told me how hard his own training had been, so I did not ask howcum he got stuck with a lousy dirtside assignment like this one.

Glad I didn't, now I think on it. He looked more like one of their ads than one of their real people. Hope I never look like an ad.

Thank you for the monies and the warm sox and Mozart's String Quintets, which I'm hearing right now. I wanna put in my bid for Luna instead of Europe next summer. Maybe . . . ? Possibly . . . ? Contingently . . . ? Huh?—If I can smash that new test you're designing for me . . . ? Anyhow, please think about it.

Your son,
Pete


"Hello. State Psychiatric Institute."

"I'd like to make an appointment for an examination."

"Just a moment. I'll connect you with the Appointment Desk."

"Hello. Appointment Desk."

"I'd like to make an appointment for an examination."

"Just a moment . . . What sort of examination?"

"I want to see Doctor Shallot, Eileen Shallot. As soon as possible."

"Just a moment. I'll have to check her schedule . . . Could you make it at two o'clock next Tuesday?"

"That would be just fine."

"What is the name, please?"

"DeVille. Jill DeVille."

"All right, Miss DeVille. That's two o'clock, Tuesday."

"Thank you."


The man walked beside the highway. Cars passed along the highway. The cars in the high-acceleration lane blurred by.

Traffic was light.

It was 10:30 in the morning, and cold.

The man's fur-lined collar was turned up, his hands were in

his pockets, and he leaned into the wind. Beyond the fence, the road was clean and dry.

The morning sun was buried in clouds. In the dirty light, the man could see the tree a quarter mile ahead.

His pace did not change. His eyes did not leave the tree. The small stones clicked and crunched beneath his shoes.

When he reached the tree he took off his jacket and folded it neatly.

He placed it upon the ground and climbed the tree.

As he moved out onto the limb which extended over the fence, he looked to see that no traffic was approaching. Then he seized the branch with both hands, lowered himself, hung a moment, and dropped onto the highway.

It was a hundred yards wide, the eastbound half of the highway.

He glanced west, saw there was still no traffic coming his way, then began to walk toward the center island. He knew he would never reach it. At this time of day the cars were moving at approximately one hundred sixty miles an hour in the high acceleration lane. He walked on.

A car passed behind him. He did not look back. If the windows were opaqued, as was usually the case, then the occupants were unaware he had crossed their path. They would hear of it later and examine the front end of their vehicle for possible signs of such an encounter.

A car passed in front of him. Its windows were clear. A glimpse of two faces, their mouths made into O's, was presented to him, then torn from his sight. His own face remained without expression. His pace did not change. Two more cars rushed by, windows darkened. He had crossed perhaps twenty yards of highway.

Twenty-five . . .

Something in the wind, or beneath his feet, told him it was coming. He did not look.

Something in the corner of his eye assured him it was coming. His gait did not alter.

Cecil Green had the windows transpared because he liked it that way. His left hand was inside her blouse and her skirt was piled up on her lap, and his right hand was resting on the lever which would lower the seats. Then she pulled away, making a noise down inside her throat.

His head snapped to the left.

He saw the walking man.

He saw the profile which never turned to face him fully. He saw that the man's gait did not alter.

Then he did not see the man.

There was a slight jar, and the windshield began cleaning itself. Cecil Green raced on.

He opaqued the windows.

"How . . . ?" he asked after she was in his arms again, and sobbing.

"The monitor didn't pick him up . . ."

"He must not have touched the fence . . ."

"He must have been out of his mind!"

"Still, he could have picked an easier way."

*It could have been any face . . . Mine?*

Frightened, Cecil lowered the seats.


Charles Render was writing the "Necropolis" chapter for *The Missing Link Is Man*, which was to be his first book in over four years. Since his return he had set aside every Tuesday and Thursday afternoon to work on it, isolating himself in his office, filling pages with a chaotic longhand.

"There are many varieties of death, as opposed to dying . . ." he was writing, just as the intercom buzzed briefly, then long, then again briefly.

"Yes?" he asked it, pushing down on the switch.

"You have a visitor," and there was a short intake of breath between "a" and "visitor."

He slipped a small aerosol into his side pocket, then rose and crossed the office.

He opened the door and looked out.

"Doctor . . . Help . . ."

Render took three steps, then dropped to one knee.

"What's the matter?"

"Come she is . . . sick," he growled.

"Sick? How? What's wrong?"

"Don't know. You come."

Render stared into the unhuman eyes.

"What kind of sick?" he insisted.

"Don't know," repeated the dog. "Won't talk. Sits. I . . . feel, she is sick."

"How did you get here?"

"Drove. Know the co, or, din, ates . . . Left car, outside."

"I'll call her right now." Render turned.

"No good. Won't answer."

He was right.

Render returned to his inner office for his coat and medkit. He glanced out the window and saw where her car was parked, far below, just inside the entrance to the marginal, where the monitor had released it into manual control. If no one assumed that control a car was automatically parked in neutral. The other vehicles were passed around it.

*So simple even a dog can drive one, he reflected. Better get downstairs before a cruiser comes along. It's probably reported itself stopped there already. Maybe not, though. Might still have a few minutes grace.*

He glanced at the huge clock.

"Okay, Sig," he called out. "Let's go."

They took the lift to the ground floor, left by way of the front entrance, and hurried to the car.

Its engine was still idling.

Render opened the passenger-side door and Sigmund leapt in. He squeezed by him into the driver's seat then, but the dog was already pushing the primary coordinates and the address tabs with his paw.

*Looks like I'm in the wrong seat.*

He lit a cigarette as the car swept ahead into a U-underpass. It emerged on the opposite marginal, sat poised a moment, then joined the traffic flow. The dog directed the car into the high-acceleration lane.

"Oh," said the dog, "oh."

Render felt like patting his head at that moment, but he looked at him, saw that his teeth were bared, and decided against it.

"When did she start acting peculiar?" he asked.

"Came home from work. Did not eat. Would not answer me, when I talked. Just sits."

"Has she ever been like this before?"

"No."

*What could have precipitated it?—But maybe she just had a bad day. After all, he's only a dog—sort of.—No. He'd know. But what, then?*

"How was she yesterday—and when she left home this morning?"

"Like always."

Render tried calling her again. There was still no answer.

"You, did it," said the dog.

"What do you mean?"

"Eyes. Seeing. You. Machine. Bad."

"No," said Render, and his hand rested on the unit of stun spray in his pocket.

"Yes," said the dog, turning to him again. "You will, make her well . . . ?"

"Of course," said Render.

Sigmund stared ahead again.


Render felt physically exhilarated and mentally sluggish. He sought the confusion factor. He had had these feelings about the case since that first session. There was something very unsettling about Eileen Shallot: a combination of high intelligence and helplessness, of determination and vulnerability, of sensitivity and bitterness.

*Do I find that especially attractive?—No. It's just the counter-transference, damn it!*

"You smell afraid," said the dog.

"Then color me afraid," said Render, "and turn the page."

They slowed for a series of turns, picked up speed again, slowed again, picked up speed again. Finally, they were traveling along a narrow section of roadway through a semi-residential area of town. The car turned up a side street, proceeded about half a mile further, clicked softly beneath its dashboard, and turned into the parking lot behind a high brick apartment building. The click must have been a special servomech which took over from the point where the monitor released it, because the car crawled across the lot, headed into its transparent parking stall, then stopped. Render turned off the ignition.

Sigmund had already opened the door on his side. Render followed him into the building, and they rode the elevator to the fiftieth floor. The dog dashed on ahead up the hallway, pressed his nose against a plate set low in a doorframe, and waited. After a moment, the door swung several inches inward. He pushed it open with his shoulder and entered. Render followed, closing the door behind him.

The apartment was large, its walls pretty much unadorned, its color combinations unnerving. A great library of tapes filled one corner; a monstrous combination-broadcaster stood beside it. There was a wide bowlegged table set in front of the window, and a low couch along the right-hand wall; there was a closed door beside the couch; an archway to the left apparently led to other rooms. Eileen sat in an overstuffed chair in the far corner by the window. Sigmund stood beside the chair.

Render crossed the room and extracted a cigarette from his case. Snapping open his lighter, he held the flame until her head turned in that direction.

"Cigarette?" he asked.

"Charles?"

"Right."

"Yes, thank you. I will."

She held out her hand, accepted the cigarette, put it to her lips.

"Thanks.—What are you doing here?"

"Social call. I happened to be in the neighborhood."

"I didn't hear a buzz, or a knock."

"You must have been dozing. Sig let me in."

"Yes, I must have." She stretched. "What time is it?"

"It's close to four-thirty."

"I've been home over two hours then . . . Must have been very tired . . ."

"How do you feel now?"

"Fine," she declared. "Care for a cup of coffee?"

"Don't mind if I do."

"A steak to go with it?"

"No thanks."

"Bacardi in the coffee?"

"Sounds good."

"Excuse me then. It'll only take a moment."

She went through the door beside the sofa and Render caught a glimpse of a large, shiny, automatic kitchen.

"Well?" he whispered to the dog.

Sigmund shook his head.

"Not same."

Render shook his head.

He deposited his coat on the sofa, folding it carefully about the medkit. He sat beside it and thought.

*Did I throw too big a chunk of seeing at once? Is she suffering from depressive side-effects—say, memory repressions, nervous fatigue? Did I upset her sensory adaptation syndrome somehow? Why have I been proceeding so rapidly anyway? There's no real hurry. Am I so damned eager to write the thing up?—Or am I doing it because she wants me to? Could she be that strong, consciously or unconsciously? Or am I that vulnerable—somehow?*

She called him to the kitchen to carry out the tray. He set it on the table and seated himself across from her.

"Good coffee," he said, burning his lips on the cup.

"Smart machine," she stated, facing his voice.

Sigmund stretched out on the carpet next to the table, lowered his head between his forepaws, sighed, and closed his eyes.

"I've been wondering," said Render, "whether or not there were any aftereffects to that last session—like increased synesthesiac experiences, or dreams involving forms, or hallucinations or . . ."

"Yes," she said flatly, "dreams."

"What kind?"

"That last session. I've dreamt it over, and over."

"Beginning to end?"

"No, there's no special order to the events. We're riding through the city, or over the bridge, or sitting at the table, or walking toward the car—just flashes, like that. Vivid ones."

"What sort of feelings accompany these—flashes?"

"I don't know. They're all mixed up."

"What are your feelings now, as you recall them?"

"The same, all mixed up."

"Are you afraid?"

"N-no. I don't think so."

"Do you want to take a vacation from the thing? Do you feel we've been proceeding too rapidly?"

"No. That's not it at all. It's—well, it's like learning to swim. When you finally learn how, why then you swim and you swim and you swim until you're all exhausted. Then you just lie there gasping in air and remembering what it was like, while your friends all hover and chew you out for overexerting yourself— and it's a good feeling, even though you do take a chill and there's pins and needles inside all your muscles. At least, that's the way I do things. I felt that way after the first session and after this last one. First times are always very special times . . . The pins and the needles are gone though, and I've caught my breath again. Lord, I don't want to stop now! I feel fine."

"Do you usually take a nap in the afternoon?"

The ten red nails of her fingernails moved across the tabletop as she stretched.

". . . Tired," she smiled, swallowing a yawn. "Half the staff's on vacation or sick leave and I've been beating my brains out all week. I was about ready to fall on my face when I left work. I feel all right now that I've rested, though."

She picked up her coffee cup with both hands, took a large swallow.

"Uh-huh," he said. "Good. I was a bit worried about you. I'm glad to see there was no reason."

She laughed.

"Worried? You've read Doctor Riscomb's notes on my analysis—and on the ONT&R trial—and you think I'm the sort to worry about? Ha! I have an operationally beneficent neurosis concerning my adequacy as a human being. It focuses my energies, coordinates my efforts toward achievement. It enhances my sense of identity . . ."

"You do have one hell of a memory," he noted. "That's almost verbatim."

"Of course."

"You had Sigmund worried today, too."

"Sig? How?"

The dog stirred uneasily, opened one eye.

"Yes," he growled, glaring up at Render. "He needs, a ride, home."

"Have you been driving the car again?"

"Yes."

"After I told you not to?"

"Yes."

174     "Why?"

"I was a, fraid. You would, not, answer me, when I talked."

"I was *very* tired—and if you ever take the car again, I'm going to have the door fixed so you can't come and go as you please."

"Sorry."

"There's nothing wrong with me."

"I, see."

"You are *never* to do it again."

"Sorry." His eye never left Render; it was like a burning lens. Render looked away.

"Don't be too hard on the poor fellow," he said. "After all, he thought you were ill and he went for the doctor. Supposing he'd been right? You'd owe him thanks, not a scolding."

Unmollified, Sigmund glared a moment longer and closed his eye.

"He has to be told when he does wrong," she finished.

"I suppose," he said, drinking his coffee. "No harm done, anyhow. Since I'm here, let's talk shop. I'm writing something and I'd like an opinion."

"Great. Give me a footnote?"

"Two or three.—In your opinion, do the general underlying motivations that lead to suicide differ in different periods of history, or in different cultures?"

"My well-considered opinion is no, they don't," she said. "Frustrations can lead to depressions or frenzies; and if these are severe enough, they can lead to self-destruction. You ask me about motivations and I think they stay pretty much the same. I feel this is a cross-cultural, cross-temporal aspect of the human condition. I don't think it could be changed without changing the basic nature of man."

"Okay. Check. Now, what of the inciting element?" he asked. "Let man be a constant, his environment is still a variable. If he is placed in an overprotective life-situation, do you feel it would take more or less to depress him—or stimulate him to frenzy— than it would take in a not so protective environment?"

"Hm. Being case-oriented, I'd say it would depend on the man. But I see what you're driving at: a mass predisposition to jump out windows at the drop of a hat—the window even opening itself for you, because you asked it to—the revolt of the bored masses. I don't like the notion. I hope it's wrong."

"So do I, but I was thinking of symbolic suicides too—functional disorders that occur for pretty flimsy reasons."

"Aha! Your lecture last month: autopsychomimesis. I have the tape. Well-told, but I can't agree."

"Neither can I, now. I'm rewriting that whole section—'Thanatos in Cloudcuckooland,' I'm calling it. It's really the death-instinct moved nearer the surface."

"If I get you a scalpel and a cadaver, will you cut out the death-instinct and let me touch it?"

"Couldn't," he put the grin into his voice, "it would be all used up in a cadaver. Find me a volunteer though, and he'll prove my case by volunteering."

"Your logic is unassailable," she smiled. "Get us some more coffee, okay?"

Render went to the kitchen, spiked and filled the cups, drank a glass of water, returned to the living room. Eileen had not moved; neither had Sigmund.

"What do you do when you're not busy being a Shaper?" she asked him.

"The same things most people do—eat, drink, sleep, talk, visit friends and not-friends, visit places, read . . ."

"Are you a forgiving man?"

"Sometimes. Why?"

"Then forgive me. I argued with a woman today, a woman named DeVille."

"What about?"

"You—and she accused me of such things it were better my mother had not borne me. Are you going to marry her?"

"No, marriage is like alchemy. It served an important purpose once, but I hardly feel it's here to stay."

"Good."

"What did you say to her?"

"I gave her a clinic referral card that said, 'Diagnosis: Bitch. Prescription: Drug therapy and a tight gag.' "

"Oh," said Render, showing interest.

"She tore it up and threw it in my face."

"I wonder why?"

She shrugged, smiled, made a gridwork on the tablecloth.

" 'Fathers and elders, I ponder,' " sighed Render, " 'what is hell?' "

" 'I maintain it is the suffering of being unable to love,' " she finished. "Was Dostoevsky right?"

"I doubt it. I'd put him into group therapy, myself. That'd be *real* hell for him—with all those people acting like his characters, and enjoying it so."

Render put down his cup, pushed his chair away from the table.

"I suppose you must be going now?"

"I really should," said Render.

"And I can't interest you in food?"

"No."

She stood.

"Okay, I'll get my coat."

"I could drive back myself and just set the car to return."

"No! I'm frightened by the notion of empty cars driving around the city. I'd feel the thing was haunted for the next two and a half weeks.

"Besides," she said, passing through the archway, "you promised me Winchester Cathedral."

"You want to do it today?"

"If you can be persuaded."

As Render stood deciding, Sigmund rose to his feet. He stood directly before him and stared upward into his eyes. He opened his mouth and closed it, several times, but no sounds emerged. Then he turned away and left the room.

"No," Eileen's voice came back, "you will stay here until I return."

Render picked up his coat and put it on, stuffing the medkit into the far pocket.

As they walked up the hall toward the elevator, Render thought he heard a very faint and very distant howling sound.

In this place, of all places, Render knew he was the master of all things.

He was at home on those alien worlds, without time, those worlds where flowers copulate and the stars do battle in the heavens, falling at last to the ground, bleeding, like so many spilt and shattered chalices, and the seas part to reveal stairways leading down, and arms emerge from caverns, waving torches that flame like liquid faces—a midwinter night's nightmare, summer go a-begging, Render knew—for he had visited those worlds on a professional basis for the better part of a decade. With the crooking of a finger he could isolate the sorcerers, bring them to trial for treason against the realm—aye, and he could execute them, could appoint their successors.

Fortunately, this trip was only a courtesy call . . .

He moved forward through the glade, seeking her.

He could feel her awakening presence all about him.

He pushed through the branches, stood beside the lake. It was cold, blue, and bottomless, the lake, reflecting that slender willow which had become the station of her arrival.

"Eileen!"

The willow swayed toward him, swayed away.

"Eileen! Come forth!"

Leaves fell, floated upon the lake, disturbed its mirror-like placidity, distorted the reflections.

"Eileen?"

All the leaves yellowed at once then, dropped down into the water. The tree ceased its swaying. There was a strange sound in the darkening sky, like the humming of high wires on a cold day.

Suddenly there was a double file of moons passing through the heavens.

Render selected one, reached up, and pressed it. The others vanished as he did so, and the world brightened; the humming went out of the air.

He circled the lake to gain a subjective respite from the rejection-action and his counter to it. He moved up along an aisle of pines toward the place where he wanted the cathedral to occur. Birds sang now in the trees. The wind came softly by him. He felt her presence quite strongly.

"Here, Eileen. Here."

She walked beside him then, green silk, hair of bronze, eyes of molten emerald; she wore an emerald in her forehead. She walked in green slippers over the pine needles, saying: "What happened?"

"You were afraid."

"Why?"

"Perhaps you fear the cathedral. Are you a witch?" he smiled.

"Yes, but it's my day off."

He laughed, and he took her arm, and they rounded an island of foliage, and there was the cathedral reconstructed on a grassy rise, pushing its way above them and above the trees, climbing into the middle air, breathing out organ notes, reflecting a stray ray of sunlight from a pane of glass.

"Hold tight to the world," he said. "Here comes the guided tour."

They moved forward and entered.

" ' . . . With its floor-to-ceiling shafts, like so many huge tree-trunks, it achieves a ruthless control over its spaces,' " he said. "— Got that from the guidebook. This is the north transept . . ."

" 'Greensleeves,' " she said, "the organ is playing 'Greensleeves' "

"So it is. You can't blame me for that though.—Observe the scalloped capitals—"

"I want to go nearer the music."

"Very well. This way then."

Render felt that something was wrong. He could not put his finger on it.

Everything retained its solidity . . .

Something passed rapidly then, high above the cathedral, uttering a sonic boom. Render smiled at that, remembering now; it was like a slip of the tongue: for a moment he had confused Eileen with Jill—yes, that was what had happened.

Why, then . . .

A burst of white was the altar. He had never seen it before, anywhere. All the walls were dark and cold about them. Candles flickered in corners and high niches. The organ chorded thunder under invisible hands.

Render knew that something was wrong.

He turned to Eileen Shallot, whose hat was a green cone towering up into the darkness, trailing wisps of green veiling. Her throat was in shadow, but . . .

"That necklace—Where?"

"I don't know," she smiled.

The goblet she held radiated a rosy light. It was reflected from her emerald. It washed him like a draft of cool air.

"Drink?" she asked.

"Stand still," he ordered.

He willed the walls to fall down. They swam in shadow.

"Stand still!" he repeated urgently. "Don't do anything. Try not even to think.

"—Fall down!" he cried. And the walls were blasted in all directions and the roof was flung over the top of the world, and they stood amid ruins lighted by a single taper. The night was black as pitch.

"Why did you do that?" she asked, still holding the goblet out toward him.

"Don't think. Don't think anything," he said. "Relax. You are very tired. As that candle flickers and wanes so does your consciousness. You can barely keep awake. You can hardly stay on your feet. Your eyes are closing. There is nothing to see here anyway."

He willed the candle to go out. It continued to burn.

"I'm not tired. Please have a drink."

He heard organ music through the night. A different tune, one he did not recognize at first.

"I need your cooperation."

"All right. Anything."

"Look! The moon!" he pointed.

She looked upward and the moon appeared from behind an inky cloud.

". . . And another, and another."

Moons, like strung pearls, proceeded across the blackness.

"The last one will be red," he stated.

It was.

He reached out then with his right index finger, slid his arm sideways along his field of vision, then tried to touch the red moon.

His arm ached, it burned. He could not move it.

"Wake up!" he screamed.

The red moon vanished, and the white ones.

"Please take a drink."

He dashed the goblet from her hand and turned away. When he turned back she was still holding it before him.

"A drink?"

He turned and fled into the night.

It was like running through a waist-high snowdrift. It was wrong. He was compounding the error by running—he was minimizing his strength, maximizing hers. It was sapping his energies, draining him.

He stood still in the midst of the blackness.

"The world around me moves," he said. "I am its center."

"Please have a drink," she said, and he was standing in the glade beside their table set beside the lake. The lake was black and the moon was silver, and high, and out of his reach. A single candle flickered on the table, making her hair as silver as her dress. She wore the moon on her brow. A bottle of Romanée-Conti stood on the white cloth beside a wide-brimmed wine glass. It was filled to overflowing, that glass, and rosy beads clung to its lip. He was very thirsty, and she was lovelier than anyone he had ever seen before, and her necklace sparkled, and the breeze came cool off the lake, and there was something—something he should remember . . .

He took a step toward her and his armor clinked lightly as he moved. He reached toward the glass and his right arm stiffened with pain and fell back to his side.

"You are wounded!"

Slowly, he turned his head. The blood flowed from the open wound in his bicep and ran down his arm and dripped from his fingertips. His armor had been breached. He forced himself to look away.

"Drink this, love. It will heal you."

She stood.

"I will hold the glass."

He stared at her as she raised it to his lips.

"Who am I?" he asked.

She did not answer him, but something replied—within a splashing of waters out over the lake:

*"You are Render, the Shaper."*

"Yes, I remember," he said; and turning his mind to the one lie which might break the entire illusion he forced his mouth to say: "Eileen Shallot, I hate you."

The world shuddered and swam about him, was shaken, as by a huge sob.

"Charles!" she screamed, and the blackness swept over them.

"Wake up! Wake up!" he cried, and his right arm burned and ached and bled in the darkness.

*   *   *

He stood alone in the midst of a white plain. It was silent, it was endless. It sloped away toward the edges of the world. It gave off its own light, and the sky was no sky, but was nothing overhead. Nothing. He was alone. His own voice echoed back to him from the end of the world: ". . . hate you," it said, ". . . hate you."

He dropped to his knees. He was Render.

He wanted to cry.

A red moon appeared above the plain, casting a ghastly light over the entire expanse. There was a wall of mountains to the left of him, another to his right.

He raised his right arm. He helped it with his left hand. He clutched his wrist, extended his index finger. He reached for the moon.

Then there came a howl from high in the mountains, a great wailing cry—half-human, all challenge, all loneliness, and all remorse. He saw it then, treading upon the mountains, its tail brushing the snow from their highest peaks, the ultimate loup-garou of the North—Fenris, son of Loki—raging at the heavens.

It leapt into the air. It swallowed the moon.

It landed near him, and its great eyes blazed yellow. It stalked him on soundless pads, across the cold white fields that lay between the mountains; and he backed away from it, up hills and down slopes, over crevasses and rifts, through valleys, past stalagmites and pinnacles—under the edges of glaciers, beside frozen river beds, and always downwards—until its hot breath bathed him and its laughing mouth was opened above him.

He turned then and his feet became two gleaming rivers carrying him away.

The world jumped backwards. He glided over the slopes. Downward. Speeding—

Away . . .

He looked back over his shoulder.

In the distance, the gray shape loped after him.

He felt that it could narrow the gap if it chose. He had to move faster.

The world reeled about him. Snow began to fall.

He raced on.

Ahead, a blur, a broken outline.

He tore through the veils of snow which now seemed to be falling upward from off the ground—like strings of bubbles.

He approached the shattered form.

Like a swimmer he approached—unable to open his mouth to speak, for fear of drowning—of drowning and not knowing, of never knowing.

He could not check his forward motion; he was swept tide-like toward the wreck. He came to a stop, at last, before it.

Some things never change. They are things which have long ceased to exist as objects and stand solely as never-to-be-calendared occasions outside that sequence of elements called Time.

Render stood there and did not care if Fenris leapt upon his back and ate his brains. He had covered his eyes, but he could not stop the seeing. Not this time. He did not care about anything. Most of himself lay dead at his feet.

There was a howl. A gray shape swept past him.

The baleful eyes and bloody muzzle rooted within the wrecked car, champing through the steel, the glass, groping inside for . . .

"No! Brute! Chewer of corpses!" he cried. "The dead are sacred! *My* dead are sacred!"

He had a scalpel in his hand then, and he slashed expertly at the tendons, the bunches of muscle on the straining shoulders, the soft belly, the ropes of the arteries.

Weeping, he dismembered the monster, limb by limb, and it bled and it bled, fouling the vehicle and the remains within it with its infernal animal juices, dripping and running until the whole plain was reddened and writhing about them.

*   *   *

Render fell across the pulverized hood, and it was soft and warm and dry. He wept upon it.

"Don't cry," she said.

He was hanging onto her shoulder then, holding her tightly, there beside the black lake beneath the moon that was Wedgwood. A single candle flickered upon their table. She held the glass to his lips.

"Please drink it."

"Yes, give it to me!"

He gulped the wine that was all softness and lightness. It burned within him. He felt his strength returning.

"I am . . ."

"—*Render, the Shaper*," splashed the lake.

"No!"

He turned and ran again, looking for the wreck. He had to go back, to return . . .

"You can't."

"I can!" he cried. "I can, if I try . . ."

Yellow flames coiled through the thick air. Yellow serpents. They coiled, glowing, about his ankles. Then through the murk, two-headed and towering, approached his Adversary.

Small stones rattled past him. An overpowering odor corkscrewed up his nose and into his head.

"Shaper!" came the bellow from one head.

"You have returned for the reckoning!" called the other.

Render stared, remembering.

"No reckoning, Thaumiel," he said. "I beat you and I chained you for—Rothman, yes, it was Rothman—the cabalist." He traced a pentagram in the air. "Return to Qliphoth. I banish you."

"This place be Qliphoth."

". . . By Khamael, the angel of blood, by the hosts of Seraphim, in the Name of Elohim Gebor, I bid you vanish!"

"Not this time," laughed both heads.

It advanced.

Render backed slowly away, his feet bound by the yellow

serpents. He could feel the chasm opening behind him. The world was a jigsaw puzzle coming apart. He could see the pieces separating.

"Vanish!"

The giant roared out its double-laugh.

Render stumbled.

"This way, love!"

She stood within a small cave to his right.

He shook his head and backed toward the chasm.

Thaumiel reached out toward him.

Render toppled back over the edge.

"Charles!" she screamed, and the world shook itself apart with her wailing.

"Then Vernichtung," he answered as he fell. "I join you in darkness."

Everything came to an end.


"I want to see Doctor Charles Render."

"I'm sorry, that is impossible."

"But I skip-jetted all the way here, just to thank him. I'm a new man! He changed my life!"

"I'm sorry, Mister Erikson. When you called this morning, I told you it was impossible."

"Sir, I'm Representative Erikson—and Render once did me a great service."

"Then you can do him one now. Go home."

"You can't talk to me that way!"

"I just did. Please leave. Maybe next year sometime . . ."

"But a few words can do wonders . . ."

"Save them!"

"I-I'm sorry . . ."


Lovely as it was, pinked over with the morning—the slopping, steaming bowl of the sea—he knew that it *had* to end.

Therefore . . .

He descended the high tower stairway and he entered the courtyard. He crossed to the bower of roses and he looked down upon the pallet set in its midst.

"Good morrow, m'lord," he said.

"To you the same," said the knight, his blood mingling with the earth, the flowers, the grasses, flowing from his wound, sparkling over his armor, dripping from his fingertips.

"Naught hath healed?"

The knight shook his head.

"I empty. I wait."

"Your waiting is near ended."

"What mean you?" He sat upright.

"The ship. It approacheth harbor."

The knight stood. He leaned his back against a mossy tree-trunk. He stared at the huge, bearded servitor who continued to speak, words harsh with barbaric accents:

"It cometh like a dark swan before the wind—returning."

"Dark, say you? Dark?"

"The sails be black, Lord Tristram."

"You lie!"

"Do you wish to see? To see for yourself?—Look then!"

He gestured.

The earth quaked, the wall toppled. The dust swirled and settled. From where they stood they could see the ship moving into the harbor on the wings of the night.

"No! You lied!—See! They are white!"

The dawn danced upon the waters. The shadows fled from the ship's sails.

"No, you fool! Black! They *must* be!"

"White! White!—Isolde! You have kept faith! You have returned!"

He began running toward the harbor.

"Come back!—Your wound! You are ill!—Stop . . ."

The sails were white beneath a sun that was a red button which the servitor reached quickly to touch.

Night fell.

# Computers Don't Argue
## Gordon R. Dickson

*Anyone who has had dealings with a book club lately will readily agree with me that this next story is frighteningly plausible.*

Mr: Walter A. Child Balance: $4.98
Dear Customer: Enclosed is your latest book selection.
"Kidnapped," by Robert Louis Stevenson.

437 Woodlawn Drive
Panduk, Michigan
Nov. 16, 1965

Treasure Book Club
1823 Mandy Street
Chicago, Illinois

Dear Sirs:

I wrote you recently about the computer punch card you sent, billing me for "Kim," by Rudyard Kipling. I did not open the package containing it until I had already mailed you my check for the amount on the card. On opening the package, I found the book missing half its pages. I sent it back to you, requesting either another copy or my money back. Instead, you have sent me a copy of "Kidnapped," by Robert Louis Stevenson. Will you please straighten this out?

I hereby return the copy of "Kidnapped."

Sincerely yours,
Walter A. Child

Treasure Book Club
SECOND NOTICE
PLEASE DO NOT FOLD, SPINDLE
OR MUTILATE THIS CARD

Mr: Walter A. Child Balance: $4.98
For "Kidnapped," by Robert Louis Stevenson
(If remittance has been made for the above, please disregard this notice)

437 Woodlawn Drive
Panduk, Michigan
Jan. 21, 1966

Treasure Book Club
1823 Mandy Street
Chicago, Illinois

Dear Sirs:
May I direct your attention to my letter of November 16, 1965? You are still continuing to dun me with computer punch cards for a book I did not order. Whereas, actually, it is your company that owes *me* money.

Sincerely yours,
Walter A. Child

Treasure Book Club
1823 Mandy Street
Chicago, Illinois
Feb. 1, 1966

Mr. Walter A. Child
437 Woodlawn Drive
Panduk, Michigan

Dear Mr. Child:
We have sent you a number of reminders concerning an amount owing to us as a result of book purchases you have made from us. This amount, which is $4.98, is now long overdue.

This situation is disappointing to us, particularly since there was no hesitation on our part in extending you credit at the time original arrangements for these purchases were made by you. If we do not receive payment in full by return mail, we will be forced to turn the matter over to a collection agency.

> Very truly yours,
> Samuel P. Grimes
> Collection Mgr.

> 437 Woodlawn Drive
> Panduk, Michigan
> Feb. 5, 1966

Dear Mr. Grimes:

Will you stop sending me punch cards and form letters and make me some kind of a direct answer from a human being?

*I* don't owe you money. *You* owe me money. Maybe I should turn your company over to a collection agency.

> Walter A. Child

## FEDERAL COLLECTION OUTFIT

> 88 Prince Street
> Chicago, Illinois
> Feb. 28, 1966

Mr. Walter A. Child
437 Woodlawn Drive
Panduk, Michigan

Dear Mr. Child:

Your account with the Treasure Book Club, of $4.98 plus interest and charges, has been turned over to our agency for collection. The amount due is now $6.83. Please send your check for this amount or we shall be forced to take immediate action.

> Jacob N. Harshe
> Vice President

## FEDERAL COLLECTION OUTFIT

> 88 Prince Street
> Chicago, Illinois
> April 8, 1966

Mr. Walter A. Child
437 Woodlawn Drive
Panduk, Michigan

Dear Mr. Child:

You have seen fit to ignore our courteous requests to settle your long overdue account with Treasure Book Club, which is now, with accumulated interest and charges, in the amount of $7.51.

If payment in full is not forthcoming by April 11, 1966, we will be forced to turn the matter over to our attorneys for immediate court action.

> Ezekiel B. Harshe
> President

## MALONEY, MAHONEY,
## MACNAMARA and PRUITT
### Attorneys

> 89 Prince Street
> Chicago, Illinois
> April 29, 1966

Mr. Walter A. Child
437 Woodlawn Drive
Panduk, Michigan

Dear Mr. Child:

Your indebtedness to the Treasure Book Club has been referred to us for legal action to collect.

This indebtedness is now in the amount of $10.01. If you will send us this amount so that we may receive it before May 5, 1966, the matter may be satisfied. However, if we do not receive satisfaction in full by that date, we will take steps to collect through the courts.

I am sure you will see the advantage of avoiding a judgment against you, which as a matter of record would do lasting harm to your credit rating.

> Very truly yours,
> Hagthorpe M. Pruitt, Jr.
> Attorney at Law

> 437 Woodlawn Drive
> Panduk, Michigan
> May 4, 1966

Mr. Hagthorpe M. Pruitt, Jr.
Maloney, Mahoney, MacNamara and Pruitt
89 Prince Street
Chicago, Illinois

Dear Mr. Pruitt:

You don't know what a pleasure it is to me in this matter to get a letter from a live human being to whom I can explain the situation.

This whole matter is silly. I explained it fully in my letters to the Treasure Book Company. But I might as well have been trying to explain to the computer that puts out their punch cards, for all the good it seemed to do. Briefly, what happened was, I ordered a copy of "Kim," by Rudyard Kipling, for $4.98. When I opened the package they sent me, I found the book had only half its pages, but I'd previously mailed a check to pay them for the book.

I sent the book back to them, asking either for a whole copy or my money back. Instead, they sent me a copy of "Kidnapped," by Robert Louis Stevenson—which I had not ordered; and for which they have been trying to collect from me.

Meanwhile, I am still waiting for the money back that they owe me for the copy of "Kim" that I didn't get. That's the whole story. Maybe you can help me straighten them out.

Relievedly yours,<br>Walter A. Child

P.S.: I also sent them back their copy of "Kidnapped," as soon as I got it, but it hasn't seemed to help. They have never even acknowledged getting it back.

MALONEY, MAHONEY,<br>
MACNAMARA and PRUITT<br>
Attorneys

89 Prince Street<br>Chicago, Illinois<br>May 9, 1966

Mr. Walter A. Child<br>
437 Woodlawn Drive<br>
Panduk, Michigan

Dear Mr. Child:

I am in possession of no information indicating that any item purchased by you from the Treasure Book Club has been returned.

I would hardly think that, if the case had been as you stated, the Treasure Book Club would have retained us to collect the amount owing from you.

If I do not receive your payment in full within three days, by May 12, 1966, we will be forced to take legal action.

Very truly yours,
Hagthorpe M. Pruitt, Jr.

## COURT OF MINOR CLAIMS
### Chicago, Illinois

Mr. Walter A. Child
437 Woodlawn Drive
Panduk, Michigan

Be informed that a judgment was taken and entered against you in this court this day of May 26, 1966, in the amount of $15.66 including court costs.

Payment in satisfaction of this judgment may be made to this court or to the adjudged creditor. In the case of payment being made to the creditor, a release should be obtained from the creditor and filed with this court in order to free you of legal obligation in connection with this judgment.

Under the recent Reciprocal Claims Act, if you are a citizen of a different state, a duplicate claim may be automatically entered and judged against you in your own state so that collection may be made there as well as in the State of Illinois.

## COURT OF MINOR CLAIMS
### Chicago, Illinois
### PLEASE DO NOT FOLD, SPINDLE
### OR MUTILATE THIS CARD

Judgment was passed this day of May 27, 1966, under Statute $15.66

Against: Child, Walter A., of 437 Woodlawn Drive, Panduk, Michigan. Pray to enter a duplicate claim for judgment

In: Picayune Court—Panduk, Michigan

For Amount: Statute 941

437 Woodlawn Drive
Panduk, Michigan
May 31, 1966

Samuel P. Grimes
Vice President, Treasure Book Club
1823 Mandy Street
Chicago, Illinois

Grimes:

This business has gone far enough. I've got to come down to Chicago on business of my own tomorrow. I'll see you then and we'll get this straightened out once and for all, about who owes what to whom, and how much!

Yours,
Walter A. Child

From the Desk of the Clerk
Picayune Court

June 1, 1966

Harry:

The attached computer card from Chicago's Minor Claims Court against A. Walter has a 1500-series Statute number on it. That puts it over in Criminal with you, rather than Civil, with me. So I herewith submit it for your computer instead of mine. How's business?

Joe

## CRIMINAL RECORDS
Panduk, Michigan
## PLEASE DO NOT FOLD, SPINDLE
## OR MUTILATE THIS CARD

Convicted: (Child) A. Walter
On: May 26, 1966
Address: 437 Woodlawn Drive
Panduk, Mich.
Crim: Statute: 1566 (Corrected) 1567
Crime: Kidnap
Date: Nov. 16, 1965
Notes: At large. To be picked up at once.

POLICE DEPARTMENT, PANDUK, MICHIGAN. TO POLICE DEPARTMENT CHICAGO ILLINOIS. CONVICTED SUBJECT A. (COMPLETE FIRST NAME UNKNOWN) WALTER, SOUGHT HERE IN CONNECTION REF. YOUR NOTIFICATION OF JUDGMENT FOR KIDNAP OF CHILD NAMED ROBERT LOUIS STEVENSON, ON NOV. 16, 1965. INFORMATION HERE INDICATES SUBJECT FLED HIS RESIDENCE, AT 437 WOODLAND DRIVE, PANDUK, AND MAY BE AGAIN IN YOUR AREA.

POSSIBLE CONTACT IN YOUR AREA: THE TREASURE BOOK CLUB, 1823 MANDY STREET, CHICAGO, ILLINOIS. SUBJECT NOT KNOWN TO BE DANGEROUS. PICK UP AND HOLD, AD-VISING US OF CAPTURE . . .

TO POLICE DEPARTMENT, PANDUK, MICHIGAN. REFER-ENCE YOUR REQUEST TO PICK UP AND HOLD A. (COMPLETE FIRST NAME UNKNOWN) WALTER, WANTED IN PANDUK ON STATUE 1567, CRIME OF KIDNAPPING.

SUBJECT ARRESTED AT OFFICES OF TREASURE BOOK CLUB, OPERATING THERE UNDER ALIAS WALTER ANTHONY CHILD AND ATTEMPTING TO COLLECT $4.98 FROM ONE SAMUEL P.

GRIMES, EMPLOYEE OF THAT COMPANY.

DISPOSAL: HOLDING FOR YOUR ADVICE.

POLICE DEPARTMENT PANDUK, MICHIGAN, TO POLICE DEPARTMENT CHICAGO, ILLINOIS

REF: A. WALTER (ALIAS WALTER ANTHONY CHILD) SUBJECT WANTED FOR CRIME OF KIDNAP, YOUR AREA, REF: YOUR COMPUTER PUNCH CARD NOTIFICATION OF JUDGMENT, DATED MAY 27, 1966. COPY OUR CRIMINAL RECORDS PUNCH CARD HEREWITH FORWARDED TO YOUR COMPUTER SECTION.

## CRIMINAL RECORDS
### Chicago, Illinois
## PLEASE DO NOT FOLD, SPINDLE
## OR MUTILATE THIS CARD

SUBJECT (CORRECTION—OMITTED RECORD SUPPLIED) APPLICABLE STATUTE NO. 1567

JUDGMENT NO. 456789

TRIAL RECORD: APPARENTLY MISFILED AND UNAVAILABLE

DIRECTION: TO APPEAR FOR SENTENCING BEFORE JUDGE JOHN ALEXANDER MCDIVOT, COURTROOM A, JUNE 9, 1966

From the Desk of
Judge Alexander J. McDivot

June 2, 1966

Dear Tony:

I've got an adjudged criminal coming up before me for sentencing Thursday morning—but the trial transcript is apparently misfiled.

I need some kind of information (Ref: A. Walter—Judgment No. 456789, Criminal). For example, what about the victim of the kidnapping. Was victim harmed?

Jack McDivot

June 3, 1966

Records Search Unit
Re: Ref: Judgment No. 456789—was victim harmed?

Tonio Malagasi<br>Records Division

June 3, 1966

To: United States Statistics Office
Attn.: Information Section
Subject: Robert Louis Stevenson
Query: Information concerning

Records Search Unit<br>Criminal Records Division<br>Police Department<br>Chicago, Ill.

June 5, 1966

To: Records Search Unit
Criminal Records Division
Police Department
Chicago, Illinois
Subject: Your query re Robert Louis Stevenson (File no. 189623)
Action: Subject deceased. Age at death, 44 yrs. Further information requested?

A. K.<br>Information Section<br>U.S. Statistics Office

June 6, 1966

To: United States Statistics Office
Attn.: Information Division
Subject: RE: File no. 189623
    No further information required.

Thank you.
Records Search Unit


Criminal Records Division
Police Department
Chicago, Illinois

June 7, 1966

To: Tonio Malagasi
Records Division
Re: Ref: Judgment No. 456789—victim is dead.

Records Search Unit


June 7, 1966

To: Judge Alexander J. McDivot's Chambers
Dear Jack:
Ref: Judgment No. 456789. The victim in this kidnap case was apparently slain.

From the strange lack of background information on the killer and his victim, as well as the victim's age, this smells to me like a gangland killing. This for your information. Don't quote me. It seems to me, though, that Stevenson—the victim—has a name that rings a faint bell with me. Possibly, one of the East Coast Mob, since the association comes back to me as something about pirates—possibly New York dockage hijackers—and something about buried loot.

As I say, above is only speculation for your private guidance.

Any time I can help . . .

Best,
Tony Malagasi
Records Division

## MICHAEL R. REYNOLDS
Attorney-at-law

49 Water Street
Chicago, Illinois
June 8, 1966

Dear Tim:

Regrets: I can't make the fishing trip. I've been court-appointed here to represent a man about to be sentenced tomorrow on a kidnapping charge.

Ordinarily, I might have tried to beg off, and Mc-Divot, who is doing the sentencing, would probably have turned me loose. But this is the damnedest thing you ever heard of.

The man being sentenced has apparently been not only charged, but adjudged guilty as a result of a comedy of errors too long to go into here. He not only isn't guilty—he's got the best case I ever heard of for damages against one of the larger Book Clubs headquartered here in Chicago. And that's a case I wouldn't mind taking on.

It's inconceivable—but damnably possible, once you stop to think of it in this day and age of machine-made records—that a completely innocent man could be put in this position.

There shouldn't be much to it. I've asked to see Mc-Divot tomorrow before the time for sentencing, and it'll just be a matter of explaining to him. Then I can discuss the damage suit with my freed client at his leisure.

Fishing next weekend?

Yours,
Mike


MICHAEL R. REYNOLDS
Attorney-at-law

49 Water Street
Chicago, Illinois
June 10

Dear Tim:

In haste—

No fishing this coming week either. Sorry.

You won't believe it. My innocent-as-a-lamb-and-I'm-not-kidding client has just been sentenced to death for first-degree murder in connection with the death of his kidnap victim.

Yes, I explained the whole thing to McDivot. And when he explained his situation to me, I nearly fell out of my chair.

It wasn't a matter of my not convincing him. It took less than three minutes to show him that my client should never have been within the walls of the County Jail for a second. But—get this—McDivot couldn't do a thing about it.

The point is, my man had already been judged guilty according to the computerized records. In the absence of a trial record—of course there never was one (but that's something I'm not free to explain to you now)—the judge has to go by what records are available. And in the case of an adjudged prisoner, McDivot's only legal choice was whether to sentence to life imprisonment, or execution.

The death of the kidnap victim, according to the statute, made the death penalty mandatory. Under the new laws governing length of time for appeal, which has been shortened because of the new system of computerizing records, to force an elimination of unfair delay and mental anguish to those condemned, I have five days in which to file an appeal, and ten to have it acted on.

Needless to say, I am not going to monkey with an appeal. I'm going directly to the Governor for a pardon— after which we will get this farce reversed. McDivot has already written the Governor, also, explaining that his sentence was ridiculous, but that he had no choice. Between the two of us, we ought to have a pardon in short order.

Then, I'll make the fur fly . . .

And we'll get in some fishing.

Best,
Mike

## OFFICE OF THE
## GOVERNOR OF ILLINOIS

June 17, 1966

Mr. Michael R. Reynolds
49 Water Street
Chicago, Illinois
Dear Mr. Reynolds:

In reply to your query about the request for pardon for Walter A. Child (A. Walter), may I inform you that the Governor is still on his trip with the Midwest Governors Committee, examining the Wall in Berlin. He should be back next Friday.

I will bring your request and letters to his attention the minute he returns.

Very truly yours,
Clara B. Jilks
Secretary to the Governor

June 27, 1966

Michael R. Reynolds
49 Water Street
Chicago, Illinois
Dear Mike:

Where is that pardon?
My execution date is only five days from now!

Walt

June 29, 1966

Walter A. Child (A. Walter)
Cell Block E
Illinois State Penitentiary
Joliet, Illinois
Dear Walt:

The Governor returned, but was called away immediately to the White House in Washington to give his views on interstate sewage.

I am camping on his doorstep and will be on him the moment he arrives here.

Meanwhile, I agree with you about the seriousness of the situation. The warden at the prison there, Mr. Allen Magruder, will bring this letter to you and have a private talk with you. I urge you to listen to what he has to say; and I enclose letters from your family also urging you to listen to Warden Magruder.

Yours,
Mike

June 30, 1966

Michael R. Reynolds
49 Water Street
Chicago, Illinois

Dear Mike: (This letter being smuggled out by Warden Magruder)

As I was talking to Warden Magruder in my cell, here, news was brought to him that the Governor has at last returned for a while to Illinois, and will be in his office early tomorrow morning, Friday. So you will have time to get the pardon signed by him and delivered to the prison in time to stop my execution on Saturday.

Accordingly, I have turned down the Warden's kind offer of a chance to escape; since he told me he could by no means guarantee to have all the guards out of my way when I tried it; and there was a chance of my being killed escaping.

But now everything will straighten itself out. Actually, an experience as fantastic as this had to break down sometime under its own weight.

Best,
Walt

## FOR THE SOVEREIGN
## STATE OF ILLINOIS

I, Hubert Daniel Willikens, Governor of the State of Illinois, and invested with the authority and powers appertaining thereto, including the power to pardon those in my judgment wrongfully convicted or otherwise deserving of executive mercy, do this day of July 1, 1966, announce and proclaim that Walter A. Child (A. Walter), now in custody as a consequence of erroneous conviction upon a crime of which he is entirely innocent, is fully and freely pardoned of said crime. And I do direct the necessary authorities having custody of the said Walter A. Child (A. Walter) in whatever place or places he may be held, to immediately free, release, and allow unhindered departure to him . . .

Interdepartmental Routing Service
### PLEASE DO NOT FOLD, MUTILATE, OR SPINDLE THIS CARD
Failure to route Document properly.
To: Governor Hubert Daniel Willikens
Re: Pardon issued to Walter A. Child, July 1, 1966

Dear State Employee:

You have failed to attach your Routing Number.

PLEASE: Resubmit document with this card and form 876, explaining your authority for placing a TOP RUSH category on this document. Form 876 must be signed by your Departmental Superior.

RESUBMIT ON: Earliest possible date ROUTING SERVICE office is open. In this case, Tuesday, July 5, 1966.

WARNING: Failure to submit form 876 WITH THE SIGNATURE OF YOUR SUPERIOR may make you liable to prosecution for misusing a Service of the State Government. A warrant may be issued for your arrest.

There are NO exceptions. YOU have been WARNED.

# Becalmed in Hell
## Larry Niven

Back to Venus, with a difference. This is the astronomical Venus, not the romantic vision of "The Doors of His Face, the Lamps of His Mouth." (But notice the sea images, even in this rationalist's view of the Planet of Love.)

Like all Larry Niven's stories, this one is solidly based on present-day science and technology, and it contains a neat, nasty problem: if something goes wrong with a spacecraft whose control system is a Cyborg—part human, part wires and transistors—is the trouble mechanical or psychological? And how do you find out before it kills you?

*I   c o u l d*   feel the heat hovering outside. In the cabin it was bright and dry and cool, almost too cool, like a modern office building in the dead of the summer. Beyond the two small windows it was as black as it ever gets in the solar system, and hot enough to melt lead, at a pressure equivalent to three hundred feet beneath the ocean.

"There goes a fish," I said, just to break the monotony.

"So how's it cooked?"

"Can't tell. It seems to be leaving a trail of breadcrumbs. Fried? Imagine that, Eric! A fried jellyfish."

Eric sighed noisily. "Do I have to?"

"You have to. Only way you'll see anything worthwhile in this—this—" Soup? Fog? Boiling maple syrup?

"Searing black calm."

"Right."

"Someone dreamed up that phrase when I was a kid, just after the news of the Mariner II probe. An eternal searing black calm, hot as a kiln, under an atmosphere thick enough to keep any light or any breath of wind from ever reaching the surface."

I shivered. "What's the outside temperature now?"

"You'd rather not know. You've always had too much imagination, Howie."

"I can take it, Doc."

"Six hundred and twelve degrees."

"I can't take it, Doc!"

This was Venus, Planet of Love, favorite of the science-fiction writers of three decades ago. Our ship hung below the Earth-to-Venus hydrogen fuel tank, twenty miles up and all but motionless in the syrupy air. The tank, nearly empty now, made an excellent blimp. It would keep us aloft as long as the internal pressure matched the external. That was Eric's job, to regulate the tank's pressure by regulating the temperature of the hydrogen gas. We had collected air samples after each ten mile drop from three hundred miles on down, and temperature readings for shorter intervals, and we had dropped the small probe. The data

211

we had gotten from the surface merely confirmed in detail our previous knowledge of the hottest world in the solar system.

"Temperature just went up to six-thirteen," said Eric. "Look, are you through bitching?"

"For the moment."

"Good. Strap down. We're taking off."

"Oh frabjous day!" I started untangling the crash webbing over my couch.

"We've done everything we came to do. Haven't we?"

"Am I arguing? Look, I'm strapped down."

"Yeah."

I knew why he was reluctant to leave. I felt a touch of it myself. We'd spent four months getting to Venus in order to spend a week circling her and less than two days in her upper atmosphere, and it seemed a terrible waste of time.

But he was taking too long. "What's the trouble, Eric?"

"You'd rather not know."

He meant it. His voice was a mechanical, inhuman monotone; he wasn't making the extra effort to get human expression out of his "prosthetic" vocal apparatus. Only a severe shock would affect him that way.

"I can take it," I said.

"Okay. I can't feel anything in the ramjet controls. Feels like I've just had a spinal anaesthetic."

The cold in the cabin drained into me, all of it. "See if you can send motor impulses the other way. You could run the rams by guess-and-hope even if you can't feel them."

"Okay." One split second later, "They don't. Nothing happens. Good thinking though."

I tried to think of something to say while I untied myself from the couch. What came out was, "It's been a pleasure knowing you, Eric. I've liked being half of this team, and I still do."

"Get maudlin later. Right now, start checking my attachments. Carefully."

I swallowed my comments and went to open the access door

in the cabin's forward wall. The floor swayed ever so gently beneath my feet.

Beyond the four-foot-square access door was Eric. Eric's central nervous system, with the brain perched at the top and the spinal cord coiled in a loose spiral to fit more compactly into the transparent glass-and-sponge-plastic housing. Hundreds of wires from all over the ship led to the glass walls, where they were joined to selected nerves which spread like an electrical network from the central coil of nervous tissue and fatty protective membrane.

Space leaves no cripples; and don't call Eric a cripple, because he doesn't like it. In a way he's the ideal spaceman. His life support system weighs only half of what mine does, and takes up a twelfth as much room. But his other prosthetic aids take up most of the ship. The ramjets were hooked into the last pair of nerve trunks, the nerves which once moved his legs, and dozens of finer nerves in those trunks sensed and regulated fuel feed, ram temperature, differential acceleration, intake aperture dilation, and spark pulse.

These connections were intact. I checked them four diferent ways without finding the slightest reason why they shouldn't be working.

"Test the others," said Eric.

It took a good two hours to check every trunk nerve connection. They were all solid. The blood pump was chugging along, and the fluid was rich enough, which killed the idea that the ram nerves might have "gone to sleep" from lack of nutrients or oxygen. Since the lab is one of his prosthetic aids, I let Eric analyse his own blood sugar, hoping that the "liver" had goofed and was producing some other form of sugar. The conclusions were appalling. There was nothing wrong with Eric—inside the cabin.

"Eric, you're healthier than I am."

"I could tell. You looked worried, son, and I don't blame you. Now you'll have to go outside."

213

"I know. Let's dig out the suit."

It was in the emergency tools locker, the Venus suit that was never supposed to be used. NASA had designed it for use at Venusian ground level. Then they had refused to okay the ship below twenty miles until they knew more about the planet. The suit was a segmented armor job. I had watched it being tested in the heat-and-pressure box at Cal Tech, and I knew that the joints stopped moving after five hours, and wouldn't start again until they had been cooled. Now I opened the locker and pulled the suit out by the shoulders and held it in front of me. It seemed to be staring back.

"You still can't feel anything in the ramjets?"

"Not a twinge."

I started to put on the suit, piece by piece like medieval armor. Then I thought of something else. "We're twenty miles up. Are you going to ask me to do a balancing act on the hull?"

"No! Wouldn't think of it. We'll just have to go down."

The lift from the blimp tank was supposed to be constant until takeoff. When the time came Eric could get extra lift by heating the hydrogen to higher pressure, then cracking a valve to let the excess out. Of course he'd have to be very careful that the pressure was higher in the tank, or we'd get Venusian air coming in, and the ship would fall instead of rising. Naturally that would be disastrous.

So Eric lowered the tank temperature and cracked the valve, and down we went.

"Of course there's a catch," said Eric.

"I know."

"The ship stood the pressure twenty miles up. At ground level it'll be six times that."

"I know."

We fell fast, with the cabin tilted forward by the drag on our tailfins. The temperature rose gradually. The pressure went up fast. I sat at the window and saw nothing, nothing but black, but I sat there anyway and waited for the window to crack. NASA had refused to okay the ship below twenty miles . . .

Eric said, "The blimp tank's okay, and so's the ship, I think. But will the cabin stand up to it?"

"I wouldn't know."

"Ten miles."

Five hundred miles above us, unreachable, was the atomic ion engine that was to take us home. We couldn't get to it on the chemical rocket alone. The rocket was for use after the air became too thin for the ramjets.

"Four miles. Have to crack the valve again."

The ship dropped.

"I can see ground," said Eric.

I couldn't. Eric caught me straining my eyes and said, "Forget it. I'm using deep infrared, and getting no detail."

"No vast, misty swamps with weird, terrifying monsters and man-eating plants?"

"All I see is hot, bare dirt."

But we were almost down, and there were no cracks in the cabin wall. My neck and shoulder muscles loosened. I turned away from the window. Hours had passed while we dropped through the poisoned, thickening air. I already had most of my suit on. Now I screwed on my helmet and three-finger gantlets.

"Strap down," said Eric. I did.

We bumped gently. The ship tilted a little, swayed back, bumped again. And again, with my teeth rattling and my armor-plated body rolling against the crash webbing. "Damn," Eric muttered. I heard the hiss from above. Eric said, "I don't know how we'll get back up."

Neither did I. The ship bumped hard and stayed down, and I got up and went to the airlock.

"Good luck," said Eric. "Don't stay out too long." I waved at his cabin camera. The outside temperature was seven hundred and thirty.

The outer door opened. My suit refrigerating unit set up a complaining whine. With an empty bucket in each hand, and with my headlamp blazing a way through the black murk, I stepped out onto the right wing.

My suit creaked and settled under the pressure, and I stood on the wing and waited for it to stop. It was almost like being under water. My headlamp beam went out thick enough to be solid, penetrating no more than a hundred feet. The air couldn't have been that opaque, no matter how dense. It must have been full of dust, or tiny droplets of some fluid.

The wing ran back like a knife-edged running board, widening toward the tail until it spread into a tailfin. The two tailfins met back of the fuselage. At the tailfin tip was the ram, a big sculptured cylinder with an atomic engine inside. It wouldn't be hot because it hadn't been used yet, but I had my counter anyway.

I fastened a line to the wing and slid to the ground. As long as we were *here* . . . The ground turned out to be a dry, reddish dirt, crumbly, and so porous that it was almost spongy. Lava etched by chemicals? Almost anything would be corrosive at this pressure and temperature. I scooped one pailful from the surface and another from underneath the first, then climbed up the line and left the buckets on the wing.

The wing was terribly slippery. I had to wear magnetic sandals to stay on. I walked up and back along the two hundred foot length of the ship, making a casual inspection. Neither wing nor fuselage showed damage. Why not? If a meteor or something had cut Eric's contact with his sensors in the rams, there should have been evidence of a break in the surface.

Then, almost suddenly, I realized that there was an alternative.

It was too vague a suspicion to put into words yet, and I still had to finish the inspection. Telling Eric would be very difficult if I was right.

Four inspection panels were set into the wing, well protected from the reentry heat. One was halfway back on the fuselage, below the lower edge of the blimp tank, which was molded to the fuselage in such a way that from the front the ship looked like a dolphin. Two more were in the trailing edge of the tailfin, and the fourth was in the ram itself. All opened, with powered screwdriver on recessed screws, on junctions of the ship's electrical system.

There was nothing out of place under any of the panels. By making and breaking contacts and getting Eric's reactions, I found that his sensation ended somewhere between the second and third inspection panels. It was the same story on the left wing. No external damage, nothing wrong at the junctions. I climbed back to ground and walked slowly beneath the length of each wing, my headlamp tilted up. No damage underneath.

I collected my buckets and went back inside.

"A bone to pick?" Eric was puzzled. "Isn't this a strange time to start an argument? Save it for space. We'll have four months with nothing else to do."

"This can't wait. First of all, did you notice anything I didn't?" He'd been watching everything I saw and did through the peeper in my helmet.

"No. I'd have yelled."

"Okay. Now get this.

"The break in your circuits isn't inside, because you get sensation up to the second wing inspection panels. It isn't outside because there's no evidence of damage, not even corrosion spots. That leaves only one place for the flaw."

"Go on."

"We also have the puzzle of why you're paralyzed in both rams. Why should they both go wrong at the same time? There's only one place in the ship where the circuits join."

"What? Oh, yes, I see. They join through me."

"Now let's assume for the moment that you're the piece with the flaw in it. You're not a piece of machinery, Eric. If

217

something's wrong with you it isn't medical. That was the first thing we covered. But it could be psychological."

"It's nice to know you think I'm human. So I've slipped a cam, have I?"

"Slightly. I think you've got a case of what used to be called trigger anaesthesia. A soldier who kills too often sometimes finds that his right index finger or even his whole hand has gone numb, as if it were no longer a part of him. Your comment about not being a machine is important, Eric. I think that's the whole problem. You've never really believed that any part of the ship is a part of *you*. That's intelligent, because it's true. Every time the ship is redesigned you get a new set of parts, and it's right to avoid thinking of a change of model as a series of amputations." I'd been rehearsing this speech, trying to put it so that Eric would have no choice but to believe me. Now I know that it must have sounded phony. "But now you've gone too far. Subconsciously you've stopped believing that the rams can *feel* like a part of you, which they were designed to do. So you've persuaded yourself that you don't feel anything."

With my prepared speech done, and nothing left to say, I stopped talking and waited for the explosion.

"You make good sense," said Eric.

I was staggered. "You agree?"

"I didn't say that. You spin an elegant theory, but I want time to think about it. What do we do if it's true?"

"Why . . . I don't know. You'll just have to cure yourself."

"Okay. Now here's *my* idea. I propose that you thought up this theory to relieve yourself of a responsibility for getting us home alive. It puts the whole problem in my lap, metaphorically speaking."

"Oh, for—"

"Shut up. I haven't said you're wrong. That would be an ad hominem argument. We need time to think about this."

\*     \*     \*

It was lights-out, four hours later, before Eric would return to the subject.

"Howie, do me a favor. Assume for awhile that something mechanical is causing all our trouble. I'll assume it's psychosomatic."

"Seems reasonable."

"It is reasonable. What can you do if I've gone psychosomatic? What can I do if it's mechanical? I can't go around inspecting myself. We'd each better stick to what we know."

"It's a deal." I turned him off for the night and went to bed. But not to sleep.

With the lights off it was just like outside. I turned them back on. It wouldn't wake Eric. Eric never sleeps normally, since his blood doesn't accumulate fatigue poisons, and he'd go mad from being awake all the time if he didn't have a Russian sleep inducer plate near his cortex. The ship could implode without waking Eric when his sleep inducer's on. But I felt foolish being afraid of the dark.

While the dark stayed outside it was all right.

But it wouldn't stay there. It had invaded my partner's mind. Because his chemical checks guard him against chemical insanities like schizophrenia, we'd assumed he was permanently sane. But how could any prosthetic device protect him from his own imagination, his own misplaced common sense?

I couldn't keep my bargain. I knew I was right. But what could I do about it?

Hindsight is wonderful. I could see exactly what our mistake had been, Eric's and mine and the hundreds of men who had built his life support after the crash. There was nothing left of Eric then except the intact central nervous system, and no glands except the pituitary. "We'll regulate his blood composition," they said, "and he'll always be cool, calm, and collected. No panic reactions from Eric!"

I know a girl whose father had an accident when he was

forty-five or so. He was out with his brother, the girl's uncle, on a fishing trip. They were blind drunk when they started home, and the guy was riding on the hood while the brother drove. Then the brother made a sudden stop. Our hero left two important glands on the hood ornament.

The only change in his sex life was that his wife stopped worrying about late pregnancy. His *habits* were developed.

Eric doesn't need adrenal glands to be afraid of death. His emotional patterns were fixed long before the day he tried to land a moonship without radar. He'd grab any excuse to believe that I'd fixed whatever was wrong with the ram connections.

But he was counting on me to do it.

The atmosphere leaned on the windows. Not wanting to, I reached out to touch the quartz with my fingertips. I couldn't feel the pressure. But it was there, inexorable as the tide smashing a rock into sand grains. How long would the cabin hold it back?

If some broken part were holding us here, how could I have missed finding it? Perhaps it had left no break in the surface of either wing. But how?

That was the angle.

Two cigarettes later I got up to get the sample buckets. They were empty, the alien dirt safely stored away. I filled them with water and put them in the cooler, set the cooler for 40° Absolute, then turned off the lights and went to bed.

The morning was blacker than the inside of a smoker's lungs. What Venus really needs, I decided, philosophizing on my back, is to lose ninety-nine percent of her air. That would give her a bit more than half as much air as Earth, which would lower the greenhouse effect enough to make the temperature livable. Drop Venus' gravity to near zero for a few weeks and the work would do itself.

The whole damn universe is waiting for us to discover antigravity.

"Morning," said Eric. "Thought of anything?"

"Yes." I rolled out of bed. "Now don't bug me with questions. I'll explain everything as I go."

"No breakfast?"

"Not yet."

Piece by piece I put my suit on, just like one of King Arthur's gentlemen, and went for the buckets only after the gantlets were on. The ice, in the cold section, was in the chilly neighborhood of absolute zero. "This is two buckets of ordinary ice," I said, holding them up. "Now let me out."

"I should keep you here till you talk," Eric groused. But the doors opened and I went out onto the wing. I started talking while I unscrewed the number two right panel.

"Eric, think a moment about the tests they run on a manned ship before they'll let a man walk into the lifesystem. They test every part separately and in conjunction with other parts. Yet if something isn't working, either it's damaged or it wasn't tested right. Right?"

"Reasonable." He wasn't giving away anything.

"Well, nothing caused any damage. Not only is there no break in the ship's skin, but no coincidence could have made both rams go haywire at the same time. So something wasn't tested right."

I had the panel off. In the buckets the ice boiled gently where it touched the surfaces of the glass buckets. The blue ice cakes had cracked under their own internal pressure. I dumped one bucket into the maze of wiring and contacts and relays, and the ice shattered, giving me room to close the panel.

"So I thought of something last night, something that wasn't tested. Every part of the ship must have been in the heat-and-pressure box, exposed to artificial Venus conditions, but the ship as a whole, a unit, couldn't have been. It's too big." I'd circled around to the left wing and was opening the number three panel in the trailing edge. My remaining ice was half water and half small chips; I sloshed these in and fastened the panel. "What cut your circuits must have been the heat or the pressure or both. I can't help the pressure, but I'm cooling these relays with ice. Let me know which ram gets its sensation back first, and we'll know which inspection panel is the right one."

"Howie. Has it occurred to you what the cold water might do to those hot metals?"

"It could crack them. Then you'd lose all control over the ramjets, which is what's wrong right now."

"Uh. Your point, partner. But I still can't feel anything."

I went back to the airlock with my empty buckets swinging, wondering if they'd get hot enough to melt. They might have, but I wasn't out that long. I had my suit off and was refilling the buckets when Eric said, "I can feel the right ram."

"How extensive? Full control?"

"No. I can't feel the temperature. Oh, here it comes. We're all set, Howie."

My sigh of relief was sincere.

I put the buckets in the freezer again. We'd certainly want to take off with the relays cold. The water had been chilling for perhaps twenty minutes when Eric reported, "Sensation's going."

"What?"

"Sensation's going. No temperature, and I'm losing fuel feed control. It doesn't stay cold long enough."

"Ouch! Now what?"

"I hate to tell you. I'd almost rather let you figure it out for yourself."

I had. "We go as high as we can on the blimp tank, then I go out on the wing with a bucket of ice in each hand—"

We had to raise the blimp tank temperature to almost eight hundred degrees to get pressure, but from then on we went up in good shape. To sixteen miles. It took three hours.

"That's as high as we go," said Eric. "You ready?"

I went to get the ice. Eric could see me, he didn't need an answer. He opened the airlock for me.

222  Fear I might have felt, or panic, or determination or self-

sacrifice—but there was nothing. I went out feeling like a used zombie.

My magnets were on full. It felt like I was walking through shallow tar. The air was thick, though not as heavy as it had been down there. I followed my headlamp to the number two panel, opened it, poured ice in, and threw the bucket high and far. The ice was in one cake. I couldn't close the panel. I left it open and hurried around to the other wing. The second bucket was filled with exploded chips; I sloshed them in and locked the number two left panel and came back with both hands free. It still looked like limbo in all directions, except where the headlamp cut a tunnel through the darkness, and—my feet were getting hot. I closed the right panel on boiling water and sidled back along the hull into the airlock.

"Come in and strap down," said Eric. "Hurry!"

"Gotta get my suit off." My hands had started to shake from reaction. I couldn't work the clamps.

"No you don't. If we start right now we may get home. Leave the suit on and come in."

I did. As I pulled my webbing shut, the rams roared. The ship shuddered a little, then pushed forward as we dropped from under the blimp tank. Pressure mounted as the rams reached operating speed. Eric was giving it all he had. It would have been uncomfortable even without the metal suit around me. With the suit on it was torture. My couch was afire from the suit, but I couldn't get breath to say so. We were going almost straight up.

We had gone twenty minutes when the ship jerked like a galvanized frog. "Ram's out," Eric said calmly. "I'll use the other." Another lurch as we dropped the dead one. The ship flew on like a wounded penguin, but still accelerating.

One minute . . . two . . .

The other ram quit. It was as if we'd run into molasses. Eric blew off the ram and the pressure eased. I could talk.

"Eric."

"What?"

"Got any marshmallows?"

"*What?* Oh, I see. Is your suit tight?"

"Sure."

"Live with it. We'll flush the smoke out later. I'm going to coast above some of this stuff, but when I use the rocket it'll be savage. No mercy."

"Will we make it?"

"I think so. It'll be close."

The relief came first, icy cold. Then the anger. "No more inexplicable numbnesses?" I asked.

"No. Why?"

"If any come up you'll be sure and tell me, won't you?"

"Are you getting at something?"

"Skip it." I wasn't angry any more.

"I'll be damned if I do. You know perfectly well it was mechanical trouble, you fool. You fixed it yourself!"

"No. I convinced you I must have fixed it. You needed to believe the rams *should* be working again. I gave you a miracle cure, Eric. I just hope I don't have to keep dreaming up new placebos for you all the way home."

"You thought that, but you went out on the wing sixteen miles up?" Eric's machinery snorted. "You've got guts where you need brains, Shorty."

I didn't answer.

"Five thousand says the trouble was mechanical. We let the mechanics decide after we land."

"You're on."

"Here comes the rocket. Two, one—"

It came, pushing me down into my metal suit. Sooty flames licked past my ears, writing black on the green metal ceiling, but the rosy mist before my eyes was not fire.

The man with the thick glasses spread a diagram of the Venus ship and jabbed a stubby finger at the trailing edge of the

224

wing. "Right around here," he said. "The pressure from outside compressed the wiring channel a little, just enough so there was no room for the wire to bend. It had to act as if it were rigid, see? Then when the heat expanded the metal these contacts pushed past each other."

"I suppose it's the same design on both wings?"

He gave me a queer look. "Well, naturally."

I left my check for $5000 in a pile of Eric's mail and hopped a plane for Brasilia. How he found me I'll never know, but the telegram arrived this morning.

>           HOWIE COME HOME ALL IS FORGIVEN
>                   DONOVANS BRAIN

I guess I'll have to.

Nebula Award, Best Novella 1965
(tied with "He Who Shapes," by Roger Zelazny)

# The Saliva Tree

## Brian W. Aldiss

*Here is the story which fought Zelazny's "He Who Shapes" to a standstill for the novella award. It is set not in the far future or even in the familiar present, but in that curiously bright and timeless late-Victorian world, glimpsed as if through the wrong end of a telescope, in which the wonderful events of H. G. Wells' stories take place.*

*The author of this brilliant pastiche was born in the mid-twenties into the East Anglia depicted as background to "The Saliva Tree," where many farms still had their own little electricity generators. He has been Literary Editor of the Oxford Mail for eight years. He made a happy second marriage in 1965, now lives in a beautiful old sixteenth-century thatched house in Oxfordshire, "seeing slightly crazy visions."*

*There is* neither speech nor language: but their voices are heard among them. Psalm XIX.

"You know, I'm really much exercised about the Fourth Dimension," said the fair-haired young man, with a suitable earnestness in his voice.

"Um," said his companion, staring up at the night sky.

"It seems very much in evidence these days. Do you not think you catch a glimpse of it in the drawings of Aubrey Beardsley?"

"Um," said his companion.

They stood together on a low rise to the east of the sleepy East Anglian town of Cottersall, watching the stars, shivering a little in the chill February air. They are both young men in their early twenties. The one who is occupied with the Fourth Dimension is called Bruce Fox; he is tall and fair, and works as junior clerk in the Norwich firm of lawyers, Prendergast and Tout. The other, who has so far vouchsafed us only an *um* or two, although he is to figure largely as the hero of our account, is by name Gregory Rolles. He is tall and dark, with gray eyes set in his handsome and intelligent face. He and Fox have sworn to Think Large, thus distinguishing themselves, at least in their own minds, from all the rest of the occupants of Cottersall in these last years of the nineteenth century.

"There's another!" exclaimed Gregory, breaking at last from the realm of monosyllables. He pointed a gloved finger up at the constellation of Auriga the Charioteer. A meteor streaked across the sky like a runaway flake of the Milky Way, and died in mid-air.

"Beautiful!" they said together.

"It's funny," Fox said, prefacing his words with an oft-used phrase, "the stars and men's minds are so linked together and always have been, even in the centuries of ignorance before Charles Darwin. They always seem to play an ill-defined role in

229

man's affairs. They help me think large too, don't they you, Greg?"

"You know what I think—I think that some of those stars may be occupied. By people, I mean." He breathed heavily, overcome by what he was saying. "People who—perhaps they are better than us, live in a just society, wonderful people . . ."

"I know, socialists to a man!" Fox exclaimed. This was one point on which he did not share his friend's advanced thinking. He had listened to Mr. Tout talking in the office, and thought he knew better than his rich friend how these socialists, of which one heard so much these days, were undermining society. "Stars full of socialists!"

"Better than stars full of Christians! Why, if the stars were full of Christians, no doubt they would already have sent missionaries down here to preach their Gospel."

"I wonder if there ever will be planetary journeys as predicted by Nunsowe Greene and Monsieur Jules Verne—" Fox said, when the appearance of a fresh meteor stopped him in mid-sentence.

Like the last, this meteor seemed to come from the general direction of Auriga. It traveled slowly, and it glowed red, and it sailed grandly towards them. They both exclaimed at once, and gripped each other by the arm. The magnificent spark burned in the sky, larger now, so that its red aura appeared to encase a brighter orange glow. It passed overhead (afterwards, they argued whether it had not made a slight noise as it passed), and disappeared below a clump of willow. They knew it had been near. For an instant, the land had shone with its light.

Gregory was the first to speak.

"Bruce, Bruce, did you see that? That was no ordinary fireball!"

"It was so big! What was it?"

"Perhaps our heavenly visitor has come at last!"

"Hey, Greg, it must have landed by your friend's farm—the Grendon place—mustn't it?"

"You're right! I must pay old Mr. Grendon a visit tomorrow and see if he or his family saw anything of this."

They talked excitedly, stamping their feet as they exercised their lungs. Their conversation was the conversation of optimistic young men, and included much speculative matter that began "Wouldn't it be wonderful if—" or "Just supposing—" Then they stopped and laughed at their own absurd beliefs.

Fox said slyly, "So you'll be seeing all the Grendon family tomorrow?"

"It seems probable, unless that red-hot planetary ship has already borne them off to a better world."

"Tell us true, Greg—you really go to see that pretty Nancy Grendon, don't you?"

Gregory struck his friend playfully on the shoulder.

"No need for your jealousy, Bruce! I go to see the father, not the daughter. Though the one is female, the other is progressive, and that must interest me more just yet. Nancy has beauty, true, but her father—ah, her father has electricity!"

Laughing, they cheerfully shook hands and parted for the night.

On Grendon's farm, things were a deal less tranquil, as Gregory was to discover.

Gregory Rolles rose before seven next morning as was his custom. It was while he was lighting his gas mantle, and wishing Mr. Fenn (the baker in whose house Gregory lodged) would install electricity, that a swift train of thought led him to reflect again on the phenomenal thing in the previous night's sky. He let his mind wander luxuriously over all the possibilities that the "meteor" illuminated. He decided that he would ride out to see Mr. Grendon within the hour.

He was lucky in being able, at this stage in his life, to please himself largely as to how his days were spent, for his father was a person of some substance. Edward Rolles had had the fortune, at the time of the Crimean War, to meet Escoffier, and with

231

some help from the great chef had brought onto the market a baking powder, "Eugenol," that, being slightly more palatable and less deleterious to the human system than its rivals, had achieved great commercial success. As a result, Gregory had attended one of the Cambridge colleges.

Now, having gained a degree, he was poised on the verge of a career. But which career? He had acquired—more as a result of his intercourse with other students than with those officially deputed to instruct him—some understanding of the sciences; his essays had been praised and some of his poetry published, so that he inclined toward literature; and an uneasy sense that life for everyone outside the privileged classes contained too large a proportion of misery led him to think seriously of a political career. In Divinity, too, he was well-grounded; but at least the idea of Holy Orders did not tempt him.

While he wrestled with his future, he undertook to live away from home, since his relations with his father were never smooth. By rusticating himself in the heart of East Anglia, he hoped to gather material for a volume tentatively entitled "Wanderings with a Socialist Naturalist," which would assuage all sides of his ambitions. Nancy Grendon, who had a pretty hand with a pencil, might even execute a little emblem for the title page . . . Perhaps he might be permitted to dedicate it to his author friend, Mr. Herbert George Wells . . .

He dressed himself warmly, for the morning was cold as well as dull, and went down to the baker's stables. When he had saddled his mare, Daisy, he swung himself up and set out along a road that the horse knew well.

The land rose slightly towards the farm, the area about the house forming something of a little island amid marshy ground and irregular stretches of water that gave back to the sky its own dun tone. The gate over the little bridge was, as always, open wide; Daisy picked her way through the mud to the stables, where Gregory left her to champ oats contentedly. Cuff and her pup, Lardie, barked loudly about Gregory's heels as usual, and he patted their heads on his way over to the house.

Nancy came hurrying out to meet him before he got to the front door.

"We had some excitement last night, Gregory," she said. He noted with pleasure she had at last brought herself to use his first name.

"Something bright and glaring!" she said. "I was retiring, when this noise come and then this light, and I rush to look out through the curtains, and there's this here great thing like an egg sinking into our pond." In her speech, and particularly when she was excited, she carried the lilting accent of Norfolk.

"The meteor!" Gregory exclaimed. "Bruce Fox and I were out last night, as we were the night before, watching for the lovely Aurigids that arrive every February, when we saw an extra big one. I said then it was coming over very near here."

"Why, it almost landed on our house," Nancy said. She looked very pleasing this morning, with her lips red, her cheeks shining, and her chestnut curls all astray. As she spoke, her mother appeared in apron and cap, with a wrap hurriedly thrown over her shoulders.

"Nancy, you come in, standing freezing like that! You ent daft, girl are you? Hello, Gregory, how be going on? I didn't reckon as we'd see you today. Come in and warm yourself."

"Good-day to you, Mrs. Grendon. I'm hearing about your wonderful meteor of last night."

"It was a falling star, according to Bert Neckland. I ent sure what it was, but it certainly stirred up the animals, that I *do* know."

"Can you see anything of it in the pond?" Gregory asked.

"Let me show you," Nancy said.

Mrs. Grendon returned indoors. She went slowly and grandly, her back straight and an unaccustomed load before her. Nancy was her only daughter; there was a younger son, Archie, a stubborn lad who had fallen at odds with his father and now was apprenticed to a blacksmith in Norwich; and no other children living. Three infants had not survived the mixture of fogs alternating with bitter east winds that comprised the typical Cottersall winter. But now the farmer's wife was unexpectedly gravid again, and would bear her husband another baby when the spring came in.

As Nancy led Gregory over to the pond, he saw Grendon with his two laborers working in the West Field, but they did not wave.

"Was your father not excited by the arrival last night?"

"That he was—when it happened! He went out with his shotgun, and Bert Neckland with him. But there was nothing to see but bubbles in the pond and steam over it, and this morning he wouldn't discuss it, and said that work must go on whatever happen."

They stood beside the pond, a dark and extensive slab of water with rushes on the farther bank and open country beyond. As they looked at its ruffled surface, they stood with the windmill black and bulky on their left hand. It was to this that Nancy now pointed.

Mud had been splashed across the boards high up the sides of the mill; some was to be seen even on the top of the nearest white sail. Gregory surveyed it all with interest. Nancy, however, was still pursuing her own line of thought.

"Don't you reckon Father works too hard, Gregory? When he's not outside doing jobs, he's in reading his pamphlets and his electricity manuals. He never rests but when he sleeps."

"Um. Whatever went into the pond went in with a great smack! There's no sign of anything there now, is there? Not that you can see an inch below the surface."

"You being a friend of his, Mum thought perhaps as you'd say something to him. He don't go to bed till ever so late—sometimes it's near midnight, and then he's up again at three and a half o'clock. Would you speak to him? You know Mother dassent."

"Nancy, we ought to see whatever it was that went in the pond. It can't have dissolved. How deep is the water? Is it very deep?"

"Oh, you aren't listening, Gregory Rolles! Bother the old meteor!"

"This is a matter of science, Nancy. Don't you see—"

"Oh, rotten old science, is it? Then I don't want to hear. I'm cold, standing out here. You can have a good look if you like but I'm going in before I gets froze. It was only an old stone out of the sky, because I heard Father and Bert Neckland agree to it."

"Fat lot Bert Neckland knows about such things!" he called to her departing back.

He looked down at the dark water. Whatever it *was* that had arrived last night, it was here, only a few feet from him. He longed to discover what remained of it. Vivid pictures entered his mind: his name in headlines in "The Morning Post," the Royal Society making him an honorary member, his father embracing him and pressing him to return home.

Thoughtfully, he walked over to the barn. Hens ran clucking out of his way as he entered and stood looking up, waiting for his eyes to adjust to the dim light. There, as he remembered it, was a little rowing boat. Perhaps in his courting days old Mr. Grendon had taken his prospective wife out for excursions on the Oast in it. Surely it had not been used in years. He dragged the boat from the barn and launched it in the shallows of the pond. It floated. The boards had dried, and water leaked through a couple of seams, but not nearly enough to deter him. Climbing delicately in among the straw and filth, he pushed off.

When he was over the approximate center of the pond, he shipped his oars and peered over the side. There was an agitation in the water, and nothing could be seen, although he imagined much.

As he stared over the one side, the boat unexpectedly tipped to the other. Gregory swung round. The boat listed heavily to the left, so that the oars rolled over that way. He could see nothing. Yet—he heard something. It was a sound much like a hound slowly panting. And whatever made it was about to capsize the boat.

"What is it?" he said, as all the skin prickled up his back and skull.

The boat lurched, for all the world as if someone invisible were trying to get into it. Frightened, he grasped the oar, and, without thinking, swept it over that side of the rowing boat.

It struck something solid where there was only air.

Dropping the oar in surprise, he put out his hand. It touched something yielding. At the same time, his arm was violently struck.

His actions were then entirely governed by instinct. Thought did not enter the matter. He picked up the oar again and smote the thin air with it. It hit something. There was a splash, and the boat righted itself so suddenly he was almost pitched into the water. Even while it still rocked, he was rowing frantically for the shallows, dragging the boat from the water, and running for the safety of the farmhouse.

Only at the door did he pause. His reason returned, his heart began gradually to stop stammering its fright. He stood looking at the seamed wood of the porch, trying to evaluate what he had seen and what had actually happened. But what had happened?

Forcing himself to go back to the pond, he stood by the boat and looked across the sullen face of the water. It lay undisturbed, except by surface ripples. He looked at the boat. A quantity of water lay in the bottom of it. He thought, all that happened was that I nearly capsized, and I let my idiot fears run away with me. Shaking his head, he pulled the boat back to the barn.

Gregory, as he often did, stayed to eat lunch at the farm, but he saw nothing of the farmer till milking time.

Joseph Grendon was in his late forties, and a few years older than his wife. He had a gaunt solemn face and a heavy beard that made him look older than he was. For all his seriousness, he greeted Gregory civilly enough. They stood together in the gathering dusk as the cows swung behind them into their regular stalls. Together they walked into the machine house next door, and Grendon lit the oil burners that started the steam engine into motion that would turn the generator that would supply the vital spark.

"I smell the future in here," Gregory said, smiling. By now, he had forgotten the shock of the morning.

"The future will have to get on without me. I shall be dead by then." The farmer spoke as he walked, putting each word reliably before the next.

"That is what you always say. You're wrong—the future is rushing upon us."

"You ent far wrong there, Master Gregory, but I won't have no part of it, I reckon. I'm an old man now. Here she come!"

The last exclamation was directed at a flicker of light in the pilot bulb overhead. They stood there contemplating with satisfaction the wonderful machinery. As steam pressure rose, the great leather belt turned faster and faster, and the flicker in the pilot bulb grew stronger. Although Gregory was used to a home lit by both gas and electricity, he never felt the excitement of it as he did here, out in the wilds, where the nearest incandescent bulb was probably in Norwich, a great part of a day's journey away.

Now a pale flickering radiance illuminated the room. By contrast, everything outside looked black. Grendon nodded in

237

satisfaction, made some adjustments to the burners, and they went outside.

Free from the bustle of the steam engine, they could hear the noise the cows were making. At milking time, the animals were usually quiet; something had upset them. The farmer ran quickly into the milking shed, with Gregory on his heels.

The new light, radiating from a bulb hanging above the stalls, showed the beasts of restless demeanor and rolling eye. Bert Neckland stood as far away from the door as possible, grasping his stick and letting his mouth hang open.

"What in blazes are you staring at, bor?" Grendon asked.

Neckland slowly shut his mouth.

"We had a scare," he said. "Something come in here."

"Did you see what it was?" Gregory asked.

"No, there weren't nothing to see. It was a ghost, that's what it was. It came right in here and touched the cows. It touched me too. It was a ghost."

The farmer snorted. "A tramp more like. You couldn't see because the light wasn't on."

His man shook his head emphatically. "Light weren't that bad. I tell you, whatever it was, it come right up to me and touched me." He stopped, and pointed to the edge of the stall. "Look there! See, I weren't telling you no lie, master. It was a ghost, and there's its wet hand-print."

They crowded round and examined the worn and chewed timber at the corner of the partition between two stalls. An indefinite patch of moisture darkened the wood. Gregory's thoughts went back to his experience on the pond, and again he felt the prickle of unease along his spine. But the farmer said stoutly, "Nonsense, it's a bit of cowslime. Now you get on with the milking, Bert, and let's have no more hossing about, because I want my tea. Where's Cuff?"

Bert looked defiant.

"If you don't believe me, maybe you'll believe the bitch. She saw whatever it was and went for it. It kicked her over, but she ran it out of here."

"I'll see if I can see her," Gregory said.

He ran outside and began calling the bitch. By now it was almost entirely dark. He could see nothing moving in the wide space of the front yard, and so set off in the other direction, down the path towards the pig sties and the fields, calling Cuff as he went. He paused. Low and savage growls sounded ahead, under the elm trees. It was Cuff. He went slowly forward. At this moment, he cursed that electric light meant lack of lanterns, and wished too that he had a weapon.

"Who's there?" he called.

The farmer came up by his side. "Let's charge 'em!"

They ran forward. The trunks of the four great elms were clear against the western sky, with water glinting leadenly behind them. The dog became visible. As Gregory saw Cuff, she sailed into the air, whirled round, and flew at the farmer. He flung up his arms and warded off the body. At the same time, Gregory felt a rush of air as if someone unseen had run past him, and a stale muddy smell filled his nostrils. Staggering, he looked behind him. The wan light from the cowsheds spread across the path between the outhouses and the farmhouse. Beyond the light, more distantly, was the silent countryside behind the grain store. Nothing untoward could be seen.

"They killed my old Cuff," said the farmer.

Gregory knelt down beside him to look at the bitch. There was no mark of injury on her, but she was dead, her fine head lying limp.

"She knew there was something there," Gregory said. "She went to attack whatever it was and it got her first. What was it? Whatever in the world was it?"

"They killed my old Cuff," said the farmer again, unhearing. He picked the body up in his arms, turned, and carried it towards the house. Gregory stood where he was, mind and heart equally uneasy.

He jumped violently when a step sounded nearby. It was Bert Neckland.

"What, did that there ghost kill the old bitch?" he asked.

"It killed the bitch certainly, but it was something more terrible than a ghost."

"That's one of them ghosts, bor. I seen plenty in my time. I ent afraid of ghosts, are you?"

"You looked fairly sick in the cowshed a minute ago."

The farmhand put his fists on his hips. He was no more than a couple of years older than Gregory, a stocky young man with a spotty complexion and a snub nose that gave him at once an air of comedy and menace. "Is that so, Master Gregory? Well, you looks pretty funky standing there now."

"I am scared. I don't mind admitting it. But only because we have something here a lot nastier than any specter."

Neckland came a little closer.

"Then if you are so blooming windy, perhaps you'll be staying away from the farm in the future."

"Certainly not." He tried to edge back into the light, but the laborer got in his way.

"If I was you, I should stay away." He emphasized his point by digging an elbow into Gregory's coat. "And just remember that Nancy was interested in me long afore you come along, bor."

"Oh, that's it, is it! I think Nancy can decide for herself in whom she is interested, don't you?"

"I'm *telling* you who she's interested in, see? And mind you don't forget, see?" He emphasized the words with another nudge. Gregory pushed his arm away angrily. Neckland shrugged his shoulders and walked off. As he went, he said, "You're going to get worse than ghosts if you keep hanging round here."

Gregory was shaken. The suppressed violence in the man's voice suggested that he had been harboring malice for some time. Unsuspectingly, Gregory had always gone out of his way to be cordial, had regarded the sullenness as mere slow-wittedness and done his socialist best to overcome the barrier between them. He thought of following Neckland and trying to make it up with him; but that would look too feeble. Instead, he followed the way the farmer had gone with his dead bitch, and made for the house.

Gregory Rolles was too late back to Cottersall that night to meet his friend Fox. The next night, the weather became exceedingly chill and Gabriel Woodcock, the oldest inhabitant, was prophesying snow before the winter was out (a not very venturesome prophecy to be fulfilled within forty-eight hours, thus impressing most of the inhabitants of the village, for they took pleasure in being impressed and exclaiming and saying "Well I never!" to each other). The two friends met in "The Wayfarer," where the fires were bigger, though the ale was weaker, than in "The Three Poachers" at the other end of the village.

Seeing to it that nothing dramatic was missed from his account, Gregory related the affairs of the previous day, omitting any reference to Neckland's pugnacity. Fox listened fascinated, neglecting both his pipe and his ale.

"So you see how it is, Bruce," Gregory concluded. "In that deep pond by the mill lurks a vehicle of some sort, the very one we saw in the sky, and in it lives an invisible being of evil intent. You see how I fear for my friends there. Should I tell the police about it, do you think?"

"I'm sure it would not help the Grendons to have old Farrish bumping out there on his pennyfarthing," Fox said, referring to the local representative of the law. He took a long draw first on the pipe and then on the glass. "But I'm not sure you have your conclusions quite right, Greg. Understand, I don't doubt the facts, amazing though they are. I mean, we were more or less expecting celestial visitants. The world's recent blossoming with gas and electric lighting in its cities at night must have been a signal to half the nations of space that we are now civilized down here. But have our visitants done any deliberate harm to anyone?"

241

"They nearly drowned me and they killed poor Cuff. I don't see what you're getting at. They haven't begun in a very friendly fashion, have they now?"

"Think what the situation must seem like to them. Suppose they come from Mars or the Moon—we know their world must be absolutely different from Earth. They may be terrified. And it can hardly be called an unfriendly act to try and get into your rowing boat. The first unfriendly act was yours, when you struck out with the oar."

Gregory bit his lip. His friend had a point. "I was scared."

"It may have been because they were scared that they killed Cuff. The dog attacked them, after all, didn't she? I feel sorry for these creatures, alone in an unfriendly world."

"You keep saying 'these!' As far as we know, there is only one of them."

"My point is this, Greg. You have completely gone back on your previous enlightened attitude. You are all for killing these poor things instead of trying to speak to them. Remember what you were saying about other worlds being full of socialists? Try thinking of these chaps as invisible socialists and see if that doesn't make them easier to deal with."

Gregory fell to stroking his chin. Inwardly, he acknowledged that Bruce Fox's words made a great impression on him. He had allowed panic to prejudice his judgment; as a result, he had behaved as immoderately as a savage in some remote corner of the Empire, confronted by his first steam locomotive.

"I'd better get back to the farm and sort things out as soon as possible," he said. "If these things really do need help, I'll help them."

"That's it. But try not to think of them as 'things.' Think of them as—as—I know, as The Aurigans."

"Aurigans it is. But don't be so smug, Bruce. If you'd been in that boat—"

"I know, old friend. I'd have died of fright." To this monument of tact, Fox added, "Do as you say, go back and sort things out as soon as possible. I'm longing for the next installment of this mystery. It's quite the jolliest thing since Sherlock Holmes."

Gregory Rolles went back to the farm. But the sorting out of which Bruce had spoken took longer than he expected. This was chiefly because the Aurigans seemed to have settled quietly into their new home after the initial day's troubles.

They came forth no more from the pond, as far as he could discover; at least they caused no more disturbance. The young graduate particularly regretted this since he had taken his friend's words much to heart, and wanted to prove how enlightened and benevolent he was towards this strange form of life. After some days, he came to believe the Aurigans must have left as unexpectedly as they arrived. Then a minor incident convinced him otherwise; and that same night, in his snug room over the baker's shop, he described it to his correspondent in Worcester Park, Surrey.

Dear Mr. Wells,

I must apologize for my failure to write earlier, owing to lack of news concerning the Grendon Farm affair.

Only today, the Aurigans showed themselves again!— If indeed "showed" is the right word for invisible creatures.

Nancy Grendon and I were in the orchard feeding the hens. There is still much snow lying about, and everywhere is very white. As the poultry came running to Nancy's tub, I saw a disturbance further down the orchard—merely some snow dropping from an apple bough, but the movement caught my eye, and then I saw a *procession* of falling snow proceed towards us from tree to tree. The grass is long there, and I soon noted the stalks being thrust aside by *an unknown agency!* I directed Nancy's attention to the phenomenon. The motion in the grass stopped only a few yards from us.

Nancy was startled, but I determined to acquit myself

243

more like a Briton than I had previously. Accordingly, I advanced and said, "Who are you? What do you want? We are your friends if you are friendly."

No answer came. I stepped forward again, and now the grass again fell back, and I could see by the way it was pressed down that the creature must have large feet. By the movement of the grasses, I could see he was running. I cried to him and ran too. He went round the side of the house, and then over the frozen mud in the farmyard. I could see no further trace of him. But instinct led me forward, past the barn to the pond.

Surely enough, I then saw the cold, muddy water rise and heave, as if engulfing a body that slid quietly in. Shards of broken ice were thrust aside, and by an outward motion, I could see where the strange being went. In a flurry and a small whirlpool, he was gone, and I have no doubt dived down to the mysterious star vehicle.

These things—people—I know not what to call them— must be aquatic; perhaps they live in the canals of the Red Planet. But imagine, Sir—an invisible mankind! The idea is almost as wonderful and fantastic as something from your novel, "The Time Machine."

Pray give me your comment, and trust in my sanity and accuracy as a reporter!

Yours in friendship,
Gregory Rolles.

What he did not tell was the way Nancy had clung to him after, in the warmth of the parlor, and confessed her fear. And he had scorned the idea that these beings could be hostile, and had seen the admiration in her eyes, and had thought that she was, after all, a dashed pretty girl, and perhaps worth braving the wrath of those two very different people for: Edward Rolles, his father, and Bert Neckland, the farm laborer.

244                    *    *    *

It was at lunch a week later, when Gregory was again at the farm, taking with him an article on electricity as a pretext for his visit, that the subject of the stinking dew was first discussed.

Grubby was the first to mention it in Gregory's hearing. Grubby, with Bert Neckland, formed the whole strength of Joseph Grendon's labor force; but whereas Neckland was considered couth enough to board in the farmhouse (he had a gaunt room in the attic), Grubby was fit only to sleep in a little flint-and-chalk hut well away from the farm buildings. His "house," as he dignified the miserable hut, stood below the orchard and near the sties, the occupants of which lulled Grubby to sleep with their snorts.

"Reckon we ent ever had a dew like that before, Mr. Grendon," he said, his manner suggesting to Gregory that he had made this observation already this morning; Grubby never ventured to say anything original.

"Heavy as an autumn dew," said the farmer firmly, as if there had been an argument on the point.

Silence fell, broken only by a general munching and, from Grubby, a particular guzzling, as they all made their way through huge platefuls of stewed rabbit and dumplings.

"It weren't no ordinary dew, that I do know," Grubby said after a while.

"It stank of toadstools," Neckland said. "Or rotten pond water."

More munching.

"It may be something to do with the pond," Gregory said. "Some sort of freak of evaporation."

Neckland snorted. From his position at the top of the table, the farmer halted his shovelling operations to point a fork at Gregory.

"You may well be right there. Because I tell you what, that there dew only come down on our land and property. A yard the other side of the gate, the road was dry. Bone dry it was."

"Right you are there, master," Neckland agreed. "And while

the West Field was dripping with the stuff, I saw for myself that the bracken over the hedge weren't wet at all. Ah, it's a rum go!"

"Say what you like, we ent ever had dew like it," Grubby said. He appeared to be summing up the feeling of the company.

The strange dew did not fall again. As a topic of conversation, it was limited, and even on the farm, where there was little new to talk about, it was forgotten in a few days. The February passed, being neither much worse nor much better than most Februaries, and ended in heavy rainstorms. March came, letting in a chilly spring over the land. The animals on the farm began to bring forth their young.

They brought them forth in amazing numbers, as if to overturn all the farmer's beliefs in the unproductiveness of his land.

"I never seen anything like it!" Grendon said to Gregory. Nor had Gregory seen the taciturn farmer so excited. He took the young man by the arm and marched him into the barn.

There lay Trix, the nannie goat. Against her flank huddled three little brown and white kids, while a fourth stood nearby, wobbling on its spindly legs.

"Four on 'em! Have you ever heard of a goat throwing off *four* kids? You better write to the papers in London about this. Gregory! But just you come down to the pig sties."

The squealing from the sties was louder than usual. As they marched down the path towards them, Gregory looked up at the great elms, their outlines dusted in green, and thought he detected something sinister in the noises, something hysterical that was perhaps matched by an element in Grendon's own bearing.

The Grendon pigs were mixed breeds, with a preponderance of Large Blacks. They usually gave litters of something like ten piglets. Now there was not a litter without fourteen in it; and one enormous black sow had eighteen small pigs swarming about her. The noise was tremendous and, standing looking down on this swarming life, Gregory told himself that he was foolish to imagine anything uncanny in it; he knew so little about farm life.

After he had eaten with Grendon and the men—Mrs. Grendon and Nancy had driven to town in the trap—Gregory went by himself to look about the farm, still with a deep and (he told himself) unreasoning sense of disturbance inside him.

A pale sunshine filled the afternoon. It could not penetrate far down into the water of the pond. But as Gregory stood by the horse trough staring at the expanse of water, he saw that it teemed with young tadpoles and frogs. He went closer. What he had regarded as a sheet of rather stagnant water was alive with small swimming things. As he looked, a great beetle surged out of the depths and seized a tadpole. The tadpoles were also providing food for two ducks that, with their young, were swimming by the reeds on the far side of the pond. And how many young did the ducks have? An armada of chicks was there, parading in and out of the rushes.

For a minute, he stood uncertainly, then began to walk slowly back the way he had come. Crossing the yard, Gregory went over to the stable and saddled Daisy. He swung himself up and rode away without bidding goodbye to anyone.

Riding into Cottersall, he went straight to the market place. He saw the Grendon trap, with Nancy's little pony, Hetty, between the shafts, standing outside the grocer's shop. Mrs. Grendon and Nancy were just coming out. Jumping to the ground, Gregory led Daisy over to them and bid them good day.

"We are going to call on my friend Mrs. Edwards and her daughters," Mrs. Grendon said.

"If you would be so kind, Mrs. Grendon, I would be very obliged if I might speak privately with Nancy. My landlady, Mrs. Fenn, has a little downstairs parlor at the back of the shop, and I know she would let us speak there. It would be quite respectable."

"Drat respectable! Let people think what they will, I say." All the same, she stood for some time in meditation. Nancy remained by her mother with her eyes on the ground. Gregory looked at her and seemed to see her anew. Under her blue coat, fur-trimmed, she wore her orange-and-brown squared gingham dress; she had a bonnet on her head. Her complexion was pure and blemishless, her skin as firm and delicate as a plum, and her dark eyes were hidden under long lashes. Her lips were steady, pale, and clearly defined, with appealing tucks at each corner. He felt almost like a thief, stealing a sight of her beauty while she was not regarding him.

"I'm going on to Mrs. Edwards," Marjorie Grendon declared at last. "I don't care what you two do so long as you behave—but I shall, mind, if you aren't with me in a half-hour, Nancy, do you hear?"

"Yes, Mother."

The baker's shop was in the next street. Gregory and Nancy walked there in silence. Gregory shut Daisy in the stable and they went together into the parlor through the back door. At this time of day, Mr. Fenn was resting upstairs and his wife looking after the shop, so the little room was empty.

Nancy sat upright in a chair and said, "Well, Gregory, what's all this about? Fancy dragging me off from my mother like that in the middle of town!"

"Nancy, don't be cross. I had to see you."

She pouted. "You come out to the old farm often enough and don't show any particular wish to see me there."

"That's nonsense. I always come to see you—lately in particular. Besides, you're more interested in Bert Neckland, aren't you?"

"Bert Neckland, indeed! Why should I be interested in him? Not that it's any of your business if I am."

"It is my business, Nancy. I love you, Nancy!"

He had not meant to blurt it out in quite that fashion, but now it was out, it was out, and he pressed home his disadvantage by crossing the room, kneeling at her feet, and taking her hands in his. "Nancy, darling Nancy, say that you like me just a little. Encourage me somewhat."

"You are a very fine gentleman, Gregory, and I feel very kind towards you, to be sure, but . . ."

"But?"

She gave him the benefit of her downcast eyes again.

"Your station in life is very different from mine, and besides—well, you don't *do* anything."

He was shocked into silence. With the natural egotism of youth, he had not seriously thought that she could have any firm objection to him; but in her words he suddenly saw the truth of his position, at least as it was revealed to her.

"Nancy—I—well, it's true I do not seem to you to be working at present. But I do a lot of reading and studying here, and I write to several important people in the world. And all the time I am coming to a great decision about what my career will be. I do assure you I am no loafer, if that's what you think."

"No, I don't think that. But Bert says you often spend a convivial evening in that there 'Wayfarer.' "

"Oh, he does, does he? And what business is it of his if I do—or of yours, come to that? What damned cheek!"

She stood up. "If you have nothing left to say but a lot of swearing, I'll be off to join my mother, if you don't mind."

"Oh, by Jove, I'm making a mess of this!" He caught her wrist. "Listen, my sweet thing. I ask you only this, that you try and look on me favorably. And also that you let me say a word about the farm. Some strange things are happening there, and I seriously don't like to think of you being there at night. All these young things being born, all these little pigs—it's uncanny!"

"I don't see what's uncanny no more than my father does. I know how hard he works, and he's done a good job rearing his animals, that's all. He's the best farmer round Cottersall by a long chalk."

"Oh, certainly. He's a wonderful man. But he didn't put seven or eight eggs into a hedge sparrow's nest, did he? He didn't fill the pond with tadpoles and newts till it looks like a broth, did

he? Something strange is happening on your farm this year,
Nancy, and I want to protect you if I can."

The earnestness with which he spoke, coupled perhaps with
his proximity and the ardent way he pressed her hand, went a
good way towards mollifying Nancy.

"Dear Gregory, you don't know anything about farm life, I
don't reckon, for all your books. But you're very sweet to be
concerned."

"I shall always be concerned about you, Nancy, you beautiful
creature."

"You'll make me blush!"

"Please do, for then you look even lovelier than usual!" He
put an arm around her. When she looked up at him, he caught
her up close to his chest and kissed her fervently.

She gasped and broke away, but not with too great haste.

"Oh, Gregory! Oh, Gregory! I must go to Mother now!"

"Another kiss first! I can't let you go until I get another."

He took it, and stood by the door trembling with excitement
as she left. "Come and see us again soon," she whispered.

"With dearest pleasure," he said. But the next visit held more
dread than pleasure.

The big cart was standing in the yard full of squealing piglets
when Gregory arrived. The farmer and Neckland were bustling
about it. The former greeted Gregory cheerfully.

"I've a chance to make a good quick profit on these little
chaps. Old sows can't feed them, but sucking pig fetches its price
in Norwich, so Bert and me are going to drive over to Heigham
and put them on the train."

"They've grown since I last saw them!"

"Ah, they put on over two pounds a day. Bert, we'd better
get a net and spread over this lot, or they'll be diving out.
They're that lively!"

The two men made their way over to the barn, clomping
through the mud. Mud squelched behind Gregory. He turned.

In the muck between the stables and the cart, footprints appeared, two parallel tracks. They seemed to imprint themselves with no agency but their own. A cold flow of acute supernatural terror overcame Gregory, so that he could not move. The scene seemed to go gray and palsied as he watched the tracks come towards him.

The carthorse neighed uneasily, the prints reached the cart, the cart creaked, as if something had climbed aboard. The piglets squealed with terror. One dived clear over the wooden sides. Then a terrible silence fell.

Gregory still could not move. He heard an unaccountable sucking noise in the cart, but his eyes remained rooted on the muddy tracks. Those impressions were of something other than a man: something with dragging feet that were in outline something like a seal's flippers. Suddenly he found his voice. "Mr. Grendon!" he cried.

Only as the farmer and Bert came running from the barn with the net did Gregory dare look into the cart.

One last piglet, even as he looked, seemed to be deflating rapidly, like a rubber balloon collapsing. It went limp and lay silent among the other little empty bags of pig skin. The cart creaked. Something splashed heavily off across the farmyard in the direction of the pond.

Grendon did not see. He had run to the cart and was staring like Gregory in dismay at the deflated corpses. Neckland stared too, and was the first to find his voice.

"Some sort of disease got 'em all, just like that! Must be one of them there new diseases from the Continent of Europe!"

"It's no disease," Gregory said. He could hardly speak, for his mind had just registered the fact that there were no bones left in or amid the deflated pig bodies. "It's no disease—look, the pig that got away is still alive."

He pointed to the animal that had jumped from the cart. It had injured its leg in the process, and now lay in the ditch some feet away, panting. The farmer went over to it and lifted it out.

"It escaped the disease by jumping out," Neckland said. "Master, we better go and see how the rest of them is down in the sties."

"Ah, that we had," Grendon said. He handed the pig over to Gregory, his face set. "No good taking one alone to market. I'll get Grubby to unharness the horse. Meanwhile, perhaps you'd be good enough to take this little chap in to Marjorie. At least we can all eat a bit of roast pig for dinner tomorrow."

"Mr. Grendon, this is no disease. Have the veterinarian over from Heigham and let him examine these bodies."

"Don't you tell me how to run my farm, young man. I've got trouble enough."

Despite this rebuff, Gregory could not keep away. He had to see Nancy, and he had to see what occurred at the farm. The morning after the horrible thing happened to the pigs, he received a letter from his most admired correspondent, Mr. H. G. Wells, one paragraph of which read: "At bottom, I think I am neither optimist nor pessimist. I tend to believe both that we stand on the threshold of an epoch of magnificent progress—certainly such an epoch is within our grasp—and that we may have reached the 'fin du globe' prophesied by our gloomier fin de siecle prophets. I am not at all surprised to hear that such a vast issue may be resolving itself on a remote farm near Cottersall, Norfolk—all unknown to anyone but the two of us. Do not think that I am in other than a state of terror, even when I cannot help exclaiming 'What a lark!' "

Too preoccupied to be as excited over such a letter as he would ordinarily have been, Gregory tucked it away in his jacket pocket and went to saddle up Daisy.

Before lunch, he stole a kiss from Nancy, and planted another on her over-heated left cheek as she stood by the vast range in the kitchen. Apart from that, there was little pleasure in the day. Grendon was reassured to find that none of the other piglets had fallen ill of the strange shrinking disease, but he

remained alert against the possibility of it striking again. Meanwhile, another miracle had occurred. In the lower pasture, in a
tumbledown shed, he had a cow that had given birth to four
calves during the night. He did not expect the animal to live,
but the calves were well enough, and being fed from a bottle by
Nancy.

The farmer's face was dull, for he had been up all night with
the laboring cow, and he sat down thankfully at the head of the
table as the roast pig arrived on its platter.

It proved uneatable. In no time, they were all flinging down
their implements in disgust. The flesh had a bitter taste for which
Neckland was the first to account.

"It's diseased!" he growled. "This here animal had the disease
all the time. We didn't ought to eat this here meat or we may
all be dead ourselves inside of a week."

They were forced to make a snack on cold salted beef and
cheese and pickled onions, none of which Mrs. Grendon could
face in her condition. She retreated upstairs in tears at the
thought of the failure of her carefully prepared dish, and Nancy
ran after her to comfort her.

After the dismal meal, Gregory spoke to Grendon.

"I have decided I must go to Norwich tomorrow for a few
days, Mr. Grendon," he said. "You are in trouble here, I believe.
Is there anything, any business I can transact for you in the city?
Can I find you a veterinary surgeon there?"

Grendon clapped his shoulder. "I know you mean well, and
I thank 'ee for it, but you don't seem to realize that vetinaries
cost a load of money and aren't always too helpful when they
do come."

"Then let me do something for you, Joseph, in return for all
your kindness to me. Let me bring a vet back from Norwich at
my own expense, just to have a look round, nothing more."

"Blow me if you aren't stubborn as they come. I'm telling
you, same as my dad used to say, if I finds any person on my

land I didn't ask here, I'm getting that there shotgun of mine down and I'm peppering him with buckshot, same as I did with them two old tramps last year. Fair enough?"

"I suppose so."

"Then I must go and see to the cow. And stop worrying about what you don't understand."

The visit to Norwich (an uncle had a house in that city) took up the better part of Gregory's next week. Consequently, apprehension stirred in him when he again approached the Grendon farm along the rough road from Cottersall. He was surprised to see how the countryside had altered since he was last this way. New foliage gleamed everywhere, and even the heath looked a happier place. But as he came up to the farm, he saw how overgrown it was. Great ragged elder and towering cow parsley had shot up, so that at first they hid all the buildings. He fancied the farm had been spirited away until, spurring Daisy on, he saw the black mill emerge from behind a clump of nearby growth. The South Meadows were deep in rank grass. Even the elms seemed much shaggier than before and loomed threateningly over the house.

As he clattered over the flat wooden bridge and through the open gate into the yard, Gregory noted huge hairy nettles craning out of the adjoining ditches. Birds fluttered everywhere. Yet the impression he received was one of death rather than of life. A great quiet lay over the place, as if it were under a curse that eliminated noise and hope.

He realized this effect was partly because Lardie, the young bitch collie who had taken the place of Cuff, was not running up barking as she generally did with visitors. The yard was deserted. Even the customary fowls had gone. As he led Daisy into the stables, he saw a heavy piebald in the first stall and recognized it as Dr. Crouchorn's. His anxieties took more definite shape.

Since the stable was now full, he led his mare across to the stone trough by the pond and hitched her there before walking over to the house. The front door was open. Great ragged dandelions grew against the porch. The creeper, hitherto somewhat sparse, pressed into the lower windows. A movement in the rank grass caught his eye and he looked down, drawing back his riding boot. An enormous toad crouched under weed, the head of a still writhing grass snake in its mouth. The toad seemed to eye Gregory fixidly, as if trying to determine whether the man envied it its gluttony. Shuddering in disgust, he hurried into the house.

Muffled sounds came from upstairs. The stairs curled round the massive chimneypiece, and were shut from the lower rooms by a latched door. Gregory had never been invited upstairs, but he did not hesitate. Throwing the door open, he started up the stairwell, and almost at once ran into a body.

Its softness told him that this was Nancy; she stood in the dark weeping. Even as he caught her and breathed her name, she broke from his grasp and ran from him up the stairs. He could hear noises more clearly now, and the sound of crying— though at the moment he was not listening. Nancy ran to a door on the landing nearest to the top of the stairs, burst into the room beyond, and closed it. When Gregory tried the latch, he heard the bolt slide to on the other side.

"Nancy!" he called. "Don't hide from me! What is it? What's happening?"

She made no answer. As he stood there baffled against the door, the next door along the passage opened and Doctor Crouchorn emerged, clutching his little black bag. He was a tall, somber man, with deep lines on his face that inspired such fear into his patients that a remarkable percentage of them did as he bid and recovered. Even here, he wore the top hat that, simply by remaining constantly in position, contributed to the doctor's fame in the neighborhood.

"What's the trouble, Doctor Crouchorn?" Gregory asked, as the medical man shut the door behind him and started down the stairs. "Has the plague struck this house, or something equally terrible?"

"Plague, young man, plague? No, it is something much more unnatural than that."

He stared at Gregory unsmilingly, as if promising himself inwardly not to move a muscle again until Gregory asked the obvious.

"What did you call for, Doctor?"

"The hour of Mrs. Grendon's confinement struck during the night," he said.

A wave of relief swept over Gregory. He had forgotten Nancy's mother! "She had her baby? Was it a boy?"

The doctor nodded in slow motion. "She bore two boys, young man." He hesitated, and then a muscle in his face twitched and he said in a rush, "She also bore seven daughters. Nine children! And they all—they all live."

Gregory found Grendon round the corner of the house. The farmer had a pitchfork full of hay, which he was carrying over his shoulder into the cowsheds. Gregory stood in his way but he pushed past.

"I want to speak to you, Joseph."

"There's work to be done. Pity you can't see that."

"I want to speak about your wife."

Grendon made no reply. He worked like a demon, tossing the hay down, turning for more. In any case, it was difficult to talk. The cows and calves, closely confined, seemed to set up a perpetual uneasy noise of lowing and uncow-like grunts. Gregory followed the farmer round to the hayrick, but the man walked like one possessed. His eyes seemed sunk into his head, his mouth was puckered until his lips were invisible. When Gregory laid a hand on his arm, he shook it off. Stabbing up another great load of hay, he swung back towards the sheds so violently that Gregory had to jump out of his way.

Gregory lost his temper. Following Grendon back into the cowshed, he swung the bottom of the two-part door shut, and bolted it on the outside. When Grendon came back, he did not budge.

"Joseph, what's got into you? Why are you suddenly so heartless? Surely your wife needs you by her?"

His eyes had a curious blind look as he turned them at Gregory. He held the pitchfork before him in both hands almost like a weapon as he said, "I been with her all night, bor, while she brought forth her increase."

"But now—"

"She got a nursing woman from Dereham Cottages with her now. I been with her all night. Now I got to see to the farm— things keep growing, you know."

"They're growing too much, Joseph. Stop and think—"

"I've no time for talking." Dropping the pitchfork, he elbowed Gregory out of the way, unbolted the door, and flung it open. Grasping Gregory firmly by the biceps of one arm, he began to propel him along to the vegetable beds down by the South Meadows.

The early lettuce were gigantic here. Everything bristled out of the ground. Recklessly, Grendon ran among the lines of new green, pulling up fistfuls of young radishes, carrots, spring onions, scattering them over his shoulder as fast as he plucked them from the ground.

"See, Gregory—all bigger than you ever seen 'em, and weeks early! The harvest is going to be a bumper. Look at the fields! Look at the orchard!" With wide gesture, he swept a hand towards the lines of trees, buried in the mounds of snow-and-pink of their blossom. "Whatever happens, we got to take advantage of it. It may not happen another year. Why—it's like a fairy story!"

He said no more. Turning, he seemed already to have forgotten Gregory. Eyes down at the ground that had suddenly achieved such abundance, he marched back towards the sheds.

Nancy was in the kitchen. Neckland had brought her in a stoup of fresh milk, and she was supping it wearily from a ladle.

"Oh, Greg, I'm sorry I ran from you. I was so upset." She came to him, still holding the ladle but dangling her arms over his shoulders in a familiar way she had not used before. "Poor Mother, I fear her mind is unhinged with—with bearing so many children. She's talking such strange stuff as I never heard before, and I do believe she fancies as she's a child again."

"Is it to be wondered at?" he said, smoothing her hair with his hand. "She'll be better once she's recovered from the shock."

They kissed each other, and after a minute she passed him a ladleful of milk. He drank and then spat it out in disgust.

"Ugh! What's got into the milk? Is Neckland trying to poison you or something? Have you tasted it? It's as bitter as sloes!"

She pulled a puzzled face. "I thought it tasted rather strange, but not unpleasant. Here, let me try again."

"No, it's too horrible. Some Sloane's Liniment must have got mixed in it."

Despite his warning, she put her lips to the metal spoon and sipped, then shook her head. "You're imagining things, Greg. It does taste a bit different, 'tis true, but there's nothing wrong with it. You'll stay to take a bite with us, I hope?"

"No, Nancy, I'm off now. I have a letter awaiting me that I must answer; it arrived when I was in Norwich. Listen, my lovely Nancy, this letter is from Dr. Hudson-Ward, an old aquaintance of my father's. He is headmaster of a school in Gloucester, and he wishes me to join the staff there as a teacher on most favorable terms. So you see I may not be idle much longer!"

Laughing, she clung to him. "That's wonderful, my darling! What a handsome schoolmaster you will make. But Gloucester—that's over the other side of the country. I suppose we shan't be seeing you again once you get there."

"Nothing's settled yet, Nancy."

"You'll be gone in a week and we shan't never see you again. Once you get to that there old school, you will never think of your Nancy no more."

He cupped her face in his hands. "Are you my Nancy? Do you care for me?"

Her eyelashes came over her dark eyes. "Greg, things are so muddled here—I mean—yes, I do care, I dread to think I'd not see you again."

Recalling her saying that, he rode away a quarter of an hour later very content at heart—and entirely neglectful of the dangers to which he left her exposed.

Rain fell lightly as Gregory Rolles made his way that evening to "The Wayfarer" inn. His friend Bruce Fox was already there, ensconced in one of the snug seats of the inglenook.

On this occasion, Fox was more interested in purveying details of his sister's forthcoming wedding than in listening to what Gregory had to tell, and since some of his future brother-in-law's friends soon arrived, and had to buy and be bought libations, the evening became a merry and thoughtless one. And in a short while, the ale having its good effect, Gregory also forgot what he wanted to say and began whole-heartedly to enjoy the company.

Next morning, he awoke with a heavy head and in a dismal state of mind. The day was too wet for him to go out and take exercise. He sat moodily in a chair by the window, delaying an answer to Dr. Hudson-Ward, the headmaster. Lethargically, he returned to a small leather-bound volume on serpents that he had acquired in Norwich a few days earlier. After a while, a passage caught his particular attention:

"Most serpents of the venomous variety, with the exception of the opisthoglyphs, release their victims from their fangs after striking. The victims die in some cases in but a few seconds, while in other cases the onset of moribundity may be delayed by hours or days. The saliva of some of the serpents contains not only venom but a special digestive virtue. The deadly Coral Snake of Brazil, though attaining no more than a foot in length, has this virtue in abundance. Accordingly, when it bites an animal or a human being, the victim not only dies in profound agony in a matter of seconds, but his interiors parts are then dissolved, so that even the bones become no more than jelly. Then may the little serpent suck all of the victim out as a kind of soup or broth from the original wound in its skin, which latter alone remains intact."

For a long while, Gregory sat where he was in the window, with the book open in his lap, thinking about the Grendon farm, and about Nancy. He reproached himself for having done so little for his friends there, and gradually resolved on a plan of action the next time he rode out; but his visit was to be delayed for some days: the wet weather had set in with more determination than the end of April and the beginning of May generally allowed.

Gregory tried to concentrate on a letter to the worthy Dr. Hudson-Ward in the county of Gloucestershire. He knew he should take the job, indeed he felt inclined to do so; but first he knew he had to see Nancy safe. The indecisions he felt caused him to delay answering the doctor until the next day, when he feebly wrote that he would be glad to accept the post offered at the price offered, but begged to have a week to think about it. When he took the letter down to the post-woman in "The Three Poachers," the rain still fell.

One morning, the rains were suddenly vanished, the blue and wide East Anglian skies were back, and Gregory saddled up Daisy and rode out along the mirey track he had so often taken. As he arrived at the farm, Grubby and Neckland were at work in the ditch, unblocking it with shovels. He saluted them and rode in. As he was about to put the mare into the stables, he saw Grendon and Nancy standing on the patch of waste ground under the windowless east side of the house. He went slowly to join them, noting as he walked how dry the ground was here, as if no rain had fallen in a fortnight. But this observation was drowned in shock as he saw the nine little crosses Grendon was sticking into nine freshly turned mounds of earth.

Nancy stood weeping. They both looked up as Gregory approached, but Grendon went stubbornly on with his task.

"Oh, Nancy, Joseph, I'm so sorry about this!" Gregory exclaimed. "To think that they've all—but where's the parson? Where's the parson, Joseph? Why are *you* burying them, without a proper service or anything?"

"I told Father, but he took no heed!" Nancy exclaimed.

Grendon had reached the last grave. He seized the last crude wooden cross, lifted it above his head, and stabbed it down into the ground as if he would pierce the heart of what lay under it. Only then did he straighten and speak.

"We don't need a parson here. I've got no time to waste with parsons. I have work to do if you ent."

"But these are your children, Joseph! What has got into you?"

"They are part of the farm now, as they always was." He turned, rolling his shirt sleeves further up his brawny arms, and strode off in the direction of the ditching activities.

Gregory took Nancy in his arms and looked at her tear-stained face. "What a time you must have been having these last few days!"

"I—I thought you'd gone to Gloucester, Greg! Why didn't you come? Every day I waited for you to come!"

"It was so wet and flooded."

"It's been lovely weather since you were last here. Look how everything has grown!"

"It poured with rain every single day in Cottersall."

"Well, I never! That explains why there is so much water flowing in the Oast and in the ditches. But we've had only a few light showers."

"Nancy, tell me, how did these poor little mites die?"

"I'd rather not say, if you don't mind."

"Why didn't your father get in Parson Landon? How could he be so lacking in feeling?"

"Because he didn't want anyone from the outside world to know. You see—oh, I must tell you, my dear—it's Mother. She has gone completely off her head, completely! It was the evening before last, when she took her first turn outside the back door."

"You don't mean to say she—"

"Ow, Greg, you're hurting my arms! She—she crept upstairs when we weren't noticing and she—she stifled each of the babies in turn, Greg, under the best goose feather pillow."

He could feel the color leaving his cheeks. Solicitously, she led him to the back of the house. They sat together on the orchard railings while he digested the words in silence.

"How is your mother now, Nancy?"

"She's silent. Father had to bar her in her room for safety. Last night she screamed a lot. But this morning she's quiet."

He looked dazedly about him. The appearance of everything was speckled, as if the return of his blood to his head somehow infected it with a rash. The blossom had gone almost entirely from the fruit trees in the orchard and already the embryo apples showed signs of swelling. Nearby, broad beans bowed under enormous pods. Seeing his glance, Nancy dipped into her apron pocket and produced a bunch of shining crimson radishes as big as tangerines.

"Have one of these. They're crisp and wet and hot, just as they should be."

Indifferently, he accepted and bit the tempting globe. At once he had to spit the portion out. There again was that vile bitter flavor!

"Oh, but they're lovely!" Nancy protested.

"Not even 'rather strange' now—simply 'lovely'? Nancy, don't you see, something uncanny and awful is taking place here. I'm sorry, but I can't see otherwise. You and your father should leave here at once."

"*Leave* here, Greg? Just because you don't like the taste of these lovely radishes? How can we leave here? Where should we go? See this here house? My granddad died here, and his father before him. It's our *place*. We can't just up and off, not even after this bit of trouble. Try another radish."

"For heaven's sake, Nancy, they taste as if the flavor was intended for creatures with a palate completely different from ours . . . Oh . . ." He stared at her. "And perhaps they are. Nancy, I tell you—"

He broke off, sliding from the railing. Neckland had come up from one side, still plastered in mud from his work in the ditch, his collarless shirt flapping open. In his hand, he grasped an ancient and military-looking pistol.

"I'll fire this if you come nearer," he said. "It goes okay, never worry, and it's loaded, Master Gregory. Now you're a-going to listen to me!"

"Bert, put that thing away!" Nancy exclaimed. She moved forward to him, but Gregory pulled her back and stood before her.

"Don't be a bloody idiot, Neckland. Put it away!"

"I'll shoot you, bor, I'll shoot you, I swear, if you mucks about." His eyes were glaring, and the look on his dark face left no doubt that he meant what he said. "You're going to swear to me that you're going to clear off of this farm on that nag of yours and never come back again."

"I'm going straight to tell my father, Bert," Nancy warned.

The pistol twitched.

"If you move, Nancy, I warn you I'll shoot this fine chap of yours in the leg. Besides, your father don't care about Master Gregory any more—he's got better things to worry him."

"Like finding out what's happening here?" Gregory said. "Listen, Neckland, we're all in trouble. This farm is being run by a group of nasty little monsters. You can't see them because they're invisible—"

The gun exploded. As he spoke, Nancy had attempted to run off. Without hesitating, Neckland fired down at Gregory's knees. Gregory felt the shot pluck his trouser leg and knew himself unharmed. With knowledge came rage. He flung himself at

Neckland and hit him hard over the heart. Falling back, Neckland dropped the pistol and swung his fist wildly. Gregory struck him again. As he did so, the other grabbed him and they began furiously hitting each other. When Gregory broke free, Neckland grappled with him again. There was more pummeling of ribs.

"Let me go, you swine!" Gregory shouted. He hooked his foot behind Neckland's ankle, and they both rolled over onto the grass. At this point, a sort of flood bank had been raised long ago between the house and low-lying orchard. Down this the two men rolled, fetching up sharply against the stone wall of the kitchen. Neckland got the worst of it, catching his head on the corner, and lay there stunned. Gregory found himself looking at two feet encased in ludicrous stockings. Slowly, he rose to his feet, and confronted Mrs. Grendon at less than a yard's distance. She was smiling.

He stood there, and gradually straightened his back, looking at her anxiously.

"So there you are, Jackie, my Jackalums," she said. The smile was wider now and less like a smile. "I wanted to talk to you. You are the one who knows about the things that walk on the lines, aren't you?"

"I don't understand, Mrs. Grendon."

"Don't call me that there daft old name, sonnie. You know all about the little gray things that aren't supposed to be there, don't you?"

"Oh, those . . . Suppose I said I did know?"

"The other naughty children will pretend they don't know what I mean, but you know, don't you? You know about the little gray things."

The sweat stood out on his brow. She had moved nearer. She stood close, staring into his eyes, not touching him; but he was acutely conscious that she could touch him at any moment.

From the corner of his eye, he saw Neckland stir and crawl

away from the house, but there were other things to occupy him.

"These little gray things," he said. "Did you save the nine babies from them?"

"The gray things wanted to kiss them, you see, but I couldn't let them. I was clever. I hid them under the good feather pillow and now even *I* can't find them!" She began to laugh, making a horrible low whirring sound in her throat.

"They're small and gray and wet, aren't they?" Gregory said sharply. "They've got big feet, webbed like frogs, but they're heavy and short, aren't they, and they have fangs like a snake, haven't they?"

She looked doubtful. Then her eye seemed to catch a movement. She looked fixedly to one side. "Here comes one now, the female one," she said.

Gregory turned to look where she did. Nothing was visible. His mouth was dry. "How many are there, Mrs. Grendon?"

Then he saw the short grass stir, flatten, and raise near at hand, and let out a cry of alarm. Wrenching off his riding boot, he swung it in an arc, low above the ground. It struck something concealed in thin air. Almost at once, he received a terrific kick in the thigh, and fell backwards. Despite the hurt, fear made him jump up almost at once.

Mrs. Grendon was changing. Her mouth collapsed as if it would run off one corner of her face. Her head sagged to one side. Her shoulders fell. A deep crimson blush momentarily suffused her features, then drained, and as it drained she dwindled like a deflating rubber balloon. Gregory sank to his knees, whimpering, buried his face in his hands, and pressed his hands to the grass. Darkness overcame him.

His senses must have left him only for a moment. When he pulled himself up again, the almost empty bag of women's clothes was still settling slowly to the ground.

"Joseph! Joseph!" he yelled. Nancy had fled. In a distracted mixture of panic and fury, he dragged his boot on again and rushed round the house towards the cowsheds.

Neckland stood halfway between barn and mill, rubbing his skull. In his rattled state, the sight of Gregory apparently in full pursuit made him run away.

"Neckland!" Gregory shouted. He ran like mad for the other. Neckland bolted for the mill, jumped inside, tried to pull the door to, lost his nerve, and ran up the wooden stairs. Gregory bellowed after him.

The pursuit took them right to the top of the mill. Neckland had lost enough wit even to kick over the bolt of the trapdoor. Gregory burst it up and climbed out panting. Throughly cowed, Neckland backed towards the opening until he was almost out on the little platform above the sails.

"You'll fall out, you idiot," Gregory warned. "Listen, Neckland, you have no reason to fear me. I want no enmity between us. There's a bigger enemy we must fight. Look!"

He came towards the low door and looked down at the dark surface of the pond. Neckland grabbed the overhead pulley for security and said nothing.

"Look down at the pond," Gregory said. "That's where the Aurigans live. My God—Bert, look, there one goes!"

The urgency in his voice made the farmhand look down where he pointed. Together, the two men watched as a depression slid over the black water; an overlapping chain of ripples swung back from it. At approximately the middle of the pond, the depression became a commotion. A small whirlpool formed and died, and the ripples began to settle.

"There's your ghost, Bert," Gregory gasped. "That must have been the one that got poor Mrs. Grendon. Now do you believe?"

"I never heard of a ghost as lived under water," Neckland gasped.

"A ghost never harmed anyone—we've already had a sample of what these terrifying things can do. Come on, Bert, shake hands, understand I bear you no hard feelings. Oh, come on, man! I know how you feel about Nancy, but she must be free to make her own choice in life."

They shook hands and grinned rather foolishly at each other.

"We better go and tell the farmer what we seen," Neckland said. "I reckon that thing done what happened to Lardie last evening."

"Lardie? What's happened to her? I thought I hadn't seen her today."

"Same as happened to the little pigs. I found her just inside the barn. Just her coat was left, that's all. No insides! Like she'd been sucked dry."

It took Gregory twenty minutes to summon the council of war on which he had set his mind. The party gathered in the farmhouse, in the parlor. By this time, Nancy had somewhat recovered from the shock of her mother's death, and sat in an armchair with a shawl about her shoulders. Her father stood nearby with his arms folded, looking impatient, while Bert Neckland lounged by the door. Only Grubby was not present. He had been told to get on with the ditching.

"I'm going to have another attempt to convince you all that you are in very grave danger," Gregory said. "You won't see it for yourselves. The situation is that we're all animals together at present. Do you remember that strange meteor that fell out of the sky last winter, Joseph? And do you remember that ill-smelling dew early in the spring? They were not unconnected, and they are connected with all that's happening now. That meteor was a space machine of some sort, I firmly believe, and it brought in it a kind of life that—that is not so much hostile to terrestrial life as *indifferent to its quality*. The creatures from that machine—I call them Aurigans—spread the dew over the farm. It was a growth accelerator, a manure or fertilizer, that speeds growth in plants and animals."

"So much better for us!" Grendon said.

"But it's not better. The things grow wildly, yes, but the taste is altered to suit the palates of those things out there. You've seen what happened. You can't sell anything. People won't touch your eggs or milk or meat—they taste too foul."

"But that's a lot of nonsense. We'll sell in Norwich. Our produce is better than it ever was. We eat it, don't we?"

"Yes, Joseph, *you* eat it. But anyone who eats at your table is doomed. Don't you understand—you are all 'fertilized' just as surely as the pigs and chickens. Your place has been turned into a superfarm, and you are all meat to the Aurigans."

That set a silence in the room, until Nancy said in a small voice, "You don't believe such a terrible thing."

"I suppose these unseen creatures told you all this?" Grendon said truculently.

"Judge by the evidence, as I do. Your wife—I must be brutal, Joseph—your wife was eaten, like the dog and the pigs. As everything else will be in time. The Aurigans aren't even cannibals. They aren't like us. They don't care whether we have souls or intelligences, any more than we really care whether bullocks have."

"No one's going to eat me," Neckland said, looking decidedly white about the gills.

"How can you stop them? They're invisible, and I think they can strike like snakes. They're aquatic and I think they may be only two feet tall. How can you protect yourself?" He turned to the farmer. "Joseph, the danger is very great, and not only to us here. At first, they may have offered us no harm while they got the measure of us—otherwise I'd have died in your rowing boat. Now there's no longer doubt of their hostile intent. I beg you to let me go to Heigham and telephone to the chief of police in Norwich, or at least to the local militia, to get them to come and help us."

The farmer shook his head slowly, and pointed a finger at Gregory.

"You soon forgot them talks we had, bor, all about the coming age of socialism and how the powers of the state was going to wither away. Directly we get a bit of trouble, you want to call in the authorities. There's no harm here a few savage dogs like my old Cuff can't handle, and I don't say as I ent going to get a couple of dogs, but you'm a fule if you reckon I'm getting the authorities down here. Fine old socialist you turn out to be!"

"You have no room to talk about that!" Gregory exclaimed. "Why didn't you let Grubby come here? If you were a socialist, you'd treat the men as you treat yourself. Instead, you leave him out in the ditch. I wanted him to hear this discussion."

The farmer leant threateningly across the table at him.

"Oh, you did, did you? Since when was this your farm? And Grubby can come and go as he likes when it's his, so put that in your pipe and smoke it, bor! Who do you just think you are?" He moved closer to Gregory, apparently happy to work off his fears as anger. "You're trying to scare us all off this here little old bit of ground, ent you? Well, the Grendons ent a scaring sort, see! Now I'll tell you something. See that shotgun there on the wall? That be loaded. And if you ent off this farm by midday, that shotgun ont be on that wall no more. It'll be here, bor, right here in my two hands, and I'll be letting you have it right where you'll feel it most."

"You can't do that, Father," Nancy said. "You know Gregory is a friend of ours."

"For God's sake, Joseph," Gregory said, "see where your enemy lies. Bert, tell Mr. Grendon what we saw on the pond, go on!"

Neckland was far from keen to be dragged into this argument. He scratched his head, drew a red-and-white spotted kerchief from round his neck to wipe his face, and muttered, "We saw a sort of ripple on the water, but I didn't see nothing really, Master Gregory. I mean, it could have been the wind, couldn't it?"

"Now you be warned, Gregory," the farmer repeated. "You

269

be off my land by noon by the sun, and that mare of yours, or I ont answer for it." He marched out into the pale sunshine, and Neckland followed.

Nancy and Gregory stood staring at each other. He took her hands, and they were cold.

"You believe what I was saying, Nancy?"

"Is that why the food did at one point taste bad to us, and then soon tasted well enough again?"

"It can only have been that at that time your systems were not fully adjusted to the poison. Now they are. You're being fed up, Nancy, just like the livestock—I'm sure of it! I fear for you, darling love, I fear so much. What are we to do? Come back to Cottersall with me! Mrs. Fenn has another fine little drawing room upstairs that I'm sure she would rent."

"Now you're talking nonsense, Greg! How can I? What would people say? No, you go away for now and let the tempest of Father's wrath abate, and if you could come back tomorrow, you will find he will be milder for sure, because I plan to wait on him tonight and talk to him about you. Why, he's half daft with grief and doesn't know what he says."

"All right, my darling. But stay inside as much as you can. The Aurigans have not come indoors yet, as far as we know, and it may be safer here. And lock all the doors and put the shutters over the windows before you go to bed. And get your father to take that shotgun of his upstairs with him."

The evenings were lengthening with confidence towards summer now, and Bruce Fox arrived home before sunset. As he jumped from his bicycle this evening, he found his friend Gregory impatiently awaiting him.

They went indoors together, and while Fox ate a large tea, Gregory told him what had been happening at the farm that day.

"You're in trouble," Fox said. "Look, tomorrow's Sunday. I'll skip church and come out with you. You need help."

"Joseph may shoot me. He'll be certain to if I bring along a stranger. You can help me tonight by telling me where I can purchase a young dog straightaway to protect Nancy."

"Nonsense, I'm coming with you. I can't bear hearing all this at secondhand anyhow. We'll pick up a pup in any event—the blacksmith has a litter to be rid of. Have you got any plan of action?"

"Plan? No, not really."

"You must have a plan. Grendon doesn't scare too easily, does he?"

"I imagine he's scared well enough. Nancy says he's scared. He just isn't imaginative enough to see what he can do but carry on working as hard as possible."

"Look, I know these farmers. They won't believe anything till you rub their noses in it. What we must do is *show* him an Aurigan."

"Oh, splendid, Bruce! And how do you catch one?"

"You trap one."

"Don't forget they're invisible—hey, Bruce, yes, by Jove, you're right! I've the very idea! Look, we've nothing more to worry about if we can trap one. We can trap the lot, however many there are, and we can kill the little horrors when we have trapped them."

Fox grinned over the top of a chunk of cherry cake. "We're agreed, I suppose, that these Aurigans aren't socialist utopians any longer?"

It helped a great deal, Gregory thought, to be able to visualize roughly what the alien life form looked like. The volume on serpents had been a happy find, for not only did it give an idea of how the Aurigans must be able to digest their prey so rapidly—"a kind of soup or broth"—but presumably it gave a clue to their appearance. To live in a space machine, they would probably be fairly small, and they seemed to be semi-aquatic. It all went to make up a picture of a strange being: skin perhaps scaled like a fish, great flipper feet like a frog, barrel-like diminutive stature, and a tiny head with two great fangs in the jaw. There was no doubt but that the invisibility cloaked a really ugly-looking dwarf!

As the macabre image passed through his head, Gregory and Bruce Fox were preparing their trap. Fortunately, Grendon had offered no resistance to their entering the farm; Nancy had evidently spoken to good effect. And he had suffered another shock. Five fowls had been reduced to little but feathers and skin that morning almost before his eyes, and he was as a result sullen and indifferent of what went on. Now he was out in a distant field working, and the two young men were allowed to carry out their plans unmolested—though not without an occasional anxious glance at the pond—while a worried Nancy looked on from the farmhouse window.

She had with her a sturdy young mongrel dog of eight months, which Gregory and Bruce had brought along, called Gyp. Grendon had obtained two ferocious hounds from a distant neighbor. These wide-mouthed brutes were secured on long running chains that enabled them to patrol from the horse trough by the pond, down the west side of the house, almost to the elms and the bridge leading over to West Field. They barked stridently most of the time and seemed to cause a general unease among the other animals, all of which gave voice restlessly this forenoon.

The dogs would be a difficulty, Nancy had said, for they refused to touch any of the food the farm could provide. It was hoped they would take it when they became hungry enough.

Grendon had planted a great board by the farm gate and on the board had painted a notice telling everyone to keep away.

Armed with pitchforks, the two young men carried flour sacks out from the mill and placed them at strategic positions across the yard as far as the gate. Gregory went to the cowsheds and led out one of the calves there on a length of binder twine under the very teeth of the barking dogs—he only hoped they would prove as hostile to the Aurigans as they seemed to be to human life.

As he was pulling the calf across the yard, Grubby appeared.

"You'd better stay away from us, Grubby. We're trying to trap one of the ghosts."

"Master, if I catch one, I shall strangle him, straight I will."

"A pitchfork is a better weapon. These ghosts are dangerous little beasts at close quarters."

"I'm strong, bor, I tell 'ee! I'd strangle un!"

To prove his point, Grubby rolled his striped and tattered sleeve even further up his arm and exposed to Gregory and Fox his enormous biceps. At the same time, he wagged his great heavy head and lolled his tongue out of his mouth, perhaps to demonstrate some of the effects of strangulation.

"It's a very fine arm," Gregory agreed. "But, look, Grubby, we have a better idea. We are going to do this ghost to death with pitchforks. If you want to join in, you'd better get a spare one from the stable."

Grubby looked at him with a sly-shy expression and stroked his throat. "I'd be better at strangling, bor. I've always wanted to strangle someone."

"Why should you want to do that, Grubby?"

The laborer lowered his voice. "I always wanted to see how difficult it would be. I'm strong, you see. I got my strength up as a lad by doing some of this here strangling—but never men, you know, just cattle."

Backing away a pace, Gregory said, "This time, Grubby, it's pitchforks for us." To settle the issue, he went into the stables, got a pitchfork, and returned to thrust it into Grubby's hand.

"Let's get on with it," Fox said.

They were all ready to start. Fox and Grubby crouched down in the ditch on either side of the gate, weapons at the ready. Gregory emptied one of the bags of flour over the yard in a patch just before the gate, so that anyone leaving the farm would have to walk through it. Then he led the calf towards the pond.

The young animal set up an uneasy mooing, and most of the beasts nearby seemed to answer. The chickens and hens scattered about the yard in the pale sunshine as if demented. Gregory felt the sweat trickle down his back, although his skin was cold with the chemistries of suspense. With a slap on its rump, he forced the calf into the water of the pond. It stood there unhappily, until he led it out again and slowly back across the yard, past the mill and the grain store on his right, past Mrs. Grendon's neglected flowerbed on his left, towards the gate where his allies waited. And for all his determination not to do so, he could not stop himself looking backwards at the leaden surface of the pond to see if anything followed him. He led the calf through the gate and stopped. No tracks but his and the calf's showed in the strewn flour.

"Try it again," Fox advised. "Perhaps they are taking a nap down there."

Gregory went through the routine again, and a third and fourth time, on each occasion smoothing the flour after he had been through it. Each time, he saw Nancy watching helplessly from the house. Each time, he felt a little more sick with tension.

Yet when it happened, it took him by surprise. He had got the calf to the gate for a fifth time when Fox's shout joined the chorus of animal noises. The pond had shown no special ripple, so the Aurigan had come from some dark-purposed prowl of the farm—suddenly, its finned footsteps were marking the flour.

Yelling with excitement, Gregory dropped the rope that led the calf and ducked to one side. Seizing up an opened bag of flour by the gatepost, he flung its contents before the advancing figure.

The bomb of flour exploded all over the Aurigan. Now it was revealed in chalky outline. Despite himself, Gregory found himself screaming in sheer fright as the ghastliness was revealed in whirling white. It was especially the size that frightened: this dread thing, remote from human form, was too big for earthly nature—ten feet high, perhaps twelve! Invincible, and horribly quick, it came rushing at him with unnumbered arms striking out towards him.

Next morning, Dr. Crouchorn and his silk hat appeared at Gregory's bedside, thanked Mrs. Fenn for some hot water, and dressed Gregory's leg wound.

"You got off lightly, considering," the old man said. "But if you will take a piece of advice from me, Mr. Rolles, you will cease to visit the Grendon farm. It's an evil place and you'll come to no good there."

Gregory nodded. He had told the doctor nothing, except that Grendon had run up and shot him in the leg; which was true enough, but that it omitted most of the story.

"When will I be up again, doctor?"

"Oh, young flesh heals soon enough, or undertakers would be rich men and doctors paupers. A few days should see you right as rain. But I'll be visiting you again tomorrow, until then you are to stay flat on your back and keep that leg motionless."

"I suppose I may write a letter, doctor?"

"I suppose you may, young man."

Directly Dr. Crouchorn had gone, Gregory took pen and paper and addressed some urgent lines to Nancy. They told her that he loved her very much and could not bear to think of her remaining on the farm; that he could not get to see her for a few days because of his leg wound; and that she must immediately come away on Hetty with a bag full of her things and stay at "The Wayfarer," where there was a capital room for which he would pay. That if she thought anything of him, she must put the simple plan into action this very day, and send him word round from the inn when she was established there.

With some satisfaction, Gregory read this through twice, signed it, and added kisses, and summoned Mrs. Fenn with the aid of a small bell she had provided for that purpose.

He told her that the delivery of the letter was a matter of extreme urgency. He would entrust it to Tommy, the baker's boy, to deliver when his morning round was over, and would give him a shilling for his efforts. Mrs. Fenn was not enthusiastic about this, but with a little flattery was persuaded to speak to Tommy; she left the bedroom clutching both letter and shilling.

At once, Gregory began another letter, this one to Mr. H. G. Wells. It was some while since he had last addressed his correspondent, and so he had to make a somewhat lengthy report; but eventually he came to the events of the previous day.

So horrified was I by the sight of the Aurigan (he wrote), that I stood where I was, unable to move, while the flour blew about us. And how can I now convey to you—who are perhaps the most interested person in this vital subject in all the British Isles—what the monster looked like, outlined in white? My impressions were, of course, both brief and indefinite, but the main handicap is that there is nothing on Earth to liken this weird being to!

It appeared, I suppose, most like some horrendous goose, but the neck must be imagined as almost as thick as the body— indeed, it was almost all body, or all neck, whichever way you look at it. And on top of this neck was no head but a terrible array of various sorts of arms, a nest of writhing cilia, antennae, and whips, for all the world as if an octopus were entangled with a Portuguese man-o'-war as big as itself, with a few shrimp and starfish legs thrown in. Does this sound ludicrous? I can only swear to you that as it bore down on me, perhaps twice my own height or more, I found it something almost too terrifying for human eyes to look on—and yet I did not see it, but merely the flour that adhered to it!

That repulsive sight would have been the last my eyes ever dwelt on had it not been for Grubby, the simple farmhand I have had occasion to mention before.

As I threw the flour, Grubby gave a great cry and rushed forward, dropping the pitchfork. He jumped at the creature as it turned on me. This put out our plan, which was that he and

Bruce Fox should pitchfork the creature to death. Instead, he grasped it as high as he possibly might and commenced to squeeze with full force of his mighty muscles. What a terrifying contest! What a fear-fraught combat!

Collecting his wits, Bruce charged forward and attacked with his pitchfork. It was his battle cry that brought me back from my paralysis into action. I ran and seized Grubby's pitchfork and also charged. That thing had arms for us all! It struck out, and I have no doubt that several arms held poisoned needle teeth, for I saw one come towards me gaping like a snake's mouth. Need I stress the danger—particularly when you recall that the effect of the flour cloud was only partial, and there were still invisible arms flailing around us!

Our saving was that the Aurigan was cowardly. I saw Bruce jab it hard, and a second later, I rammed my pitchfork right through its foot. At once it had had enough. Grubby fell to the ground as it retreated. It moved at amazing speed, back towards the pool. We were in pursuit! And all the beasts of the barnyard uttered their cries to it.

As it launched itself into the water, we both flung our pitchforks at its form. But it swam out strongly and then dived below the surface, leaving only ripples and a scummy trail of flour.

We stood staring at the water for an instant, and then with common accord ran back to Grubby. He was dead. He lay face up and was no longer recognizable. The Aurigan must have struck him with its poisoned fangs as soon as he attacked. Grubby's skin was stretched tight and glistened oddly. He had turned a dull crimson. No longer was he more than a caricature of human shape. All his internal substance had been transformed to liquid by the rapid-working venoms of the Aurigan; he was like a sort of giant man-shaped rotten haggis.

There were wound marks across his neck and throat and what had been his face, and from these wounds his substance drained, so that he slowly deflated into his trampled bed of flour and dust. Perhaps the sight of fabled Medusa's head, that turned

277

men to stone, was no worse than this, for we stood there utterly paralyzed. It was a blast from Farmer Grendon's shotgun that brought us back to life.

He had threatened to shoot me. Now, seeing us despoiling his flour sacks and apparently about to make off with a calf, he fired at us. We had no choice but to run for it. Grendon was in no explaining mood. Good Nancy came running out to stop him, but Neckland was charging up too with the pair of savage dogs growling at the ends of their chains.

Bruce and I had ridden up on my Daisy. I had left her saddled. Bringing her out of the stable at a trot, I heaved Bruce up into the saddle and was about to climb on myself when the gun went off again and I felt a burning pain in my leg. Bruce dragged me into the saddle and we were off—I half unconscious.

Here I lie now in bed, and should be about again in a couple of days. Fortunately, the shot did not harm any bones.

So you see how the farm is now a place of the damned! Once, I thought it might even become a new Eden, growing the food of the gods for men like gods. Instead—alas! the first meeting between humanity and beings from another world has proved disastrous, and the Eden is become a battleground for a war of worlds. How can our anticipations for the future be anything other than gloomy?

Before I close this over-long account, I must answer a query in your letter and pose another to you, more personal than yours to me.

First, you question if the Aurigans are entirely invisible and say—if I may quote your letter—"Any alteration in the refractive index of the eye lenses would make vision impossible, but without such alteration the eyes would be visible as glassy globules. And for vision it is also necessary that there should be visual purple behind the retina and an opaque cornea. How then do your Aurigans manage for vision?" The answer must be that they do without eyesight as we know it, for I think they naturally maintain a complete invisibility. How they "see" I know not, but whatever sense they use, it is effective. How they communicate I know not—our fellow made not the slightest sound when I speared his foot!—yet it is apparent they must communicate effectively. Perhaps they tried originally to communicate with us through a mysterious sense we do not possess and, on receiving no answer, assumed us to be as dumb as our dumb animals. If so, what a tragedy!

Now to my personal inquiry. I know, sir, that you must grow more busy as you grow more famous; but I feel that what transpires here in this remote corner of East Anglia is of momentous import to the world and the future. Could you not take it upon yourself to pay us a visit here? You would be comfortable at one of our two inns, and the journey here by railway is efficient if tedious—you can easily get a regular wagon from Heigham station here, a distance of only eight miles. You could then view Grendon's farm for yourself, and perhaps one of these interstellar beings too. I feel you are as much amused as concerned by the accounts you receive from the undersigned, but I swear not one detail is exaggerated. Say you can come!

If you need persuasion, reflect on how much delight it will give to

Your sincere admirer,
Gregory Rolles.

Reading this long letter through, scratching out two superfluous adjectives, Gregory lay back in some satisfaction. He had the feeling he was still involved in the struggle although temporarily out of action.

But the later afternoon brought him disquieting news. Tommy, the baker's boy, had gone out as far as the Grendon farm. Then the ugly legends circulating in the village about the place had risen in his mind, and he had stood wondering whether he should go on. An unnatural babble of animal noise came from the farm, mixed with hammering, and when Tommy crept forward and saw the farmer himself looking as black as a puddle and building a great thing like a gibbet in the yard, he had lost his nerve and rushed back the way he came, the letter to Nancy undelivered.

Gregory lay on the bed worrying about Nancy until Mrs. Fenn brought up supper on a tray. At least it was clear now why the Aurigans had not entered the farmhouse; they were far too large to do so. She was safe as long as she kept indoors—as far as anyone on that doomed plot was safe.

He fell asleep early that night. In the early hours of the morning, nightmare visited him. He was in a strange city where all the buildings were new and the people wore shining clothes. In one square grew a tree. The Gregory in the dream stood in a special relationship to the tree: he fed it. It was a job to push people who were passing by the tree against its surface. The tree was a saliva tree. Down its smooth bark ran quantities of saliva from red lips like leaves up in the boughs. It grew enormous on the people on which it fed. As they were thrown against it, they passed into the substance of the tree. Some of the saliva splashed on to Gregory. But instead of dissolving him, it caused everything he touched to be dissolved. He put his arms about the girl he loved, and as his mouth went towards hers, her skin peeled away from her face.

He woke weeping desperately and fumbling blindly for the ring of the gas mantle.

Dr. Crouchorn came late next morning and told Gregory he should have at least three more days complete rest for the recovery of the muscles of his leg. Gregory lay there in a state of acute dissatisfaction with himself. Recalling the vile dream, he thought how negligent he had been towards Nancy, the girl he loved. His letter to her still lay undelivered by his bedside. After Mrs. Fenn had brought up his dinner, he determined that he must see Nancy for himself. Leaving the food, he pulled himself out of bed and dressed slowly.

The leg was more painful than he had expected, but he got

himself downstairs and out to the stable without too much trouble. Daisy seemed pleased to see him. He rubbed her nose and rested his head against her long cheek in sheer pleasure at being with her again.

"This may be the last time you have to undertake this particular journey, my girl," he said.

Saddling her was comparatively easy. Getting into the saddle involved much bodily anguish. But eventually he was comfortable and they turned along the familiar and desolate road to the domain of the Aurigans. His leg was worse than he had bargained for. More than once, he had to get the mare to stop while he let the throbbing subside. He saw he was losing blood plentifully.

As he approached the farm, he observed what the baker's boy had meant by saying Grendon was building a gibbet. A pole had been set up in the middle of the yard. A cable ran to the top of it, and a light was rigged there, so that the expanse of the yard could be illuminated by night.

Another change had taken place. A wooden fence had been built behind the horse trough, cutting off the pond from the farm. But at one point, ominously, a section of it had been broken down and splintered and crushed, as if some monstrous thing had walked through the barrier unheeding.

A ferocious dog was chained just inside the gate, and barking its head off, to the consternation of the poultry. Gregory dared not enter. As he stood wondering the best way to tackle this fresh problem, the door of the farmhouse opened fractionally and Nancy peeped out. He called and signalled frantically to her.

Timidly, she ran across and let him in, dragging the dog back. Gregory kissed her cheek, soothed by the feel of her sturdy body in his arms.

"Where's your father?"

"My dearest, your leg, your poor leg! It's bleeding yet!"

"Never mind my leg. Where's your father?"

281

"He's down in South Meadow, I think."

"Good! I'm going to speak with him. Nancy, I want you to go indoors and pack some belongings. I'm taking you away with me."

"I can't leave Father!"

"You must. I'm going to tell him now." As he limped across the yard, she called fearfully, "He has that there gun of his'n with him all the time—do be careful!"

The two dogs on a running chain followed him all the way down to the side of the house, nearly choking in their efforts to get at him, their teeth flashing uncomfortably close to his ankles. He noticed Neckland below Grubby's little hut, busy sawing wood; the farmer was not with him. On impulse, Gregory turned into the sties.

It was gloomy there. In the gloom, Grendon worked. He dropped his bucket when he saw Gregory there, and came forward threateningly.

"You came back? Why don't you stay away? Can't you see the notice by the gate? I don't want you here no more, bor. I know you mean well, and I intend you no harm, but I'll kill 'ee understand, kill 'ee if you ever come here again. I've plenty of worries without you to add to them. Now then, get you going!"

Gregory stood his ground.

"Mr. Grendon, are you as mad as your wife was before she died? Do you understand that you may meet Grubby's fate at any moment? Do you realize what you are harboring in your pond?"

"I ent a fule. But suppose them there things do eat everything, humans included? Suppose this is now their farm? They still got to have someone to tend it. So I reckon they ent going to harm me. So long as they sees me work hard, they ent going to harm me."

"You're being fattened, do you understand? For all the hard work you do, you must have put on a stone this last month. Doesn't that scare you?"

Something of the farmer's pose broke for a moment. He cast a wild look round. "I ent saying I ent scared. I'm saying I'm doing what I have to do. We don't own our lives. Now do me a favor and get out of here."

Instinctively, Gregory's glance had followed Grendon's. For the first time, he saw in the dimness the size of the pigs. Their great broad black backs were visible over the top of the sties. They were the size of young oxen.

"This is a farm of death," he said.

"Death's always the end of all of us, pig or cow or man alike."

"Right-ho, Mr. Grendon, you can think like that if you like. It's not my way of thinking, nor am I going to see your dependents suffer from your madness. Mr. Grendon, sir, I wish to ask for your daughter's hand in marriage."

For the first three days that she was away from her home, Nancy Grendon lay in her room in "The Wayfarer" near to death. It seemed as if all ordinary food poisoned her. But gradually under Doctor Crouchorn's ministration—terrified perhaps by the rage she suspected he would vent upon her should she fail to get better—she recovered her strength.

"You look so much better today," Gregory said, clasping her hand. "You'll soon be up and about again, once your system is free of all the evil nourishment of the farm."

"Greg, dearest, promise me you will not go to the farm again. You have no need to go now I'm not there."

He cast his eyes down and said, "Then you don't have to get me to promise, do you?"

"I just want to be sure we neither of us go there again. Father, I feel sure, bears a charmed life. It's as if I was now coming to my senses again—but I don't want it to be as if you was losing yours! Supposing those things followed us here to Cottersall, those Aurigans?"

"You know, Nancy, I've wondered several times why they remain on the farm as they do. You would think that once they found they could so easily defeat human beings, they would attack everyone, or send for more of their own kind and try to invade us. Yet they seem perfectly content to remain in that one small space."

She smiled. "I may not be very clever compared with you, but I can tell 'ee the answer to that one. They ent interested in going anywhere. I think there's just two of them, and they come to our little old world for a holiday in their space machine, same as we might go to Great Yarmouth for a couple of days for our honeymoon. Perhaps they're on their honeymoon."

"On honeymoon! What a ghastly idea!"

"Well, on holiday then. That was Father's idea—he says as there's just two of them, treating Earth as a quiet place to stay. People like to eat well when they're on holiday, don't they?"

He stared at Nancy aghast.

"But that's horrible! You're trying to make the Aurigans out to be *pleasant!*"

"Of course I ent, you silly ha'p'orth! But I expect they seem pleasant to each other."

"Well, I prefer to think of them as menaces."

"All the more reason for you to keep away from them!"

But to be out of sight was not to be out of mind's reach. Gregory received another letter from Dr. Hudson-Ward, a kind and encouraging one, but he made no attempt to answer it. He felt he could not bear to take up any work that would remove him from the neighborhood, although the need to work, in view of his matrimonial plans, was now pressing; the modest allowance his father made him would not support two in any comfort. Yet he could not bring his thoughts to grapple with such practical problems. It was another letter he looked for, and the horrors of the farm that obsessed him. And the next night, he dreamed of the saliva tree again.

In the evening, he plucked up enough courage to tell Fox and Nancy about it. They met in the little snug at the back of "The Wayfarer's" public bar, a discreet and private place with red plush on the seats. Nancy was her usual self again, and had been out for a brief walk in the afternoon sunshine.

"People wanted to give themselves to the saliva tree. And although I didn't see this for myself, I had the distinct feeling that perhaps they weren't actually killed so much as changed into something else—something less human maybe. And this time, I saw the tree was made of metal of some kind and was growing bigger and bigger by pumps—you could see through the saliva to big armatures and pistons, and out of the branches steam was pouring."

Fox laughed, a little unsympathetically. "Sounds to me like the shape of things to come, when even plants are grown by machinery. Events are preying on your mind, Greg! Listen, my sister is going to Norwich tomorrow, driving in her uncle's trap. Why don't the two of you go with her? She's going to buy some adornments for her bridal gown, so that should interest you, Nancy. Then you could stay with Greg's uncle for a couple of days. I assure you I will let you know immediately the Aurigans invade Cottersall, so you won't miss anything."

Nancy seized Gregory's arm. "Can we please, Gregory, can we? I ent been to Norwich for long enough and it's a fine city."

"It would be a good idea," he said doubtfully.

Both of them pressed him until he was forced to yield. He broke up the little party as soon as he decently could, kissed Nancy good-night, and walked hurriedly back down the street to the baker's. Of one thing he was certain: if he must leave the district even for a short while, he had to have a look to see what was happening at the farm before he went.

The farm looked in the summer's dusk as it had never done before. Massive wooden screens nine feet high had been erected and hastily creosoted. They stood about in forlorn fashion, intended to keep the public gaze from the farm, but lending it unmeaning. They stood not only in the yard but at irregular intervals along the boundaries of the land, inappropriately among fruit trees, desolately amid bracken, irrelevantly in swamp. A sound of furious hammering, punctuated by the unwearying animal noises, indicated that more screens were still being built.

But what lent the place its unearthly look was the lighting. The solitary pole supporting the electric light now had five companions: one by the gate, one by the pond, one behind the house, one outside the engine house, one down by the pig sties. Their hideous yellow glare reduced the scene to the sort of unlikely picture that might be found and puzzled over in the eternal midnight of an Egyptian tomb.

Gregory was too wise to try and enter by the gate. He hitched Daisy to the low branches of a thorn tree and set off over waste land, entering Grendon's property by the South Meadow. As he walked stealthily towards the distant outhouses, he could see how the farm land differed from the territory about it. The corn was already so high it seemed in the dark almost to threaten by its ceaseless whisper of movement. The fruits had ripened fast. In the strawberry beds were great strawberries like pears. The marrows lay on their dunghill like bloated bolsters, gleaming from a distant shaft of light. In the orchard, the trees creaked, weighed down by distorted footballs that passed for apples; with a heavy autumnal thud one fell over-ripe to the ground. Everywhere on the farm, there seemed to be slight movement and noise, so much so that Gregory stopped to listen.

A wind was rising. The sails of the old mill shrieked like a gull's cry as they began to turn. In the engine house, the steam engine pumped out its double unfaltering note as it generated power. The dogs still raged, the animals added their uneasy chorus. He recalled the saliva tree; here as in the dream, it was as if agriculture had become industry, and the impulses of nature swallowed by the new god of Science. In the bark of the trees rose the dark steam of novel and unknown forces.

He talked himself into pressing forward again. He moved carefully through the baffling slices of shadow and illumination created by the screens and lights, and arrived near the back door of the farmhouse. A lantern burnt in the kitchen window. As Gregory hesitated, the crunch of broken glass came from within.

Cautiously, he edged himself past the window and peered in through the doorway. From the parlor, he heard the voice of Grendon. It held a curious muffled tone, as if the man spoke to himself.

"Lie there! You're no use to me. This is a trial of strength. Oh God, preserve me, to let me prove myself! Thou has made my land barren till now—now let me harvest it! I don't know what You're doing. I didn't mean to presume, but this here farm is my life. Curse 'em, curse 'em all! They're all enemies." There was more of it; the man was muttering like one drunk. With horrid fascination, Gregory was drawn forward till he had crossed the kitchen flags and stood on the verge of the larger room. He peered round the half open door until he could see the farmer, standing obscurely in the middle of the room.

A candle stood in the neglected hearth, its flickering flame glassily reflected in the cases of maladroit animals. Evidently the house electricity had been cut off to give additional power to the new lights outside.

Grendon's back was to Gregory. One gaunt and unshaven cheek was lit by candle-light. His back seemed a little bent by the weight of what he imagined his duties, yet looking at that leather-clad back now Gregory experienced a sort of reverence for the independence of the man, and for the mystery that lay under his plainness. He watched as Grendon moved out through the front door, leaving it hanging wide, and passed into the yard, still muttering to himself. He walked round the side of the house and was hidden from view as the sound of his tread was lost amid the renewed barking of dogs.

The tumult did not drown a groan from near at hand. Peering into the shadows, Gregory saw a body lying under the table. It rolled over, crunching broken glass as it did so, and exclaimed

287

in a dazed way. Without being able to see clearly, Gregory knew it was Neckland. He climbed over to the man and propped his head up, kicking away a stuffed fish as he did so.

"Don't kill me, bor! I only want to get away from here."

"Bert? It's Greg here. Bert, are you badly hurt?"

He could see some wounds. The fellow's shirt had been practically torn from his back, and the flesh on his side and back was cut from where he had rolled in the glass. More serious was a great weal over one shoulder, changing to a deeper color as Gregory looked at it.

Wiping his face and speaking in a more rational voice, Neckland said, "Gregory? I thought as you was down Cottersall? What you doing here? He'll kill you proper if he finds you here!"

"What happened to you, Bert? Can you get up?"

The laborer was again in possession of his faculties. He grabbed Gregory's forearm and said imploringly, "Keep your voice down, for Christ's sake, or he'll hear us and come back and settle my hash for once for all! He's gone clean off his head, says as these pond things are having a holiday here. He nearly knocked my head off my shoulder with that stick of his! Lucky I got a thick head!"

"What was the quarrel about?"

"I tell you straight, bor, I have got the wind up proper about this here farm. They things as live in the pond will eat me and suck me up like they done Grubby if I stay here any more. So I run off when Joe Grendon weren't looking, and I come in here to gather up my traps and my bits and leave here at once. This whole place is evil, a bed of evil, and it ought to be destroyed. Hell can't be worse than this here farm!"

As he spoke, he pulled himself to his feet and stood, keeping his balance with Gregory's aid. Grunting, he made his way over to the staircase.

"Bert," Gregory said, "supposing we rush Grendon and lay him out. We can then get him in the cart and all leave together."

Neckland turned to stare at him, his face hidden in shadows, nursing his shoulder with one hand.

"You try it!" he said, and then he turned and went steadily up the stairs.

Gregory stood where he was, keeping one eye on the window. He had come to the farm without any clear notion in his head, but now that the idea had been formulated, he saw that it was up to him to try and remove Grendon from his farm. He felt obliged to do it; for although he had lost his former regard for Grendon, a sort of fascination for the man held him, and he was incapable of leaving any human being, however perverse, to face alone the alien horrors of the farm. It occurred to him that he might get help from the distant houses, Dereham Cottages, if only the farmer were rendered in one way or another unable to pepper the intruders with shot.

The machine house possessed only one high window, and that was barred. It was built of brick and had a stout door which could be barred and locked from the outside. Perhaps it would be possible to lure Grendon into there; outside aid could then be obtained.

Not without apprehension, Gregory went to the open door and peered out into the confused dark. He stared anxiously at the ground for sight of a footstep more sinister than the farmer's, but there was no indication that the Aurigans were active. He stepped into the yard.

He had not gone two yards before a woman's screams rang out. The sound seemed to clamp an icy grip about Gregory's ribs, and into his mind came a picture of poor mad Mrs. Grendon. Then he recognized the voice, in its few shouted words, as Nancy's. Even before the sound cut off, he began to pelt down the dark side of the house as fast as he could run.

Only later did he realize how he seemed to be running against a great army of animal cries. Loudest was the babel of the pigs; every swine seemed to have some message deep and

289

nervous and indecipherable to deliver to an unknown source; and it was to the sties that Gregory ran, swerving past the giant screens under the high and sickly light.

The noise in the sties was deafening. Every animal was attacking its pen with its sharp hooves. One light swung over the middle pen. With its help, Gregory saw immediately how terrible was the change that had come over the farm since his last visit. The sows had swollen enormously and their great ears clattered against their cheeks like boards. Their hirsute backs curved almost to the rafters of their prison.

Grendon was at the far entrance. In his arms he held the unconscious form of his daughter. A sack of pig feed lay scattered by his feet. He had one pen gate half open and was trying to thrust his way in against the flank of a pig whose mighty shoulder came almost level with his. He turned and stared at Gregory with a face whose blankness was more terrifying than any expression of rage.

There was another presence in the place. A pen gate near Gregory swung open. The two sows wedged in the narrow sty gave out a terrible falsetto squealing, clearly scenting the presence of an unappeasable hunger. They kicked out blindly, and all the other animals plunged with a sympathetic fear. Struggle was useless. An Aurigan was there; the figure of Death itself, with its unwearying scythe and unaltering smile of bone, was as easily avoided as this poisoned and unseen presence. A rosy flush spread over the back of one of the sows. Almost at once, her great bulk began to collapse; in a moment, her substance had been ingested.

Gregory did not stay to watch the sickening action. He was running forward, for the farmer was again on the move. And now it was clear what he was going to do. He pushed into the end sty and dropped his daughter down into the metal food trough. At once, the sows turned with smacking jaws to deal with this new fodder. His hands free, Grendon moved to a bracket set in the wall. There lay his gun.

Now the uproar in the sties had reached its loudest. The sow whose companion had been so rapidly ingested broke free, and burst into the central aisle. For a moment she stood—mercifully, for otherwise Gregory would have been trampled—as if dazed by the possibility of liberty. The place shook and the other swine fought to get to her. Brick crumbled, pen gates buckled. Gregory jumped aside as the second pig lumbered free, and next moment the place was full of grotesque fighting bodies, fighting their way to liberty.

He had reached Grendon, but the stampede caught them even as they confronted each other. A hoof stabbed down on Grendon's instep. Groaning, he bent forward, and was at once swept underfoot by his creatures. Gregory barely had time to vault into the nearest pen before they thundered by. Nancy was trying pitifully to climb out of the trough as the two beasts to which she had been offered fought to kick their way free. With a ferocious strength—without reason—almost without con-sciousness—Gregory hauled her up, jumped until he swung up on one of the overhead beams, wrapped a leg round the beam, hung down till he grasped Nancy, pulled her up with him.

They were safe, but the safety was not permanent. Through the din and dust, they could see that the gigantic beasts were wedged tightly in both entrances. In the middle was a sort of battlefield, where the animals fought to reach the opposite end of the building; they were gradually tearing each other to pieces—but the sties too were threatened with demolition.

"I had to follow you," Nancy gasped. "But Father—I don't think he even recognized me!"

At least, Gregory thought, she had not seen her father tram-pled underfoot. Involuntarily glancing in that direction, he saw the shotgun that Grendon had never managed to reach still lying across a bracket on the wall. By crawling along a traverse beam, he could reach it easily. Bidding Nancy sit where she was, he wriggled along the beam, only a foot or two above the heaving backs of the swine. At least the gun should afford them some protection: the Aurigan, despite all its ghastly differences from humanity, would hardly be immune to lead.

As he grasped the old-fashioned weapon and pulled it up, Gregory was suddenly filled with an intense desire to kill one of the invisible monsters. In that instant, he recalled an earlier hope he had had of them: that they might be superior beings, beings of wisdom and enlightened power, coming from a better society where higher moral codes directed the activities of its citizens. He had thought that only to such a civilization would the divine gift of traveling through interplanetary space be granted. But perhaps the opposite held true: perhaps such a great objective could be gained only by species ruthless enough to disregard more humane ends. As soon as he thought it, his mind was over-powered with a vast diseased vision of the universe, where such races as dealt in love and kindness and intellect cowered forever on their little globes, while all about them went the slayers of the universe, sailing where they would to satisfy their cruelties and their endless appetites.

He heaved his way back to Nancy above the bloody porcine fray.

She pointed mutely. At the far end, the entrance had crumbled away, and the sows were bursting forth into the night. But one sow fell and turned crimson as it fell, sagging over the floor like a shapeless bag. Another, passing the same spot, suffered the same fate.

Was the Aurigan moved by anger? Had the pigs, in their blind charging, injured it? Gregory raised the gun and aimed. As he did so, he saw a giant hallucinatory column in the air; enough dirt and mud and blood had been thrown up to spot the Aurigan and render him partly visible. Gregory fired.

The recoil nearly knocked him off his perch. He shut his eyes, dazed by the noise, and was dimly aware of Nancy clinging to him, shouting, "Oh, you marvellous man, you marvellous man! You hit that old bor right smack on target!"

He opened his eyes and peered through the smoke and dust.

The shade that represented the Aurigan was tottering. It fell. It fell among the distorted shapes of the two sows it had killed, and corrupt fluids splattered over the paving. Then it rose again. They saw its progress to the broken door, and then it had gone.

For a minute, they sat there, staring at each other, triumph and speculation mingling on both their faces. Apart from one badly injured beast, the building was clear of pigs now. Gregory climbed to the floor and helped Nancy down beside him. They skirted the loathsome messes as best they could and staggered into the fresh air.

Up beyond the orchard, strange lights showed in the rear windows of the farmhouse.

"It's on fire! Oh, Greg, our poor home is afire! Quick, we must gather what we can! All Father's lovely cases—"

He held her fiercely, bent so that he spoke straight into her face. "Bert Neckland did this! He did it! He told me the place ought to be destroyed and that's what he did."

"Let's go, then—"

"No, no, Nancy, we must let it burn! Listen! There's a wounded Aurigan loose here somewhere. We didn't kill him. If those things feel rage, anger, spite, they'll be set to kill us now— don't forget there's more than one of 'em! We aren't going that way if we want to live. Daisy's just across the meadow here, and she'll bear us both safe home."

"Greg, dearest, this is my home!" she cried in her despair.

The flames were leaping higher. The kitchen windows broke in a shower of glass. He was running with her in the opposite direction, shouting wildly, "I'm your home now! I'm your home now!"

Now she was running with him, no longer protesting, and they plunged together through the high rank grass.

When they gained the track and the restive mare, they paused to take breath and look back.

The house was well ablaze now. Clearly nothing could save it. Sparks had carried to the windmill, and one of the sails was ablaze. About the scene, the electric lights shone spectral and pale on the tops of their poles. An occasional running figure of a gigantic animal dived about its own purposes. Suddenly, there was a flash of lightning and all the electric lights went out. One of the stampeding animals had knocked down a pole; crashing into the pond, it short-circuited the system.

"Let's get away," Gregory said, and he helped Nancy on to the mare. As he climbed up behind her, a roaring sound developed, grew in volume, and altered in pitch. Abruptly it died again. A thick cloud of steam billowed above the pond. From it rose the space machine, rising, rising, rising, suddenly a sight to take the heart in awe. It moved up into the soft night sky, was lost for a moment, began dully to glow, was seen to be already tremendously far away.

Desperately, Gregory looked for it, but it had gone, already beyond the frail confines of the terrestrial atmosphere. An awful desolation settled on him, the more awful for being irrational, and then he thought, and cried his thought aloud, "Perhaps they were only holiday-makers here! Perhaps they enjoyed themselves here, and will tell their friends of this little globe! Perhaps Earth has a future only as a resort for millions of the Aurigan kind!"

The church clock was striking midnight as they passed the first cottages of Cottersall.

"We'll go first to the inn," Gregory said. "I can't well disturb Mrs. Fenn at this late hour, but your landlord will fetch us food and hot water and see that your cuts are bandaged."

"I'm right as rain, love, but I'd be glad of your company."

"I warn you, you shall have too much of it from now on!"

The door of the inn was locked, but a light burned inside, and in a moment the landlord himself opened to them, all eager to hear a bit of gossip he could pass on to his custom.

"So happens as there's a gentleman up in Number Three wishes to speak with you in the morning," he told Gregory.

"Very nice gentleman come on the night train, only got in here an hour past, off the wagon."

Gregory made a wry face.

"My father, no doubt."

"Oh, no, sir. His name is a Mr. Wills or Wells or Walls— his signature was a mite difficult to make out."

"Wells! Mr. Wells! So he's come!" He caught Nancy's hands, shaking them in his excitement. "Nancy, one of the greatest men in England is here! There's no one more profitable for such a tale as ours! I'm going up to speak with him right away."

Kissing her lightly on the cheek, he hurried up the stairs and knocked on the door of Number Three.

# The Drowned Giant
## J. G. Ballard

*With its cool, detached style and its disturbing images, this story is as mysteriously compelling as Kafka's* Metamorphosis, *and I think it may be remembered as long.*

O n   t h e   morning after the storm the body of a drowned giant was washed ashore on the beach five miles to the northwest of the city. The first news of its arrival was brought by a nearby farmer and subsequently confirmed by the local newspaper reporters and the police. Despite this the majority of people, myself among them, remained skeptical, but the return of more and more eyewitnesses attesting to the vast size of the giant was finally too much for our curiosity. The library where my colleagues and I were carrying out our research was almost deserted when we set off for the coast shortly after two o'clock, and throughout the day people continued to leave their offices and shops as accounts of the giant circulated around the city.

By the time we reached the dunes above the beach a substantial crowd had gathered, and we could see the body lying in the shallow water 200 yards away. At first the estimates of its size seemed greatly exaggerated. It was then at low tide, and almost all the giant's body was exposed, but he appeared to be a little larger than a basking shark. He lay on his back with his arms at his sides, in an attitude of repose, as if asleep on the mirror of wet sand, the reflection of his blanched skin fading as the water receded. In the clear sunlight his body glistened like the white plumage of a sea bird.

Puzzled by this spectacle, and dissatisfied with the matter-of-fact explanations of the crowd, my friends and I stepped down from the dunes onto the shingle. Everyone seemed reluctant to approach the giant, but half an hour later two fishermen in wading boots walked out across the sand. As their diminutive figures neared the recumbent body a sudden hubbub of conversation broke out among the spectators. The two men were completely dwarfed by the giant. Although his heels were partly submerged in the sand, the feet rose to at least twice the fishermen's height, and we immediately realized that this drowned leviathan had the mass and dimensions of the largest sperm whale.

Three fishing smacks had arrived on the scene and with keels raised remained a quarter of a mile offshore, the crews watching from the bows. Their discretion deterred the spectators on the shore from wading out across the sand. Impatiently everyone stepped down from the dunes and waited on the shingle slopes, eager for a closer view. Around the margins of the figure the sand had been washed away, forming a hollow, as if the giant had fallen out of the sky. The two fishermen were standing between the immense plinths of the feet, waving to us like tourists among the columns of some water-lapped temple on the Nile. For a moment I feared that the giant was merely asleep and might suddenly stir and clap his heels together, but his glazed eyes stared skyward, unaware of the minuscule replicas of himself between his feet.

The fishermen then began a circuit of the corpse, strolling past the long white flanks of the legs. After a pause to examine the fingers of the supine hand, they disappeared from sight between the arm and chest, then re-emerged to survey the head, shielding their eyes as they gazed up at its Grecian profile. The shallow forehead, straight high-bridged nose, and curling lips reminded me of a Roman copy of Praxiteles, and the elegantly formed cartouches of the nostrils emphasized the resemblance to sculpture.

Abruptly there was a shout from the crowd, and a hundred arms pointed toward the sea. With a start I saw that one of the fishermen had climbed onto the giant's chest and was now strolling about and signaling to the shore. There was a roar of surprise and triumph from the crowd, lost in a rushing avalanche of shingle as everyone surged forward across the sand.

As we approached the recumbent figure, which was lying in a pool of water the size of a field, our excited chatter fell away again, subdued by the huge physical dimensions of this dead colossus. He was stretched out at a slight angle to the shore, his legs carried nearer the beach, and this foreshortening had disguised his true length. Despite the two fishermen standing on his abdomen, the crowd formed itself into a wide circle, groups of people tentatively advancing toward the hands and feet.

My companions and I walked around the seaward side of the giant, whose hips and thorax towered above us like the hull of a stranded ship. His pearl-colored skin, distended by immersion in salt water, masked the contours of the enormous muscles and tendons. We passed below the left knee, which was flexed slightly, threads of damp seaweed clinging to its sides. Draped loosely across the midriff, and preserving a tenuous propriety, was a shawl of heavy open-weave material, bleached to a pale yellow by the water. A strong odor of brine came from the garment as it steamed in the sun, mingled with the sweet, potent scent of the giant's skin.

We stopped by his shoulder and gazed up at the motionless profile. The lips were parted slightly, the open eye cloudy and occluded, as if injected with some blue milky liquid, but the delicate arches of the nostrils and eyebrows invested the face with an ornate charm that belied the brutish power of the chest and shoulders.

The ear was suspended in mid-air over our heads like a sculptured doorway. As I raised my hand to touch the pendulous lobe, someone appeared over the edge of the forehead and shouted down at me. Startled by this apparition, I stepped back, and then saw that a group of youths had climbed up onto the face and were jostling each other in and out of the orbits.

People were now clambering all over the giant, whose reclining arms provided a double stairway. From the palms they walked along the forearms to the elbows and then crawled over the distended belly of the biceps to the flat promenade of the pectoral muscles which covered the upper half of the smooth hairless chest. From here they climbed up onto the face, hand over hand along the lips and nose, or forayed down the abdomen to meet others who had straddled the ankles and were patrolling the twin columns of the thighs.

We continued our circuit through the crowd, and stopped to examine the outstretched right hand. A small pool of water lay in the palm, like the residue of another world, now being

301

kicked away by people ascending the arm. I tried to read the palmlines that grooved the skin, searching for some clue to the giant's character, but the distention of the tissues had almost obliterated them, carrying away all trace of the giant's identity and his last tragic predicament. The huge muscles and wristbones of the hand seemed to deny any sensitivity to their owner, but the delicate flexion of the fingers and the well-tended nails, each cut symmetrically to within six inches of the quick, argued refinement of temperament, illustrated in the Grecian features of the face, on which the townsfolk were now sitting like flies.

One youth was even standing, arms wavering at his side, on the very tip of the nose, shouting down at his companions, but the face of the giant still retained its massive composure.

Returning to the shore, we sat down on the shingle and watched the continuous stream of people arriving from the city. Some six or seven fishing boats had collected offshore, and their crews waded in through the shallow water for a closer look at this enormous storm catch. Later a party of police appeared and made a halfhearted attempt to cordon off the beach, but after walking up to the recumbent figure, any such thoughts left their minds, and they went off together with bemused backward glances.

An hour later there were a thousand people present on the beach, at least two hundred of them standing or sitting on the giant, crowded along the arms and legs or circulating in a ceaseless melee across his chest and stomach. A large gang of youths occupied the head, toppling each other off the cheeks and sliding down the smooth planes of the jaw. Two or three straddled the nose, and another crawled into one of the nostrils, from which he emitted barking noises like a demented dog.

That afternoon the police returned and cleared a way through the crowd for a party of scientific experts—authorities on gross anatomy and marine biology—from the university. The gang of youths and most of the people on the giant climbed down, leaving behind a few hardy spirits perched on the tips of the toes and on the forehead. The experts strode around the giant, heads nodding in vigorous consultation, preceded by the policemen who pushed back the press of spectators. When they reached the outstretched hand the senior officer offered to assist them up onto the palm, but the experts hastily demurred.

After they returned to the shore, the crowd once more climbed onto the giant, and was in full possession when we left at five o'clock, covering the arms and legs like a dense flock of gulls sitting on the corpse of a large fish.

I next visited the beach three days later. My friends at the library had returned to their work, and delegated to me the task of keeping the giant under observation and preparing a report. Perhaps they sensed my particular interest in the case, and it was certainly true that I was eager to return to the beach. There was nothing necrophilic about this, for to all intents the giant was still alive for me, indeed more alive than many of the people watching him. What I found so fascinating was partly his immense scale, the huge volumes of space occupied by his arms and legs, which seemed to confirm the identity of my own miniature limbs, but above all, the mere categorical fact of his existence. Whatever else in our lives might be open to doubt, the giant, dead or alive, existed in an absolute sense, providing a glimpse into a world of similar absolutes of which we spectators on the beach were such imperfect and puny copies.

When I arrived at the beach the crowd was considerably smaller, and some two or three hundred people sat on the shingle, picnicking and watching the groups of visitors who walked out across the sand. The successive tides had carried the giant nearer the shore, swinging his head and shoulders toward the beach, so that he seemed doubly to gain in size, his huge body dwarfing the fishing boats beached beside his feet. The uneven contours of the beach had pushed his spine into a slight arch, expanding his chest and tilting back the head, forcing him into a more expressly heroic posture. The combined effects of sea water and the tumefaction of the tissues had given the face a sleeker and less youthful look. Although the vast proportions of the features made it impossible to assess the age and character of the giant, on my previous visit his classically modeled mouth and nose suggested that he had been a young man of discreet and modest temper. Now, however, he appeared to be at least in early middle age. The puffy cheeks, thicker nose and temples, and narrowing eyes gave him a look of well-fed maturity that even now hinted at a growing corruption to come.

The accelerated post-mortem development of the giant's character, as if the latent elements of his personality had gained sufficient momentum during his life to discharge themselves in a brief final résumé, continued to fascinate me. It marked the beginning of the giant's surrender to that all-demanding system of time in which the rest of humanity finds itself, and of which, like the million twisted ripples of a fragmented whirlpool, our finite lives are the concluding products. I took up my position on the shingle directly opposite the giant's head, from where I could see the new arrivals and the children clambering over the legs and arms.

Among the morning's visitors were a number of men in leather jackets and cloth caps, who peered up critically at the giant with a professional eye, pacing out his dimensions and making rough calculations in the sand with spars of driftwood. I assumed them to be from the public works department and other municipal bodies, no doubt wondering how to dispose of this monster.

Several rather more smartly attired individuals, circus proprietors and the like, also appeared on the scene, and strolled slowly around the giant, hands in pockets of their long overcoats, saying nothing to one another. Evidently its bulk was too great even for their matchless enterprise. After they had gone the children continued to run up and down the arms and legs, and the youths wrestled with each other over the supine face, the damp sand from their feet covering the white skin.

\*     \*     \*

The following day I deliberately postponed my visit until the late afternoon, and when I arrived there were fewer than 50 or 60 people sitting on the shingle. The giant had been carried still closer to the shore, and was now little more than 75 yards away, his feet crushing the palisade of a rotting break-water. The slope of the firmer sand tilted his body toward sea, the bruised swollen face averted in an almost conscious gesture. I sat down on a large metal winch which had been shackled to a concrete caisson above the shingle, and looked down at the recumbent figure.

His blanched skin had now lost its pearly translucence and was spattered with dirty sand which replaced that washed away by the night tide. Clumps of seaweed filled the intervals between the fingers and a collection of litter and cuttlebones lay in the crevices below the hips and knees. But despite this, and the continuous thickening of his features, the giant still retained his magnificent Homeric stature. The enormous breadth of the shoulders, and the huge columns of the arms and legs, still carried the figure into another dimension, and the giant seemed a more authentic image of one of the drowned Argonauts or heroes of the *Odyssey* than the conventional portrait previously in my mind.

I stepped down onto the sand, and walked between the pools of water toward the giant. Two small boys were sitting in the well of the ear, and at the far end a solitary youth stood perched high on one of the toes, surveying me as I approached. As I had hoped when delaying my visit, no one else paid any attention to me, and the people on the shore remained huddled beneath their coats.

The giant's supine right hand was covered with broken shells and sand, in which a score of footprints were visible. The rounded bulk of the hip towered above me, cutting off all sight of the sea. The sweetly acrid odor I had noticed before was now more pungent, and through the opaque skin I could see the serpentine coils of congealed blood vessels. However repellent it

305

seemed, this ceaseless metamorphosis, a macabre life-in-death, alone permitted me to set foot on the corpse.

Using the jutting thumb as a stair rail, I climbed up onto the palm and began my ascent. The skin was harder than I expected, barely yielding to my weight. Quickly I walked up the sloping forearm and the bulging balloon of the biceps. The face of the drowned giant loomed to my right, the cavernous nostrils and huge flanks of the cheeks like the cone of some freakish volcano.

Safely rounding the shoulder, I stepped out onto the broad promenade of the chest, across which the bony ridges of the rib cage lay like huge rafters. The white skin was dappled by the darkening bruises of countless footprints, in which the patterns of individual heel marks were clearly visible. Someone had built a small sand castle on the center of the sternum, and I climbed onto this partly demolished structure to get a better view of the face.

The two children had now scaled the ear and were pulling themselves into the right orbit, whose blue globe, completely occluded by some milk-colored fluid, gazed sightlessly past their miniature forms. Seen obliquely from below, the face was devoid of all grace and repose, the drawn mouth and raised chin propped up by gigantic slings of muscles resembling the torn prow of a colossal wreck. For the first time I became aware of the extremity of this last physical agony of the giant, no less painful for his unawareness of the collapsing musculature and tissues. The absolute isolation of the ruined figure, cast like an abandoned ship upon the empty shore, almost out of sound of the waves, transformed his face into a mask of exhaustion and helplessness.

As I stepped forward, my foot sank into a trough of soft tissue, and a gust of fetid gas blew through an aperture between the ribs. Retreating from the fouled air, which hung like a cloud over my head, I turned toward the sea to clear my lungs. To my surprise I saw the the giant's left hand had been amputated.

I stared with shocked bewilderment at the blackening stump,

while the solitary youth reclining on his aerial perch a hundred feet away surveyed me with a sanguinary eye.

This was only the first of a sequence of depredations. I spent the following two days in the library, for some reason reluctant to visit the shore, aware that I had probably witnessed the approaching end of a magnificent illusion. When I next crossed the dunes and set foot on the shingle, the giant was little more than 20 yards away, and with this close proximity to the rough pebbles all traces had vanished of the magic which once surrounded his distant wave-washed form. Despite his immense size, the bruises and dirt that covered his body made him appear merely human in scale, his vast dimensions only increasing his vulnerability.

His right hand and foot had been removed, dragged up the slope, and trundled away by cart. After questioning the small group of people huddled by the breakwater, I gathered that a fertilizer company and a cattle-food manufacturer were responsible.

The giant's remaining foot rose into the air, a steel hawser fixed to the large toe, evidently in preparation for the following day. The surrounding beach had been disturbed by a score of workmen, and deep ruts marked the ground where the hands and foot had been hauled away. A dark brackish fluid leaked from the stumps, and stained the sand and the white cones of the cuttlefish. As I walked down the shingle I noticed that a number of jocular slogans, swastikas, and other signs had been cut into the gray skin, as if the mutilation of this motionless colossus had released a sudden flood of repressed spite. The lobe of one of the ears was pierced by a spear of timber, and a small fire had burned out in the center of the chest, blackening the surrounding skin. The fine wood ash was still being scattered by the wind.

A foul smell enveloped the cadaver, the undisguisable signature of putrefaction, which had at last driven away the usual gathering of youths. I returned to the shingle and climbed up onto the winch. The giant's swollen cheeks had now almost closed his eyes, drawing the lips back in a monumental gape. The once straight Grecian nose had been twisted and flattened, stamped into the ballooning face by countless heels.

When I visited the beach the following day I found, almost with relief, that the head had been removed.

Some weeks elapsed before I made my next journey to the beach, and by then the human likeness I had noticed earlier had vanished again. On close inspection the recumbent thorax and abdomen were unmistakably manlike, but as each of the limbs was chopped off, first at the knee and elbow, and then at shoulder and thigh, the carcass resembled that of any headless sea animal—whale or whale shark. With this loss of identity, and the few traces of personality that had clung tenuously to the figure, the interest of the spectators expired, and the fore shore was deserted except for an elderly beachcomber and the watchman sitting in the doorway of the contractor's hut.

A loose wooden scaffolding had been erected around the carcass, from which a dozen ladders swung in the wind, and the surrounding sand was littered with coils of rope, long metal-handled knives, and grappling irons, the pebbles oily with blood and pieces of bone and skin.

I nodded to the watchman, who regarded me dourly over his brazier of burning coke. The whole area was pervaded by the pungent smell of huge squares of blubber being simmered in a vat behind the hut.

Both the thighbones had been removed, with the assistance of a small crane draped in the gauzelike fabric which had once covered the waist of the giant, and the open sockets gaped like barn doors. The upper arms, collarbones, and pudenda had likewise been dispatched. What remained of the skin over the thorax and abdomen had been marked out in parallel strips with a tar-brush, and the first five or six sections had been pared away from the midriff, revealing the great arch of the rib cage.

As I left, a flock of gulls wheeled down from the sky and alighted on the beach, picking at the stained sand with ferocious cries.

Several months later, when the news of his arrival had been generally forgotten, various pieces of the body of the dismembered giant began to reappear all over the city. Most of these were bones, which the fertilizer manufacturers had found too difficult to crush, and their massive size, and the huge tendons and discs of cartilage attached to their joints, immediately identified them. For some reason, these disembodied fragments seemed better to convey the essence of the giant's original magnificence than the bloated appendages that had been subsequently amputated. As I looked across the road at the premises of the largest wholesale merchants in the meat market, I recognized the two enormous thighbones on either side of the doorway. They towered over the porters' heads like the threatening megaliths of some primitive druidical religion, and I had a sudden vision of the giant climbing to his knees upon these bare bones and striding away through the streets of the city, picking up the scattered fragments of himself on his return journey to the sea.

A few days later I saw the left humerus lying in the entrance to one of the shipyards. In the same week the mummified right hand was exhibited on a carnival float during the annual pageant of the guilds.

The lower jaw, typically, found its way to the museum of natural history. The remainder of the skull has disappeared, but is probably still lurking in the waste grounds or private gardens of the city—quite recently, while sailing down the river, I noticed two ribs of the giant forming a decorative arch in a waterside garden, possibly confused with the jawbones of a whale. A large square of tanned and tattooed skin, the size of an Indian blanket, forms a back cloth to the dolls and masks in a novelty shop near the amusement park, and I have no doubt that elsewhere in the city, in the hotels or golf clubs, the mummified nose or ears of the giant hang from the wall above a fireplace. As for the immense pizzle, this ends its days in the freak museum of a circus which travels up and down the northwest. This monumental apparatus, stunning in its proportions and sometime potency, occupies a complete booth to itself. The irony is that it is wrongly identified as that of a whale, and indeed most people, even those who first saw him cast up on the shore after the storm, now remember the giant, if at all, as a large sea beast.

The remainder of the skeleton, stripped of all flesh, still rests on the seashore, the clutter of bleached ribs like the timbers of a derelict ship. The contractor's hut, the crane and scaffolding have been removed, and the sand being driven into the bay along the coast has buried the pelvis and backbone. In the winter the high curved bones are deserted, battered by the breaking waves, but in the summer they provide an excellent perch for the sea-wearying gulls.

We hope you enjoy this first edition from Stealth Press.

Stealth was conceived and created with a simple premise in mind: that good books matter, and that good books deserve to be in print in the finest form possible, for as long as possible, for the betterment of all.

Privately owned and independently funded, Stealth specializes in high quality, hardcover editions from proven and talented writers, printed on acid-free paper and finely bound, and made directly available to our readers via the Internet.

Stealth believes that every book is a one-on-one experience for author and audience alike. We are dedicated to fostering the most direct and positive connection possible between writers and readers, and all who love books.

Our web site is constantly updated with information on our authors and our latest editions of their work. You can contact the author of this book directly at **www.stealthpress.com**

The revolution will not be televised.